The Days of My Life by Margaret Oliphant

An Autobiography

Margaret Oliphant Wilson was born on April 4th, 1828 to Francis W. Wilson, a clerk, and Margaret Oliphant, at Wallyford, near Musselburgh, East Lothian.

Her youth was spent in establishing a writing style and by 1849 she had her first novel published: Passages in the Life of Mrs. Margaret Maitland.

Two years later, in 1851 Caleb Field was published and also an invitation gained to contribute to Blackwood's Magazine; the beginning of a lifelong business relationship.

In May 1852, Margaret married her cousin, Frank Wilson Oliphant. Their marriage produced six children but, tragically, three died in infancy. When her husband developed signs of the dreaded consumption (tuberculosis) they moved to Florence, and then to Rome where, sadly, he died.

Margaret was naturally devastated but was also now left without support and only her income from writing to support the family. She returned to England and took up the burden of supporting her three remaining children by her literary activity.

Her incredible and prolific work rate increased both her commercial reputation and the size of her reading audience. Tragedy struck again in January 1864 when her only remaining daughter, Maggie, died.

In 1866 she settled at Windsor to be closer to her sons, who were being educated at near-by Eton School.

For more than thirty years she pursued a varied literary career but family life continued to bring problems. Cyril Francis, her eldest son, died in 1890. The younger son, Francis, who she nicknamed 'Cecco', died in 1894.

With the last of her children now lost to her, she had little further interest in life. Her health steadily and inexorably declined.

Margaret Oliphant Wilson Oliphant died at the age of 69 in Wimbledon on 20th June 1897. She is buried in Eton beside her sons.

Index of Contents
BOOK I
THE FIRST DAY
THE SECOND DAY
THE THIRD DAY
THE FOURTH DAY
THE FIFTH DAY

BOOK I

THE FIRST DAY

I was going home from the village, and it was an autumn evening, just after sunset, when every crop was cut and housed in our level country, and when the fields of stubble and browned grass had nothing on them, except here and there, a tree. They say our bare flats, in Cambridgeshire, are neither picturesque, nor beautiful. I cannot say for that—but I know no landscape has ever caught my eye e like the long line of sunburnt, wiry grass, and the great, wide arch above, with all its shades of beautiful color. There were no hedgerows to skirt the path on which I was, and I saw nothing between me and the sky, save a solitary figure stalking along the highway, and in the other direction the clump of trees which surrounded Cottiswoode; the sky, in the west, was still full of the colors of the sunset, and from the horizon it rose upward in a multitude of tints and shades, the orange and red melting into a rosy flush which contrasted for a while, and then fell into the sweet, calm, peaceful tone of the full blue. In the time of the year, and the look of the night, there was alike that indescribable composure and satisfaction which are in the sunny evenings after harvest; the work was done, the day was fading, everything was going home; the rooks sailed over the sky, and the laborer trudged across the moor. Labor was over, and provision made, and the evening and the night, peace and refreshment, and rest were coming for every man. I do not suppose I noticed this at the time, but I have the strongest impression of it all in my remembrance now.

And I was passing along, as I always did, quickly and, perhaps, with a firmer and a steadier step than was usual to girls of my years, swinging in my hand a bit of briony, which, for the sake of its beautiful berries, I was carrying home, but which stood a good chance of being destroyed before we got there—not taking leisure to look much about me, thinking of nothing particular, with a little air of the superior, the lady of the manor, in my independent carriage—a little pride of proprietorship in my firm footstep.

I was going home—when there suddenly appeared two figures before me, advancing on my way. I say two figures, because in our country everything stands out so clear upon the great universal background of sky, that I could not so truly say it was a man and a boy, as two dark outlines, clearly marked and separated from the low, broad level of the country, and the arch of heaven, which now approached upon me. I cannot help an unconscious estimate of character from the tricks of gesture and carriage, which, perhaps, could not have been so visible anywhere else, as here, upon this flat, unbroken road. One of these figures was a stooping and pliant one, with a sort of sinuous twisting motion, noiseless and sidelong, as if his habit was to twist and glide through ways too narrow to admit the passage of a man; the other form was that of a boy—a slight figure, which, to my perfect health and girlish courage, looked timid and hesitating; the brightness of the sky behind cast the faces of the strangers into shadow—but my eye was caught by the unfamiliar outlines; they were strangers, that was sure.

We gradually approached nearer, for I was walking quickly, though their pace was slow; but before we met my thoughts had wandered off from them, and I was greatly astonished by the sudden address which brought me to an abrupt pause before them. "Young lady," the man said, with an awkward bow, "what is your name?"

I was a country girl, and utterly beyond the reach of fear from impertinence. I was my father's daughter, moreover, and loftily persuaded that nothing disrespectful could approach me. I answered immediately with a little scorn of the question—for to be unknown in my own country was a new sensation—"I am Hester Southcote, of Cottiswoode," and having said so, was about to pass on.

"Ah, indeed! it is just as I thought, then," said the stranger, wheeling his young companion round, so as to place him side by side with me. "We are going back to Cottiswoode—we will have the pleasure of your company; I am quite happy we have met."

But my girlish disdain did not annihilate the bold intruder; it only brought a disagreeable smile to his mouth which made him look still more like some dangerous unknown animal to me. I was not very well versed in society, nor much acquainted with the world, but I knew by intuition that this person, though quite as well dressed as any one I had ever seen, was not a gentleman; he was one of those nondescripts whom you could not respect either for wealth or poverty—one of those few people you could be disrespectful to, without blushing for yourself.

"Do you want any thing at Cottiswoode?" I asked accordingly, not at all endeavoring to conceal that I thought my new companion a very unsuitable visitor at my father's house.

"Yes! we want a great deal at Cottiswoode," said the stranger, significantly; and as I raised my head in wonder and indignation, I could not but observe how the boy lagged behind, and how his companion constantly attempted to drag him forward close to me.

With an impatient impulse, I gathered up the folds of my dress in my hand and drew another step apart. I was the only child of a haughty gentleman. I did not know what it was to be addressed in the tone of a superior, and I was fully more annoyed than angry—but with a young girl's grand and innocent assumption, I held my head higher. "You are not aware whom you are speaking to," I said, proudly; but I was very much confused and disconcerted when the stranger answered me by a laugh—and the laugh was still less pleasant than the smile, for there was irritation mingled with its sneer.

"I am perfectly aware whom I am speaking to, Miss," he said, rather more coarsely than he had yet spoken; "better aware than the young lady is who tells me so, or than my lord himself among the trees yonder," and he pointed at Cottiswoode, to which we were drawing near. "But you will find it best to be friends," he continued, after a moment, in a tone intended to be light and easy, "look what I have brought you—here's this pretty young gentleman is your cousin."

"My cousin!" I said, with great astonishment, "I have no cousin."

"Oh, no! I dare say!" said the man, with such a sneer of insinuation, that in my childish passion I could have struck him, almost. "I'd disown him, out and out, if I were you."

"What do you mean, sir?" I said, stopping short and turning round upon him; then my eye caught the face of the boy, which was naturally pale, but now greatly flushed with shame and anger, as I thought; he looked shrinking, and timid, and weak, with his delicate blue-veined temples, his long, fair hair, and refined mild face. I felt myself so strong, so sunburnt, so ruddy, and with such a strength and wealth of life, in presence of this delicate and hesitating boy. "What does he mean," I repeated, addressing him, "does he mean that I say what is not true?"

"I will tell you what I mean, my dear young lady," said the man, suddenly changing his tone, "I mean what I have just been to tell your amiable father; though, of course, both yourself and the good gentleman have your own reasons for doubting me—I mean that this is your cousin, Mr. Edgar Southcote, the son of your father's elder brother, Brian Southcote, who died in India ten years ago—that's what I mean!"

The man had his eyes fixed upon me with a broad full gaze, as if he expected a contradiction; but, of course, after hearing this, I did not care in the least how the man looked, or what he had to do with it—I turned very eagerly to look at the boy.

"Are you really my cousin?" said I, "have you just come from India? why did we never know before? and your name is Edgar?—a great many of the Southcotes have been called Edgar—how old are you?—I never knew I had a cousin, or any near friends, and neither did papa; but I have heard every body talk of uncle Brian. Poor boy! you have no father—you are not so happy as I—"

But to my great amazement, and just at the moment I was holding out my hand to him, and was about to say that my father would love him as he did me—my new cousin, a boy, a man—he ought to have had more spirit!—suddenly burst into a great fit of tears, and in the strangest passionate manner, cried out to the man, "I cannot bear it, Saville—Saville, take me away!"

I had no longer any curiosity or care about the man; but I was very much surprised at this, and could not understand it—and I was a little ashamed and indignant besides to see a boy cry.

"What is the matter?" I asked again, with some of my natural imperiousness, "why do you cry—is anything wrong? Is your name Edgar Southcote, and yet you cry like a child? Do you not know we are called the proudest house in the country; and what is this man doing, or what does he want here? why should he take you away? you ought to be at Cottiswoode if you are Edgar Southcote—what do you mean?"

"Cheer up, Master Edgar—your cousin is quite right, you ought to be at Cottiswoode, and nowhere else, my boy," said the man, giving him such a blow on the shoulders, in encouragement, that the delicate boy trembled under it. "Why, where is your spirit! come, come, since the young lady's owned you, we'll go straight to the old gentleman again; and you'll see what papa will say to you, Miss, when he sees what you bring him home."

I did not answer, but turned away my head from this person, who filled me with disgust and annoyance: then their slow pace roused me to impatience. I was always a few steps before them, for Saville's gliding pace was uniformly slow, and the pale boy, who was called my cousin, lingered still more than his companion. He never answered me—not a word, though I put so many questions to him, and he seemed so downcast and sad, so unlike a boy going home—so very, very unlike me, that I could not understand him. I was so very eager to return to tell my father, and to ask him if this was truly an Edgar Southcote, that our slow progress chafed me the more.

We were now drawing very near to Cottiswoode; every dark leaf of the trees was engraved on the flush of many colors which still showed in the sky the road where the sun had gone down—and among them rose my father's house, the home of our race, with its turrets rising gray upon the sky like an old chateau of France or Scotland, without a hill in sight to harmonize that picturesque architecture: nothing but the elm trees and the olive shade of the great walnut, with the flat moors and sunburnt grass, running away in vast level lines into the sky. Cottiswoode, the house of all our ancestors, where every room was a chapter in the history of our name, and every Southcote of renown still lived upon the ancient walls—I could not fancy one of us approaching, without a flush and tremor, the family dwelling-place. But Edgar Southcote's pale cheek was not warmed by the faintest color—I thought he looked as if he must faint or die—he no longer glanced at me or at his companion; and when I turned to him, I saw only the pale eyelids with their long lashes, the drooping head, and foot that faltered now at every step—a strange boy! could he be of our blood after all?

The front of Cottiswoode was somewhat gloomy, for there was only a carriage-road sweeping through the trees, and a small shrubbery thickly planted with evergreens before the great door. When we were near enough, I saw my father pacing up and down hurriedly through the avenue of elms which reaches up to the shrubbery. When I saw him, I became still more perplexed than before—my father was reserved, and never betrayed himself or his emotions to the common eye; I could not comprehend why he was here, showing an evident agitation, and disturbed entirely out of his usual calm.

And as quickly as I did, the stranger noticed him. This man fixed his eye upon my father with a sneer, which roused once more to the utmost, my girlish passion. I could not tell what it meant, but there was an insinuation in it, which stung me beyond bearing, especially when I saw the trouble on my father's face, which was generally so calm. I hurried forward anxious to be first, yet involuntarily waiting for my strange companions. The man too quickened his pace a little, but the boy lagged behind so drearily, and drooped his head with such a pertinacious sadness—though the very elm trees of Cottiswoode were rustling their leaves above him—that in my heat, and haste, and eagerness, I knew not what to do.

"Papa!" I said anxiously; my father heard me, and turned round with a sudden eager start, as though he was glad of my coming; but when he met my glance, and saw how I was accompanied, I cannot describe the flash of resentment, of haughty inquiry, and bitterness that shone from my father's eye—I saw it, but was too much excited to ask for an explanation. "Papa," I cried, again springing forward upon his arm, "this is Edgar Southcote, my cousin—did they tell you? I am sorry he does not seem to care for coming home, but he has been all his life in India, I suppose—Uncle Brian's son, papa—and his name is Edgar! did you send him to meet me? tell him you are glad that he has come home; look at Cottiswoode, Edgar—dear Cottiswoode, where all the Southcotes lived and died. What ails him? I believe he will faint. Papa—papa, let the boy know he is welcome home!"

"Hester!" said my father in an ominous cold tone, "restrain your feelings—I have no reason to believe there is an Edgar Southcote in existence. I do not believe my brother Brian left a son—I cannot receive this boy as Edgar Southcote—he may be this man's son for aught I know."

The boy's wan face woke up at these words; he shook his long hair slightly back upon the faint wind, and raised his eyes full of sudden light and courage. I understood nothing of my father's reluctance to acknowledge the stranger. I pleaded his cause with all my heart.

"He is not this man's son," I exclaimed eagerly, "papa, he is a gentleman! Look, he has been so sad and downcast till now, but he wakes when you accuse him—he is an orphan, poor boy, poor boy! say he is welcome home."

"You had best," said Saville, and the contrast between my own voice of excitement, and these significant tones with their constant sneer and insinuation of evil, struck me very strangely, "the young lady is wise—it is your best policy, I can tell you, to receive him well in his own house."

My father's haughty face flushed with an intolerable sense of insult, and I saw Edgar shrink as if something had stung him. "Hester, my love, leave me!" said my father, "I will deal with this fellow alone. Go, keep your kind heart for your friends. I tell you these pretensions are false—do you hear me, child?"

I never doubted my father before; when I looked from his face which was full of passion, yet clouded with an indescribable shadow of doubt, to the insolent mocking of the man beside him, I grew bewildered and uncertain; did my father believe himself? Yet I neither could nor would put faith in the elder stranger. I had been so constantly with my father, and had so much licence given me, that I could not obey him; and I did what I have always done—I suddenly obeyed my own sudden impulse, and turned to the boy.

"I do not believe what he will say," I said rapidly, "but I will trust you; are you Edgar Southcote? are you my cousin? you will not tell a lie."

The boy paused, hesitated; but he had raised his eyes to mine, and he did not withdraw them. His face crimsoned over with a delicate yet deep flush, like a girl's—then he grew pale—and then he said slowly—

"I cannot tell a lie—my father's name was Brian Southcote, I am Edgar; I will not deny my name."

I cried out triumphantly, "Now, papa!" but my father made an impatient gesture commanding me away; it was so distinctly a command now, that I was awed and dared not disobey him. I turned away very slowly through the thick evergreens, looking back and lingering as I went. I was just about to turn round by the great Portugal laurel, which would have hid from me these three figures standing together among the elm trees and against the sky, when my father called me to him again. I returned towards him gladly, for I had been very reluctant to go away.

"Hester, these gentlemen will accompany you," he said, with a contemptuous emphasis, "show them to my library, and I will come to you."

I cannot tell to what a pitch my anxiety and excitement had risen—it was so high, at least, that without question or remark, only very quickly and silently, I conducted my companions to the house, and introduced them to my father's favorite room, the library. It was a very long, large room, rather gloomy in the greater part of it, but with one recessed and windowed corner as bright as day. My life had known no studies and few pleasures, that were not associated with this un-bright corner, with its cushioned window-seat and beautiful oriel. When we entered, it was almost twilight by my father's writing-table, behind which was the great window with the fragrant walnut foliage overshadowing it like a miniature forest—but a clear, pale light, the evening blessing—light, as sweet and calm as heaven itself, shone in upon my little vase of faint, sweet roses—roses gathered from a tree that blossomed all the year through, but all the year through was sad and faint, and never came to the flush of June. Edgar Southcote sank wearily into a chair almost by the door of the library, but Saville, whom I almost began to hate, bustled about at once from one window to another, looking at everything.

"Fine old room—I'd make two of it," said this fellow; "have down a modern architect, my boy, and make the place something like. Eh, Edgar! what, tired? you had better pluck up a spirit, or how am I to manage this worthy, disinterested uncle of yours?"

I could not let the man think I had heard him, but left the room to seek my father—what could he mean? I met my father at the door, and with a slight wave of his hand bidding me follow him, he went on before me to the dining parlor, the only other room we used; my excitement had deepened into painful anxiety—something was wrong—it was a new thought and a new emotion to me.

"What is the matter, papa?" I said, anxiously, "what is wrong? what has happened? do you think this is not my cousin, or are you angry that he has come? Father, you loved my uncle Brian, do you not love his son?"

"Hester!" said my father, turning away his troubled face from my gaze and the light, "I will not believe that this boy is my brother Brian's son."

"But he says he is, papa," I answered, with eagerness; I did not believe in lying, and Edgar Southcote's pale face was beyond the possibility of untruth.

"It is worth his while to say it," my father exclaimed hurriedly; then a strange spasm of agitation crossed his face—he turned to me again as if with an irrestrainable impulse to confide his trouble to me. "Hester! Brian was my elder brother," he said in a low, quick whisper, and almost stealthily. I did not comprehend him. I was only a child—the real cause of his distress never occurred to me.

"I know it would be very hard to take him home to Cottiswoode for a Southcote, and then to find out he was not uncle Brian's son," I said, looking up anxiously at my father, "and you know better than I, and remember my uncle; but papa—I believe him—see! I knew it—he is like that picture there!"

My father turned to the picture with a start of terror; it was an Edgar Southcote I was pointing to—a philosopher; one of the few of our house, who loved wisdom better than houses or lands, one who had died early after a sad short life. My father's face burned as he looked at the picture; the refined visionary head drooping over a book, and the large delicate eyelids with their long lashes were so like, so very like!—it struck him in a moment. "Papa, I believe him," I repeated very earnestly. My father started from me, and paced about the room in angry agitation.

"I have trained you to be mistress of Cottiswoode, Hester," he said, when he returned to me. "I have taught you from your cradle to esteem above all things your name and your race—and now, and now, child, do you not understand me? if this boy is Brian's son, Cottiswoode is his!"

It was like a flash of sudden lightning in the dark, revealing for an instant everything around, so terribly clear and visible—I could not speak at first. I felt as if the withering light had struck me, and I shivered and put forth all my strength to stand erect and still; then I felt my face burn as if my veins were bursting. "This was what he meant!"

"What, who meant? Who?" cried my father.

"You believe he is Edgar Southcote, papa?" said I, "you believe him as I do; I see it in your face—and the man sneers at you—you, father! because it is your interest to deny the boy. Let us go away, and leave him Cottiswoode if it is his; you would not do him wrong, you would not deny him his right—father, father, come away!"

And I saw him, a man whose calm was never broken by the usual excitements of life, a man so haughty and reserved that he never showed his emotions even to me—I saw him dash his clenched hand into the air with a fury and agony terrible to see. I could not move nor speak, I only stood and gazed at him, following his rapid movements as he went and came in his passion of excitement, pacing about the room; the every day good order and arrangement of every thing around us; the calm light of evening, which began to darken; the quiet house where there was no sound of disturbance, but only the softened hum of tranquil life—the trees rustling without, the grass growing, and night coming softly down out of the skies; nothing sympathized with his fiery passion, except his daughter who stood gazing at him, half a woman, half a child—and nothing at all in all the world sympathized with me.

Very gradually he calmed, and the paroxysm was over; then my father came to me, and put his hands on my shoulders, and looked into my strained eyes; I could not bear his gaze, though I had been gazing at him so long, and thick and heavy, my tears began to fall; then he stooped over me and kissed my brow. "My disinherited child!" that was all he said—and he left me and went away.

Then I sat down on the carpet by the low window, and cried—cried "as if my heart were breaking," but hearts do not break that get relief in such a flood of child's tears. I felt something in my hand as I put it up to my wet eyes. It was the bit of briony which I had carried unwittingly a long, long way, through all my first shock of trouble. Yes! there were the beautiful tinted berries in their clusters uninjured even by my hand—but the stem was crushed and broken, and could support them no longer; the sight of it roused me out of my vague but bitter distress—I spread it out upon my hand listlessly, and thought of the low hedge from which I had pulled it, a bank of flowers the whole summer through. It was our own land—our own land—was it ours no longer now?

In a very short time, I was disturbed by steps and voices, and my father came into the room with Edgar and his disagreeable companion; then came Whitehead, bringing in the urn and tea-tray, and I had to make tea for them. I did not speak at all, neither did my new cousin; and my father was polite, but very lofty and reserved, and behaved to Saville with such a grand courtesy, as a prince might have shown to a peasant; the man was overpowered and silenced by it, I saw, and could no longer be insolent, though he tried. My father took his cup of tea very slowly and deliberately, and then he rose and said, "I am quite at your service," and Saville followed him out of the room.

We two were left together; my new cousin was about my own age I thought—though indeed he was older—but while I had the courage of health and high spirits, of an unreproved and almost uncontrolled childhood, the boy was timid as a weak frame, a susceptible temper, and a lonely orphanhood could make him. We sat far apart from each other, in the large dark room, and did not speak a word; a strange sudden bitterness and resentment against this intruder had come to my heart. I looked with contempt and dislike at his slight form and pallid face. I raised my own head with a double pride and haughtiness—this was the heir of Cottiswoode and of the Southcotes, this lad whose eye never kindled at sight of the old house—and I was disinherited!

It grew gradually dark, but I sat brooding in my bitterness and anger, and never thought of getting lights. The trees were stirring without, in the faint night wind which sighed about Cottiswoode, and I could see the pensive stars coming out one by one on the vast breadth of sky—but nothing stirred within. Edgar was at one end of the room, I at the other—he did not disturb me, and I never spoke to him, but involuntarily all this time, I was watching him—he could not raise his hand to his head but I saw it; he could not move upon his chair without my instant observation; for all so dark as the room was, and so absorbed in my own thoughts as was I.

At length my heart beat to see him rise and approach towards me. I was tempted to spring up, to denounce and defy the intruder, and leave him so—but I did not—I only rose and waited for him, leaning against the window. He came up with his soft step stealing through the darkness. "Cousin," he said, in a low voice, which sounded very youthful, yet had a ring of manhood in it, too, "cousin, it is not Edgar Southcote who has come to Cottiswoode, but a great misfortune—what am I to do?—you took part with me, you believed me, Hester: tell me what I am to do to make myself something else than a calamity to my Uncle and to you?"

He spoke very earnestly, but his voice did not touch my heart, it only quickened my resentment. "Do nothing except justice," said I, in my girlish, passionate way. "We are Southcotes, do you think we cannot bear a misfortune? but you do not know your race, nor what it is. If you are the heir of Cottiswoode do you think anything you could do, would make my father keep what is not his? No, you can do nothing except justice. My father is not a man to be pitied."

"Nor do I mean to pity him," said the boy, gently, "I respect my father's brother, though my father's brother doubts me. Will you throw me off then? you judge of me, perhaps, by my companion. Ah! that would be just; I do not care for justice, cousin Hester; I want that which you reject so bitterly—pity, compassion, love!"

"Pity is a cheat," said I, quoting words which my father had often said, "and when you have justice you will not need pity."

He stood looking at me for a moment, and though my pride would not give way, my heart relented. "When I have justice—is that when I have my father's inheritance?" said Edgar, slowly, "that will not give me a father, or a mother, or a friend. I will need pity more, and not less, than now."

He did not speak again, and I could not answer him; no, I could not answer his gentle words, nor open my heart to him again. A stranger, an unknown boy; and he was to take from my father his ancestral house, his lands, his very rank and degree! I clasped my hands and hardened my heart; let him have justice, I said within myself—justice—we would await it proudly, and obey it without a murmur; but we rejected the sympathy of our supplanter; let him, as we did, stand alone.

But I could not help a wistful look after him as Edgar went away with his most unsuitable companion along the level, dark, long road to the village inn. My father stood with me at the door gazing after them, with a strange, fascinated eye, and when they passed into the distance out of our sight, he drew a long breath of relief, and, in a faint voice, bade me come in. I followed him to the library where lights were burning. The large, dim room looked chill and desolate as we entered it, and I saw a chair thrust aside from the table, where Saville had been sitting opposite my father. I stood beside him now, for he held my hand and would not let me go. He had been quite dignified and self-possessed when we parted with the strangers, but now his face relaxed into a strange ease and weariness. We were alone in the world, my father and I, but his thoughts were not often such as could be told to a girl like me; and I think I had never felt such a thrill of affectionate delight as now, when I saw him yield before me to his new trouble—when he took his child into his confidence, and suffered no veil of appearance to interpose between us.

"Hester," he said, holding my hand lightly in his own; "I have heard all this story; the man is a relation, he tells me, of Brian's wife; and though I cannot understand how my brother should so have demeaned himself, yet the story, I cannot dispute, has much appearance of truth. I like to be prepared for the worst—Hester! I wish you to think of it. Do you understand at all what will happen to us if this be true?"

"Scarcely, papa," said I.

"Cottiswoode will be ours no longer; the rank and consideration we have been accustomed to, will be ours no longer," said my father, with a slight shudder. "Hester, do you hear what I say?"

"Yes, I am thinking, papa," said I, "poverty, want—I know the words; but I do not know what they mean."

"We shall not have poverty or want to undergo," said my father quickly, with a little impatience, "we will have to endure downfall, Hester—overthrow, exile and banishment—worse things than want or poverty. We shall have to endure—child, child, go to your child's rest, and close those bright, questioning eyes of yours! You do not understand what this grievous calamity is to me!"

I withdrew from him a little, pained and cast down, while he rose once more, and paced the room with measured steps. I watched his lofty figure retiring into the darkness and returning to the light with reverence and awe. He was not a country gentleman dispossessed of his property to my overstrained imagination, but a king compelled to abdicate, a sovereign prince banished from his dominions; and his own feelings were as romantic, as exalted, I might say as exaggerated as mine.

After a little while he returned to me, restored to his usual composure.

"It is time to go to rest, Hester—good-night. In the morning I will know better what this is; and to-morrow—to-morrow," he drew a long breath as he stooped over me, "to-morrow we will gird ourselves for our overthrow. Good-night!"

And this was now the night-fall on the first day which I can detach and separate from all the childhood and youthful years before it—the beginning of the days of my life.

THE SECOND DAY

It was late in October, and winter was coming fast; in all the paths about Cottiswoode the fallen leaves lay thick, and every breath of air brought them down in showers. But though these breezes were so melancholy at night when they moaned about the house, as if in lamentation for us, who were going away, in the morning when the sun was out the chilled gale was only bracing and full of wild pleasure, as it blew full over the level of our moors, with nothing to break its force for miles.

My own pale monthly rose had its few faint blossoms always; but I do not like the flowers of autumn, those ragged dull chrysanthemums and grand dahlias which are more like shrubs than flowers. The jessamine that waved into my window was always wet, and constantly dropping a little dark melancholy leaflet upon the window-ledge—and darker than ever were the evergreens—those gloomy lifeless trees which have no sympathy with nature. Before this, every change of the seasons brought only a varied interest to me; but this year, I could see nothing but melancholy and discouragement in the waning autumn, the lengthening nights and the chilled days. I still took long rambles on the flat high roads, and through the dry stubble fields and sun-burnt moors—but I was restless and disconsolate; this morning I returned from a long walk, tired, as it is so unnatural to feel in the morning—impatient at the wind that caught my dress, and at the leaves that dropped down upon me as I came up the avenue—wondering where all the light and color had gone which used to flush with such a splendid animation the great world of sky, where everything now was cold blue and watery white—looking up at Cottiswoode, where all the upper windows were open, admitting a damp unfriendly breeze. Cottiswoode itself, for the first time, looked deserted and dreary; oh, these opened windows! how comfortless they looked, and how well I could perceive the air of weary excitement about the whole house—for we were to leave it to-day.

The table was spread for breakfast in the dining-parlor; but already a few things were away, an old-fashioned cabinet which had been my mother's and the little book-case where were all the books in their faded pretty bindings which had been given to her when she was a young lady and a bride—these were mine, and had always been called mine, and the wall looked very blank where they had stood; and my chair, with the embroidered cover of my mother's own working; I missed it whenever I came into the room. There were other things gone too, everything which was my father's own, and did not belong to Cottiswoode, and everybody knows how desolate a room looks which has nothing but the barely necessary furniture—the table and the chairs. To make it a little less miserable, a fire had been lighted; but it was only raw, and half kindled, and, I think, if possible, made this bare room look even less like home. My tears almost choked me when I came into it; but I was very haughty and proud in my downfall and would not cry, though I longed to do it. My father was still in the library, and I went to seek him there. He was sitting by his own table doing nothing, though he had writing materials by him, and a book at his hand. He was leaning his head upon both his hands, and looking full before him into the vacant air, with the fixed gaze of thought—I saw, that from his still and composed countenance, his proud will had banished every trace of emotion—yet I saw, nevertheless, how underneath this calm exterior, his heart was running over with the troubles and remembrances of his subdued and passionate life.

For I knew my father was passionate in everything, despite his habitual restraint and quietness—passionate in his few deep-seated and unchanging loves—and passionate in the strong, but always suppressed resentment which he kept under as a Christian, but never subdued as a man. I stood back as I looked, in reverence for the suffering it must have cost him to retrace, as I saw he was doing, all his life at Cottiswoode; but he heard the rustle of my dress, and, starting with an impatient exclamation, called me to him. "Breakfast, papa," said I, hesitating, and with humility—a strange smile broke on his face.

"Surely, Hester, let us go to breakfast," he said, rising slowly as if his very movements required deliberation to preserve their poise and balance—and then he took me by the hand, as he had done when I was a child, and we went from the one room to the other, and sat down at a corner of the long dining-table—for our pleasant round table at which we usually breakfasted, had, like the other things, been taken away.

My father made a poor pretence to eat—and kept up a wavering conversation with me about books and study. I tried to answer him as well as I was able; but it was strange to be talking of indifferent things the day we were to leave Cottiswoode, and my heart seemed to flutter at my throat and choked me, when I ventured a glance round the room. More than a month had passed since that visit of misfortune had brought a new claimant upon our undisturbed possession, and Edgar Southcote's rights had been very clearly made out, and this was why we were to leave to-day.

We were still sitting at the breakfast-table, when the letters were brought in. My father opened one of them, glanced over it, and then tossed it to me. It was a letter from my cousin, such a one as he had several times received before, entreating him with the most urgent supplications to remain in Cottiswoode. It was a very simple boyish letter, but earnest and sincere enough to have merited better treatment at our hands—I have it still, and had almost cried over it, when I saw it the last time—though I read it with resentment this morning, and lifted my head haughtily, and exclaimed at the boy's presumption: "I suppose he would like to give us permission to stay in Cottiswoode," I said bitterly, and my father smiled at me as he rose and went back to the library—I knew him better than to disturb him again, so I hurried out of the room which was so miserable to look at, and went to my own chamber up-stairs.

My pretty room with its bright chintz hangings, and its muslin draperies which I did not care for, and yet loved! for I was not a young lady at this time, but only a courageous independent girl, brought up by a man, and more accustomed to a library than a boudoir; and feminine tastes were scarcely awakened in me. I was more a copy of my father than anything else; but still with a natural love of the beautiful, I liked my pretty curtains, and snowy festoons of muslin—I liked the delicacy and grace they gave—I liked the inferred reverence for my youth and womanhood which claimed these innocent adornments; and more than all I loved Alice, who provided them for me. Alice was my own attendant, my friend and guide and counsellor; she was a servant, yet she was the only woman whom I held in perfect respect, and trusted with all my heart. After my father, I loved Alice best of all the world; but with a very different love. In my intercourse with my father, he was the actor and I the looker-on, proud when he permitted me to sympathize with him, doubly proud when he opened his mind, and showed me what he felt and thought. To bring my little troubles and annoyances, my girlish outbreaks of indignation or of pleasure to disturb his calm, would have been desecration—but I poured them all in the fullest detail into the ear of Alice, and with every one of the constant claims I made upon her sympathy, I think Alice loved me better. When I was ill, I would rather have leaned upon her kind shoulder than on any pillow, and nothing ever happened to me or in my presence, but I was restless till Alice knew of it. I think, even, her inferior position gave a greater charm to our intercourse—I think an old attached and respected servant is the most delightful of confidants to a child; but, however that may be, Alice was my audience, my chorus, everything to me.

Alice was about forty at this time, I suppose; she had been my mother's maid, and my nurse, always an important person in the house; she was tall, with rather a large face, and a sweet bright complexion, which always looked fresh and clear like a summer morning; she was not very remarkable for her taste in dress—her caps were always snow-white, her large white aprons so soft and spotless, that I liked to lay my cheek on them, and go to sleep there, as I did when I was a child; but the gown she usually wore was of dark green stuff, very cold and gloomy like the evergreens, and the little printed cashmere shawl on her shoulders would have been almost dingy, but for the white, white muslin kerchief that pressed out of it at the throat and breast. She had large hands, brown and wrinkled, but with such a soft silken touch of kindness;—and this was my Alice as she stood folding up the pretty chintz curtains in my dismantled room.

"Oh, Alice! isn't it miserable?" I cried while I stood by her side, looking round upon the gradual destruction—I did not want to cry; but it cost me a great effort to keep down the gathering tears.

"Sad enough, Miss Hester," said Alice, "but, do you know, if you had been brought up in a town, you would not have minded a removal; and you shall soon see such a pretty room in Cambridge that you will not think of Cottiswoode—"

"No place in the world can ever be like Cottiswoode to me," said I with a little indignation that my great self-control should be so little appreciated. "Of course, I should not wish to stay here when it is not ours," I went on, rubbing my eyes to get the tears away, "but I will always think Cottiswoode home—no other place will ever be home to me."

"You are very young, my dear," said Alice quietly. I was almost angry with Alice, and it provoked me so much to hear her treating my first grief so composedly that the tears which I had restrained, came fast and thick with anger and petulance in them.

"Indeed, it is very cruel of you, Alice!" I said as well as I was able, "do you think I do not mean it?—do you think I do not know what I say?"

"I only think you are very young, poor dear!" said Alice, looking down upon me under her arm, as she stretched up her hands to unfasten the last bit of curtain, "and I am an old woman, Miss Hester. I saw your poor mamma come away from her home to find a new one here; it was a great change to her, for all so much as her child likes Cottiswoode—she liked her own home very dearly, Miss Hester, and did not think this great house was to be compared to it—but she came away here of her own will after all—"

"But that was because she was married, Alice," said I hastily.

"Yes! it was because she was married, and because it is the common way of life," said Alice; "but, the like of me, Miss Hester, that has parted with many a one dear to me, never to see them again, thinks little, darling, of parting with dead walls."

"Alice, have you had a great deal of grief," said I reverently; my attention was already diverted from the main subjects of my morning's thoughts—for I was very young, as she said, and had a mind open to every interest, that grand privilege of youth.

"I have lost husband and children, father and mother, Miss Hester," said Alice quietly; she had her back turned to me, but it was not to hide her weeping, for Alice had borne her griefs with her for many, many years. I knew very well that it was as she had said, for she had often told me of them all, and of her babies whom she never could be quite calm about—but she very seldom alluded to them in this way, and never dwelt upon her loss, but always upon themselves. I did not say anything, but I felt ashamed of my passion of grief for Cottiswoode. If I should lose Alice—or, still more frightful misfortune, lose my father, what would Cottiswoode be to me.

"But, my dear young lady was pity herself," said Alice, after a short pause, "I think I can see her now, when I could not cry myself, how she cried for me; and I parted with her too, Miss Hester. I think she had the sweetest heart in the world; she could not see trouble, but she pitied it, and did her best to help."

"Alice," said I hastily, connecting these things by a sudden and involuntary conviction, "why is it that papa says: 'pity is a cheat.'"

"It is a hard saying, Miss Hester," said Alice, pausing to look at me; and then she went on with her work, as if this was all she had to say.

"He must have reason for it," said I, "and when I think of that Edgar Southcote presuming to pity us, I confess it makes me very angry—I cannot bear to be pitied, Alice!"

But Alice went on with her work, and answered nothing; I was left to myself, and received no sympathy in my haughty dislike of anything which acknowledged the superiority of another. I was piqued for the moment. I would a great deal rather that Alice had said, "no one can pity you"—but Alice said nothing of the kind, and after a very little interval my youthful curiosity conquered my pride.

"You have not answered me, but I am sure you know," said I, "Alice, what does papa mean?"

Alice looked at me earnestly for a moment. "I am only a servant," she said, as if she consulted with herself, "I have no right to meddle in their secrets—but I care for nothing in the world but them, and I have served her all her days. Yes, Miss Hester, I will tell you," she concluded suddenly, "because you'll be a woman soon, and should know what evil spirits there are in this weary, weary life."

But though she said this, she was slow to begin an explanation—she put away the curtains first, carefully smoothed down and folded into a great chest which stood open beside us, and then she began to lift up my few books, and the simple furniture of my toilette-table, and packed them away for the removal. It was while she was thus engaged, softly coming and going, and wiping off specks of dust in a noiseless, deliberate way, that she told me the story of my father and mother.

"My young lady was an only child, like you, Miss Hester," said Alice, "but her father's land was all entailed, and it has passed to a distant cousin now, as you know. I think she was only about eighteen when the two young gentlemen from Cottiswoode began to visit at our house. Mr. Brian came as often as your father—they were always together, and I remember very well how I used to wonder if both of the brothers were in love with Miss Helen, or if the one only came for the other's sake. Mr. Brian was a very different man from your papa, my dear—there was not such a charitable man in the whole country, and he never seemed to care for himself—but somehow, just because he was so good, he never seemed in earnest about anything he wished—you could not believe he cared for anything so much, but he would give it up if another asked it from him. It's a very fine thing to be kind and generous, Miss Hester, but that was carrying it too far, you know. If I had been a lady I never would have married Mr. Brian Southcote, for I think he never would have loved me half so much as he would have loved the pleasure of giving me away.

"But you know how different your papa was; I used to think it would be a pleasure to trust anything to Mr. Howard, because whatever he had and cared for, he held as fast as life; and my young lady thought so too, Miss Hester. They were both in love with Miss Helen, and very glad her papa would have been had she chosen Mr. Brian, who was the heir of all. It used to be a strange sight to see them all, poor Mr. Brian so pleasant to everybody, and Mr. Howard so dark and passionate and miserable, and my sweet young lady terrified and unhappy—glad to be good friends with Mr. Brian, because she did not care for him; and so anxious about Mr. Howard, though she scarcely dared to be kind to him, because she thought so much of him in her heart. Your papa was very jealous, Miss Hester, it is his temper, and I am not sure, my dear, that it is not yours; and he knew Mr. Brian was pleasanter spoken than he was, and that everybody liked him—so, to be sure, he thought his brother was certain to be more favored than he—which only showed how little your papa knows, for all so learned a man as he is," said Alice, shifting her position, and turning her face to me to place a parcel of books in the great chest; "for Mr. Brian was a man to like, and not to love."

She was blaming my father, and, perhaps, she had more blame to say; but her blame inferred more than praise, I thought, and I listened eagerly. Yes! my father was a man to love and not to like.

"They say courting time is a happy time," said Alice with a sigh, "it was not so then, Miss Hester. However, they all came to an explanation at last. I cannot tell you how it came about, but we heard one day that Mr. Brian was going abroad, and that Mr. Howard was betrothed to Miss Helen. I knew it before any one else, for my young lady trusted me; and when I saw your papa the next day, his face was glorious to behold, Miss Hester. I think he must have had as much joy in that day as most men have in all their lives, for I don't think I ever saw him look quite happy again."

"Alice!"

"My dear, it is quite true," said Alice quietly, and with another sigh: "I could not tell for a long time what it was that made him so overcast and moody, and neither could my young lady. It could not be Mr. Brian, for Mr. Brian gave her up in the kindest and quietest way; you could not have believed how glad he was to sacrifice himself to his brother—and went away to the West Indies where your grandmamma had an estate, to look after the poor people there; so then the marriage was over very soon, and your grandpapa Southcote took the young people home to live with him at Cottiswoode, and any one that knew how fond he was of Miss Helen, would have thought Mr. Howard had got all the desire of his heart. But he had not, Miss Hester! The heart of man is never satisfied, the Bible says—and I have often seen your papa's face look as black and miserable after he was married, as when he used to sit watching Mr. Brian and my poor dear young lady. Your mamma did not know what to think of it, but she always hung about him with loving ways and was patient, and drooped, and pined away till my heart was broken to look at her. Then she revived all at once, and there was more life in the house for a little while—she had found out what ailed him: but oh! Miss Hester, a poor woman may set her life on the stake to change a perverse fancy, and never shake it till she dies. Your papa had got it into his head that my young lady had married him out of pity; and all her pretty ways, and her love, and kindnesses, he thought them all an imposition, my dear—and that is the reason why he says that hard, cruel saying, 'Pity is a cheat!'"

"And then, Alice?" said I, eagerly.

"And then? there was very little more, Miss Hester—she was hurried out of this world when you were born; she had never time to say a word to him, and went away with that bitterness in her heart, that the man she had left father and mother for, never understood her. Death tries faith, my dear, though you know nothing of it! think how I stood looking at her white face in her last rest! Thinking of her life and her youth, and that this was the end of all; so carefully as she had been trained and guarded from a child, and all her education and her books, and such hopes as there were of what she would be when she grew up a woman; but soon I saw that she grew up only to die—God never changes, Miss Hester— he tries a poor woman like me very like the way he tried Abraham—and that was what I call a fiery passage for faith!"

"And my mother, Alice? and poor, poor papa! oh! how did he ever live after it?" cried I, through my tears.

"He lived because it was the will of God—as we all do," said Alice, "a sad man, and a lonely he is to this day: and will never get comfort in his heart for the wrong he did my dear young lady—never till he meets her in heaven."

At that moment Alice was called and went away. Poor, poor papa! he was wrong; but how my heart entered into his sufferings. I did not think of the bitterness of love disbelieved and disturbed, of my mother's silent martyrdom—I thought only of my father, my first of men! He loved her, and he thought she pitied him. I started from my seat at the touch of this intolerable thought. I realized in the most overwhelming fulness, what he meant when he said, "Pity is a cheat!" Pity! it was dreadful to think of it—though it was but a mistake, a fancy—what a terrible cloud it was!

I will not say that this story filled my mind so much, that I do not recollect the other events of that day; on the contrary, I recollect them perfectly, down to the most minute detail; but they are all connected in my mind with my grief for my father—with the strange, powerful compassion I had for him, and some involuntary prescience of my own fate. For it was him I thought of, and never my mother, whom I had never seen, and whose gentle, patient temper was not so attractive to my disposition. No—I never thought he was to blame! I never paused to consider if it was himself who had brought this abiding shadow over his life. I only echoed his words in my heart, and clung to him, in secret, with a profound and passionate sympathy. Pity! I shuddered at the word. I no longer wondered at his haughty rejection of the slightest approach to it—for did not I myself share—exaggerate this very pride.

This mournful tedious day went on, and its dreary business was accomplished: all our belongings were taken away from Cottiswoode, and Alice and another servant accompanied them to set our new house in order before we came. Just before she went away, at noon, when the autumn day was at its brightest, I found Alice cutting the roses from my favorite tree. I stood looking at her, as she took the pale faint flowers one by one, but neither of us spoke at first: at last I asked her, "why do you take them, Alice?" and I spoke so low, and felt so reverential that I think I must have anticipated her reply.

I had to bend forward to her, to hear what she said. "They were your mother's," said Alice, "I decked her bride chamber with them, and her last bed. They are like what she was when trouble came."

She had only left one rose upon the tree, a half blown rose, with dew still lying under its folded leaves, and she went away, leaving me looking at it. I felt reproved, I know not why, as if my young mother was crying to me for sympathy, and I would not give it. No! I went back hastily to the dreary half-emptied library where my father sat. My place was by him—this solitary man, who all his life had felt it rankling in his heart, that he was pitied where he should have been loved.

In the evening, just before sunset, I heard wheels approaching, and on looking out, saw the post-chaise which was to take us to Cambridge coming down the avenue. My father saw it also; we neither of us said anything, but I went away at once to put on my bonnet. It was dreadful to go into these desolate rooms, which were all the more desolate because they were not entirely dismantled, but still had pieces of very old furniture here and there, looking like remains of a wreck. After I had left my own room—a vague dusty wilderness now, with the damp air sighing in at the open lattice, and the loose jessamine bough beating against it, and dropping its dreary little leaves—I stole into the dining parlor for a moment to look at that picture which was like Edgar Southcote. I looked up at it with my warm human feelings, my young, young exaggerated emotions, full of resentful dislike and prejudice; it looked down on me, calm, beautiful, melancholy, like a face out of the skies. Pity, pity, yes! I hurried away stung by the thought. Edgar Southcote had the presumption to pity my father and me.

With a last compunctious recollection of my poor young mother, I went to the garden and tenderly brought away that last rose. I could cry over it, without feeling that I wept because Cottiswoode was my cousin's and not mine. "I will always keep it!" I said to myself, as I wrapped some of the fragrant olive-colored leaves of the walnut round its stalk; and then I went in to my father to say I was ready. He had left the library, and was walking through the house—I could hear his slow heavy footsteps above me as I listened breathlessly in the hall. Whitehead, and the other servants, had collected there to say good-bye. Whitehead, who was an old man, was to remain in charge of the house; but all the others, except his niece Amy, were to go away this very night. While I stood trying to speak to them, and trying very hard not to break down again, my father came down stairs, went into the dining-parlor, and passed through the window into the garden. I thought he wished to escape the farewell of the servants, so I said good-bye hurriedly and followed him; but he was only walking up and down, looking at the house. He took my hand mechanically, as I came up to him, and led me along the walk in silence; then I was very much startled to find that he took hold of my arm, and leaned on it as if he wanted a support. I looked up at him wistfully when he paused at last—he was looking up at a window above; but he must have felt how anxiously my eyes sought his face, for he said slowly, as if he were answering a question, "Hester, I have lived here." I did not dare to say anything, but I held very close to my heart my mother's rose; he was thinking of her then, he was not thinking of pity nor of any bitterness.

In a few minutes he was quite himself once more, and drew my hand upon his arm, and went in with me to say farewell to the servants; he did so with grace and dignity like an old knight of romance—for he was never haughty to his inferiors, and they all loved him. They were crying and sobbing, every one of them—even old Whitehead—and I cried too, I could not help it; but my father was quite unmoved. He put me into the chaise, took his seat beside me, waved his hand out of the window, smiling as he did so—and then he closed the blinds rapidly on that side, and the carriage drove away. It was all over like a dream. I dared not and could not, look back upon the home which had been the centre of my thoughts all my life; and with the cold night wind blowing in our faces, we were hurrying to a new life, altogether severed from our old existence, and from Cottiswoode.

Yes! the wind was in our faces, fresh and cold—and I never feel it so now without an instant recollection of that long silent drive to Cambridge, through the darkening October night. The long dark levels of the fields rushed past us so swiftly, and with such a desolate quietness; and the long luminous line of the horizon, and the dull clouds of night kept us company with such a ghost-like constancy, travelling at as quick a pace as ours. I was soon tired of weeping under my veil, for I had all the restlessness of my years; and I can see now how the darkness brooded upon the flat meadows, how there seemed no human divisions of fence or hedge upon them, but only one blank line of grass from which the night had taken all color, and of ploughed land stretching back its lessening furrows over many acres, which the eye ached to see. Sometimes miles away, a pollard willow bristled up upon the sky, showing its every twig with a strange exaggeration as it stood guarding some dreary point of road—and the solitary haystack which belonged to some one of those poor stray cottages belated among the fields, threw up its bulk like a goblin against that clear universal background—that pale line of sky which brought out every outline with such a ghostly distinction. Distance, space, the wild idea of an unending and unreposing journey, are the very spirit and sentiment of this country—I think sometimes its dull unfeatured outline is half sublime; there are no mountain heights to attain to, no sweet valleys charming you to rest; only the long lines converging into the infinite sky—the fresh breeze in your face—and the rushing of your own footsteps through the silence, crying—on—on!

There was not a word exchanged between us all the way—my father sat quite still, looking out from one window, engaged I know not how, while I looked from the other, feeling a strange enjoyment in the mere motion and progress, and in the silence and dreamy dreariness of all those flat, unvarying lines, that glided past us in the twilight and the night.

There were neither moon nor stars, yet it was not very dark, even when we reached Cambridge—I had been in the town before, but I knew little of it, and I had no knowledge of where we were, when we stopped beside the old church of St. Benet, and my father assisted me to alight. I was surprised, for there were only some mean houses and a shop before us—but he drew my hand within his arm, and led me along a paved and narrow lane, on one side of which was the churchyard. The light seemed quite shut out here—it was like descending a well to go boldly into that darkness; but we went on, past the little new houses on the one hand, and the old conventual buildings, which loomed on us so strangely from the other, till we paused at a door where some one stood with a lantern. As the man raised his lantern and the light flashed up, I saw that we were to enter under this arched doorway, which had a coat of arms in the keystone. There were two or three steps to descend, and then the door was closed, and we went along a narrow path, where there was a blank wall covered with ivy on one side, and the house on the other. The light of the lantern gleamed in those dark glistening ivy leaves, and in the square projecting windows of this new home of ours. I was glad to see how different from the massy glories of Cottiswoode, was this strange house, with its two projections, one supported on dark oaken beams, and the other built up from the ground. The building was only wood, and lath and plaster, except the heavy and unlighted ground story, which was grey and aged stone; and the broad square windows on the upper floor which filled the whole front of each projecting part, were formed of small diamond panes. But I saw no mode of entrance, nothing but tall ungainly rose bushes, and withered creepers nestling up against the walls, till we turned a corner and came to a door in the end of the house, where Alice was standing to receive us. We had to make our way in here through a ragged regiment of tall straggling hollyhocks—I have hated them ever since that night.

But my father had not once addressed me yet, and my own mind was so full, that I had never observed his silence. He spoke now when we were on the threshold, and I started at the sound of his voice. He only said, "Hester, this is your new home!" but I think there was the most wonderful mixture of emotions in his voice that I had ever heard—determined composure, and yet highly excited feeling—disdain of this poor place he brought me to, yet a fixed resolution to show content in it, and stronger and greater pride than ever. My heart echoed the resolution and the pride, as I sprang in—but my heart was young and full of the pleased excitement of novelty and change. I knew nothing of what he felt as he followed me with his slow and stately step—nothing, for I was impatient to see all these rooms that we were to live in, and to make acquaintance with my new home.

So I ran on, leaving him to follow me—I could not have done better, had I been laboring to find something which would comfort and cheer him. My eagerness gave a certain interest to the poor house. I remember that he held me back for a moment, and looked into my face with a slow smile gradually breaking upon his own. Mine, I know, was full of light and animation—I remember how my cheeks glowed from the wind, and how the warmth and the lights had brought water into my eyes; and, I suppose, I looked quite as bright and eager as if I had never known the girlish heroical despair for leaving Cottiswoode which possessed me an hour ago. I ran from one apartment to another, exclaiming at everything, sometimes with pleasure, sometimes with astonishment. The two broad windows which I had seen outside, represented two large apartments, occupying the whole breadth of the house, and each with a window at the other end, looking out upon a great dim silent garden, fenced in by other gardens, and on one side by a dark mass of building, along which a light twinkled here and there. These rooms were not fully furnished, but they were already in a habitable state, and in one of them a bright fire blazed pleasantly, sparkling in the old silver kettle and tea-pot, and antique china, which we always used at home—at home! The words meant these strange rooms, and had no other reference now for my father and me.

But when I went to lay aside my bonnet, I found a room prepared for me, prettier, if that were possible, than the pretty chamber at Cottiswoode, where Alice had tended me all my life. The white draperies were so white, and full, and soft—the pretty chintz hangings were so fresh with their new bands of ribbons, and there was so much care and tenderness in the hands which had restored my old room perfect and unbroken, yet made it brighter than ever, that I clung to Alice with an April face where the tears had somehow lost their bitterness, and the smile its pride. Now and then in my life, I have found out suddenly, in a moment, of how little importance external things were to me. The conviction came upon my mind at this instant, like a sunbeam. What did it matter to me standing here in my triumphant youthfulness, with my father to be loved and cared for, and Alice to love and care for me—what did it matter who lost or who won such outside and external matters as houses and lands? I threw off my mantle upon the kind arm of Alice, and danced away to make tea for my father. In proportion to the depth of my sadness at leaving Cottiswoode, was the height of my exhilaration now to find another home. We had expected this to be a very dreary evening—instead of that I had seldom been so happy, so vivacious, so daring, in my girl's talk; and there sat my father, his face brightening in the firelight, smiling at my boldness, my enthusiasms, my denunciations, my girlish superlative emotion. When tea was over, he fell into a fit of musing, and was not to be disturbed, I knew—and then I examined the room with its wainscot pannels, its carved mantel-shelf, and its pannel pictures, hard flat portraits, which had no pretension to the roundness or the breadth of life, but were as level as the Cambridgeshire flats, and almost as much like each other. And then I went to the further window, and coiled myself up upon the bench within the curtains, to solace myself with my own thoughts. The garden lay dark beneath, with shadowy bare trees here and there, lifting up their branches to the sky, and some fantastic little green-house, or summer-house, half way down, showing a dull glimmer of glass under the boughs. But insensibly my eyes turned from the garden and the darkness, to count the scattered lights in the windows of this dark building, which marked its embrasures upon the sky at my right hand. A light in a window is a strange lure to imagination—I watched them with interest and pleasure—they were unknown, yet they were neighbors—and it was pleasant from hearing the wind without, and seeing the dark, to turn upon the glimmering tapers with a certain friendly warmth and satisfaction, as though some one had said good-night.

And so we were settled to our new beginning, and our new home.

THE THIRD DAY

I was in the garden, where I almost lived in the sweet summer days in those times of my youth; it was June, and I did not fear the windows of Corpus, which looked out upon the trees with their numberless leaves, the trees which were quite shelter enough for me. If I had begun to have visions of the universal romance of youth, my thoughts were much too exalted to think of vulgar fallings in love, and though I constantly hailed as neighbors these kindly lights in the windows of the collegiate buildings, I was troubled by no thought of the young gownsmen, the possible possessors of the same; and so it came about that I went as freely to the garden of our quaint old house, overlooked by the windows of Corpus Christi College as I had been used to go in the garden of Cottiswoode, which was not overlooked by anything within a dozen miles, save the fruit trees in the orchard, and the great walnut by the house.

This was now the second summer since we came to Cambridge, and this garden was no longer the wilderness which it was when I saw it first. My father had a peculiar fancy in gardening—everything in this sunny strip of land was enclosed in a soft frame of greensward—where a path was indispensable, it was a hard, yellow sandy path that glistened in the sun, and threw off the moisture; but instead of geometrical divisions and cross-roads through our garden, you could scarcely see either gravel or soil for the velvet turf that pressed over the roots of the trees, and round the flower-beds; and for the thick and close luxuriance of the flowers that grew within. The one or two Cambridge ladies who came to see me sometimes, shook their heads at our grassy garden, and hoped I took care never to go out when the turf was damp; but, indeed, I took no such care, and was very proud of our full and verdant enclosure in comparison with other people's flower-beds, where nothing grew so well as ours, though everything had more room to grow. On this day of which I am now speaking, the sweet greensward was warm with sunshine in every corner. It was afternoon, and the streets were sultry, the wayfarers flushed and weary, the fields parched and dry; but the sun was playing in the leaves about me, and making playful figures with his light and shadow on the grass under my feet—figures which changed and varied with sweet caprice as the wind swayed the leaves about, and as the sun stole by invisible degrees towards the west—and everything was fresh and sweet and full of fragrance in this charmed country of mine. I was within the little fanciful greenhouse which was no less a bower for me, than a shelter for the rarer flowers, and I was busy about some of my favorites, which I used to care for with great devotion by fits, making up for it by such negligence at other times, that this pretty place would soon have been a very woeful one had it been left to me. Just on the threshold of this green-house door, was the stool on which I had been sitting, with a piece of embroidery at which I had been working thrown down upon it, and beyond that, on the grass, was a book which I had not been reading; for it was not in my girlish, impatient nature to dally with anything readable—I either devoured it, or I let it alone. I was busy among the plants, and so enclosed by them that I was not visible from the garden—but at this moment I was not aware of that.

I did not hear their footsteps upon the soft grass, but I heard the voices of my father and his friend, Mr. Osborne, a fellow of Corpus, who visited us constantly, and always seemed in my father's confidence. They came to the green-house door and lingered there, and Mr. Osborne stood before the door, with his gown streaming and rustling behind him, effectually concealing me if I had not been concealed already. I had no reason to suppose that their talk concerned me; nor was I much interested to listen to it. I went on with my occupation, plunging some slips of favorite plants into little pots of rich vegetable mould, and singing to myself half under my breath. I was quite unsuspicious and so were they.

"No," said my father, "Hester does not know of it. Hester is a girl, Osborne—I have no desire to make a woman of her before her time."

"Yet girls find out for themselves what interest they have in these matters," said Mr. Osborne, in his quiet, half sarcastic tone, "and have speculations in those quiet eyes of theirs, whether we will or no, my friend."

"There are few girls like Hester," said my father, proudly; "pardon me, Osborne, but you have no child—I want to preserve her as she is—why should I bring a disturbing element into our peaceful life?"

"Why? do you think your little girl is safely through her probation, when she has had the measles and the hooping-cough?" said Mr. Osborne, laughing. "Nonsense, man—d'ye think ye save her from the epidemic of youth by shutting her up in this garden here? Take my word for it, these obnoxious things that you call the world and society, are much better preventives than this leisure and solitude. Why look at these windows, and be a sensible man, Southcote; d'ye think nobody in Corpus but an old fellow like me has seen your Proserpine among the flowers? How old is the child? tell me that, and I will tell you how soon there will be moonlight meditations, and breaking hearts, disturbing your peaceful life for you. Hester is a very good girl—of course, she is—but what is that to the question, I should be glad to know?"

I was very indignant by this time. I had very nearly caught his streaming gown, and shaken it with vehement displeasure, but, withal, I was very curious to know what was the origin of this conversation, and I subsided into a perfect guilty silence, and listened with all my might.

"You do not understand Hester, Osborne," said my father.

"Granted," said his friend, quickly, "and perhaps the young lady is not quite an orthodox subject of study, I allow you; but pray what do you intend to do with her? is she to live in this garden for ever, like that fantastic boy's lady of Shalott?"

My father paused and I listened eagerly. It was some time before he answered, and there was hesitation in his usually firm tones.

"Life has deluded me," he said, slowly. "I am at a loss to know how to guard Hester, that it may not delude her also."

"Southcote," said his companion, earnestly, "listen to me a moment. Life deludes no man. You are a self-devourer. You have deluded yourself; nay, take offence and, of course, I have done at once. I do not know the innocent mind of a young girl, very true; but I know that imagination is the very breath of youth—it must look forward, and it must dream—what is Hester to dream about, think you? not of the triumph of an examination, I suppose, nor of going in for honors; you have not even tried to kill the woman in her, and make her a scholar. The child is shamefully ignorant, Southcote. Why here's this feminine rubbish lying under my very feet—look here!" and he pulled up my mangled embroidery. "I should not be surprised now if it pleased your fancy to see her bending her pretty head over this stuff—what's she thinking of all this time, my friend? Nothing, eh? or only how to arrange the stitches, and make one little turn the same as another? I'll trust Hester for that."

There was another pause, and there he stood turning over my work, and I not able to rush forward and snatch it out of his hand. My cheeks burned with shame and anger—how dared any man discuss my thoughts and fancies so!

"Well, here is the real matter," said my father, slowly; "Edgar Southcote, it appears, is eighteen—two years older than my Hester, and old enough, he thinks, as he tells me, to decide upon the most important event of his life for himself—so he sends me a formal proposal for the hand of his cousin. My difficulty is not whether to accept the proposal—you understand that, Osborne—but whether, before giving it a peremptory and decided negative, I ought to make it known to Hester?"

"I understand. Well now, waiving that principal difficulty, might one ask why this young man's very reasonable proposal should have such a peremptory negative?" said Mr. Osborne; "for my own part I do not see that this is at all a necessary conclusion."

"I am afraid it must suffice that I think it so," said my father, in his firmest and coldest tone.

"On your high horse again, Southcote? Patience a little, now. Your brother Brian was not a strong-minded man—but a very good fellow for all that. What's your objection now to his son?"

I almost trembled for this cool scrutinizing of my father's motives and opinions, which he never revealed to any one—yet I too listened with interest for the answer. No answer came. My father spoke hurriedly and with irritation; but he did not reply.

"I presume you will permit us some little exercise of our own will as to the person whom we admit into our family," he said; "but enough of this. Do you advise me to tell Hester, or to dispose of the affair on my own responsibility?"

Mr. Osborne seemed bent upon provoking my father's slumbering resentment.

"Well," he said with a pause of much consideration, "had the boy proposed to you, the answer would have lain with you of course—but I think it quite possible that some time or other in her life, Hester might remember that her old home in all its revenues, and, I have no doubt, a very worthy and generous youth along with them, had been laid at her feet, and her father, on his own responsibility, threw them away."

"Osborne!" cried my father—I almost expected he would command him away, and bid him never more enter our house. I am sure I felt that I never could address him with ordinary civility again—but instead of that, after a moment's pause, my father resumed, in vehement tones certainly, but not in tones of anger at the speaker. "Generous! and you think I would give my daughter to one who sought her from a generous impulse; you forget my life and you forget me."

How my heart throbbed and resounded in its quick and painful beating!—I cannot tell how strangely I felt the possibility that I myself might one day or other realize in my own person the misfortune of my father's life. Yes, Mr. Osborne was right thus far, I had not been thinking of nothing while I sat in the sunshine working at my embroidery. I had already seen dimly through the golden mists the hero, the prince, the red cross knight. I had already seen myself worshipped with the pure devotedness of chivalry. I had already, like a true girl and woman, imagined all manner of glories and honors won for me by my true knight, and prized because they made him nobler, and not because they exalted me. Yes! I had been dreaming innocent, beautiful, unworldly dreams—when lo! there fell upon me a vision of my cousin Edgar, and his generous impulse. I clenched my hands upon my little plant in a passion of indignation. The words stung me to the heart.

"Well—I am not astonished that you regard it in this light," said Mr. Osborne, "but you must confess, at the same time, Southcote, that there is a more common sense way of looking at it. The boy is a good boy, and feels that he has been the means of injuring his cousin—what more natural than that the two branches of the family should unite their claims in this most satisfactory way—what is your objection to it? A punctilio? Come, don't talk of it to Hester yet—let's have a fight, old friend. I flatter myself you were none the worse in the old days of arguing out the matter with Frank Osborne. Now, then, for your arguments. Heigho! Howard, my boy, do you recollect the last time?"

There was so long a pause that I could not help stealing forward to look what was the reason. My father's face was as black as night, and he stood opposite his friend in a rigid fixed attitude, vacantly looking at him—then he turned suddenly on his heel, "Excuse me—I am faint—I will return to you instantly," he said, as he hurried in. Mr. Osborne shrugged his shoulders, gazed after him, shrugged again, began to whistle, and then suddenly turning round found himself face to face with me.

For the first moment I think I was the least disconcerted—for I was very angry and indignant beyond measure; but, as his face gradually brightened into its usual expression of shrewdness and good-humored sarcasm, my own courage fell. I had been eavesdropping, finding out my father's secrets without his knowledge—playing a very shabby part—I who piqued myself upon my sense of honor.

"So!" said Mr. Osborne, "your father is right, young lady. I see I did not understand Hester; pray what may you be doing here?"

And I, who had intended to denounce his paltry views, and to pour out the full tide of my indignation upon him for thwarting and chafing my father—I was ready to cry with vexation and mortified pride. "I did not intend to listen—I was only here by chance—and, at first, I thought you knew I was here," said I, making a pause between each sentence, swallowing down my ire and my humiliation. After all I had heard, to have to excuse myself to him!

"Well, your father's run away," said Mr. Osborne; "suppose we finish the argument, Hester. It is your concern after all; but I suppose such a thing as a sweetheart, or the dim possibility of being wooed and married never entered your guileless thoughts at all?"

I did not answer him—my girlish pride was on fire, and my cheeks burnt, but I could find nothing sufficiently annihilating to reply to Mr. Osborne.

We heard the noise of an opened door just then, and of a footstep in the passage which led to the garden. Mr. Osborne glanced hastily round him, and then bent forward to me.

"Hester, attend to me. You are very young, and have had a wild education; try, if you can think before you permit your father to decide on this. Do you mark me? I know this boy—he is a better boy than you are, and he has a fantastic fancy for you, as great as you could desire. Hester, here's your father. I'll keep your secret, and do you think of what I say."

My father joined us immediately. If it surprised him to find me there, he took no notice of it, and I was glad to pick up my embroidery and hurry away. I was impressed with an uncomfortable necessity for thinking about it, from what Mr. Osborne had said, and I went to my own room to recollect myself. I could not deny either that I was a little excited and agitated about this new appearance of Edgar Southcote. It did not soften my heart to him, but it awoke my curiosity, and it made a step in my life. I said to myself with a beating heart—a heart disturbed with wonder, with anger, with surprise, and something like affright, that I was no longer a girl, but a woman now, standing upon the threshold of my life. I was sixteen. I thought I was rapidly maturing and growing old, for in this old house of ours, so quiet and withdrawn from common company, the days were peopled with fancies and imaginary scenes, and I did not know how very, very young and girlish were my secret conceptions of life and of the world.

Life! Here was my father, a man in whom I could see no blemish—what was his existence? Such as it was, he lived it in his library, among his books; talking with me now and then, and coming forth to take a long silent solitary walk, or a stroll in the garden in the evening, once or twice a week. Was this all? yes! and I said within myself in reverent explanation of it, that his life had been blighted and cast down by one wrong that always gnawed at his heart; he had married for love; but my mother had married him for pity. Was not this enough to account for the sombre shade in which he lived and walked? I said yes, yes! in eager youthful enthusiasm—yes, this was surely enough to decide for good or evil the whole tenor of a life.

And then there was Alice! Nothing in this house or about it, not even the sunshine, cheered my heart like the smile of Alice; yet she was not merry, and had little to be merry for. Alice was like one who had come out of a desert, leaving all her loves and treasures there behind her—she had lost everything, everything but her life—what had she to live for? I shuddered while I said so; for without Alice how dreary would my days be; and then I paused to recollect that on the borders of this grand and momentous existence, where my father had failed in his own enterprise for happiness, and in which Alice had lost all she loved, my own feet were standing now.

This was what I thought on the subject which Mr. Osborne recommended to my consideration; when I thought again of Edgar, it was with a renewed flush of anger and mortification. My cousin pitied me, who dreamed of inspiring some true knight with the loftiest ambitions, and rewarding him sufficiently with a smile. I was to be subjected to the humiliating proposals which Edgar Southcote's "generous impulse" suggested to him! These were unfortunate words—how often they have clamored in my ear, and haunted me since then.

I did not go into the garden again that day; not even when it was twilight, and the dews were culling out the odors, and the murmur of hushed sounds and distant voices from the quiet town charmed the dim air into an enchanted calm. In my new-born consciousness, I walked up and down the dim close, at the other side of the house, where there were no windows overlooking the high walls and its glistening ivy. I would be no Proserpine among the flowers, to any foolish boy who dared spy upon my retirement from the college windows. Proserpine! if Mr. Osborne had known I heard him, he never would have called me by that name, nor supposed that any gownsman of Corpus could ever interest me! I had a great contempt for my next neighbors in my girlish loftiness and maturity. I could not have been more insulted than by such an insinuation as this.

And then I went to the drawing-room, and stationed myself at my usual place in the window; the long room was nearly dark, though the pale half-light streamed through it from window to window, and it was strange to look across the whole length of the room to the ivy leaves faintly quivering on the wall at the other side. My father and Mr. Osborne, who had dined with us, were walking in the garden, talking earnestly, and with some indignation I watched them, wondering if they still talked of me. Then there came out, one by one, these lights in the windows, some of them looking faint and steady like true students' lamps, some suspiciously bright as though there was merry-making within. It pleased me to watch them, as window after window brightened on the night. I scorned the inmates; but I did not scorn these neighborly and kindly lights.

My father came in very soon, and Mr. Osborne called me to say good-night; I went down to him where he stood at the door, and he held my hand a moment, and looked into my face. "Now, Hester, good night—think of what I said," he repeated. These words induced me to return very quickly upstairs, where my father had gone, following Alice with the lamp. When she had placed it on the table and left the room, I went to my father and stood beside him, till he lifted his eyes from the book. He looked at me with a kind loving look, as if he had pleasure in seeing me—a look not very usual to my father—and took my hand as he always used to do, when I stood at his knee, to ask anything of him as a child, and said, "Well, Hester?" I was full of excitement and resolution, and came to my subject at once, without remembering that I might be blamed for what I had to say first. "I was in the greenhouse, papa, when you were talking there with Mr. Osborne to-day," I said, firmly—and then I paused with a sudden recollection that this was not quite consistent either with my father's code of honor or my own.

"I did not intend to listen—it was very wrong—but I could not conceal it from you, now it is done," I proceeded hurriedly, "and I have come to say, papa, that I heard what you told Mr. Osborne about Edgar Southcote. I wonder how he dares presume upon us so; I think a true gentleman would be sorry to let us see that he was able to be generous to us; and I hope you will write to him at once, papa, and if it is necessary to say anything from me, let it be that I hope there never will be any communication between us, nor any need for me to tell him what I think in plain words."

My father continued to smile upon me, holding my hand, but without speaking—then he said, still with a smile—"This is a very enigmatical message, Hester—I am afraid I must make it plainer; for this young man, your cousin, has not dared nor presumed so much as you seem to think, my love; I am to tell him that we cannot entertain any proposal for an alliance between the rival branches of the house of Southcote, that we beg his overtures may not be repeated, and though sensible of the great honor he does us, we must beg to decline any further correspondence on the subject—is that what you mean, Hester? I think that is about as much as we are entitled to say."

I was scarcely pleased at the playful manner in which my father now treated a matter which he evidently had not looked on in a playful light a few hours ago; but, at the same time, his tone made me ashamed of my own vehemence, and I assented hastily. He still held my hand, and his face became quite grave—he seemed to see that I was surprised, and wanted explanation of what he had said.

"I am afraid we are thinking of this young man with a little bitterness, Hester," said my father, raising his lofty head, "which is not very creditable to us, I fear, my love;—that he has claimed and won what is justly his own, can be no wrong or offence to us. It is rather my part to thank him that he has set me right, than to imply that he has injured me. This last is by no means a dignified assumption, Hester, and it is more or less implied in every harsh judgment we give against your cousin—whereas he is simply indifferent to us, and in rejecting this proposal, I do it with civility, you perceive, just as I would any proposal which was distasteful, from whomsoever it came."

This speech of my father's impressed me very greatly; I left him holding my head erect, yet feeling humbled. Yes, I had been very bitter in my heart against Edgar Southcote—I had felt resentment against him, strong and violent, as the supplanter of my father; but it was mean to dislike him on such a ground—it was what Alice called "a poor pride;" yet I confess, it was somewhat difficult to rise, in anything but words, to the altitude of the other pride, and say "he is quite indifferent to me—he has done me no wrong—it is not possible that I can have any grudge against my cousin."

It was thus that I returned to my window-seat; when I placed myself in my favorite corner, I looped up the curtain, so that I could look in as well as out. The room was dim with that summer dimness which only the evening firelight drives away, and the mild light of the lamp shone softly in the middle of the silent apartment, throwing every piece of furniture near in shadows on the carpet, and leaving all the corners in a faint half-shade of darkness. The point of light in the room was my father's high white forehead, looking like marble with that illumination on it, and contrasting so strangely with his black hair. I looked at him as I might have looked at a picture. On one of his thin white fingers he had a ring, a very fine diamond in a slender circle of gold, which flashed and shone in the light as he raised his hand, now and then, to turn a leaf—behind him and around him there was shadow and darkness, but the light had gathered on his face, and shone there like a star to me, as I lay within the curtain looking out into the stillness: and on my other hand was the soft gloom of a summer night lying close with its downy plumes upon the trees, and the soft pale skies with a faint star in them here and there, and the lights in the college windows glowing upon youth and untried strength like mine. Rest and calm, and the mild oblivion of the night enclosed us like the arms of angels, but did not silence the swell of the rising tide in my heart.

THE FOURTH DAY

It was winter again, a gloomy November day, ungenial and cold. The rain was beating on the dark buildings of the college, and saturating the dreary greensward in our garden, till it sunk under the foot like a treacherous bog. There was not a leaf on the trees, and the ivy on the high wall of the close at the other side, glistened and fluttered under the rain. There was nothing very cheerful to be seen out of doors. I was alone in our drawing-room, and it was still early, and nothing had occurred to break the morning torpor of this unbrightened day. I was sitting at the table, working with great assiduity, with scraps of my materials lying round me on every side. My occupation was not a very serious one, though I pursued it with devotion. I was only dressing a doll for a little girl, who was niece to Alice, and named after me; but as it did not consist with my ambitious desires to have a doll of my dressing arrayed like a doll which could be bought by any one, I was attiring this one in elaborate historical costume, like a lady of the age of Elizabeth, or even—so stiff and so grand was she—like that grim and glorious sovereign herself.

The fire burned with a deep red glow, so full that it warmed and reddened the very color of the room; and though it was a very subdued and gloomy light which came through the rain, from those heavy leaden skies, there was a warmth and comfort in the stillness here, which was rather increased than diminished by the dreary prospect without. It was very still—the great old clock ticking on the stair, the rain pattering upon the gravel and on the broad flag-stones at the kitchen door below, the faint rustle of the ivy leaves upon the wall, and sometimes the footsteps of Alice, or of Mary, as they went up and down about their household work, were all the sounds I could hear; and as the excitement of my enterprise subsided, and my occupation itself was almost done, I began to be restless in the extreme quietness. It is true, I was very well used to it, and made up to myself largely by dreams and by visions; but I am not sure that I was much of a dreamer by nature. I had a strong spirit of action and adventure stirring within me. I was moved by the swiftest and most uncontrollable impulses, and had such a yearning upon me to do something now and then, that there was about the house a score of things begun, which it was impossible I could ever finish, and which, indeed, I never tried to finish, except under a momentary inspiration. If any one had tried to direct me, I might have applied to better purpose my superfluous energy—but no one did—so I wasted it in wild fancies, and turbulent attempts at doing something, and sometimes got so restless with the pressure of my own active thoughts and unemployed faculties, that I could rest nowhere, but wandered about as perverse and unreasonable as it was possible for a lonely girl to be, and generally ended by quarrelling with Alice, and finding myself to be in the wrong, and miserable to my heart's content.

This stillness! it began to get intolerable now—to sit and look at these ivy leaves, and at the rain soaking into the spongy grass—to feel the warm full glow of the fire actually make me sleepy in the vacancy of my life—I started up in high disdain, and threw down the doll which caricatured Queen Elizabeth. I wanted something to do—something to do—I was sixteen and a half, high spirited, warm tempered, a Southcote! and I had nothing better to do with my youth and my strength, than to fall asleep over the fire, before it was noon in the day! I rushed down stairs immediately, with one of my sudden impulses to make some sort of attack upon Alice. I would have been glad to think that it was somebody's fault that my life was of so little use; and I ran along the passage leading to the kitchen with an impatient step; on the same floor was my father's study, and a little odd parlor where we now and then sat; but I did not disturb my father with my perverse thoughts.

The kitchen was not very large, but looked so cheerful, that it always reminded me of Alice. The walls of the ground floor of the house were founded on some tiers of massy stonework, and I suppose that gave it a look of warmth and stability—and in the side of the room, which was of this same old masonry almost to the roof, there was a little high window with an arched top, which threw a strange stream of sunlight into the room, and constantly annoyed Alice, in the summer, by putting out her fire. There was no sun to put out anybody's fire to-day, but the rain beat against the panes instead, and the high straggling head of a withered hollyhock nodded at the window-sill, with the dreariest impertinence. In the breadth of the kitchen, however, looking out on the garden, was a broad low lattice, quite uncurtained, which gave the fullest light of which the day was capable to this cheerful apartment; and at the great table which stood by it, Alice was standing making some delicate cakes, in the manufacture of which she excelled. I came up to her hastily, and threw myself upon the wooden chair beside her. I was full of those endless metaphysical inquiries which youth—and especially youth that has nothing to do, abounds in—what was life for—what was it—what was the good of me, my particular self, and for what purpose did I come into the world? Before now, I had poured my questionings into the ears of Alice, but Alice was very little moved by them, I am constrained to say.

"Have you done, Miss Hester?" said Alice, for I had taken her into my counsels to discuss the momentous question of the doll's costume, and of what period it was to be.

"Oh, yes! I am done," said I; "only think, Alice, nothing better to do all this morning than dress a doll; and now I have nothing at all to do."

"Dear Miss Hester, you never can want plenty of things to amuse you," said Alice; "don't speak to me so—it's unkind to your papa."

"I don't want things to amuse me," said I, "I want something to do, Alice. What is the use of me—it is very well for you—you are always busy—but I want to know what's the good of me!"

"You must not say that, dear! don't now," said Alice, "you're but a child—you're only coming to your life—"

"I don't think life is much better, Alice," said I. "Mr. Osborne and my father dispute for hours about passages in Greek books; are books life? I don't think there's any satisfaction in them, more than in dressing a doll."

"You did not think so on Tuesday night, my dear," said Alice quietly, "when the light was in your window half through the night, and I know you were sitting up reading one."

"Ah! but that was a novel," I cried, starting up, "that is the very thing! May I send Mary to the library? I will have one to-day."

So I ran up stairs to make a list of certain desirable volumes, and sent off Mary forthwith; then I returned to the table, where Alice made her cakes, and to my wooden chair.

"No, there is no satisfaction in them," said I, "even a novel has an end, Alice; but do you think that reading pages of printed paper is all that people need to care for—do you think that is life?"

"Life is not one thing, but a many things, Miss Hester," said Alice. "Dear, you're a-coming to it now."

"What am I coming to—only to breakfast, and dinner, and supper, over and over again, Alice," said I. "I don't think it was so at Cottiswoode, but it is so here, I know—then you have to work all day to cook for us, and we have to eat what you cook—and that is our life."

"Don't speak so, Miss Hester," entreated Alice once more, "it is not a poor woman like me that can tell you what life is; there were ten years or more in my life that were full of great things happening to me; but little happened to me before or after—you would think it was not worth my while living after these years."

I confessed to my thought. "Yes, Alice! I am afraid I did think so; though I would be a very desolate girl, I am sure, without you."

It seemed to move her a little, this that I said. Her cheeks reddened, and she paused in her work.

"If you were older, you would know better," said Alice. "After the last of them were gone, it was a dreary, dreary time. I rose to do my work, Miss Hester, and laid me down to sleep and forget what a lonesome woman I was. What was it you said this morning about the new day cheering you, and the fresh spirit you had when you woke, howsoever you had been at night? I know what that is—but after my troubles, when I opened my eyes, and saw the daylight, it made me sick—I used to turn my face to the wall, and wish and wish that I might sleep on, and never wake to think about what had befallen me; but still I lived, and still I lived, and the breakfast and the dinner and the common ways were what God had appointed me. If I said life was trouble and sorrow, would you like it better than when its only comfort was quiet, and reading books as it is with you?"

"But it was not all trouble and sorrow, Alice, in these ten years?"

Her face changed again a little. I knew I was urging her to a painful subject, yet I did not pause; and I do not think my questions grieved her, even though they revived her grief.

"When joy turns to sorrow, it's the sorest grief of all, Miss Hester," said Alice; "no, I was happy beyond the common lot of women, but one by one everything I rejoiced in was taken away. Yes, that was life—I had babies in my arms, and plans for them in my heart; I was working and contriving for their schooling and their clothing, and laying by for them and considering in my mind how to train them up. We were walking together, striving for them, using all our strength, my husband and me; ay, that was life!"

I was a little awed by the words and said nothing. All this had ceased for Alice—absolutely ceased—yet left a far sorer blank than if it had never been. As I looked at her, going on very hurriedly with her work, something I had been reading came to my mind. I said it aloud, watching her, and wondering if it was true—

"I hold it true whate'er befall, I feel it when I sorrow most; 'Tis better to have loved and lost Than never to have loved at all."

Alice turned round to me eagerly with a tear shining in her eye.

"Don't you think I'd rather have been without them, Miss Hester; don't you think it now! it's hard to lose, but it's blessed to have; that's true—that's true! I would not have been without one, though they're all gone: I have read in books many a time, good books, books that were written on purpose to comfort the sorrowful," said Alice, sinking to her usual quietness of tone, "that God did but lend our treasures to us, to take them back at His pleasure. No, Miss Hester, no!—as sure as they are His, my darling, His first and His always, so sure do I know that He's keeping them for me."

I was silenced again, and had nothing to say, for the name of God then was nothing but a sound of awe to me. I held it in the deepest reverence, this wonderful great name—but Him, the august and gracious Person to whom my poor Alice lived, her bereaved and pious life, was unknown to me.

And Alice, I believe, had reproached herself already, for bringing her real griefs, or the shadow of them, to eclipse my cherished discontent. She returned to me with her face lighting up again in its cheerful kind humility.

"Ay, Miss Hester, that's life to a woman," said Alice, "and, my dear, in a year or two, you will find it waiting for you."

But this did not at all chime in with the current of my thoughts.

"Do you think, Alice, that a woman is fit for nothing but to be married?" I exclaimed, fiercely. Poor Alice was taken by surprise: she had not expected such a flush of sudden displeasure—she paused in her work, and looked at my crimsoned face with a glance of real apprehension. Alice was old-fashioned and held by many primitive notions—she did not understand what I could mean.

"Miss Hester, if it's the nuns you're thinking of, I'll break my heart," said Alice.

"I'm not thinking of the nuns," cried I, indignantly, "why should a lady be married any more than Mr. Osborne? do you mean I could not be as well by myself as he is? I do not think you can have any woman-pride when you speak so, Alice."

Alice smiled with her eyes when I made this speech, but kept her gravity otherwise. "To be like Mr. Osborne is nothing much to wish for, my dear," said Alice, quietly, "but I can tell you, Miss Hester, it is not Mr. Osborne's fault that he is living lone in his rooms, a college gentleman, instead of having his own house, and a happy family round him—if it had pleased God. Ah! if Mr. Osborne had been the man!"

"What do you mean?" said I, quickly; I had an instinctive suspicion as she spoke.

"Long days ago, before ever your papa knew my dear young lady, Mr. Osborne came a-courting to her," said Alice, "and if you'd have told that merry young gentleman what he was to come to, he'd have laughed in your face then; he did not choose for himself in those days to be living all by himself as he does now."

"Mamma again," said I under my breath, with wonder and curiosity, "did she break his heart too?"

"To tell the truth I do not think she did, Miss Hester," said Alice, with a smile, "it's only a heart here and there, my dear, that breaks when it's crossed in love."

"Alice!" cried I, horror-stricken at her want of feeling—for I had a very poor opinion of any heart which would not break instantly for such a weighty reason.

"She did not break his heart, dear; she only disappointed him," said Alice, "and I never heard how it was that he took so much to learning and settled down here; but he never had any grudge at Miss Helen, though I can see he likes you the better for it, that you sometimes have a look like her sweet face."

"She was my mother," said I doubtfully, "but it was cruel of her to marry papa, Alice. Why was it, I wonder, that so many people cared for her?"

"It was because she deserved better love than she ever got in this world," said Alice, with a start; "why was it cruel of her to marry your papa, Miss Hester? It was cruel of him—she never gave him cause to doubt her, she waited on his will as if he had been a king; oh! my dear, your papa was hard upon my young lady, and all for a fancy of his own."

"It has blighted his life, Alice," said I.

"Your papa is my master, Miss Hester," said Alice, with some pride, "and you and I can only speak of him as his servant and his daughter should—but I would have you think upon your mamma sometimes—your dear, sweet, innocent young mother; she never did harm to any living creature; she was always a delight to look upon till—"

"Till what, Alice?"

"My dear, till her heart broke."

Alice moved away without saying another word; this was a perplexing new light upon my meditations, but I was very reluctant to receive it. If it should happen that my mother had been misconceived and misinterpreted—that she, after all, was the wronged person, and that my father was to blame, it might have made a great difference in the influences which just then were moulding my mind and life; but I rejected this unwelcome conclusion—I would not permit myself to be convinced of it. I clung over again to my father, and made my stand by him, and so went on, unconsciously determining and ripening for my fate.

"Don't take it ill of me, Miss Hester," said Alice, coming back, and I thought her voice trembled slightly, "but never distrust one that cares for you, dear—don't do it—you can't tell what ill comes of it in a house; and when any one speaks to you of a blighted life, be you sure it's his own doing more or less, and not another's. Take heed to your way, darling, there's not a speck on your life yet; but the cloud rises like a man's hand, Miss Hester. Pray that it may never come to you."

"Alice, how can it come to me?" cried I, trying to smile at her earnestness, yet I was angry for her implied blame of my father, and at the moment Edgar Southcote's rejected overtures flashed upon my mind. Yes! if by any chance these had been accepted, the curse of my father's life would have come to me. I was silent, oppressed by a vague discomfort; it was foolish, but I could not overcome it, and Alice did not answer my question, but returned to her work once more.

When Mary came back with the novel I wanted, I confess that I ran up stairs with it, and that there ensued an immediate dispersion of my thoughts—nor did I recal them much till the evening when I had galloped through the three volumes, and was left sitting by the fire in the sudden reaction of excitement, to cogitate upon the disagreeable necessity common to stories, of coming to an end. My father, who, from habit and punctilio, never returned to the library in the evening, sat at the table as usual with his book, and after a little pause of impatience at the conclusion of my tale, I resumed the thread of my previous meditations. I had been a little startled and shaken to-day in my thoughts. To say that I was inclined to scoff at the youthful notion of a life determined once and for ever by the misfortune which Alice mentioned as being "crossed in love," would be to say what was not true—for my ideal belief in this extraordinary and all-powerful unknown influence was as devout as that of any girl or boy of my years, and I had an equal admiration for that melancholy constant faithful lover, doomed to be unrequited, and never to overcome his disappointment, of whose existence many a romance had made me aware. But I was misanthropical to-night from the abrupt ending of my novel—and there was still the greater part of the evening left vacant with no new story to begin—so I speculated with a more sceptical mind than usual upon my great problem. Was it my mother, so many years ago—twenty years or more, a fabulous and unappreciable period, before I was born—whose rejection of him had fixed Mr. Osborne in his rooms at Corpus, and made the records of his life little better than a library catalogue?

Was it my mother, and his disappointment in her, which had cast my father into his existence of aimless and sombre dignity? Was all this the single work of a young girl who died nearly seventeen years ago, and who was not much more than twenty when she died?

I was much perplexed to answer this question; though it flattered my pride as a woman shortly to enter upon the field myself, and perhaps make decisions of equally momentous result to somebody, it sadly bewildered my perceptions of right and wrong. I felt humbled rather than exalted in my own self-opinion by the idea, that anything I said or did could produce such consequences; and I could not understand about Mr. Osborne. He, with his shrewd merry eyes, his regard for all his own comforts and luxuries, his want of sentiment and melancholy—that he should be the disappointed lover, almost exceeded my powers of belief. I was glad to think that he must have "got over it," but I was greatly puzzled to make the conclusion whether it could be this that decided the manner of his life.

My father was extremely absorbed in his book to-night—more than usually so I thought; and I am afraid that circumstance made me still more disposed to question him, unoccupied and idle as I was. I had disturbed him two or three times already by stirring the fire, and moving my seat, and had perceived his quick upward glance of impatience, but I was not deterred from beginning my investigations.

"Papa, have you known Mr. Osborne a very long time?" said I, looking at his face in the lamplight, and at the ray of reflection which came from the diamond on his finger. He looked up sharply as if not quite comprehending.

"Known Mr. Osborne?—yes, a long time, Hester—since I was a boy."

"And do you know why he lives here—why he is not married, papa?" I continued quietly.

My father looked up with a smile. "He is not married because he did not choose it, I suppose; and because he is a fellow, and has his income on that condition. Osborne is a scholar, and not a family man."

"I wonder now what is the good of being a scholar," said I. "Is Mr. Osborne poor? Does he do it for the sake of his income? Yes! I know all these colleges are for making scholars—but then, what is the good of it, papa?"

"Hester, you speak like a child," said my father with a little anger; "you might say in the same foolish words what is the good of anything—what is the good of life?"

"And so I do," said I with a little terror, and in an undertone.

"So! I have a young misanthrope on my hands—have I?" said my father; "we will not enter on that question, but return to Mr. Osborne, if you please, for I am busy. Are you very sorry for Mr. Osborne, Hester?"

"No, papa," said I.

"I am glad to hear it—there is no such prolific source of evil in the world," said my father gradually becoming vehement, "as false and injudicious pity—take care you never let that fictitious principle sway your conduct, Hester. Justice—let every man have justice—and he who is not content with that deserves no more."

He ceased abruptly, and returned to his book with a stern face. This was enough for me; all my questionings disappeared at once, in the greatness of my sympathy for my father. I thought again upon Edgar Southcote, and upon his "generous impulse." I unconsciously associated myself with my father, and took his place, and tried to fancy the intolerable misery with which I should feel the substitution of pity and generosity in my own case, for that unknown love, that wonderful visionary influence which was in my favorite stories, and in my girlish dreams—and my heart returned to its former confidence in my father, and passionate feeling of his great wrong. His life had been blighted—who could deny it! he who was so well worthy of the loftiest affection, he had found nothing better than pity in its place.

It is not my wish to trace all we did hour by hour in our solitary house, or I might record many a day like this. This was not a day of very vital moment in my life—but it was one which confirmed into singular strength and obstinacy, the influences which have guided and led me through many a more momentous day.

THE FIFTH DAY

All this day, with a degree of expectation and excitement, of which I felt somewhat ashamed, I had been preparing for a party to which, at the instance of Mr. Osborne, I was to go in the evening. It was a ridiculous thing for a girl of nineteen—that was my age now—to think so much of a party which was by no means a great party, nor had anything remarkable about it; but, though I was so old, I had never been out anywhere before, and much as I denied it to myself, this was really an event for me. Our days were all so like each other, of such a uniform color and complexion, that it was something to be roused even to anxiety for a becoming dress. We were not precisely poor—this old house in which we lived was my father's property, and though I did not know what was the amount of the income which he inherited, along with this house, from his mother, I knew it was enough to maintain us in comfort, and that nothing in the household was ever straitened. But, I had never gone out in the evening before, and I did not very well know what to wear. Alice and I had a great many consultations on the subject. For my own part, I thought white muslin was only suitable for girls, and very young people, and at nineteen I no longer thought myself very young; and I had no patience for the pink and blue in which dolls were dressed as well as young ladies—it was very hard to please me—and the question remained still undecided, even to the afternoon of this very day—

When I went up to my room and summoned Alice for our last deliberation. I found a white muslin dress elaborately propped up on a chair, waiting my inspection at one side of my dressing-table; and at the other: yes, I was no stoic, I confess to a throb of pleasure which I can still recollect and feel—at the other, rich full folds of silk, of what I thought, for a moment, the most beautiful color in the world, a soft creamy amber crossed with white, attracted my delighted eye. Alice stood behind me, watching the effect it would have, and Alice, I am sure, had no reason to be disappointed; but when I cried eagerly, "Where did you get it, Alice?" the smile faded from her kind face.

"My dear, it was given to your mamma just before you were born," said Alice, "and she would not permit it to be made, for I don't doubt, Miss Hester, she had a thought how it was to happen with her— and from that day to this, I have kept it safe, and nobody has ever known of it but me; and I thought I would take upon me to have it made, Miss Hester. Dear! you have very few things that were your mamma's."

I expressed no more delight after that. I almost think she thought me angry, her explanation silenced me so suddenly; but she said no more, and neither did I. There were other little things arranged for me on my table which I turned to with measured satisfaction. I think poor Alice was disappointed now, for I saw her cast furtive glances at me as she smoothed down the silk with a tender hand, trying as I thought to draw my attention to it; and I would gladly have spoken, if I could, to please her; but I was strangely moved by this occurrence, and could not speak.

And when I came up again to dress, and Alice began to brush out my hair, I saw her face in the glass, and that it was troubled and tears were in her eyes. She did not think I saw her, while she stood behind me busy with my hair, and when she looked up and saw that my eyes were fixed upon her in the glass, she started and reddened, and was painfully confused for a moment. I knew what she was thinking—she was pained in her good heart for what she thought the hardness of mine.

When I was dressed and looked in the mirror again, I scarcely knew myself in my unusual splendor. Yet I was not very splendid—I had not a single ornament, not so much as a ring or bracelet—and I am not sure the color of my dress was the best in the world for my brown hair; but, I had a very fair complexion, Alice said, and some color in my cheeks, though I was not ruddy; and my uncovered arms, with their very short sleeves and rich frill of lace, and the unusual elaboration of my hair, and the beautiful material of my dress, made me look a very different person from the plain everyday girl who had entered the room an hour before.

"There is one thing I would like to have," said I, as I contemplated my own appearance, and saw with how much proud, yet tremulous satisfaction, Alice stood behind, arranging the folds of my dress, and regulating, with anxious touches, the beautiful trimmings of lace, and the braids of my hair.

"What is that, dear?" cried Alice eagerly.

"One of the roses that you brought from Cottiswoode—one from that tree—to put here at my breast," said I. "Alice, I will think all to-night, that this dress is from mamma."

Alice kissed me suddenly before I had finished speaking.

"Lord bless my darling!" she said in a low voice, turning her face away from me; I knew she did so that I might not see how very near crying she was.

When I went to show myself to my father—he was not going—but a lady, a friend of Mr. Osborne's, was to come for me—he looked at me with some surprise.

"What fairy princess gave you your gown, Hester?" he said, with a smile. I could not help hesitating and looking embarrassed, when I answered almost under my breath,

"Alice had it, papa."

He became grave immediately, and the color flushed to his cheek. Then he opened a cabinet which always stood in his library, both here and at Cottiswoode, and took out a box.

"These are yours, Hester—it is time they were given to you," he said, almost with coldness; "you will use your own discretion in wearing them, only I beg you will not show them to me to-night. Good-night, my love, take what pleasure you can, and be ready when your friend calls for you—good-night."

I carried the box away mechanically, and returned to the drawing-room to wait for Mrs. Boulder. I was surprised, but still sufficiently curious to open the box at once. It contained a number of smaller morocco jewel cases, which I examined eagerly; I was as ignorant as my father of the ancient fashion of these ornaments, but I think an uncultivated and savage taste such as mine was, is generally disappointed with the appearance of precious stones. I was extremely interested, but I did not admire them, and that I should wear them did not occur to me at the first moment. But there was one little spot of quivering living light which changed my opinion; it was a small diamond pendant attached to a very little chain, which puzzled me into a deliberation whether it was intended for the neck or the arm. I tried it on, however, and settled the question in the most satisfactory manner possible; and then there was a bracelet of pearls, and then—but Mrs. Boulder's carriage came up to the door with a great rush and din, and I hurried away my store of treasures, and suffered myself to be wrapped up, and went away to make my first entrance into the world.

The world! had I been a boy I would have been an adventurer, and sought my fortunes in toils, and fights, and travel: but it was strange to look round upon this Cambridge drawing-room, and think of it and of its well-dressed, commonplace company as representing the great stormy universe, of which I had my grand thoughts, like every other inexperienced spirit. There was a large company, I thought, being unused to evening parties. Mr. Osborne and a few more of his rank and standing, scholars who looked shorn and diminished for want of their habitual cap and gown, some young undergraduates, and a background of county people made up the number—and a stray lion from London, who had been caught in the neighborhood, was reported to be somewhere in the room. My chaperone, Mrs. Boulder, was a professor's wife, and herself a scientific person, who seldom condescended to talk of anything but literature, geology, and the gossip of the colleges; she was very much interested about this unknown author. From the sofa where she had established herself, and where her professional black satin swept its ample folds over my pretty dress, she was constantly thrusting her head into the groups of people who gathered before her, searching with her spectacles for somebody who might be the distinguished visitor.

"That must be he, talking to the Master," she exclaimed, "no, there is another stranger, I declare, a very remarkable looking personage, beside Mr. Selwyn. I wonder why nobody brings him to me. Mr. Osborne—Mr. Osborne! Professor! I cannot make any of them hear me; my love, would you mind stepping to Mr. Osborne? There he is talking to that very old Fellow. Call him to me."

I rose with considerable trepidation to obey—an old Fellow, it must be understood, is by no means a contemptuous expression in a University town; and this was a very old white-haired man with whom Mr. Osborne was engaged. He held out his hand when I came up to him, and looked at me with a glance of pleased satisfaction, almost as if he were proud of me, which warmed my heart in spite of myself. I told my message, but he made no haste to obey it. He only nodded his head, with a smile, in answer to Mrs. Boulder's urgent beckoning.

"Should you like to see him, Hester?" said Mr. Osborne, "there he is, that young dandy there, among all the young ladies—he prefers worshippers to critics, like a sensible man. Should you like to hear the great lion roar, Hester?"

"I am very glad to have seen him," said I, "but he has enough of worshippers. No, thank you: but Mrs. Boulder wants to see him, Mr. Osborne."

"Presently," he said, once more nodding at that tantalized and impatient lady, "presently—and how do you like the party, Hester?"

"I like very well to look at it," said I, glancing round the handsome, well-proportioned, well-lighted room, "it is a picture, but I do not know any one here."

"We will remedy that, by and by," said Mr. Osborne, "see there is something to look at in the meantime; and I will bring Mrs. Boulder to you here."

As he spoke, he wheeled in a chair for me, close to a table, covered with plates and drawings. I could not help being pleased at the kindness of his manner and tone, and at the pride he seemed to have in me, as if he wished other people to see that I belonged to him. A young man was standing at the table, minutely examining some of the prints—at least, I supposed so, they occupied him so long; and the old gentleman who had been speaking to Mr. Osborne, remained by me when he went to Mrs. Boulder, and said a word now and then, to encourage me, and set me at my ease I thought—for I was shy and embarrassed, and not very comfortable at being left alone. The young man on the other side of the table—how very long he held that print! it made me impatient to watch his examination of it, and ashamed of myself for finding so little in the others to detain me. When he laid it down at last—it was one of those street landscapes of the old quaint Flemish towns—the old gentleman made some remark upon it, and the young one replied. They had both been there. I have no doubt that was the reason why he looked at it so long.

"These Low Countries—you have not seen them, Miss Southcote?" said Mr. Osborne's friend, "they are about as dull and unimpressive as our own Cambridgeshire." I had a great deal of local pride and was piqued at this—it restored me to my self-possession better than his kindness had done. "Do you think Cambridgeshire is unimpressive?" I asked quickly, looking up at him.

"Why, yes, I confess I think so," said the old Fellow. "I have forgotten my native fells a little, after living here nearly fifty years; but I have never learned yet to find any beauty in the country here. Pray what are its impressive features, Miss Southcote?"

I paused a moment that I might not be angry. "There is the sky," said I.

The youth, on the other side of the table, bent towards me to listen; the old gentleman laughed a polite little critical laugh. "The sky is scarcely a part of the Cambridgeshire scenery, I am afraid," he said.

As I paused, not quite knowing what to answer, the young man came to my aid. "I am not sure of that, sir," he said, with a look of eagerness, which struck me with some wonder. "The sky is as much a portion of the Cambridgeshire scenery as Michael Angelo's roof is a part of the Sistine chapel. Where else have you such an extent of cloud and firmament? You must yield us the sky."

"The sky belongs equally to every county in England, and to every country in the world," said our white-haired critic. "I will yield you no such thing—there is but one Sistine chapel in the world, and one roof belonging to it. You must find a better argument."

"You can see so far—you are bounded by nothing but heaven," said I.

"Yes," said my new supporter, "there is the true sense of infinitude in that wonderful vast blank of horizon; you never find the same thing in a hilly country, and it is perfect of its kind."

"My young assailants," said the old gentleman, smiling, "if you mean to maintain that your county has no features at all, I have no controversy with you; that is exactly my own opinion."

It happened that as we both glanced up indignantly, and both paused, hesitating what next to say to such an obdurate infidel, our eyes met. He looked at me earnestly, almost sadly, and with a rising color—I felt my cheeks burn, yet could not help returning his gaze for an instant. It was a contemplative face, with fine and regular features, and large dark blue eyes; the oval outline of the cheeks was quite smooth, and the complexion dusky and almost colorless; but I was surprised to find myself wondering over this stranger's features, as if they were familiar to me. Where was it possible I could have seen them before? but, indeed, if he was a Cambridgeshire man, as his words implied, it was easy to account for having seen him.

For the moment, looking at each other, we forgot the cause we were defending, and our antagonist stood contemplating us with a pleasant smile; he did not say anything, but when I looked up and caught his eye, I withdrew my own in confusion. I did not know why, and there was, indeed, no cause, but though I could not explain, I felt a strange embarrassment, and hastened to speak to shake it off.

"I know what I mean, though I may not be able to say it," said I; "I think in our country you are never master of the landscape—you can never see it all, as you could if it was shut in with hills; it is always greater than you—and it is because our eyes are not able, and not because there is any obstacle in nature, that we cannot see twice as far—to the end of the world."

"It is quite true," said the young man hurriedly, "these flat fields are boundless like the sky—or like a man's desires which are limited by nothing but heaven."

"My dear boy, a man's desires are limited by very trifles, sometimes," said our old friend; "happy are they whose wishes reach like your Cambridge fields as far as the horizon. If you come to that," he continued, going on with a smile, "and give a figurative significance to those dreary levels, I will not quarrel with you. In my north country, which, by the way, I have quite lost acquaintance with—the extent of our ambition is, to have our hills recognised as mountains, and get to the top of them; but your land, I confess, Miss Southcote, gets to the sky as soon as we do; there is no dispute about that."

I was obliged to be content with this, satirical as it was, and began to occupy myself immediately with the prints on the table. The old gentleman fell back a step, and began conversing with some one else. The youth still stood opposite, holding an engraving in his hands and going over it minutely. It was very strange—I cannot tell how it came about—but in this crowded room, and among all these echoes of conversation, I felt myself in some extraordinary way alone with this young stranger. I never lifted my eyes from the picture before me, yet I was aware of every motion he made—and though he did not once look up, I felt his eye upon me. We did not exchange a single word, but we remained opposite each other perfectly still, watching each other with a sort of fascination. I do not know how the time went for those few moments—I know it looked like an hour to me before Mrs. Boulder came back; yet when she did come back, she exclaimed at having lost sight of me for full ten minutes, and began to overpower me with an account of the unknown lion, and the clever things he said—and to pull about and turn over the prints which had been passing so slowly and so unwittingly through my hands.

Mrs. Boulder had not been seated by our table for five minutes when she had a ring of potent people round her, whom she had called out of the crowd. I sat by her timidly on a stool, which some one brought me when I gave up my easy chair to the great lady—and bent my head, half with awkwardness and half to find breathing room, oppressed as I was by the bulky figure of the Professor leaning over me in earnest discussion with another pillar of learning. Mr. Osborne was not far off; but though this might be pleasant enough for Mrs. Boulder, who was the centre of the group, it was very much the reverse for me, stifled and overwhelmed by half-a-dozen people pressing over me to pay their court to the eminent woman, who had taken charge of a bewildered and shy girl to her own inconvenience, and who, if she ever thought of me at all, thought no doubt that I was only too greatly privileged, had I been entirely, instead of only half, stifled with the pressure of this learned crowd. But the young stranger whom I followed, not with my eyes, but with my attention, remained still very near us, and still I felt strongly that though our eyes had only met once, we had been observing each other all the time.

I saw Mr. Osborne speak to him, as to a familiar acquaintance—I saw him honored with a nod from Mrs. Boulder—and I wondered greatly who he was. He was certainly not older than myself, and of a slight youthful figure, which made him look even younger, I thought—was he a Cambridge man? a traveller, though so young, and a scholar too, of course, or he would not be here. I was very curious about this young man; would he speak to me again? what could we have to do with each other which could account for this strange mutual attraction? for I felt sure that he was wondering and inquiring in his own mind about me, as I was about him.

After a little while, he drew nearer to us, and joined our little circle, and turning round to answer some question for Mr. Osborne, I was surprised to find him still by my side. Then, still under cover of the prints, he spoke to me. I would have gladly spoken to any one else, but I was uncomfortably embarrassed, I could not tell why, in speaking to him. He began to tell me of those Dutch towns, and then we returned to talk of our own country, and insensibly grew into a kind of acquaintance. Then when the greater people dispersed, Mrs. Boulder perceived him, and entered into a condescending conversation with him, touching, in a professional tone, on the progress of his studies, and putting hard questions to him, which puzzled and somewhat irritated me. He answered them quietly and with a smile, and was evidently in great favor with her; and still I sat by watching him, and still he stood at my side observing me.

"How well he gets on!" said Mrs. Boulder, in a loud whisper to Mr. Osborne, behind her chair. Mrs. Boulder did not think it necessary to conceal her favorable judgment from the happy object of it.

"Who? oh! Harry Edgar," said Mr. Osborne, glancing at him; "that will be a distinguished man!"

I had nothing to do with it, yet it pleased me, and set me on a new train of questions—how would he distinguish himself? Not after the fashion of my heroes—not like Columbus or Buonaparte—in books then, I supposed. Now I had few literary tastes, though I read novels with devotion; yet I paused to marvel what kind of books they could be, which should distinguish this youth; but without finding any answer to my secret question. More than ever now was I anxious about him. I wondered what he was thinking now—what he would think to-morrow. I felt a great desire to see into the mind of my new acquaintance, not by any means to see how he thought, or if he thought at all, of me; it was simply himself whom I wanted to understand. Harry Edgar—I did not think it was a Cambridgeshire name—it sounded hard to me, like a north country one; but it did not throw the least light upon who he was.

When Mr. Osborne put me into Mrs. Boulder's carriage at the door, I saw Mr. Edgar's face again turned towards us for a moment. He, too, was going away—and when Mr. Osborne asked me how I liked the party, it was with difficulty I restrained the words on my lips: "I wonder who he is!" I had no doubt he was thinking the same of me; yet I am sure we were not attracted by each other, as people might suppose, who heard what I say. For my part, it was a species of fascination. I did not either like or dislike this stranger; but somehow I wanted to penetrate his thoughts, and to know what manner of man he was.

Alice, of course, was waiting for me, and a fire was burning in my room, to make it more cheerful. When Alice loosed off the great shawl I was wrapped in, I could not comprehend, for a moment, what caused her sudden exclamation of pleasure, and the heavy sigh with which it was followed. It was the little diamond ornament which I wore round my neck. I had forgotten it. Yes, this had been my mother's too; but I was tired and sleepy, and not communicative. Had I liked the party? Yes, I thought I had—pretty well—quite as much as I expected; sometimes it was very pretty, that was taking it in the picture point of view—for I did not think it necessary to tell Alice how I had been interested by the stranger. What a pity, I thought, that he was a young man! for people would laugh at me, if I expressed any interest in him.

So I lay down to rest in the firelight, to watch the ruddy shadows dancing on the walls, and wakefully and long to consider this evening and all its novelties. It was all novel to me. My dress and my jewels were enough to have woke me for a little out of the usual torpor of my life; but this party which I had been rather ashamed of desiring to go to, I felt I should never forget it now. Why? I could not tell why— but I went to sleep wondering which was Harry Edgar's college, and what he might be thinking of. I even looked into the future with a little eagerness, marvelling what sort of career his was to be, and if I should ever know more of him. It was very strange—for certainly his thoughts, and the subjects they might be occupied with, were nothing to me.

THE SIXTH DAY

I was out upon a household errand to order something for Alice. My father and Alice conspired to keep me still as free of cares and almost of duties, as a child. Alice attended to everything; she was a good careful housekeeper, long accustomed to our house and ways, and needed no help in the administration of our domestic economy; though, perhaps, it would have been better for me, if I had been led to these homely occupations, and found something tangible to employ my mind and thoughts. It was Spring, one of those fresh, sunny, showery, boisterous days, which are so pleasant to youth. I liked my quiet walk along the narrow, old-fashioned streets—I liked the wind which blew my hair loose from my bonnet, and swept the clouds along the blue, blue sky, rushing past the turrets and pinnacles of the collegiate buildings. I was young, and my heart rose with the vague and causeless exhilaration of youth. I scarcely cared to think, but went on with a pure delight in the motion and life which I had within me. I was pleased to feel the shawl escaping from my hand, and my hair curling upon the breeze; and if my step was not quite so bold as its girlish freedom permitted five years ago, it was as firm a tread as it had been among our own fields, or in the lanes that led to Cottiswoode.

I had done my errand and was going home; but I was scarcely contented to return so soon, and would have walked a mile or two with pleasure. When I came to the paved alley, by St. Benet's, which was the nearest way to our house, I paused a moment in uncertainty, thinking where I should go—but just as I was about to return in the opposite direction, I started to hear Mr. Osborne's voice behind me. "Running away, Hester?—nay, I want you at home to-day; come back and tell me how your father is."

I turned round—Mr. Osborne was not alone—standing a little apart from him, out of regard to his meeting with me, was the young man who had so strangely interested me at the party. I glanced at him involuntarily, and so did he at me; but we had no warrant for knowing each other, and I drew apart as he did, as if by instinct. Mr. Osborne was not paying the least attention to his companion, and seemed quite careless of him, whether he stayed or went away, and the wind at that moment was playing very strange pranks with the elder gentleman's gown, so that, what with keeping it in order, and addressing me, Mr. Osborne had quite enough to do.

"My father is very well," I said. "He is at home, of course; are you going to see him?"

"I am going to tell him how his daughter behaved on her entrance into the world," said Mr. Osborne with much importance. "Were you very much impressed by your first experiences, Hester? There now, that is a little better. We are, at least, out of the road of that vagabond breeze."

We had turned into the alley, and I had been waiting for Mr. Osborne's young acquaintance to leave us; but he walked on steadily at the other side, and showed no disposition to go away. I did not quite like answering Mr. Osborne's questions before this stranger; he made me feel so strangely conscious of all my own words and movements. I no longer did anything easily, but became aware of every step I made.

"Have you not seen him since that night?" said I, "it is quite a long time ago."

"That night—so it did make some impression on my young debutante," said Mr. Osborne, with a smile. "Do you know I have been out of Cambridge for nearly three weeks, you forgetful young lady? Well, Hester, what of that night?"

"What of it, Mr. Osborne?" said I, with some little indignation. "I suppose there was nothing very extraordinary about it."

Mr. Osborne laughed, and I was provoked. "There only was a crowd of people—there is nothing remarkable in a crowd," said I, impetuously. "Why should I think about it—you do not suppose that I take a party like that for the world?"

"What do you call the world then, Hester?" said Mr. Osborne.

"I do not know," said I, hesitating a little. "I cannot tell," I repeated, after another pause, "but I suppose there is as much of it here as there was yonder. I think so, at least."

"So that is the verdict of youth, is it?" said Mr. Osborne. "Henry, my boy, what say you?"

I could not help turning my head quickly towards him, but I did not raise my eyes; how I wondered what he would say.

"The party has sometimes more influence on a life than the street can have," said the young man, with hesitation, "otherwise, I have no doubt, a thronged and busy street in London would look more like the world than a Cambridge drawing-room—but sometimes the drawing-room makes a greater mark in a life."

"My good youth, you are less intelligible than Hester," said Mr. Osborne, "but the young lady has no metaphysical bias that I know of, so we will not discuss the question. So we were very prosy, were we, the other night? and you were nearly smothered under the Professor's shadow, and had nothing but pictures to look at, poor child! The next one will be better, Hester, do not be dismayed."

I made no answer. I was piqued at Mr. Osborne's mockery; but I wondered over what the other had said—what did he mean by the drawing-room making a mark in his life. Had it made any mark in mine? why should it? and why was he walking along so quietly by Mr. Osborne's side, without the least intention of going away? I saw that he kept his eyes away from me, as carefully as I kept mine from him; but how I observed him for all that. His walk was rather slow and steady—he was not quick and impetuous as I was—I wanted to hasten on, for I was embarrassed a little, not knowing anything about "society," and being quite at a loss to know whether I was acquainted with this stranger or not; but, of course, Mr. Osborne continued his leisurely pace, and so did his young companion. They made me impatient and almost irritated me; they went on so quietly.

When we came to the door, I opened it hastily, for it was an old-fashioned, unsuspicious door, and opened from the outside. Then in my awkwardness I went down the two steps which led from it, and stood below in the door, waiting for Mr. Osborne. I was in a little tremor of expectation—what was he going to do?

"I think I may presume on your father and yourself, Hester, so far as to ask my young friend to come in with me," said Mr. Osborne, "for we have some business together. This is Mr. Harry Edgar, Miss Southcote—will you admit him within your precincts."

Of course I had to make a little awkward bow to him, and I do not think his was much more graceful; and then I hurriedly led the way into the house. Mr. Osborne went directly to the library, and I called Alice to show Mr. Edgar up-stairs, then I ran to my own room to take off my bonnet. Must I go to the drawing-room where he was sitting alone—I thought it was very unpleasant—I felt extremely confused and awkward, yet I smoothed my hair, and prepared to go.

When I went into the room, he was looking at the pictures—those dark, hard panel portraits on the wall, and with some interest as I thought—though when I came, he, too, grew a little embarrassed like me. I went to my work-table immediately to look out some work, for I could not sit idle and talk to him. There were countless little bits of work lying half completed on my work-table, I had no difficulty in finding occupation, and when I had selected one, I sat down by the window and wished for Mr. Osborne. He ought to know better, than to leave me alone here.

There was nothing at all to keep us from the necessity of talking to each other, for he immediately gave up looking at the portraits, and the room was in fatal good order, and all the books put away. After the first awkward pause, he said something about the pictures: "they were family portraits, no doubt."

"No," said I, "that is, they are not Southcotes; they are portraits of grandmamma's family, I suppose; but we always count our family on the other side."

Then we came to another dead pause, and Mr. Edgar advanced to the window where I sat.

"How fresh and green your garden looks," he said, after the fashion of people who must say something, "what a good effect the grass has—are there really blossoms on the trees? how early everything is this year!"

"We are well sheltered," said I, in the same tone. "Our trees are always in blossom before our neighbors'."

"And that is old Corpus," he said, glancing out at the little gleaming windows of the College, "all this youth and life out of doors, contrasts strangely enough, I am sure, with the musty existence within."

"The books may be musty, but I don't think the existence is," said I, rashly; "everybody ought to be happy that has something to do."

"Yes. I always envy a hard student who has an object," said Mr. Edgar, rather eagerly seizing upon this possibility of conversation—"he is a happy fellow who has a profession to study for, otherwise it is vanity and vexation of spirit."

Now I had a strong instinct of contradiction in me—a piece of assertion always provoked me to resistance.

"I do not know how that can be," said I. "I suppose Mr. Osborne only lives for his books, and his spirit shows very little vexation or vanity, and papa does nothing else but study, and cannot have any object in it—I fancy a good thing ought to be good for its own sake."

"Mr. Osborne is a very busy man—he has a great many pursuits," said my new friend, "he is not a fair example. We have an enthusiasm for books when we are young, and suck inspiration from them, and then we come back to them that they may deaden our own feelings and recollections after we have had a life of our own—when we are old."

"You are not old, to be aware of that," cried I, though I secretly thought that, at least, in my father's case this might be true.

"I have lived a very solitary life," he said, "which is almost as good as grey hairs."

After that we paused again, very conscious of our silence, but finding conversation a very difficult matter. I was more at my ease than I had expected. I observed him, but not with the same intense observation. A person I knew by name, and spoke to in my father's house, was a less mysteriously interesting person than the stranger who had attracted my notice so much, when all were strangers. At last, Mr. Edgar began to talk again—it was only to ask me if I had seen the great author who was at the party when he met me first—he did not say "had the pleasure to meet."

"I saw him, but I did not speak to him—nor even hear him speak," said I.

Another pause—what were we to say? "Do you like his books?" said the young man.

"I do not care for any books but novels," said I bluntly. I am afraid I was not above a wish to shock and horrify him.

Mr. Edgar laughed a little, and his color rose. I am sure I did what I could to give him an unfavorable impression of me, in this our first interview. He said—

"You are very honest, Miss Southcote."

I cannot tell how it was either that he presumed so far, or that I suspected it—but I certainly did think he had a great mind to say Hester, instead of Miss Southcote, and only checked himself by an effort. It was very strange—I felt haughty immediately, but I scarcely felt displeased; but I am sure there was a consciousness in the deep color that rose upon his face, and in my tone as I answered him.

"I am only telling the truth," said I. "I cannot help it—when it is only thinking about a thing, I would rather think myself. A story is a different matter; I am very sorry for my dulness, but I think there are no really pleasant books except those which tell a story."

"Even that limit reaches to something more than novels," said Mr. Edgar; "there is history, and biography besides."

"Yes—but then I only care for them for the mere story's sake," said I, "and not because they are true or good, or for any better reason. I suppose a man's life is often more like a novel than like anything else—only, perhaps, not so well arranged. The misfortunes do not come in so conveniently, and neither do the pleasures. I think reading a novel is almost next best to having something to do."

"I am afraid some of us think it a superior good, now and then," said my companion.

And so our talk came to an abrupt conclusion again. It was my turn to make a new beginning, and I could not. I did not like to ask him any questions about himself—which was his college, or if he was a Cambridgeshire man, or any of the things I wished to know; and, as I glanced up at his thoughtful face, I once more fell a-pondering what he could be thinking of. I do not recollect that I had ever had much curiosity about other people's thoughts before. My father always had a book before him, which he read, or made a pretence of reading, and my father's meditations were sacred to me. I guessed at them with reverence, but it would have been sacrilege to inquire into them. As my established right, I claimed to know what Alice was thinking of, and did not need to wonder; but here, with the full charm of a mystery which I could not inquire into, came back upon me my first curiosity about this stranger. Either his face did express what was in his mind, or I was not acquainted with its language. What was he thinking of?—what did he generally think of? I wondered over his thoughts so much that I had no leisure to think of himself who was standing beside me, though still I was strongly aware of every movement he made.

Just then I heard my father and Mr. Osborne ascending the stairs. I was half sorry, and yet altogether glad that they were coming; and I was a little curious how my father would receive my new acquaintance. My father received him with stately politeness, distant but not ungracious, and as Mr. Osborne and he took their usual places, they began their ordinary conversation. When Mr. Edgar joined in it, I discovered from what they said that he was a student of Corpus, a close neighbor, and it amused me a little to watch the three gentlemen as they talked; of course, my father and Mr. Osborne were in the daily habit of talking, without any greater reference to me than if I had been a very little girl with a doll and a pinafore. I was not intellectual. I did not care for their discussions about books—and I expected no share in their conversation, nor wished it. I was quite pleased to sit by, with the ring of their voices in my ear, doing my needlework. I always worked at something, during these times; and thinking my own thoughts. But Mr. Edgar, who was unused to this, and perhaps did not think me quite so little a girl as my father and his friend did, was puzzled and disconcerted, as I saw, by my exclusion from the stream of talk. I had a certain pleasure in showing him how much a matter of course this was. I had never known a young man of rank and age before, but I had a perverse delight in making myself appear something different to what I was. I turned half aside to the window, and hemmed as only demure little girls can hem, when grave talk is going on over their heads. But I saw very well how uncertainly he was regarding me—how puzzled he was that I should be left out of the conversation, and how he wanted to be polite and amiable, and draw me in.

"How is the garden, Hester?" said Mr. Osborne at last, rising and coming towards me with a subject adapted to the capacity of the little girl, "what! blossom already on that little apple tree—what a sturdy little fellow it is! Now, Southcote, be honest—how many colds has Hester taken this winter in consequence of your trap for wet feet—that grass crotchet of yours?"

"Hester is a sensible girl in some respects," said my father, "she never takes cold—and your argument against my grass is antiquated and feeble. I will not plan my garden by your advice, Osborne."

"My advice is always to be depended on," said Mr. Osborne; "you have taken it in more important matters, and I think I know some matters in which it would be very well you took it again."

"That is my affair," said my father coldly. "Advice is a dangerous gift, Mr. Edgar," he continued, with a somewhat sarcastic smile, "every man who has the faculty thinks himself infallible—and when you bring yourself ill fortune by following good advice and friendly counsel, you are in a dangerous dilemma—to hide your failure or to lose your friend."

"What do you mean, Southcote?" cried Mr. Osborne with a look of great surprise and almost anxiety in his face.

"Nothing but my old opinion," said my father, "that every man must stand on his own ground, consult his own discretion, and build only upon his own merits. I have no faith in the kindness and compassion of friends; a kind act, done with the noblest good intentions, may make a man's life miserable. No, no, justice, justice—what you deserve and no galling boon of pity—all is dishonest and unsatisfactory but this."

Mr. Edgar and Mr. Osborne exchanged a slight rapid glance, and I saw the color rise over the young man's broad white brow; but I was too much concerned and moved by what my father said to observe the others much. His friend even did not comprehend him, I alone knew what he referred to. I alone could enter into his feelings, and understand how deep the iron had gone into his soul.

After that Mr. Edgar was very silent, and listened to what was said, rather than took part in it—so that when Mr. Osborne spoke of going away, the young man had subsided into a chair, as humble and unconsidered as I was. He did not come to talk to me—he sat quite silent looking on—looking round at the pictures sometimes, with a quiet sweep of his eyes, often looking at the speakers, and sometimes examining curiously my work-table. I was sitting close by it, but he never looked at me nor did I look at him.

When they were going away, my father, to my great surprise, bade him return. "Come again, I will be glad to see you," said my father. I looked up almost with consternation, and Mr. Edgar, though he looked gratified, was surprised too, I could see—however, he answered readily, and they went away.

My father did not leave me immediately after they were gone; he walked up and down the room for a while, pausing sometimes to look at the ivy leaves which waved and rustled as much as the fine tendrils clasping the wall would let them, in the fresh spring breeze. My father seemed to have a certain sympathy with these clusters of ivy—he always went to that window in preference to this one where I was seated, and which looked into the free and luxuriant garden. After standing there for some time, he suddenly turned and addressed me.

"Since you went out, Hester," said my father, "I have had another letter from your persevering cousin. He is at Cottiswoode, and would fain 'be friends,' as he says; though I will not permit him to be anything warm. He is of age—he has entered upon his inheritance—though I hear no one has seen him yet; and he does us the honor to desire to become acquainted with us, whom he calls his nearest relations. What do you say?"

"You will not let him come, papa," cried I, "why should he come here? Why should he trouble us? We do not want him—you surely will tell him so."

"I am glad you agree with me so thoroughly, Hester," said my father. "Osborne is a great advocate for this young man. He has been urging me strongly to receive him—and had you been of his opinion, Hester, I am not sure that I could have held out."

This was so singular a confession from my father, that I looked up in alarm and dismay. My opinion! what was that in comparison with his will?

He caught my look, and came towards me slowly, and with a step less firm than usual—then he drew a chair near me, and sat down.

"What I have to say, I must say in so many words," said my father. "My health is declining, Hester. I have exhausted my portion of life. I do not expect to live long."

"Papa!" I exclaimed, starting up in sudden terror—the shock was so great that I almost expected to see him sink down before me then. "Papa! shall I send for the doctor? what shall I do? are you ill, father, are you ill? oh! you do not mean that, I know."

"Sit down, my love—I am not ill now—there is nothing to be done," said my father; "only you must listen calmly, Hester, and understand what I mean. You will not be destitute when I die, but you will be unprotected. You will be a very lonely girl, I am afraid. Ignorant of society, and unaccustomed to it; and I have no friend with whom I could place you. This was the argument which Mr. Osborne urged upon me, when he advised me to receive your cousin."

"Mr. Osborne was very cruel," I exclaimed, half blinded by tears, and struggling with the hysterical sobbing which rose in my throat. "He knows nothing of me if he thinks—Oh! papa, papa! what would my life be to me if things were as you say?"

My father smiled upon me strangely. "Hester, you will grieve for me, I know," he said, in his quiet, unmoved tones; "but I know also the course of time and nature; and in a little while, my love, your life will be as much to you, as if I had never been."

I could not utter the passionate contradiction that came to my lips. This composed and philosophic decision struck me dumb. I would rather he had thought of his daughter and of her bitter mourning for him, than of the course of time and nature. But I sat quite silent before him, trembling a great deal, and trying to suppress my tears. This doctrine, that grief is not for ever—that the heavy affliction which it is agony unspeakable to look forward to, will soften and fade, and pass away, is a great shock to a young heart. I neither could nor would believe it. What was my after life to me? But for once, I exercised self-denial, and did not say what I thought.

"Shall I say any more, Hester? Can you hear me? or is this enough for a first warning?" said my father.

"Oh! say all, papa, say all!" cried I. "I can bear anything now—anything after this."

"Then I may tell you, Hester, plainly, that it would give me pleasure to see you 'settled,' as people call it—to see you married and in your own house, before I am removed from mine. Circumstances," said my father, slowly, "have made me a harsh judge of those romantic matters that belong to youth. I am not sure that it would much delight me to suppose my daughter the heroine of a passionate love-story. Will you consent to obey me, Hester, in an important matter as readily as in the trifling ones of your childhood? I have no proposal to make to you. I only desire your promise to set my mind at ease, and obey me when I have."

My face burned, my head throbbed, my heart leaped to my throat. Shame, pride, embarrassment, and the deeper, desolate fear of what was to happen to my father, contended within me. I could not give an assent to this strange request. I could not say in so many words that I gave up utterly to him the only veto a woman has upon the fashion of her life. Yet I could not refuse to do what, under these circumstances, he asked of me. I made him no answer. I clasped my hands tightly over my brow, where the veins seemed full to bursting. For an instant I felt, with a shudder, what a grand future that was, full of all joyous possibilities, which I was called upon to surrender. I had thought to myself often that my prospects were neither bright nor encouraging; at this moment I saw, by a sudden light, what a glorious uncertainty these prospects were, and how I clung to them. They were nothing, yet the promise of everything was in them; and my father asked me to give them up—to relinquish all that might be. It was a great trial; and I could not answer him a word.

"You do not speak, Hester," he said. "Have you no reply, then, to my question?"

"I want no protector, father," I cried, almost with sullenness. "If I must be left desolate, let me be desolate. Do not mock me with false succor. I want no home. Let Alice take care of me. I will not want very much. Alice is fond of me, though I do not deserve it. Let her take care of me till I die."

I was quite overcome. I fell into a violent outbreak of tears as I spoke. I could command myself no longer. I was not made of iron to brave such a shock as this "with composure," as my father said. He rose and went away from me towards the other window, where he stood looking out. Looking after him through my tears, I fancied that already I could see his step falter, and his head droop with growing weakness. I cried out, "Oh, my father! my father!" with passionate distress. Perhaps he had never seen me weeping before since I was a child. Now, at least, he left me to myself, as I could remember him doing when I was a little girl, when I used to creep towards him very humbled and penitent after the fit was over, and sit down at his feet, and hold his hand, and after a long time get his forgiveness. I could not do that now. I sat still, recovering myself. I was no longer a child, and I had a stubborn spirit. It wounded me with a dull pain that he should care so little for my distress.

He did not return to me. He left the room, only saying as he went away, "You will tell me your decision, Hester, at another time;" and when the door closed upon him I gave way to my tears, and let them flow. If he had only said a word of consolation to me—if he had only said it grieved him to see my grief! But he treated it all so coldly. "The course of time and nature!"—they were bitter in their calmness, those dreadful words.

I wept long; but my tears did not help me. I did not feel it possible to make this promise. To be given to somebody who would take care of me, as if I was a favorite spaniel! I could not help the flush of indignation and discontent which came over me at the thought. And then I began to think of my father's real state of health in this revulsion of feeling. He was mistaken—he must be mistaken. When I thought over the subject I could find no traces of illness, no change upon him. He was just as he had always been. The longer I considered, the more I convinced myself that he was wrong; and somewhat relieved by this, I went to my room to bathe my eyes and arrange my dress for dinner. How I watched my father while we dined!—how tremulously I noted every motion of his hand, every change of his position. His appetite was good—rather greater than usual; and he had more color in his face. I was sure he had been deceived. He spoke very little during that meal. For the first time a sort of antagonism had risen between my father and me. I could not consent to what he asked of me; and, even if I could have consented, I could not be the first to enter upon the subject again.

And when I crept into my window-seat in the twilight, and watched as I had watched so often, the lights gleaming in the windows of the College, I wondered now with a strange sense of neighborhood and friendship, which of them shone upon the thoughtful face and dark blue eyes of my new friend. I had made many a story in my own mind about the lights; and there was one favorite one, which was lighted sooner, and burned longer than any of the others, which I immediately fixed upon as his. I thought I could fancy him sitting within its steady glow, reading books which I knew nothing of, writing to friends unknown to me, thinking thoughts which I could not penetrate. As I sat still in the darkness, with my eyes upon that little gleaming window, I found a strange society and fellowship in looking at it. If I had had a brother now, like this student, how much happier would I have been. As it was, the idea of him was a relief to me. I forgot my own perplexity as I wondered and pondered about him.

My father came into the drawing-room, as I sat thus in the corner of the window-seat, leaning my cheek upon my hand, and looking out upon the little shining windows of Corpus—he was displeased that the lamp was not lighted, and rang the bell hurriedly; and it was only by some sudden movement I made, that, with a start, he discovered me. "So, Hester, you are thinking," he said, in a low tone. I started up, emboldened by my own thoughts.

"Papa—papa! you were mistaken in what you said this morning," I exclaimed eagerly, "you are not ill—how firm your hand is, and I never saw your eyes so bright—you are mistaken, I am sure you are."

"Do me justice, Hester," said my father, in a voice which chilled me back out of all my hopes. "I took care not to speak of this till I was sure that I could not be mistaken. Trust me, I have a fearful warrant for what I say."

His voice neither paused nor faltered—it was a stoic speaking of the mortal pain he despised; but it was hard and bitter, and so cold—oh! so cold! If he had no pity for himself, he might have had pity for me.

I held his hand, grasped it, and clung to it; but I did not cry again, for I felt that he would have been displeased, and it was a long time before his fingers closed upon mine with any return of my eager clasp. "You have been thinking, Hester, of what I said to you—what have you to tell me now?"

"I cannot do it, papa," I said, under my breath.

He did not answer anything at first, nor loose my hand, nor put me away from him. But after a little while he spoke in his measured low melodious tones. "You think it better to risk your all upon a chance, do you, Hester? Such a chance—happiness never comes of it. It is always an unequal barter—but you prefer to risk that rather than to trust to me."

"I want to risk nothing—I need nothing!" cried I, "while I have my father, I want no other, and do not bid me think of such misery—do not, papa! You will live longer than I shall—oh! I hope, I pray you will. Papa, do not urge me, I cannot anticipate such a calamity!"

"This is merely weakness; is it compassion for my feelings?" said my father. "I tell you this calamity, if it is a calamity, is coming rapidly, and you cannot stay it. What will you do then?"

"I do not care what I do then," I said, scarcely knowing what my words were, "but I would rather you left me desolate than gave me to somebody to protect me. Oh! father, I cannot do it—I cannot consent."

He said nothing more, but turned away from me, and went to his usual seat at the table, and to his book. I sat still in my corner, once more venturing to weep, and struck with a hundred compunctions; but I steadily resisted the strong impulse which came upon me to go to his feet and promise anything he wished—I could not do this—it would kill the very heart in me, and surely I was right.

THE SEVENTH DAY

It was now nearly Midsummer, the crown of the year. I was sitting in my own room by the window, idly musing, when Alice came in with some of my light muslin dresses to put them away. I had neither book nor work to veil my true occupation. I was leaning my head upon both my hands, sometimes vacantly looking out at the windows, sometimes closing my fingers over my eyes. I had both scenery and circumstances in my dream—I wanted nothing external to help me in the meditations with which my mind had grown familiar now.

I was not unaware of the entrance of Alice, but I only changed my position a little, and did not speak, hoping to be undisturbed. I saw, with a little impatience, how careful she was about the dresses—how she smoothed down their folds, and arranged them elaborately, that they might not be crushed in the drawer; but she certainly took more time than was necessary for this simple operation, and though Alice had no clue to my thoughts, I scarcely liked, I cannot tell why, to continue them in her presence. But when the drawers were closed at last, Alice still did not go away—she came to the dressing-table, and began to arrange and disarrange the pretty toilette boxes which she kept in such good order, and to loop up and pull down the muslin draperies of the table and the mirror; at last she gathered courage and came close to me.

"May I speak to you, Miss Hester?" said Alice, but it was in a disturbed and nervous tone.

Now I was annoyed to have my own thoughts, which had a great charm for me at that time, interrupted and broken. I looked up with a little petulance—"What is it, Alice?"

She came still closer to where I was sitting, and her bright good face was troubled. "Miss Hester, my darling, I want to consult you," said Alice, and I thought I saw a tear trembling in her eye. "I am afraid your papa is ill. I am afraid he is very bad. The doctor comes and goes, and he never lets you know; and I have said to myself this three months back: 'it's cruel to keep it from her—the longer she is of knowing the worse it will be.' And now, dear, I've taken heart and come myself to tell you. He's very bad, Miss Hester, he has a deal of trouble; and it'll come hard—hard upon you."

I felt that my face was quite blanched and white. What a contrast was this to the terror of my own thoughts! I shrank within myself with a guilty consciousness, that while I had been running in these charmed ways, my father had suffered in secret, making no sign. I cannot say I was startled—Alice's words fell upon me with a dull heavy pang—I felt as if a blow which had long been hanging over me had fallen at last.

"But Alice, Alice, I see no change in him," cried I, for a moment struggling against the truth.

"If you went to him as I sometimes go, you would see a change, Miss Hester," said Alice; "it is not your fault, dear. Well I know that—but the light in his eye and the color in his cheek—hush—that's the hectic, darling, you've heard of that," and Alice turned to me a glance of fright, and sunk her voice to a whisper, as if this was some deadly enemy lurking close at hand.

And fever and faintness came upon me as she spoke. I rose and threw up the window for a moment's breath, and then I turned to Alice, and cried upon her shoulder and asked her what I was to do—what I was to do?

With her kind hand upon my head, and her kind voice blessing her "dear child," Alice soothed and calmed me—and the tears gave me some relief, and I gradually composed myself. "Do you think he will let me nurse him, Alice? He told me he was ill long ago, but I persuaded myself he was mistaken; and you think he is very bad—in great pain? oh! do you think he will let me nurse him, Alice?"

"I cannot tell. Miss Hester," said Alice, "but, dear, you must try—did he tell you he was ill?—and I was doing him wrong, thinking he was too proud to let his own child see him in weakness: oh, we're hard judges, every one of us. When was it, dear?"

"In spring, a long time ago; and we were not quite friends then," said I. "I thought he was cruel; he spoke to me about—about—I mean he told me that I must soon be left alone, and that he wanted to find some one to take care of me. I cannot tell you about it, Alice; and I refused—I said no to my father; and we have never been very good friends since then."

"Do you mean that your papa wanted you to marry, Miss Hester?" asked Alice.

"I suppose so—yes!" I said, turning away my head—she was looking full at me, and looking very anxiously—she had always been greatly privileged. I feared I might have been questioned, had she caught the expression of my eye.

"And did he say who? Was it M—? Was it your cousin?" said Alice.

"No, it was not my cousin; but why do you speak of that? Alice, let me go to my father," said I.

"He does not want you now, darling," said Alice, detaining me. "Dear Miss Hester, don't you think it wrong of me—you're my own child. I took you out of your mother's arms. Speak to me just one word. Is there any one, darling, any one?—Miss Hester, you'll not be angry with me?"

"Then do not ask me such questions, Alice," I said, in great shame and confusion, with a burning flush upon my cheek, "does it become us to speak of things like this, when my father so ill—why do you say he does not want me now! he may want me this very moment, let me go."

"Dear, he's sleeping," said Alice, "he has been very ill, and now he's at rest and easy, and lying down to refresh himself—you can't go now, Miss Hester, for it would only disturb him—poor gentleman—won't you stay, dear, and say a word to me?"

"I have nothing to say to you, Alice," said I, half crying with vexation and shame and embarrassment, "why do you question me so? I have done nothing wrong—you ought rather to tell me how my father is, if you will not let me go to see."

"The pain is here," said Alice, putting her hand to her side, "here at his heart. I know what trouble at the heart is, Miss Hester, and your papa has known it many a day, but it isn't grief or sorrow now, but sickness, and if the one has brought the other, I cannot tell. It comes on in fits and spasms, and is very bad for a time, and then it goes off again, and he is as well to look at as ever he was. But every time it comes he's weaker, and it's wearing out his strength day by day. Yes, dear, it's cruel to say it, but it's true."

"And are you with him when he is ill, Alice?" said I anxiously.

"He rings his bell when he feels it coming," said Alice, "though I know he has many a hard hour all by himself; and anxiety on his mind is very bad for him, dear," she continued, looking at me wistfully, "and he is troubled in his spirit about leaving you. If you can give in to him, Miss Hester, dear, if it's not against your heart—if you're fancy-free, and think no more of one than of another—oh! darling, yield to him anything you can. He's a suffering man, and is your father, and pride is the sin of the house; every one has it, less or more; and there are only two of you in the world, and you are his only child!"

Alice ran breathlessly through this string of arguments, while I listened with a disturbed and a rebellious heart. No, if this was true,—if my father was slowly dying—if he would soon be beyond the reach of all obedience and duty, I would not deny him anything—not even this. It was hard, unspeakably hard, to think of it. I could not see why he should ask such a bitter sacrifice from me. I knew of no self-sacrifice in his history—why should he think it was easy in mine?

Alice left me like a skilful general, when she had made this urgent appeal, and went away down stairs, saying she would call me when my father awoke. I remained at my window, where I had been dreaming before, but what a harsh interruption had come to my dreams—the sunshine without streamed down as full and bright as ever over the trees and flowers, and fresh enclosing greensward of our pretty garden; half an hour of time had come and gone, but it might have been half a year for the change it made in me. Alice had come to my Bower of Bliss, like Sir Guyon, and driven me forth from among the flowers and odors of the enchanted land. My heart became very heavy, I could not tell why. I resolved upon making my submission to my father, if I had an opportunity, and telling him to do what he would with me. This was not a willing or tender submission, but a forced and reluctant one; and I did not try to conceal from myself that I felt it very hard, though when I thought again of his recent suffering, and of the fantastic paradise of dreams in which I was wandering, while he wrestled with his mortal enemy, I felt suddenly humiliated and subdued. My father! my father! I had belonged to him all my life, I had no right to any love but his; I had lived at ease in his care, and trusted to him with the perfect confidence of a child. But now, when it was at last of importance that I should trust him, was this the time to follow my own fancies and leave him to suffer alone?

At that moment Alice called me, and I immediately went down stairs. I went with a tremulous and uncertain step, and an oppressed heart—to make any sacrifice he wished or asked—to do anything he desired of me. When I entered the library, my father looked up from his book with a momentary glance of surprise and inquiry; and with a heart beating so loud and so uneasily as mine it was hard to look unembarrassed and natural. I said breathlessly: "May I sit beside you, papa? I want to read a little," but I did not dare to look at him as I spoke—the calm everyday tone of his voice struck very strangely upon my excited ear as he answered me: "Surely, Hester," he said, with a slight quiet astonishment at the unnecessary question. He was perfectly unexcited—I could see neither care, nor anxiety, nor suffering in his calm and equable looks; and he did not perceive nor suspect the tumult and fever in my mind. Prepared as I was to yield to him with reluctance, and a feeling of hardship, I felt a shock of almost disappointment when I found that nothing was to be asked of me—I sank into the nearest chair and took up the first book I could find to cover my trembling and confusion. The stillness of the room overpowered me—I could hear my heart beating in the silence, and as my eye wandered over all these orderly and ordinary arrangements, and to the calm bright sunshine out of doors, and the shadow of the trees softly waving across the window, I was calmed into quieter expectancy and clearer vision. My father sat in his usual place at his usual studies, with the summer daylight full upon his face, and everything about him arranged with scrupulous propriety and care; if any of his habitual accessories had been disturbed—if he had occupied another seat, or sat in a different attitude, or if I could have detected the slightest sign of faltering or weakness in his manner, I would not have felt so strongly my sudden descent from the heights of terror, anxiety, and expectation, to the everyday level of repose and comfort; but there was no change in his stately person or dress, no perceptible difference in his appearance. He was not old—at this present moment he looked like a man in his prime, handsome, haughty, reserved, and fastidious. As I observed him under the shadow of my book, I felt like a spy watching to detect incipient weakness—was I disappointed that he did not look ill? Was this the man who half an hour ago was sleeping the sleep of exhaustion after a deadly struggle with his malady? I could not believe myself, or Alice—she was mistaken—for it was impossible to reconcile what she told me with what I saw.

But the stillness of the room and his steady occupation influenced me like a spell—I did not go away— and when a slight movement he made startled me into a momentary fear that he might perceive I was watching him, I began to read in earnest the book which, all this time, I had been holding in my hands. It had been lying on the top of a pile of others, and was quite a new book, not entirely cut up, a very unusual thing here. My eye had already travelled vacantly two or three times to the end of the page without knowing a syllable of the lines which I went over mechanically—but now I caught the name of the book, and it strangely awed and startled me. I could almost have cast it from me like a horrible suggestion when I saw that title. It was a medical treatise, and its subject was "Sudden Death"—the words were like a revelation to me—this was why he sat so composed and stately, ready to meet the last enemy like a brave man; this was why he suffered no trace of agitation or of languor to come into this solemn room which at any moment, as my excited fancy whispered, might become the chamber of death. I could almost fancy I saw the shadowy sword suspended over my father's head, and in another instant it might fall.

My terror now, for himself and for him only, was as insane and wild as it seemed visionary and baseless; for I had seen nothing as yet to point to him as one of the probable victims of this sudden conclusion. But the very manner of the book convinced me of what he thought himself. I went on reading it, scarcely sensible now how my hands trembled, nor how easily he would find me out, if he happened to glance at me. Yes! here was abundant confirmation of my fears. I read with a breathless and overwhelming interest cases and symptoms—to my alarmed fancy, every one seemed to bear some likeness to what I knew of his; I never read a drama or a tale with such profound excitement as I read this scientific treatise—there seemed to be life and death in its pages—the authoritative mandate which should forbid hope, or silence fear.

"Hester!" said my father. I started violently and looked up at him, I felt the heat and flush of my intense occupation upon my cheek, and I almost expected to see him faint or fall as I sprang towards him. He held up his hand half impatient, half alarmed, at my vehemence. "What are you reading? what has excited you, Hester?" he said.

I retired very rapidly and quietly to my chair, and put my book away with nervous haste. "Nothing, papa," I said, bending my head to escape his eye.

"Nothing! that is a child's answer," said my father, and I felt that he smiled; "I have been watching you these five minutes, Hester, and I know that 'nothing' could not make you so earnest. What is it you have been reading—tell me."

"It is only a book—a new book," I said slowly.

"I thought so—almost the only new book in my library, is it not?" said my father, in a singular tone, "what do you think of it, Hester?"

I lifted my hands in entreaty—I could not bear to hear him speaking thus.

"It is true," he said quietly, "and you perceive it does not disturb me—this is what you must make up your mind to, Hester. It will be a trial for you—but not a long and tedious one—and you must hold yourself prepared for it as I do."

"But father—father! you are not ill. You are not so ill—I cannot believe it," I cried, scarcely knowing what I said.

"It will prove itself by and by," he answered calmly, and returned to his book as if we had been speaking of some indifferent matter. I could not think of it so coolly—I cried: "Papa, listen to me, I will do anything, everything you want—do you hear me, papa?"

He looked up at me for a moment—was it suspicion? he certainly seemed to have forgotten that he had ever asked anything of me which I had refused.

"I require nothing, Hester," he said, "nothing, my love, and I perfectly believe in your willingness to serve me. Lay down the book, it is not for you, and go out and refresh yourself. I am pleased that you know what may come, but I shall not be pleased if you brood upon it. Now leave me, Hester, but come again when you will, and I will never exclude you. Pshaw, child! it is the common lot. What do you tremble for? what is it you want to do?"

"Is there nothing you wish, papa—nothing I could do to please you?" I said, under my breath. I could not allude more plainly to the former question between us.

"It is time enough to ask such questions," he said, with a momentary jealousy of my intention, "I am not dying yet."

He did not understand me—he had forgotten! I hurried out grieved, overwhelmed, yet in spite of myself relieved on this one point. I thought myself the meanest wretch in the world, to be able to derive satisfaction from it at such a moment. Yet I was so! I felt a thrill of delight that I was free, in the midst of my terrors and dismay at the doom which hung over our house. I tried to conceal it from myself, but I could not. I was free to mourn for my dear father for ever, and admit no human consolation. I was not bound under a promise to commit myself to somebody's hands to be taken care of. I was afflicted, but at liberty.

Alice waited eagerly to speak to me when I came from the library, but I only could speak two or three words to her, and then hastened out, to relieve the oppression on my spirit if I could. It was a dreadful thought to carry with me and ponder upon, and when I was walking fast along a lonely wood, half a mile out of Cambridge, it suddenly occurred to me what danger there was in leaving home, even for an hour. Before I returned, the blow might fall—it might be falling even now. I turned at once and went hastily homewards, my heart sick with anxiety and terror. When I nearly reached the house, I met Mr. Osborne; though I knew he would detain me, I was yet very anxious to speak to him, for perhaps he would give me some hope. He was speaking to some one, but he saw that I waited for him, and immediately left his former companion and came to me. "No other young lady in the world would do me so much honor," said Mr. Osborne, in the gay good-humored tone which was usual to him, but which jarred so much upon my feelings. "Oh! Hester, what's this? why do you look so much excited? Have you something important to tell me? I have almost expected it, do you know."

I was very sorry, but I could not help the burning heat which came to my face; and I could not lift my eyes for the moment to meet his saucy eyes which seemed to read my thoughts. What had I to do with such thoughts! I cast them from me with bitter self-indignation, and looked up at him at last with a face so grave that he smiled on me no more.

"I want to speak to you about papa, Mr. Osborne," I said. "Will you tell me?—you must know. He thinks he is very ill. He thinks—oh! tell me if you think he is so bad as that."

For an instant his face grew very serious. "I am not qualified to give an opinion," he said, first; and then, regaining his usual look, with an effort, he continued, "He is not well, Hester; but quite well and very ill are a long way from each other. I do not think he is very bad—I do not, indeed. I see no need for your alarming yourself."

"But he speaks of danger and of sudden—" I could not say the fatal word. "Has he any foundation for it; do you think he is right, Mr. Osborne?" I continued with a shudder.

"I do not think he is right, Hester. I think that you ought not to be frightened with such a ghastly doubt as this," said Mr. Osborne, seriously, "your father has fancies, as every man in weak health has; but I know enough of his illness, I think—I am almost sure—to give you confidence on this point. If anything sudden should occur, it will not be without long and abundant warning—a sudden or immediate blow is not to be feared. I assure you I am right, Hester, you may trust to me."

I did trust to him with gratitude, and a feeling of relief. He walked home with me, moderating my pace, and leading my mind to ordinary subjects. He was very kind to me. He said nothing to embarrass or distress; but calmed my excitement, and made me feel a real confidence in him. When we got home, nothing had happened. The quiet house was as quiet and undisturbed as ever it had been. Mr. Osborne went to the library; and I went up-stairs to the window-seat in the drawing-room. And I do not venture to say that I did not go back to my dreams.

THE EIGHTH DAY

Alice had sent me out to walk at sunset—she said I was breaking her heart with my white thin face, and woful looks. I had spent all that afternoon in the garden watching my father at his window. I could do little else but watch him, and listen, and wait near the library; the constant strain of anxiety almost wore me out; yet I had a fond persuasion at the bottom of my heart, that my fears were groundless, and I think I almost kept up my anxiety on purpose as a sort of veil for this hope. Since I had been so much afraid for him, he seemed to have grown better every day—he had begun to take his walks again, and had never had another attack since the time Alice warned me how ill he was.

I obeyed her now tacitly and went out; though it was a beautiful night, few people were walking when I went to walk by the river side, where the last rays of the sun were shining gloriously through the half transparent leaves of the lime-trees. The tender slanting golden light was very sweet to see, as it touched upon the green surface of the lawn at some single ripple or eddy, and left all beside in the deep shadow of the coming twilight. In those great trees overhead, the wind was sighing with a gentle rustle, shaking the leaves against each other, swaying the sunny branches into the shade, and thrusting now and then a dark parcel of leaves into the sunshine, when they suddenly became illuminated and showed you all the life in their delicate veins, quivering against the light. On the one bank of the river was a trim slope of grass descending to the water, and on the other, withdrawn over broad lawns of greensward, with shadows of trees lying on the grass, and the light falling on it aslant and tardily, stood the stately College buildings, noble and calm in the sweet leisure of the evening rest. I came here because I saw it solitary; no one interrupted me as I wandered along the broad sandy footpath; no one disturbed my thoughts as I pursued my dream. Sometimes a bird fluttered through the leaves from one branch to another, going home; and there was a low sweet twittering of welcome from the tiny household deep in the heart of the green lime, a forest all bedewed and shining with the last smiles of the sun; but I heard no other sound except my own footsteps, at which I sometimes could almost have blushed and stepped aside, afraid of some spectator of my maiden meditations, or some passer-by who might guess at the secret of my dream.

When I first saw him coming on the same solitary road, no one here but he and I, my first impulse was to turn back and escape. I trembled and blushed, and shrank with conscious conviction, believing he could read all my thoughts whenever he met my eyes. Then I paused and stumbled, and felt how ashamed and hesitating my face had become, and wondered what he would think was the occasion of this nervous foolishness. But I do not think he took time to observe, for he was hastening towards me, with an eager haste which only made me shrink the more. I could not turn back, I could not go steadily onward; I almost thought all nature which had made this seem so beautiful, and all Cambridge who had left it to us, were in a conspiracy against me. On came his light active figure, pushing through the trees, and I with my faltering steps advanced slowly, going towards him, because I could not help myself. When we met at last, he turned and went on with me; I was not able to object to this, and even he did not say anything about it, but merely turned by my side, subdued his hasty pace to my slow one, and accompanied me as though it had been quite a matter of course. I do not think we said much to each other. I do not recollect anything that passed between us—I remember only the twittering of the birds, the rustle of the leaves, the light stealing off the dewy greensward and the darkening river, all those soft sweet distant sounds that belong to a summer's night were ringing with a subdued and musical echo in the air around us; our own steps upon the path—the beating of our own hearts—these, and not words from each other, were what we listened to.

Then he suddenly seemed to rouse himself, and began to speak—suddenly, in a moment, when I was quite unprepared for it. I cannot tell how I felt while I listened. We went on mechanically, I am sure, not knowing or caring whither we went. He was speaking to me, pleading with me, entreating me; and I listened with a vague, secret delight, half pain, half pleasure, when his voice stopped at last. I became aware how I was hanging upon it—what a great shock and disappointment it was that it should cease. But still, in my trance of embarrassment, in my agitation and perplexity, it never occurred to me that it was I who must speak now—that it was I who had to decide and conclude upon this strange eventful question, and that with still greater excitement than that with which I had listened to him, he was waiting to hear me.

I did not speak—I went slowly on with the echo of his words ringing into my heart—then came his voice again, agitated and breathless. "Hester, have you nothing to say to me?"

I cannot tell why, at this moment, our first conversation together, when he came to our house with Mr. Osborne, returned to my memory. I did not turn towards him nor lift my eyes, but I asked in a tone as low and hurried as his own, "Almost the first time you ever spoke to me, you were going to call me Hester—why was that?"

He did not answer me immediately. "Because your name became the sweetest sound in the world to me, the first time I heard it," he said, after a moment's pause. I believed him—I was not vain of it, it seemed to be a merit in him to think so of me, but no merit in me.

"Not a word—not a word—must I go away then—will you answer me nothing?" he said, at last, after another interval, with other wild words of tenderness, such as had never been said to me before, and such as no woman can tell again. I was roused by his outcry, I turned for an instant to look at him, and then I suddenly felt my face burn and my brow throb, and then—it seemed he was satisfied, and wanted no more words from me.

And we wandered on together, out from the shadows of the trees, where the sun came gleaming and glistening upon us like a friend who had found us out. I think there never was such a night of content, and satisfaction, and peace; there was the calm of night, and the flush of hope for another day upon the heavens; and the sweet light blessed the earth, and the earth lay still under it in a great joy, too deep to be expressed. I was leaning with my hand upon his arm—I was leaning my heart upon him, so that I could have wept for the delight of this sweet ease and rest. Yes! it was the love of the Poets that had overtaken us, and put our hands together. As he clasped both his hands over one of mine, he said it was for ever and for ever—for ever and for ever, and lingered on the words. I said nothing—but the clasp of his hands holding me, stirred the very depths in my heart. I was alone no longer, I wanted to tell him everything—my secret thoughts, my fears—all that had ever happened to me. I could not tell him my fancies about himself, though I listened so eagerly to all he said of me, but all my life came brightening up before me, I was eager to show it all to him—I was jealous of having anything in which he had no share.

We went up and down—up and down—the same bit of enchanted ground, and it was only when I felt a chill breath of air, and slightly shivered at it, and when he put up my shawl upon my shoulders, and drew it round me so anxiously and tenderly, that I glanced up at the sky to escape his eyes which were gazing full upon me, and saw that it was getting quite dark, and must be late. "Is it late?" I said, starting suddenly at the thought of my father; "they will wonder where I am—oh! I must go home."

"Time has not been to-night," he said, with the smile upon his lip quivering as if the tears were in his eyes as well as in mine. "Once more, Hester, let me look at this glorious bit of road that has brought me fortune. Here—it was just here—winter should never come to this spot; and there is a faint timid footstep in the sand. My sovereign lady was afraid of me! If you had but known what a poor coward I was, how I trembled for those words which would not come, and how you held my fate in your hand, and played with it. Love is quite bad enough—but Love and Fear! how is a single man to stand against them!"

"I do not think you looked very much afraid," said I.

"You cannot tell—you never vouchsafed me a glance," said Harry, "and Fear is the very soul of daring; when a man will rather hear the worst than hear nothing, Hester, his courage is not very cool, I can tell you. And how unmindful you were!"

"Hush! hush! I am sure it is very late," said I, "I must go home."

"But not without me, Hester," said my companion.

I did not want him to leave me, certainly; but I was a little startled. My father! what would he say? how would he receive this unexpected accomplishment of his desires? The idea agitated and excited me. I suddenly felt as if this meeting of ours had been clandestine and underhand. I did not know what I could say to my father, and Alice would be anxious about myself already.

"You would not prolong my suspense, Hester," said Harry, as we slowly took the way home; "you know I cannot rest till I have spoken to your father—have I a rival, then—do you see difficulties? or is it that you would rather tell him with your own sweet lips what you have never yet told me?"

"No—no—I do not want to speak to him first," said I, hurriedly, "but he is not well—he is not strong—agitation hurts him; yet perhaps this would not agitate him," I continued with involuntary sadness—"perhaps, indeed, it is better he should know."

"I think it will not agitate him. I think, perhaps, he will not be much surprised, except indeed that I should have won what I have long aimed at," said Harry. "I met his eye the last time I saw him, Hester!"

"And what then?" I asked eagerly.

"Nothing much, except that I think that he knew the sad condition I was in," said Harry, with a smile, "and remembered somebody who was the light of his eyes in his own youth—for I think he did not look unkindly on me."

"But he never could suspect anything," said I.

"Did you never suspect anything, you hard heart?" he said; "you would not shake hands with me. You would not look at me. You never would come frankly out into the garden where a poor fellow could see you. Do you mean to tell me now that you were not afraid of me, and did not feel that I was your fate?"

"Hush! hush!" I repeated again. "And Mr. Osborne and Alice—you do not mean that everybody knew?"

"You must not be angry with me, if I confess that Mr. Osborne was in my confidence," said Harry, looking into my face, with some alarm, as I thought. "I was shy of whispering my name of names to any other man; but I betrayed myself once by saying Hester to your old friend. Hester—Hester! Homer never knew the sweet sounds of these two syllables, yet they used to glide in upon his page, and no more intelligence was left in it. Ah! you do not know what you have to answer for. And Alice!—Alice loves you too well not to suspect anybody who approaches you, Hester. She has been very curious about me for a long time. I think she approves of me now at last."

"It is very strange," I said, with a little pique and offended dignity, "everybody seems to have been aware except—"

I paused, being so sincere that I could not imply what was not true. Had not I been aware? or what were all my dreams about for many a day?

"Except the person most concerned? I suppose it is always so," said Harry. "But do not blame me for that. If my queen was not aware of her devoted servant's homage—it was no fault of mine. Ah! Hester! so many jealous glances I have given to this closed door."

For we had reached home; and with a beating heart I opened the door and entered before him. It was so dark here in the close, that I could only hear, and could not see the ivy rustling on the wall; and the air was chill, though it was August; and I trembled with a nervous shiver. He held me back for a moment as I was about to hasten in. "Hester, give me your hand, give me your promise," he said, in a low, passionate tone. "Your father may not be content with me; but you—you will not cast me off? You will give me time to win him to my side? Say something to me, Hester—say a kind word to me!"

I could see, even in the darkness, how he changed color; and I felt his hands tremble. I gave him both mine very quietly; and I said: "He will consent." Then we parted. I hurried in, and called Alice to show Henry to the drawing-room where my father was; and, without pausing to meet her surprised and inquiring look, I ran up-stairs, and shut myself into my own room. I wanted to be alone. It was not real till I could look at it by myself, and see what it was.

Yes! there was the dim garden underneath, with the trees rising up solemnly in the pale summer night, and all the color and the light gone out of this flowery little world. There were the lights in the little gleaming windows of Corpus like so many old friends smiling at me. I had come home to my own familiar room; but I was not the same Hester Southcote, who had lived all her life in this environment. In my heart, I brought another with me into my girlish bower. The idea of him possessed all my thoughts—his words came rushing back, I think almost every one of them, into my ears. I dropped upon my seat with the shawl he had placed there still upon me, without removing my bonnet or doing anything. I sat down and began to live it over again, all this magical night. It stood in my memory like a picture, so strange, so beautiful, so true! could it be true? Did he think me the first, above all others? and all these words which sent the blood tingling to the very fingers he had clasped, had he really spoken them, and I listened? and all this wonderful time had been since I left the little dark room, where I had even now again to look at my altered fate. All the years before were nothing to this single night.

And then I remembered where he was, and how occupied now. He was telling my father—asking my father to give up his only child.

My father was ill—in danger of his life—and was I willing to leave him alone? but then the proud thought returned to me—not to leave him alone—to add to him a better companion than I, a friend, a son, a man of nature as lofty as himself; but I was not willing to enter into details, and as I thought upon the interview going on so near me, I grew nervous once more. Then I heard a step softly approaching my door. Then a light gleamed through it, and I went to open it with a great tremor. It was Alice, with a light, and she said my father had sent for me to come to him now.

Alice did not ask me why I sat in the dark with my bonnet on; instead of that she helped to take off my walking dress, and kept her eyes from my face, in her kindness—for she must have seen how the color went and came, how I trembled, and how much agitated I was. She brushed back my hair with her own kind hands, and took a rose out of a vase on the table, and fastened it in my dress.

I had been so full of my own thoughts, that I had not observed these roses, but I knew at once when she did this. They were from my own tree at Cottiswoode. I did not ask Alice how she got them, yet I had pleasure in the flower. It reminded me of my mother—my mother—if I had a mother now!

"They are waiting for you, Miss Hester," said Alice—they? how strange the combination was—yet I lingered still. I could not meet them both together. I could have borne to hear my father discuss it afterwards; but to look at each of them in the other's presence, was more than I thought I could endure. I went away slowly, Alice lingering over me, holding the light to show me the way I knew so well, and following me with her loving ways. My Alice, who had nobody but me! I turned round to her suddenly, for a moment, and leaned upon her breast, and sought her kiss upon my cheek—then I went away comforted. It was all the mother-comfort I had ever known.

When my hand touched the drawing-room door, it was suddenly thrown open to me, and there he stood to receive me with such joy and eagerness, that I shrunk back in terror for my father. My father was not there.

"We are alone," said Henry, "your father would not embarrass you, Hester, and he gives his consent under the most delightful of all conditions. Do you think me crazy? indeed, I will not answer for myself, for you belong to me, Hester, you are lawfully made over—my wife!"

I was almost frightened by his vehemence; and though I had feared it so much, I was sorry now that my father did not stay. "Did it trouble him? Was he disturbed? What did he say?" I asked eagerly.

"I am not to tell you what he said—he will tell you himself," said Henry, "but the condition—have you no curiosity to hear what this condition is?"

"No," I said, "it seems to please you. I am glad my father cared to make conditions; and you are sure he was not angry? What did he say?"

"I will tell you what I said," was all the answer I got; "but all the rest you are to hear from himself. Now, Hester," he continued, pleadingly, holding my hands and looking into my face, "don't be vexed at the condition. I don't expect you are to like it as well as I do; but you will consent, will you not? You can trust yourself to me as well as if you knew me another year? Hester! don't turn away from me. There is your father coming; and I promised to leave you when I heard him. It is very hard leaving you; but I suppose I must not break my word to him. I am to come to-morrow. You will say good-night to me, surely—good-night to your poor slave. Princess—good-night!"

My father was just at the door, when at last he left me. There was a brief leave-taking between them; and then I heard his rapid step descending the stair, and my father entered the room. I had gone to my usual seat at the table, and scarcely ventured to look up as he entered. I thought he hesitated for a moment as he stood at the door looking in upon me. Perhaps he thought of giving me a kinder greeting; but, if he did, he conquered the impulse, and came quietly to his chair opposite me, and, without saying a word, took his place there, and closed the book which had been lying open upon the table. Then he spoke. My heart beat so loud and wild that it almost took away my breath. He was my father—my father! and I wanted to throw myself at his feet, and pour out all my heart to him. I wanted to say that I never desired to leave him—never! and that I would rather even give up my own happiness than forsake him now.

He gave me no opportunity; he spoke in his grave, calm tone of self-possessed and self-commanded quietness, which chilled me to the heart. "Hester!" he said, "I have been listening to a young man's love-tale. He is very fervid, and as sincere as most youths are, I have no doubt. He says he has thought of nothing but how to win you, since we first admitted him here; and he says that you have promised him your hand if he can gain my consent. I have no doubt you recollect, Hester, the last conversation we had on this subject. You have chosen for yourself, what you would not permit me to choose for you, and I hope your choice will be a happy one. I have given my consent to it. What he says of his means seems satisfactory; and I waive the question of family, in which his pretensions, I presume, are much inferior to your own. But I earnestly desire that you should have a proper protector, Hester! and I give my consent to your marriage, on condition—" he paused, and I glanced up at him, I know not with what dismayed and apprehensive glance; for his solemn tone struck me with terror: "on condition," he continued, with a smile. "Do not fear—it is nothing very terrible—on condition that your marriage takes place within three weeks from this time."

"Papa!"

I started to my feet, no longer shrinking and embarrassed. Oh! it was cruel—cruel! To seize the first and swiftest opportunity to thrust me from him, while he was ill, perhaps dying, and when he knew how great my anxiety was. I could not speak to him; I burst into a passionate fit of tears. I was wounded to the heart.

"I suppose it is natural that you should dislike this haste, Hester," said my father, in a slightly softened tone; "I can understand that it is something of a shock to you; but I cannot help it, my love. The circumstances are hard, and so is the necessity. I yield to you in the more important particulars; you must yield to me in this."

"Papa! I cannot leave you. Do not bid me," I cried, eagerly, encouraged by his tone; "to go away now would kill me. Father, father! have you no pity upon me? you cannot have the heart to send me away!"

"I have the heart to do all I think right, Hester!" said my father, sternly. "I am the last man in the world to speak to of pity. Pity has ruined me; and I will do what is right, and not a false kindness to my only child. This lover of yours is your own choice—remember at all times he is your own choice. I might have made a wiser selection. I might not have made so good a one. The probability is in your favor; but, however it happens, recollect it is your own election, and that I wash my hands of the matter. But I insist on the condition I have told you of. What we have to do, we must do quickly. There is time enough for all necessary preparations, Hester."

I had taken my seat again in the dull and mortified sullenness of rejected affection and unappreciated feelings. Preparations! was it that I cared for? I had no spirit to speak again. I rather was pleased to give up with a visible bad grace all choice and wish in the matter.

"You do not answer me," said my father; "is my substantial reason too little to satisfy your punctilio, Hester? are you afraid of what the world will say?"

"No! I know no world to be afraid of," said I, almost rudely, but with bitter tears coming to my eyes; "if you care so little for me, I do not mind for myself if it was to-morrow."

"I do not choose it to be to-morrow, however," said my father, with only a smile at my pique, "there are some things necessary beforehand besides white satin and orange flowers. Alice has arranged your dress before, you had better consult with her, and to-morrow I will give you a sum sufficient for your equipment; that is enough, I think, Hester. Neither of us seems to have any peculiar delight in the subject. I consider the matter settled so far as personal discussion between us goes—matters of arrangement we can manage at our leisure."

He drew his book to him, and opened it as he spoke. When he began to read, he seemed to withdraw from me into his retirement, abstracted and composed, leaving me in the tumult of my thoughts to subside into quietness as I best could. I sat still for some time, leaning back in my chair, gnawing at my heart; but I could not bear it—and then I rose up to walk up and down from window to window, my father taking no note of me—what I did. As I wandered about in this restless and wretched way, I saw the lights in the college windows, shining through the half-closed curtain. He was there, brave, generous, simple heart! I woke out of my great mortification and grief, to a delight of rest and relaxation. Yes, he was there; that was his light shining in his window, and he was sitting close by it looking out upon this place which enclosed me and mine. I knew his thoughts now, and what he was doing, and I knew he was thinking of me.

When my heart began to return to its former gladness, I went away softly to my own room, thinking that no one would hear me, and that I might have a little time to myself; but when I had just gone, and was standing by the window, leaning my head upon it, looking out at his window, and shedding some quiet tears, Alice once more appeared upon me, with her candle in her hand. She did not speak at first, but went about the room on several little pretences, waiting for me to address her; then she said, "Will I leave the light, Miss Hester?" and stood gazing at me wistfully from beside the dressing-table. I only said, "Stay, Alice," under my breath, but her anxious ear heard it. She put down the light at once, and went away to a distant corner of the room, where she pretended to be doing something, for she would not hasten me, though she was very anxious—it was pure love and nothing else, the love of Alice.

"Alice!"

She came to me in a moment. I had just drawn down the blind, and I crept close to her, as I used to do when I was a child. "Do you know what has happened, Alice?" I said.

"Dear, I have had my thoughts," said Alice, "is it so then? and does your papa give his consent?"

"Oh! papa is very cruel—very cruel!" cried I bitterly, "he does not care for me, Alice. He cares nothing for me! he says it must be in three weeks, and speaks to me as if punctilio and preparations were all I cared for. It is very hard to bear—he will force me to go away and leave him, when perhaps he is dying. Oh! Alice, it is very hard."

"Yes, my darling—yes, my darling!" said Alice vaguely; "and will I live to dress another bride? oh! God bless them—God bless them! evil has been in the house, and distress, and sorrow—oh! that it may be purged and cleansed for them."

"What do you mean? what house, Alice?" I cried in great astonishment.

Alice drew her hand slowly over her brow and said, "I was dreaming, do not mind me, Miss Hester. I dressed your mamma, darling, and you'll let me dress my own dear child."

"No one else shall come near me, Alice; but think of it," cried I in despair, "in three weeks—and it must be. I think it will kill me. My father used to care for me, Alice, but now he is only anxious to send me away."

"Miss Hester, it is your father's way; and he has his reasons," said my kind comforter; "think of your own lot, how bright it is, and your young bridegroom that loves you dearly; think of him."

"Yes, Alice," I said very humbly, but I could not help starting at the name she gave him, it was so very sudden: every time I thought of it, it brought a pang to my heart.

But then she began to talk of what things we must get immediately—and I was not very old nor very wise—I was interested about these things very soon, and regarded this business of preparation with a good deal of pleasure; the white silk dress, and the veil, and the orange blossoms—it may be a very poor thing to tell of myself, but I had a flutter of pleasure thinking of them; and there we sat, full of business, Alice and I, and Alice went over my wardrobe in her imagination, and began to number so many things which I would require—and it was so great a pleasure to her, and I was so much softened and cheered myself, that when I rose, after she had left me, to wave my hand in the darkness, at the light in his window, I had almost returned to the deep satisfaction of my first joy.

But when I returned to the drawing-room—returned out of my own young blossoming life, with all its tumult of hopes, to my father, sitting alone at his book, all by himself, abstracted and solitary, like one whom life had parted from and passed by—I could not resist the sudden revulsion which threw me down once more. But now I was very quiet. I bent down my head into my hands where he could not see me weeping. I forgot he had wounded or injured me—I said, "My father! my dear father!" softly to myself; and then I began to dream how Harry would steal into his affections—how we would woo him out of his solitude; how his forsaken desolate life would grow bright in our young house; and I began to be very glad in my heart, though I did not dry my tears.

When we were parting for the night, my father came slowly up to me, and with a gesture of fondness put his hands on my head. "Hester," he said, in a low steady voice, "you are my only child"—that was all—but the words implied everything to me. I leaned upon his arm to hide my full eyes, and he passed his hand softly over my hair—"My only child! my only child!" he repeated once or twice, and then he kissed my cheek, and "God bless you, my love!" and sent me away.

I was very sad, yet I was very happy when I lay down to rest. The blind was drawn up, and I could see the light still shining in Harry's window; and I was not afraid now to put his name beside my father's when I said my prayers. It was very little more than saying my prayers with me. I had known no instruction, and in many things I was still a child. Just when I was going to sleep, some strong associations brought into my mind what Alice had told me of my father; how rejoiced he looked on the day of his betrothal, and how she never saw him look happy again—it was a painful thought, and it came to me as a ghost might have come at my bedside; I could not get far from it. I had no fear for myself, yet this haunted me. Ah, my dear father, how unhappy he had been!

THE NINTH DAY

It was the first of September, a brilliant sunshiny autumn day. The light streamed fall into my chamber window, and upon the figure of Alice standing before it, with her white apron and her white cap, so intensely white under the sunshine. She was drawing out rolls of white ribbon, and holding them suspended in the light for me to see them. They were dazzling in their silken snowy lustre. It was difficult to make a choice while this bright day glorified them all.

The room was not in disorder, yet it was littered everywhere with articles of dress. On my dining-table was a little open jewel-case with the bit of gold chain and the little diamond pendant which I had worn the first time I saw Harry—and the jewels were sparkling quietly, to themselves, in the shade. There were other ornaments, presents from him, lying beside this; and they made a subdued glow in the comparative dimness of that corner of the room. On my bed, catching a glance of sunshine, lay my bridal dress, its rich full folds and white brocaded flowers glistening in the light. On the little couch near the window were all the pretty things of lace which graced my trousseau—the veil arranged by Alice's own hand over a heap of rich purple silk which lay there for my approval, and which brought out to perfection the delicate pattern of the lace. And this was not all, for every chair held something—boxes of artificial flowers, so beautifully made, that it was impossible not to like them, exquisite counterfeits of nature—boxes of gloves, in delicate pale colors, fit for a bride—and last of all, this box of snowy-white ribbons, from which we found it so difficult to choose.

People speak of the vanity of all these bridal preparations. I have heard often how foolish was all this display and bustle about a marriage. I do not think it. It is the one day in a woman's life when everything and every one should do her honor. As I stood with Alice in my bright room, half blinded with the intense light upon the white ribbons, I was pleased with all the things about me. I had license to like everything, and to be interested with all the additions to my wardrobe. Only once in one's life can one be a bride. And all these white, fine, shining dresses—all these flowers and draperies of lace and pretty ornaments—they are not minutes of vanity always, but expressions of a natural sentiment—and they were very pleasant to me.

"I'll come out of the light, Miss Hester—here, dear, you can see them better now: though I like to see them shining in the sunshine. There is a beauty! will this one do?"

"Do you think that is the best?" said I, "then I will take it, Alice; and some for your cap now; here is a satin one, and here is gauze, but I must choose them myself; and you are to have your silk gown made and wear it—you are not to put it away in your drawer."

Alice looked down at her dark green stuff gown, hanging quite dead and unbrightened even in that fervid sunshine, and shook her head with a smile of odd distress. "It is much too fine for me, I was never meant to be a lady," said Alice, "but I'd wear white like a girl, sooner than cross you, my darling; and that is for me—bless your dear heart! that is a ribbon fit for a queen!"

"But the queen is not to be here," said I, "so you must wear it, Alice; and I do not want you to be without your apron. I like that great white apron. I wonder if I will like to lay down my head upon it, Alice, when I am old?"

"When you are old, Alice will not be here, Miss Hester," she said, with a smile; "you are like other young things, you think you will not be a young lady when you are married; but my darling, married or not married, the years take their full time to come."

"Ah, I will never be a girl again," said I, sighing with one of the half mock, half real sentimentalities of youth. "Alice, do you think, after all, my father is pleased?"

"I think," she began, but she stopped and paused, and evidently took a second thought; "yes, Miss Hester, I think he is pleased," she said, "he has every reason—yes, dear, don't fear for your papa; it is all good—all better than anybody could have planned it—I know it is."

"Do you know that you speak very oddly sometimes, Alice," said I; "you speak as if you were a prophet, and knew something about us, that we did not ourselves know."

"Don't you think such things, Miss Hester," said Alice, hurriedly, and her face reddened, "as I am no gipsy nor fortune-teller either, not a bit."

"Are you angry?" said I, "angry at me, Alice?" I was a little surprised, and it was quite true that two or three times I had been at a loss to know what she meant.

"Angry at you—no, darling, nor never was all your life," said Alice, "for all you have your own proud temper, Miss Hester—for I never was one to flatter. Will I send the box away? look, dear, if you have got all."

I had got all that we wanted, and when she went away, I drew my chair to the window, and began a labor of love. Alice never changed the fashion of her garments, and while she labored night and day for me, I was making a cap for her, and braiding a great muslin apron, which she was to wear on the day. I was very busy with the apron, doing it after a fashion of my own, and in a pattern which Alice would think all the more of because it was my own design, though I am not very sure that it gained much in effect by that circumstance. I drew my seat near to the open window, into the sunshine, and began to work, singing to myself very quietly but very gladly, as the pattern grew under my fingers. My heart rejoiced in the beautiful day, and in its own gladness; and I do not know that this joy was less pleasant for the tremor of expectation, and the flutter of fear, which my strange new circumstances brought me. I glanced from the window, hearing a step in the garden, and there was Harry, wandering about looking up at me.

When he caught my eye, he began to beckon with all his might, and try to get me to come down to him. I had seen him already this morning, so I knew it was not because he had anything to say to me, and I shook my head, and returned to my work. Then he began to telegraph to me his despair, his impatience, his particular wish to talk to me—and kept me so occupied smiling at him, and answering his signals, that the apron did not make much more progress than if I had gone down. At last, however, Alice came back, and I looked from the window no more, but went on soberly with my occupation. I had no young friends to come to see my pretty things, so Alice began to put them away.

A fortnight was gone, since that day when we were engaged, as Alice called it; and in a week, only a week now, the other day was to come.

"You have never told me yet, Miss Hester," said Alice, as she passed behind me, "where you are going, after—"

I interrupted her hurriedly. I was frightened for a mention of this dreadful ceremony, in so many words; and the idea of going away was enough to overset my composure at any time—I who had never left home before, and such a going away as this!

"We are to go abroad," I answered hurriedly; "but only for a few weeks, and then to have a house in Cambridgeshire, if we can find one very near at hand, Alice."

"Yes," answered Alice.

There was so much implied in this "yes," it seemed so full of information and consciousness, as if she could tell me more than I told her, that I was annoyed and almost irritated. In the displeasure of the moment I could not continue the conversation; it was very strange what Alice could mean by these inferences, and then to look so much offended when I spoke to her about them. I saw that Harry was still in the garden, looking up, and beckoning to me again, when he saw me look out—so I put away my work, and went down to hear what he had to say.

He had not anything very particular to say; but it was not disagreeable, though there was little originality in it, and I had heard most of it before; and he helped me with some flowers in the green-house which had been sadly neglected, and we cut some of the finest of them in the garden, for the vase upon my little table upstairs; and he told me I ought to wear flowers in my hair, and he said he would bring me a wreath of briony. "I should like to bind the beautiful clustered berries over those brown locks of yours, Hester," he said. "I will tell you some day how I came to know the briony first, and fell in love with it—it was one of the first incidents in my life."

"Tell me now then," said I.

But he shook his head and smiled. "Not now—wait till I can get a wreath of it fresh from a Cambridgeshire hedgerow, and then I will tell you my tale."

"I shall think it is a tale about a lady, if you speak of it so mysteriously," said I, and when I turned to him I saw he blushed. "It was so then," I said, with the slightest pique possible. I was not quite pleased.

"There never was but one in the world to me, Hester," he said, and I very soon cast down my eyes, "so it could not be about a lady, unless it happened in a dream, and the lady was you."

I looked at him with a strange perplexity, he was almost as hard to understand as Alice was—but he suddenly changed the conversation, and made me quite helpless for any further controversy by talking about what we were to do next week, after—I was always silenced in a moment by a reference to that.

Then my father looked out from the library window and called to us. My father had been a good deal occupied with Harry, and I pleased myself with thinking that he began to like him already. They seemed very good friends, and Harry showed him so much deference and was so anxious to follow his wishes in everything, that I was very grateful to him; and all the more because I thought it was from his own natural goodness he did this, fully more than from a wish to please me.

We went in together to the library. My father was reading papers, some of those long straggling papers tied together at the top, which always look so ominous, and are so long-winded. His book was put away, and instead he had pen and ink and his great blotting-book before him. My father had been writing much and reading little, during these two weeks; the occupation of his life was rudely broken in upon by these arrangements, and though I could not understand how it was that he had so much business thrown upon him, the fact seemed to be certain. There was more life even in the room, it was less orderly, and there was a litter of papers upon the table. My father looked well, pale, and self-possessed, but not so deadly calm, and he called Harry to him with a kind and familiar gesture. I had not yet overcome the embarrassment which I always felt when I was with them both; and when I saw that my father was pointing out sundry things in the papers to Harry, that they were consulting about them, and that I was not a necessary spectator, I turned over some books for a few minutes, and then I turned to go away. When he saw me moving towards the door, my father looked up. "Wait a little, Hester, I may want you by and by," he said. I was obedient and came back, but I did not like being here with Harry. I did not feel that our young life and our bright prospects were fit to intrude into this hermit's room, and I wondered if it would look drearier or more solitary—if my father would feel any want of me in my familiar place, when I went away.

But I had very little reason to flatter myself that he would miss me. He conducted all these matters with a certain satisfaction, I thought. He was glad to have me "settled;" and though I think he had been kinder than usual ever since that night, he had never said that it would grieve him to part with me, or that the house would be sad when I was gone.

There was a pause in their consultation. I heard, for I did not see, because I had turned to the window, and they were behind me, and then my father said—"Come here, Hester, we have now talked together of these arrangements—sit down by me, here, and see if it will not distress you too much to hear the programme of the drama in which you are to be a principal actor—here is a chair, sit down."

I turned, and went slowly to the seat he pointed out to me. I was very reluctant, but I could not disobey him, not even though I saw Harry's face bending forward eagerly to know if this was disagreeable to me.

"In the first place," said my father with a smile, "it is perhaps well that Hester is no heiress, as she once was supposed to be. Had my daughter inherited the family estate, her husband must have taken her name, and that is a harder condition than the one I stipulated for."

As there was no answer for a moment, I glanced shyly under the hand which supported my head at Harry. To my great surprise, he seemed strangely and painfully agitated. There was a deep color on his face. He did not lift his eyes, but shifted uneasily, and almost with an air of guilt, upon his chair; and he began to speak abruptly with an emotion which the subject surely did not deserve.

"Hester is worth a greater sacrifice than that of a name like mine," he said; "it would give me pleasure to show my sense of the honor you do me by admitting me into your family. I have no connexions whom I can gain by abandoning my own name, and I have no love for it, even though Hester has made it pleasanter to my ear. Let me be called Southcote. I would have proposed it myself had I thought it would be agreeable to you. You have no son. When you give Hester to me, make me altogether your representative. I will feel you do me a favor. Pray let us settle it so."

My father looked at him with more scrutinizing eyes—"When I was your age, young man, not for all the bounties of life, would I have relinquished my name."

Once more Harry blushed painfully. I too, for the moment, would rather that he had not made this proposal, yet how very kind it was of him! and I could not but appreciate the sacrifice which he made for me.

"Your name was the name of a venerable family, distinguished and dear to you," he said, after a little pause. "I am an orphan, with no recollections that endear it to me. Nay, Mr. Southcote, do not fear, I have no antecedents which make me ashamed of it; but for Hester's sake and yours, I will gladly relinquish this name of mine. If you do not wish it, that is another question."

There was a suppressed eagerness in his tone which impressed me very strangely. I could understand how, in an impulse of generosity, he could make the proposal; but I could not tell why he should be so anxious about it. It was very strange.

"I have not sufficient self-denial to say that," said my father. "I do wish it. It will gratify me more than anything else can, and I do not see indeed why, being satisfied on every other point, I should quarrel with you for proposing to do what I most desire; but regard for his own name is so universal in every man, I confess in other circumstances I should have been disposed to despise the man who accepted my heiress and her name with her. You, of course, are in an entirely different position. I can only accept your offer with gratitude. It is true, as you say, I have no son—you shall be my representative—yes, and I will be glad to think," said my father, with a momentary softening, and in a slow and lingering tone, "that she is Hester Southcote still."

Ah, those lingering touches of tenderness, how they overpowered me! I did not wish to let my father see me cry, like a weak girl; but I put my hands on my eyes to conceal my tears. He did care for me, though he expressed it so little; and when he said that, I was glad too, that I was still to bear my father's name—glad of this one proof of Harry's regard, and proud of the self-relinquishment—the devotion he showed to me.

There was a considerable pause after that—we did not seem at our ease, any one of us, and when I glanced up again, Harry, though he looked relieved, was still heated and embarrassed, and watched my father eagerly. He cleared his voice a great many times, as if to speak—changed his position, glanced at me; but did not seem able to say anything after all. My father had a faint smile upon his face—though it was a smile, I did not think it a pleasant one—and I was quite silent, with a vague fear of what was to follow.

But nothing followed to confirm my alarm. When my father spoke again it was quite in his usual tone.

"Then, with this one change—which, by the bye, requires our instant attention as to the papers and everything necessary—our arrangements stand as before; and you leave Cambridge on Tuesday, and return in a month, either here or to some house which Mr. Osborne may find for you. Osborne is your agent, I understand? You leave these matters in his hands? Now, I must know the hour you will leave me—how you are to travel, and where you will go first; and if I may depend certainly on the time of your return?"

"We will fix it for any time you choose," said Harry, quickly and with an air of relief. "I will be only too proud to bring Hester home, and to see her in her own settled house; but you must give us our moon; we have a right to that—I have a right to that. You will not grudge us our charmed holiday. I shall be content to have no other all my life."

My father looked at him with a smile, almost of scorn, but it soon settled into a fixed and stern gravity. "I will not grudge your pleasure—no," he said, in the tone of a monitor who means to imply "it is all vanity," "but I wish to have your assurance that I may trust your word. And you, Hester, are you nearly ready to go away from me?"

"Oh! papa, papa!" I cried wildly. Was he disposed to regret me at last?

"Nay, nay, child, we must have no lamentations," said my father, "no weeping for the house you leave behind. On the verge of your life be sparing of your tears, Hester—if you have not occasion for them all one day or another you will be strangely favored. Are you ready? tell me? I have been hard upon you sometimes; I am not a man of genial temper, and what kindness was in me was soured. There—I apologize to you, Hester, for wounding your sensibilities—they distress me; and now answer my question."

"I will be ready," I said. This dreadful coldness of his always drove me into a sullen gloom.

"Very well, you have chosen each other," said my father gravely; "and now you are about to begin your life. I am no dealer in good advice or moral maxims. I only bid you remember that it is of your own free will you bind yourselves in this eternal contract. This union, on which you are entering, has a beginning, but no end. Its effects are everlasting; you can never deliver yourself from its influences, its results. On the very heart and soul of each of you will be the bonds of your marriage; and neither separation, nor change, nor death, can obliterate the mark they will make. I do not speak to discourage you. I only bid you think of the life before you, and remember that you pursue it together of your own free choice."

"We do not need that you should use such solemn words; they are not for us, father," said Harry, advancing to my side, and drawing my hand within his arm. He was afraid that I could not bear this, when he saw me drooping and leaning on the chair from which I had just risen. He did not know what a spirit of defiance these words roused in me. "Hester trusts me and does not fear that I will make her life wretched; and, as for me, my happiness is secure when I claim the right thus to stand by her, and call her mine. There are no dark prognostics in our lot—think not so. We will fear God and love each other; and I desire to feel the bonds of my marriage in my very soul and heart. I do not care to have a thought that is not hers—not a wish that my wife will not share with me. Say gentler words to us, father! Bless us as you bless her in your heart. She is a young, tender, delicate woman. She trembles already; but you will not speak only those words which make her tremble more?"

My father stood by himself, stooping slightly, leaning his hands upon the table before him, and looking at us. Harry's firm voice shook a little as he ended; his eyes were glistening, and there was a noble tender humility about his whole look and attitude, which was a very great and strange contrast to the cold, self-possessed man before him. I saw that my father was struck by it. I saw that the absence of any thought for himself—that his care and regard for me moved with a strange wonder my father's unaccustomed heart. The young man's generous life and love, the very strength of all the youthful modest power of which he would make no boast—his entire absence of offence, yet firm and quiet assertion of what was due to our young expectations and hopes, and perhaps the way in which we stood together, my arm in his, leaning upon him, impressed my father. He looked at us long, with a steady, full look; and then he spoke.

"You are right—it does not become me to bode evil to my own child, nor to her bridegroom. God bless you! I say the words heartily; and now leave me, I am weary, and will call you if I need you, Hester! I am not ill, do not fear for me."

He took our hands, Harry's and mine, and held them tightly within his own; then he said again, "Children, God bless you!" and sent us away.

We went up to the drawing-room together; Harry had spent almost all of the day with us for at least a week past, and even now he did not seem disposed to go away. When I told him that I had something to do, he bade me bring it and work beside him—he would like to see me working, so I did what he said— and while I was busy with Alice's apron, he talked to me, for I did not speak a great deal myself. My mind was somewhat troubled by what my father had said. I had an uneasy sense of something doubtful and uncertain in our circumstances, of some event or mystery, though I could not tell what it was. I do not think I was pleased that Harry should be so willing to resign his name. It was one of those concessions that a woman does not like to have made to her. A true woman is far happier to receive rank than to confer it. When she is placed in these latter circumstances, she is thrown upon the false expedient of undervaluing herself, and what she has to bestow. I would much rather have felt that Harry was quite superior to me in the external matters—then we could have stood on our natural ground to each other, and I should have been proud of his name; but it was not a pleasant thought to me that he himself thought it unworthy, and that he was to adopt mine.

"You are very grave, Hester; are you thinking of what your father said?" he asked me at last.

"I do not quite know what I am thinking of," I said, with a faint sigh.

"No, it is a summer cloud," said Harry, "something floating over this beautiful sky of our happiness; but it will not last, Hester. I know you may trust yourself; your sweet young life and all its hopes. I think you need not fear to trust them with me."

"I have no fear—it is not that," said I; "do not heed me. I cannot tell what it is that troubles me."

He bent down upon his knee to see my face, which was stooping over Alice's apron, and he put his hand upon mine, and arrested my fingers, which were playing nervously with the braid. "Do you remember the compact you made with me, Hester? 'Cannot tell' is for other people; but what troubles you should trouble me also."

"Nay, I would not have that," said I, hurriedly, "that would be selfish, but indeed I don't know what it is—I rather feel as if there was something which I did not know—as if there was a secret somewhere which somebody ought to tell me; I cannot guess what or where it is, but I think there is surely something. Do you know of anything, Harry?"

He continued to kneel at my knee, holding my hand, and looking up in my face, and I gazed at him wistfully, wondering to see the color rise to his very hair. He did not remove his eyes from me, but what could it be that brought that burning crimson to his face?

But I did not wait for his answer. In my womanish foolishness, afraid that I was grieving him, I took away the opportunity, that opportunity—what misery it might have saved me: and spoke myself, wearing the time away till he had quite recovered himself. "I do not think you would hide anything from me, Harry, which I ought to know; my father scarcely knows that I am a woman now; it is hard for him to get over the habit of thinking me a child, but you are no older than I am; we are equal then—and you would not use me as if I was unfit to know all that concerns us both."

"We are equal then," he said, repeating my words hurriedly, but without any answer to the meaning of them; "but I do not think we are nearly equals in anything else, Hester. Your sincere heart—oh, if I begin to speak of that, I will soon make myself out a poor fellow, and I would rather you did not think me so just yet; equal! why I am justly entitled to call myself your superior in that particular at least, for do you know I am two or three years older than you are?"

"I was not speaking of that," said I gravely.

"I know you were not speaking of that," said Harry, "you were speaking of the summer cloud. See, Hester, there is another on the sky; look how it floats away with the sunshine and the wind. There shall be neither secret nor mystery between us, trust me. I want your help and sympathy too much for that."

"There shall be!" I said to myself in an under tone. I was quite satisfied; this promise was fortunate, and Henry did not say: "there is not."

But at this moment we heard the door open below, and Mr. Osborne's voice asking for my father.

I rose in great haste and ran up stairs. I forgot everything of more importance, and only remembered how embarrassed and uncomfortable I should be, if Mr. Osborne came in and found us together. I went back again to my room with my heart beating quick. The vague and uncertain doubtfulness which had taken possession of me did not prompt any distrust of Harry. It was not that I found that he was deceiving me, or that I dreamed of such a possibility. The utmost length to which my suspicions went, was to a little jealousy of something which I did not know, and was not told of, and when I reflected over it in my own room, I found no particular foundation for these doubts of mine; but still I should have much preferred that Harry had not offered to take our name. It was generous like himself. I was no heiress that he should have done it for the land, or for the rank I brought him. Instead of that, he did it for pure love; but I was perverse still, and I was not pleased.

When I went down stairs, I found that Mr. Osborne was to dine with us, and that Harry had not gone away; and after a little time, I found that I was very glad of Mr. Osborne's presence at table. My father spoke very little, and seemed more abstracted than usual. Harry was almost talkative, on the contrary, but he was less easy than I had seen him; and as for me, I said nothing, but watched them with a strange fascination, as if I was the spectator of some drama of which I must find out the secret. It was a relief to see Mr. Osborne's uninterrupted spirits, his usual manner and bearing. I wonder if they are happier than other people, those men who have nobody to disturb their equanimity, no one to put them out of temper, or break their hearts—but at any rate, it was a comfort to look at Mr. Osborne, and to see, whatever change might be in us, that there was none in him.

After dinner, Harry left us, though only for a time, and when I had been by myself in the drawing-room for nearly an hour, Mr. Osborne came in, and approached me with something in his hand. When he opened it, it turned out to be another little gold chain with something hanging from it, very much like my little diamond ornament; but this was a very small miniature of a very young sweet face, so smiling, and loving, and gentle, that it was pleasant to look at it. "I think this is the fittest present I can make you," said Mr. Osborne. "You know who it is, Hester?"

"No," I said; though from the look he gave me, I guessed at once.

"It is very like her," he said in a low voice; "like what she was when I had a young man's fancy for that pretty sweet young face. No, Hester, you need not glance at me so wistfully, she did not break my heart; but I love you the better, my child, that she was your mother."

"And this is my mother!" I said. It was younger than me, this innocent simple girlish face—my heart was touched by its gentleness, its happiness, the love and kindness in its sweet eyes—my tears began to fall fast upon the jewelled rim—this was my mother! and it was not a face to make any one unhappy. I did not think of thanking Mr. Osborne, I only thought of her.

"She must have been very happy," I said, softly; we sank our voices speaking of her.

"She was very happy then," said Mr. Osborne; "the sunshine was her very life, Hester; and when it faded away from her, she died."

These words recalled me to myself. I could not permit him to go on, perhaps to blame my father—so I interrupted him to thank him very gratefully for his present.

"She used to wear an ornament like this; and the miniature is from a sketch I myself made of her in her first youth," said Mr. Osborne. "I know your father has no portrait, but there is one in the possession of her friends."

"Her friends! has she friends living?" I asked eagerly; "I do not know what it is to have relations. I wonder if they know anything of us."

"You have one relation at least, Hester," said Mr. Osborne; "is it possible, after all his attempts to become acquainted with you, that you have never given a kind thought to your cousin?"

"I do not know my cousin, sir," I answered rather haughtily, "I do not wish to know him; we have nothing in common with each other, he and I."

"How do you know that?" said my companion. "Hester, when you do know him, do him justice. I have seen Edgar Southcote; I know few like him, and he ill deserves unkindness, or distrust, or resentment at your hands. Now hear me, Hester. I have given you this portrait of your mother, because I loved her in my youth; and because you are as dear to me as if you were my own child; but I give it you also as a charm against the cruel injustice, the suspicion, and the pride of your race. A false conception of her motives, obstinately held and dwelt upon, killed your poor mother. Yes! I do not want to mince words. It made her wretched first, and then it killed her. Hester, beware! your husband's happiness depends as much on you as yours does on him. He is himself a noble young man, worthy the regard of any woman; and I have had a higher opinion of yourself ever since I saw that you valued him. When you leave your father's house, take this sweet counsellor with you. Remember the cause that broke her young heart, and left you without a mother in the world. Let the glance of the sweet frank eyes teach you a woman's wisdom, my dear child. Forgive what is wrong—foster what is right. Hester! I am making a long speech to you. It is the first and last preachment you will hear from an old friend."

I had risen while he was speaking, and stood before him a little proud, a little indignant, waiting till he should come to an end. Then I said: "Mr. Osborne, I cannot hear you blame my father."

"I am not blaming your father, Hester. I am warning you," he answered; "and I do it because you are as a child to me."

I thanked him again, kissed the little miniature, and put it round my neck. But Mr. Osborne would not suffer this. "Time enough," he said, "when you go away. Do not awake too strongly your father's recollections. He is not in a fit state for that."

"He is not worse!" I exclaimed eagerly.

"No, Hester, he is not worse—but he is not strong, you know. Now go and put this away, and remember my words like a good child."

When I took it upstairs Alice was in the room; and when she saw it, Alice wept on it, and exclaimed how like it was. Then she clasped it on my neck, and kissed me, and cried, and said how glad she was that I should have such a token of my mother; and then Alice, too, began to admonish me. "Oh! think of her sometimes, Miss Hester! Think how her young life and all her hopes were lost. It was no blame of her's, my sweet young lady! Oh! think of your mother, dear child." I was strangely shaken by all these admonitions. I did not know whether to reject this indignantly, or to sit down on the floor, and cry with mortification and annoyance. What occasion had they all to be afraid of my spirit or temper? I put away this beautiful little portrait, at last, with a vexed and sullen pain. Why did everybody preach to me on this text? I had never harmed my mother, and how could my circumstances possibly resemble those she was placed in? If this sweet, gentle smile of hers was to be a perpetual reproach to me, how could I have any pleasure in it? I was annoyed and vexed with everybody, and though in the rebound my heart clung to my father, I could not go to him to seek for sympathy. I wandered out into the garden, into the twilight, thinking with a deeper pity of his disappointed heart. I forgave him all his hard words and coldness, thinking mysteriously of the darkness which had fallen over all his life; and I could not be patient with my advisers who had been warning me by his example. How could they tell what he had suffered? What was it to them that he had looked for love, and had not found it? In imagination, I stood by my father's side, vindicating and defending, and said to myself with indignant earnestness: "Nobody shall blame him to me."

I was not even satisfied with Harry. He had not answered me plainly, and he had gone away. I paced up and down the springy, fragrant grass with short, impatient steps. I forgot that the night-wind was chill, and that I had nothing to protect me from it. I was not at all in a sweet or satisfactory mood of mind; and when I thought of the continual happy smile of the miniature, it rather chafed and annoyed than calmed me. While I was thus unhappily wandering in the garden, at issue with myself and every one around, I suddenly heard a step behind, and as suddenly felt a great, soft shawl thrown over me. I resisted my first impatient impulse to throw it off, and submitted to have myself wrapped in it, and a fold of it thrown over my head like a hood—the warmth and shelter it seemed to give, had something strangely pleasant in them. I was soothed against my will—and Harry drew my arm through his, and we continued our walk in silence. It was pleasant to be taken possession of so quietly—it was pleasant to feel that some one had a right to take care of me, whether I would or no.

And then Harry had all the talk to himself for a long time, though it was not the less agreeable on that account; and then my troubled mood went away, and I told him of Mr. Osborne's present, and how they had been cautioning me on his behalf—and, indeed, with a confession of the temper I was in when he came to me—things were very different now. I perceived it was a beautiful dewy Autumn night, with a young moon in the sky, and pale silvery stars half lost in the mist of the Milky Way, and there was a breath of faint fragrance in the air, and one by one the lights were beginning to shine in the college windows—these friendly lights which I had watched so long—then my father's lamp was lighted in the library. In the stillness and darkness we wandered through the garden, speaking little, finding no great necessity to speak. Out of all the agitation of the day, it happened to me now to become very quiet, and very happy; my heart beat quick, yet softly; I no longer felt the chill evening breath, or chafed at what had been said to me—what mattered all that had been said to me? When Harry and I were together, I knew nothing could ever step in between us. Nobody else understood me as he did. Nobody else, like me, trusted in him.

THE TENTH DAY

It was my marriage day.

I awoke when the morning was breaking with its chill harmony of tints in the east. I went to my window, to watch the song-thrushes rising upon the grey of the dawn; to look upon those long wide lines of clouds which seemed to stretch out their vain ineffectual barriers to keep down the rising day. I lingered till the early sunshine came down aslant upon the top-most boughs, and woke the birds to twitter their good-morrow—till the darkness in the garden paths underneath yielded and fled before this sweet invasion, and took a momentary refuge in the depths of dreary shadow, under the three elm trees at the boundary wall. No one was astir but I—there was not a sound but the chirp of little housewives in their leafy nests, up betimes to seek the day's provisions. I saw nothing but the sky, the clouds, the early light, the dew glistening on the trees, and the sunshine touching the little deep-set windows of Corpus, and the morning mist just clearing from the brown outline of its wall.

It was my wedding-day—the first grand crisis of my life—and I had no lack of material for my thoughts; but I was not thinking as I knelt by the window in my white dressing-gown, vacantly looking out upon the rising day. My mind was full of a vague tumult of imagination. I myself was passive and made no exertion, but looked at the floating pictures before me, as I might have looked in a dream. My fancy was like the enchanted mirror in the story; out of the mist, scenes and figures developed themselves for a moment, and faded into vapor once more. The scenes were those of my girlish life; so many recollections of it came back upon me; so many glimpses I had of that careless sunshine, those unencumbered days! when I was a child at Cottiswoode, where I was the young lady of the Manor, and knew all these lands over which I looked in my frank girlish pride to be our own. Then the time when the new heir came—and then all those years and days which had gone over me here. I saw myself in the garden on which I was looking now with dreamy eyes—I saw myself in the corner of the window-seat looking out upon the twinkling lights of Corpus, and thinking to myself in my silence and solitude of the owners of these lights; and then Harry glided in upon my dreams, and I woke with a startling flush of consciousness to remember what day this was, and to know that I myself was a bride!

Yes, a bride! to go away from my father's house in a few hours, never to come back to it again as to my home. To take farewell of all my girlish loneliness, and retirements, and wild fancies—to give up all the involuntary romancings and possibilities, the uncommunicated and self-contained life of my youth. I almost fancied, with a sudden shrinking and tremor, that this was the last hour of all my life in which I should be alone. I buried my face in my hands at the thought, though there was no one there to see me; I felt my face burn with a hot heavy glow. I had in me a restless sense of excitement, a reluctant heart, and yet a passive consciousness of certainty, of necessity, of something fixed and absolute, from which there was neither way nor means to recede. A thing which must be, always roused a little defiance, a little resistance; and the morning of a bridal is seldom a time of perfect happiness to anybody concerned. I lay with my head upon the cushion of my chair, kneeling before it. I tried to say my prayers, but my thoughts wandered off from the familiar words. My thoughts seemed wandering everywhere, and would not be composed into steady attention for a moment; and after I had said the words, I knew with a certain shock and distress that I had meant nothing by them, and that those childish sentences that claimed sincerity more than the most elaborate compositions could have done, were only a cover for a tumult of agitating thoughts. After this, in real distress at my involuntary mocking of prayer, I spoke aloud, and trembling, with my face still hidden, what plain words I could think of, asking for a blessing. "Oh, Lord, bless us, bless us." I almost think that was all that I could keep my mind to; and after I had made this child's outcry, I lay still, kneeling, hiding my face, in this little pause of vacant time, on the threshold of my fate.

When I heard some one stirring below, and after an interval, when Alice's step approached my door, I rose up hurriedly, that she might not see me thus. Alice could not tell whether to smile or to cry as she came towards me. It was a true April face, beaming and showery, that stooped towards me as she kissed my cheek. "Bless you, my darling!" said Alice, and with the words the tears fell, but she recovered immediately and set me down in the old-fashioned easy chair, and drew a little table before me, and brought me some tea; and henceforward I delivered myself up into the hands of Alice, and was served and waited upon as if I had been a child.

It was still only seven o'clock, and there was no haste, yet we began my solemn toilet immediately. I became quite calm under the sway of Alice. When she brushed my hair over my shoulders, I shook it round me like a veil, and defied her to reduce it into order. I was relieved and eased by her company. I had no longer the opportunity of bewildering myself with my own thoughts, and as Alice brushed and braided, she told me stories, as she had been used to do, of many another bride.

"For nobody makes much account of the bridegroom, Miss Hester," said Alice; "though the wedding wouldn't be much of a wedding without him, and though a handsome young gentleman like our Mr. Harry is a pleasure to see in the day of his joy; but even if it's a poor country maid, instead of a young lady, every one wants a look at the bride. The married folks think of their young days, and the young folks of what's to come; and I think there's never a mortal, unless he's quite given over to the evil one, but has a kind thought for a bride."

To this I answered nothing, but only played with a superb bracelet Harry had given me, sliding it on and off my arm, and watching the glitter of the light in the precious stones.

"But, my darling, you hav'n't half the company you should have had," continued Alice, smoothing my hair with her large kind hand, in a caressing motion. "Half-a-dozen pretty young bridesmaids at the least, ought to have gone with you—all in their pretty gowns and their white ribbons; and now there's only Mr. Osborne's niece, just for the name of the thing, and not another woman but me."

"That is because I know no one, Alice," said I.

"But you should have known some one, dear," said Alice. "It's not in nature for a young thing to be so lonesome; but that's all to be mended now. You'll not make light of the country people, Miss Hester, as your papa did? Promise me now, my dear young lady, that you'll think well of them, for his sake, when you get home."

"What country people, Alice? I don't suppose we will be rich enough to keep company with great people," said I, "but you always speak as if you knew quite well where I was to live, when the truth is, that nobody knows, and that Mr. Osborne is to find a house for us, if he can."

Alice made no immediate reply. I liked her pleasant talk and recollections, and I did not like to bring them to an end, so I resumed the conversation by a question. "I never asked you, Alice, how you got those roses from Cottiswoode, that night, you remember, three weeks ago?"

"I have some more to-day, Miss Hester," said Alice.

"Have you? how did you get them? I hope the master of the house does not think that his flowers are stolen for us," said I, with a little indignation. "You ought to take care, Alice, that you do not compromise my father and me."

"There is no fear, Miss Hester," said Alice, almost with a little bitterness. "The young Squire, your cousin, would never believe your papa nor you to stoop out of your pride for a fancy like that. No, a friend brought me the flowers for my own pleasure, and if you'd rather not have them, I'll take them back to my own room."

"Why, Alice, how foolish you are," said I, turning back in surprise to look at her. "I wonder now why you should care for my cousin. I don't see how he can be anything to you."

"Kindness is a deal to me, dear; I never like to see a kind meaning despised," said Alice.

"You flatter me, Alice," said I, with some pique; "you think it was a kind meaning that my cousin should propose to share his new inheritance with me; perhaps you think it is a kind meaning which moves Harry too?"

"Oh, Miss Hester!" cried Alice, with a subdued groan, "don't talk in that way, it's just as your papa did. You'll break my heart."

"Alice, you don't know—no one knows, what papa has had to suffer," said I. "He gave her all his heart, and she took it, because she was sorry for him! Never say that to me again; I would rather die—I would rather die, than be so bitterly deceived!"

Again I heard the groaning sigh with which Alice had answered me, but this time she did not say anything. I was somewhat excited. I did not now attempt to resume our talk again. I was annoyed and distracted to hear my cousin's "generous" proposal brought before me this morning. I felt myself humiliated by it. I felt as if it were a scoff at Harry to say that any one had entertained compassion for his bride—and it occurred to me, that I would like to meet Edgar Southcote, perhaps in a year or two, and show him how far I was from being such a one as he would pity. This idea possessed me immediately, and I said in the impulse of the moment—"By and bye, Alice, I will have no objection to see my cousin."

Why or for what reason I could not fancy, but I felt the hand of Alice tremble as she arranged the last braids of my hair; and she answered me in the strangest, subdued, troubled voice, "And when you know him, Miss Hester—when you know him—oh! be kind to the poor young gentleman—if it were only for your mother's sake."

"For my mother's sake! are you crazy, Alice?" I said, turning round upon her with utter amazement, "how is it possible that you can connect my mother with him?"

Alice seemed greatly disconcerted at my sudden question. She retreated a step or two, as if I had made a real attack upon her, and said in a faltering apologetic voice, "I'll maybe never have to wait upon you, and talk to you another morning, Miss Hester—you oughtn't to be hard on poor old Alice to-day."

"Why should you never wait upon me, and talk to me again?" I said. "You are full of whims this morning, Alice! Shall I not find you here when we come back again? You do not mean that you will not come to me?"

"I never will leave your papa while he has need of me, dear," said Alice, humbly.

"Ah, he will permit you to stay with him—he will not permit me," said I, "but papa will get strong, and then you will come. I wish you would not be mysterious, Alice. I wish you would not give me these prophetic warnings. Do you really think I have such a dreadful temper that I will make everybody unhappy, or what do you mean?"

"It's not that, Miss Hester," said Alice hurriedly, retreating once more before me, and taking out of its folds the dress which I was about to put on.

"Because if you think so," I said, recovering from my momentary anger, "you should not speak to me about it, you ought to warn the person most concerned."

I smiled at the thought—to warn Harry of my hereditary pride and my faulty character—to caution him how to deal with me—with a proud assurance which warmed my very heart, I smiled at the thought. Yes, I was secure and blessed in my firm persuasion of what I was to Harry. I was his lady of romance— his perfect ideal woman—his first love—and I rejoiced in him because he thought so. It did not make me vain, but it made him the ideal lover, the true knight.

There came a message to the door that my father was in the dining-room and wished to see me. I was fully dressed. Can a bride forget her ornaments? I thought they were very dazzling as I saw them in my mirror. I could not help pausing to look at myself, at the lustre of my dress, and the glow of Harry's bracelet on my arm; and I was about to go away so, to see my father—but Alice stopped me to wrap a large light shawl over my splendor—"Dear, he'll feel it," said Alice. I was struck with the delicacy which both Alice and Mr. Osborne, though they condemned him, showed to my father and his feelings. I wrapped the shawl closer over my arms, and with a subdued step left my own room. I wondered what he was thinking of. I wondered if this day recalled to him the freshness of those hopes which had been dead and withered for many a year, and when I went in at last, I went very softly and humbly, like a timid child.

He was pale and his eyes were hollow—he looked rather worse than usual to-day—and before I reached the door of the room, I had heard his slow measured footsteps pacing from window to window. He very seldom did this, and I knew it was a sign of some excitement and agitation in his mind. I was pleased it should be so. I was pleased that he did not send me away with his perfect cold self-possession, as if I had been a book or a picture. He turned towards me when I went in, but did not look at me for a moment! and when I met his eye, I saw by his momentary glance of relief, that he was glad not to see me in my full bridal dress. But this was only for a moment; he came towards me steadily, and with his own hands removed the shawl. I hung my head under his full serious gaze. I felt the color burning on my cheek and the tears coming to my eyes. A few hours and I would be away from him. A few hours, and it might be, I would never see him again.

But my tears were checked by the touch of his cold firm hand upon my head. "God bless you, Hester!" he said, slowly. "My own life has been unfortunate and aimless. I think all my better ambition died on my wedding-day. I gave myself over to the bitterest feeling in the world, a sense of wrong and injury, while I was still young, and reckoned happy. I would fain hope your life is to be happier than mine has been; but in any case, do not follow my example. I care not who blames or justifies me, but I have not made so much by my experiment that I should recommend it to my child—forgive when you are wronged—endure when you are misunderstood—if you can, at all times be content. I believe a woman finds it easier to attain these passive heroisms, and heaven knows I have profited little by my resistance to the mild fictions of ordinary life. Remember, Hester, what I say; take whose example you will to form your life by, only do not take mine."

I cannot tell how this strange repetition of the advice which I had already heard so often, overpowered me. Where was the opportunity for my following my father's example? I saw no circumstances at all like his in the promise of my life. I could not suspect any compassion in Harry's regard for me. It was pure, manly affection, and no feigning. I felt as if all this was a conspiracy to drive me into the very suspiciousness from which they sought to guard me. What temper must I be of when everybody thought these cautions necessary; I felt humiliated and degraded by the constant counsel. The tears gathered in my eyes—large tears of mortification and bitterness—but my pride was roused at the same time, and they did not fall.

All this while, when I was swallowing down as I best could the sob in my throat, my father looked at me steadily, then he suddenly threw the shawl over me again. "I did not think, Hester, that you had been like your mother," he said, in a tone so cold and rigid that I saw at once it was the extreme control he exercised over some violent and passionate emotion which alone could express itself in these tones, and then he stooped, kissed my forehead gently, and began once more with hasty and irregular steps to pace the room from end to end. I stood where he had left me for a moment, and then I left the room and retired to my own.

The sun was rising higher—the world was all astir—it was very near the time. I went back and sat down at my chamber window to wait for the hour. Alice would not leave me; she remained in the room wandering about in a restless state of excitement, dressed and ready, but she did not speak, nor disturb my thoughts; and Harry had now arrived and was with my father, she told me—but that made no impression on my abstracted mood. I sat as in a dream, looking out upon all these familiar objects; there seemed to me a languid pause of expectation upon everything. I myself, as still as if I had been in a trance, watched at the window; but my senses were nervously quick and vivid. I thought I heard every step and movement below—and long before anybody else heard them, I felt that this was Mr. Osborne and the young lady, who was to be my bridesmaid, who alighted at the outer door, and came gaily talking through the close—then I knew that the time of my reverie was over. When Alice left me to bring Miss Osborne upstairs, I tried to shake myself free from my lethargy—it required an effort. I felt like the enchanted lady in the tale, as if I had been fixed in that magic chair, and could have slept there for a hundred years.

I was abruptly disturbed by the entrance of Miss Osborne—she was older than I, and used to such things—she did not understand the intense secret excitement which I had reached to by this time. She came up to me in a flutter of silk, and lace, and ribbons; she laid cordial hands upon me and kissed me. Having neither mother, sisters, nor female friends, I was very shy of the salutations which are current among young ladies. I felt myself shrink a little from the kiss, and my color rose in spite of myself. Miss Osborne laughed, and was astonished, and tried to encourage me. "Don't give way, there's a dear; poor little thing, how nervous you look, come lean on me, love, and get ready; where's some gloves? and her handkerchiefs? she must keep up her heart now, must she not?"

This was addressed in a half-satirical tone to Alice, and Alice as well as myself was considerably discomposed by the cool activity and gaiety of our visitor. "Dear, there is the carriage waiting for you at the door," whispered Alice in my ear. "Don't tremble, darling—don't now, it'll be all over before you know."

And when I went down stairs, I did not see either Harry or Mr. Osborne, though I suppose they were both there; I saw only my father's white thin hand take mine and lead me away—and then we drove from the door. I recollect quite well seeing the people in the streets as we drove along, and being struck with a vague wonder whether this day was really the same as any other day to all those strangers. Then came the church, a confused and tremulous picture—and then a voice addressed us, and I had to say something and so had Harry, and the scene suddenly cleared up, and became distinct for an instant before me, when with a shock and start I found my hand put into his hand; and by and bye all was over, and we came away.

And now we were again at home—at home—no longer home to me. And Alice with her silk gown and her great white muslin apron which I had braided for her, with the cap of lace and white ribbons which I had made, and her little white shawl fastened with a brooch which Harry had given her, and which contained some of my hair. Alice stood by my chair, sometimes forgetting that she had to attend to the party at table, and only remembering that she had to cry over, and comfort, and encourage me. Harry was in wild spirits, too joyous, almost flighty—like a man who has just achieved some wonderful triumph; but is scarcely quite aware of it yet. His name was Southcote now, and my name was unchanged. My father sat at the head of the table, beside us—he was grave, but much calmer than he had been in the morning, and I thought he watched Harry, and Harry avoided his eye in a manner which was strange to me. Mr. Osborne and his niece were a great relief to us—this event, which was so momentous to us, was nothing to them but a little occasion of festivity to which they had to contribute a reasonable portion of gaiety. They came to rejoice with those who did rejoice, and they were certainly the most successful in the company. The table was gay with flowers, and there were the sweet pale Cottiswoode roses, like friends from home, with dew upon their leaves, and the faint fragrance stealing through the room. I wondered once more where Alice had got them—for my own part I was not now excited; I had fallen into a lull of composure, and was watching everybody. I remember the little speech Mr. Osborne made—full of real kindness; but with a little mock formality in it, as if a large party had been present, when he drank our healths; and I remember the glow upon Harry's face, and the gleam in his eyes, when he without any mockery stretched out his hand to him, and thanked him. Miss Osborne sat by me in her rustle and flutter of finery, whispering jokes and kind words into my ear; telling me not to look so pale—not to blush so much—to compose myself and a great many other young lady-like sayings, and I began to think that though it was not very comfortable, it might be very good to be "supported" by Miss Osborne, since I carefully strove to banish all trace of feeling from my face, that I might be saved from her criticisms. We sat at table an unmercifully long time; but though I could see Harry was as impatient as I was, and though he was constantly looking at his watch, and whispering that it would soon be time to go away, no one else seemed disposed to release us. At length my father rose, and we all went into the drawing-room, where the table was covered with cards and envelopes. My father lifted one of the little packets and took a note from it to show to me. It was addressed to my cousin, and very formally and politely informed him of what had taken place to-day. "I thought it right to let him know; what do you think, Harry?" said my father, turning round to him somewhat sharply. Harry came up to see what it was. "It is to Hester's cousin, once a pretender for her hand. I ought to let him know it is disposed of, ought I not?" said my father, and he lifted the cover, which was addressed to "Edgar Southcote, Esq., Cottiswoode." My father was looking full at him, and I saw once more that burning flush rise to Harry's hair, and cover his whole face. Their eyes met; I do not know, and have never known what was in the glance; but Harry never spoke, he turned to me immediately, and took my hand, and said hoarsely with an extraordinary suppressed emotion, "Hester—my wife! Hester—it is time to go away." I thought he rather wished to draw me from my father's side, to keep me from much conversation with him; but he looked up again at me with recovered composure, and turned again boldly to my father. "All this only agitates and distresses me," he said, holding out his hand; "let me take her away, it is our time."

My father slowly extended his hand to him. "Take her away!" he said, "she is yours, and I do not dispute with you the triumph you have gained. Hester, my love, go and get ready. I will detain you no longer; Osborne, take leave of her, she is going away."

Then Mr. Osborne came forward and took both my hands and looked into my face. I was surprised to see that a tear twinkled in his sunny bright gray eye. "So you are going away," he said; "well, it is the course of nature; but Cambridge will be all the duller, Hester, when you are not to be met with in the streets. Good-bye! my dear child, I wished for this, but it costs me a pang notwithstanding. Good-bye, Hester! and don't let anything persuade you to be offended with your old friend."

With an old-fashioned graceful courtesy, he kissed my hand. I think I never felt so strong a momentary impulse to cling to any one, as at that time I did cling to him. He said it grieved him that I should go away; but, alas! there was no tear for me in my father's thoughtful eye. I had to restrain whatever I felt; my eyes were blinded with tears; but Miss Osborne was rustling forward to support me and give me her arm upstairs, and I would not call forth her common-place coldness, should I not even have ten minutes with Alice, all by ourselves.

But Alice contrived this, and, as I changed my dress, Alice wept over me. "The house will be desolate— desolate, darling," said Alice, "but I see nothing but happiness for you. It makes my heart light to think on what's before you. He's a noble young gentleman, Miss Hester; I never saw one was equal to him. Now, darling, you're ready, and here's the picture, my sweet young lady's sweet face to be your counsellor, my own child, and blessing and prosperity and joy be with you. Farewell, farewell;—I'll not cry now. I'll not shed tears on the threshold the bride steps over, and there's himself waiting for you."

Yes! there he was, without the door, standing waiting for my coming forth. I came out of my pretty room, the bower of my youth, and gave my husband my hand. Still my eyes were blind with tears, but I did not shed them, and in the close was my father, walking quickly up and down waiting to take leave of me. He took me in his arms for a moment, kissed my forehead again—said once more, "God bless you, my love, God bless my dear child!" and then put my hand again in Harry's. I was lifted into the carriage; I caught a last glimpse of the face of Alice, struggling with tears, and smiling; and then I fell into a great fit of weeping, I could control myself no longer. Harry did not blame me, he said I had been a hero, and soothed and calmed, and comforted me, with some bright moisture in his own eyes, and I awoke to remember him, and think of myself no longer; and this was how I left my home.

BOOK II

THE FIRST DAY

It is rather difficult for a girl, after all her solemn and awful anticipations of the wonderful event of her marriage, to find after it is over that she is precisely the same person as she was before—that instead of the sudden elevation, the gravity, and decorum, and stateliness of character which would become the mature stage of her existence, she has brought all her girlish faults with her, all her youth and extravagance, and is in reality, just as she was a few months ago, neither wiser, nor older, nor having greater command of herself, than when she was a young unwedded girl. After I became accustomed to Harry's constant companionship, and got over the first awe of myself and my changed position, I was extremely puzzled to find myself quite unchanged. No, I had not bidden a solemn adieu to my youth when I left my father's house; I was as young as ever, as impulsive, as eager, as ready to enjoy as to be miserable. I could fancy, indeed, with all this, and the gay foreign life around me, and Harry's anxiety to please, and amuse, and keep me happy—I who knew life only as it passed in our lonely drawing-room and garden, or in the dull streets of Cambridge—that youth, instead of being ended, was only beginning for me.

I was in vigorous health, and had an adventurous spirit. Long rapid journeys had in them a strange exhilaration for me. I liked the idea of our rapid race over states and empires; the motion, and speed, and constant change made the great charm of travel. I did not care for museums and picture-galleries: but I cared for a bright passing glimpse of an old picturesque town, a grand castle or cathedral; and though the road we travelled was a road which people called hackneyed and worn out, the resort of cockney tourists, and all manner of book-makers—yet it was perfectly fresh to me.

This day was in the early part of October, chill, bracing, and sunshiny. A very wearisome journey on the day before, had brought us to an old German town, where there was neither tourist nor English; but old embattled walls—Gothic houses, and churches dating far back—those picturesque rude centuries, when they knew the art of building, whatever other arts they did not know. Young and light of heart as we were, our fatigue vanished with the night, and when we had taken our coffee and our hard leathery rolls in the light, cold, carpetless salle of our inn, we went out arm in arm for one of our long rambles, with no cicerone to disturb our enjoyment. We were not model sightseers—we did not find out what was to be admired beforehand, nor seek the lions—we were only two very young people much delighted with these novel scenes, and with each other, who were in no mood to be critical. We delighted to lose ourselves in these quaint old streets—to trace their curious intricacies, to find out the noble vistas here and there, when the high houses stretched along in perched and varied lines to the golden way, where there was some smoke and a great deal of sunshine, behind which lay the sky. We saw the churches, and admired and wondered at them, but our great fascination was in the streets, where everything savored of another land and time; the peasant dress, the characteristic features, the strange tongue, which, except when Harry spoke, was unintelligible to me, made all these streets animated pictures to my eager observation.

I was a very good walker, and not easily wearied, and Harry was only too eager to do every thing I pleased. We came and went, enjoying every thing, and I think our fresh young English faces, our freedom, and vigor, and youthful happiness attracted some wistful glances from under the toil-worn, sun-burnt brows of these peasant people, about whom I was so curious; our enjoyment was so frank and honest, that it pleased even the unenjoying bystanders; and all the young waiters at the inn, who shook their heads at my elaborately conned questions in German, and drove me desperate with the voluble and anxious explanations of which I could not understand a word, had now a French dictionary on the side-table in the salle, which some one was always studying for my especial benefit—what with smiles and signs, and my English-French, and their newly acquired phrases, we managed to do a little conversation sometimes, though whether I or my young attendants would have been most barbarous to a Parisian, even I cannot tell—though I dare say the palm would have been given to me.

Although my dress was quite plain, and we flattered ourselves that it was not easy to find out that this was our wedding tour, it was strange what a sympathetic consciousness every one seemed to have that I was a bride. The people were all so wonderfully kind to us—we travelled in the simplest way without either maid or man. We had nothing to limit or restrain us, no need to be at any certain place by any certain day, no necessity to please any one's convenience but our own; so we rambled on through these old picturesque streets, the bright autumn day floating unnoted over our heads, and life running on with us in an enchanted stream. There was the chill of early winter in the air already; and in those deep narrow lanes, where the paths looked like a deep cut through the houses rather than a road, on each side of which they had been built, were parties of wood-sellers chopping up into lengths for fuel great branches and limbs of trees. Everybody seemed to be laying in their winter stock, the streets resounded with the ringing of the hatchet, the German jokes and gossip of the operators, and the hoarse rattle of the rope or chain by which the loaded bucket was drawn up to the highest story, the storeroom of these antique houses. As we threaded these deep alleys arm in arm, catching peeps of interiors and visions of homely housewifery, we caught many smiling and kindly glances, and I do not doubt that many a brave little woman called from the door to her mother when she saw us coming, that here were the young Englishers again—for we had store of kreutzers and zwangzigers, and these small people very soon found it out.

We had just emerged upon one of the principal streets, when Harry uttered a surprised and impatient exclamation, and turned me hastily around again, to go in another direction. "What is the matter?" cried I, in alarm. "Nothing," he said, quietly, "only a great bore whom I knew when I was last in Germany. Here, Hester, let's avoid him if we can."

We turned up a steep street leading to one of the gates of the town, and Harry hurried me along at a great pace. "We are running away," said I, laughing, and out of breath. "You are a true Englishman, Harry, you flee before a bore when you would face an enemy; who is this formidable stranger?"

"He is a professor at Bonn," said Harry, in a disturbed and uneasy tone. "I was there some time, you know—and knew him pretty well, but if he finds us out here, we will never get rid of him, unless we leave the town in desperation. Come, Hester, a race for it, you are not too old or too sedate for that. An army of bores would conquer with a look, like Cæsar—nothing could stand before them. Come, Hester!"

We ran across the bridge of planks which stretched over the peaceful moats, now a garden of rich verdure, full of tobacco plants and plum-trees, from the Thiergarten Thor. There we continued our ramble without the walls. At a little distance was a peaceful old churchyard, where some great people were lying, and where many unknown people slept very quietly with love-wreaths and scattered flowers over their humble tombstones. Some one had been laid down in that quiet bed even now, and we two, in our youth and flush of happiness, stood by, and saw the flowers showered down in handfuls and basketfuls upon the last enclosure of humanity. The rude earth was not thrown in till this sweet bright coverlid lay thick and soft upon the buried one—buried in flowers. We came away very softly from this scene—it touched our hearts, and awed us with a sense of our uncertain tenure of our great happiness. We clung close to each other, and went on with subdued steps, saying nothing; and there on our way, at regular intervals, were those rude frames of masonry, enclosing each its piece of solemn sculpture, its groups of Jews and Romans looking on, and its one grand central figure, thorn-crowned and bearing the cross. I remember the strange emotion which crept upon me as we went along this sunny road. I had heard of the great sorrows of life, with the hearing of the ear, but I knew them not—and it struck me with a dull and strange wonder to see these pictures of the mortal agony which purchased life and hope and comfort for this latter world. I shrank closer to my husband and clasped his arm, and turned my eyes from those dark and antique pictures. I knew not Him who stooped under his tremendous burden, in this sublime and voluntary anguish. I was awestruck at the thought, but I turned away from it. I was glad to talk again of what we had been seeing, of where we were to go next. We were going back to our hotel in the first place, and when we returned by another gate, I woke once more to amusement, when I saw how jealously Harry looked about to see if his bore was still in our way.

And as it happened, when we had almost reached our inn, and turned a sharp corner on our way to it, we suddenly met this dreaded stranger face to face; there was no escaping then; after a moment's pause, he rushed upon Harry with the warmest solicitations, addressing him in very deliberate and laborious English, by his present name, which he called "Soutcote," and seemed quite to claim the standing of an old friend.

I was amused, yet I was annoyed, at Harry's appearance and manner. He was more than constrained, he was embarrassed, one moment cordial, the other, cold and repellant, and though he submitted to an affectionate greeting himself, it was in the proudest and briefest manner in the world that he introduced me. My new acquaintance was a middle-aged gentleman, abundantly bearded, with an immense cloak over his arm, and an odor of cigars about his whole person—but that odor of cigars was in the very atmosphere. I am sorry to confess that even Harry had it; and the Professor had bright, twinkling, sensible eyes, and his face, though it was large and sallow, was good-humored and pleasant, so much as you could see of it, from its forest of hair. He did not look at all like a bore, and he spoke very good slow English, and I was surprised at Harry's dislike of him. He asked where we were living, and with a very bad grace Harry told him; then he volunteered to call on us. I had to answer myself that we would be glad to see him, for Harry did not say a word, and then he apologized for some immediate engagement he had, and went away.

"He does not seem a bore," said I; "why did you run away from him, Harry? and if you only give him time enough, he speaks very good English. It is pleasant to hear some one speaking English. I hope he will come to-night."

"O inconsistent womanhood!" said Harry, hiding a look of great annoyance under a smile, "how long is it since you told me that you liked to be isolated from all the world, and that it was very pleasant for two people to have a language all to themselves?"

"That was a week ago," I said, "and I like it still, and yet I like to hear somebody speak English; why do not you like him? I think he looks very pleasant for a German. You ought to be glad to have some one else to speak to than always me."

"Do you judge by yourself?" said Harry, smiling; "as for me, Hester, I am no more tired of our tête-à-tête than I was the day we left Cambridge—so pray be thankful on your account and not mine."

"Are you vexed, Harry?" asked I.

"I am annoyed to have this presuming intruder thrust upon us," said Harry. "I know he is not easily discouraged, and I did know him very well, and went to his house, so that I should not like quite to be rude to him; and foreigners are so ignorant of our English habits in England, our friend would not understand that people who have only been three weeks married, prefer their own society to anybody else; but everything is so different here."

"Perhaps he does not know how short a time it is," said I, "but he called you Southcote, Harry; did you write to him, or how does he know?"

"Oh! from the papers, of course," said Harry, hurriedly, "you know what linguists these Germans are, and how they like to show their proficiency in our language: and, of course, there are lots of English fellows in Bonn; and where there are English, there is generally a Times. Why, the professor has become quite a hero, Hester; come in and dine, and forget that our solitude has been disturbed; what a bloom you have got—I think they will vote me thanks when I take you home."

So speaking, Harry hastened me in to arrange my dress. I could not understand his embarrassment, his perplexity, his dislike of the stranger. Why receive him less cordially than he had been used to do; why introduce him to me so stiffly; a person who knew so much about him, that he was even aware of his change of name, though he did not seem equally aware of his marriage. It was very odd altogether—my curiosity was piqued, and I think I should have been very much disappointed if the stranger had not come that night.

We had another long ramble after dinner, for our hotel apartments, great gaunt rooms, with rows of many windows, and scanty scattered morsels of furniture, were not very attractive, and when we finally came in again very tired, Harry wrapped my shawl round me, had a crackling explosive wood fire lighted in the stove, made me rest upon the sofa, and finally told me that he would "take a turn" for ten minutes and have a cigar. I was a little disappointed—he seldom did it, and I did not like to be without him, even for ten minutes; however, I was reasonable, and let him go away.

When he was gone, I lay quite still in the great darkening room; there were five windows in it, parallel lines of dull light coming in over the high steep roof of a house opposite, where there were half-a-dozen stories of attic windows, like a flight of steps upon the giddy incline of those mossed tiles. The whole five only made the twilight visible, and disclosed in dark shadow the parallel lines of darkness in the spaces between them; and the great green porcelain stove near which I lay, gave no light, but only startling reports of sound to the vacant solitary apartment. I was glad to hear the crackling of the wood—it was "company" to me—and I began to think over Alice's last letter, with its consolatory assurance that my father was well. He wrote himself, but his letters said nothing of his health, and I was very glad of the odd upside down epistle of Alice, which told me plainly in so many words what I wanted to know. In another week we were to go home, but Harry had said nothing yet of where we were to go to; he had received a letter from Mr. Osborne, about the house, and I concluded we would go first to Cambridge, and there find a place for ourselves.

It brought the color to my cheek to think of going home with Harry, and taking my husband with me to the dwelling of my youth. I was shy of my father and Alice, under my new circumstances. If I had the first meeting over, I did not think I would care for the rest—but the first meeting was a very embarrassing thought. I was occupying myself with boding of these pleasant troubles, when I heard voices approaching the door; the Herr Professor's solemn English, and Harry's tones, franker and less embarrassed than before. I got up hastily, and they entered; the stranger came and took a seat by me; he began to tell me he had once been in London, and what a wonderful place he thought it; his manner of speaking was amusing to me—it was very slow, as if every word had to be translated as he went on— but it was very good English notwithstanding, and not merely German translated into English words; and the matter was very good, sprightly and sensible; and I was very much amused by his odd observations upon our habits, and the strange twist the most familiar things acquired when looked at through his foreign spectacles. He had a great deal of quiet humor, and made quaint grave remarks, at which it was very hard to keep one's gravity. I thought he was the last person in the world whom any one could call a bore.

All this time Harry sat nervous and restless, with a flush upon his face, taking little part in the conversation; but watching the very lips of the stranger, as it seemed to me, to perceive the words that they formed before he uttered them. I was very anxious that he should speak rather of Harry, than of

London. I should have liked so much to hear if he was very popular among his companions, and very clever as a student; but when I saw how very nervous and fidgety Harry was, I did not like to ask, but sat in discomfort and strange watchfulness, my attention roused to every word the professor said. I could not perceive that he said anything of importance, and I really was very much disturbed and troubled by the look of Harry.

Then suddenly the stranger turned round and began to speak to him in German. Why in German? when he could speak English perfectly well, and evidently liked to exhibit his acquirements. This put the climax to my astonishment, and it did more than that, it woke a vague pang in my heart, unknown before, which I suppose was that little thing called jealousy; had Harry gone out on purpose to meet and warn him? was it at Harry's request, and that I might not understand, that they spoke in German? A sudden suspiciousness sprang up within me—was there, indeed, some secret which Harry did not want me to know?—I who would have counted it the greatest hardship in the world to have anything to conceal from him.

I sank into sudden and immediate silence—I watched Harry. I was mortified, grieved, humiliated—I could have left the room and gone away somewhere to cry by myself; but this would only make matters worse, and I did not wish Harry to think me unreasonable or exacting. But he saw that I grew very pale, he saw the tears in my eyes, and how firmly my hands clasped each other. He suddenly said something in English—the stranger answered, and this cause of distress to me was gone; but now the Professor was speaking of having visited Harry in England. "And that house you were speaking of," said the German, "that, ho—I know not your names—did you never go to live in it then?"

"No, no, I have never been there," said Harry, hastily, "a place I was thinking of—of settling in, Hester," he explained to me in a very timid way, "when you are next in England you must see a true English home, Professor—no bachelor's quarters now."

"Ah, my young friend, I have not forgot what you did say about la belle cousine," said the Professor, with a smile at me.

I sat as still as if I had been made of stone. I saw Harry's face flush with a violent color; but no color came to my cheek—I felt cold, rigid, desolate. I shivered over all my frame with the chill at my heart. For he had said so often that I was the only one who had ever entered his heart—that he had known no love of any kind till he knew me. Alas! were these all vain words; the common deceits of the world—and what was I to believe or trust in, if my faith failed in Harry? I tried to believe it was some foolish jest, but though I might have persuaded myself so from the unconscious smile of the Professor, there was guilt on Harry's brow. I did not change my position in the slightest gesture. I sat very still, scarcely drawing my breath. The momentary pause that followed was an age to me. While the silence lasted, I had already tried to persuade myself that whatever might have been, Harry loved me only now—but I could not do it—I was sick to my very heart.

I heard him dash into conversation again, into talk upon general subjects, vague and uninteresting. I listened to it all with the most absorbing interest to find something more on this one point, if I could. Then, by and bye, the stranger went away. I bade him good-night mechanically, and sat still, hearing the wood crackling in the stove, and Harry's footsteps as he returned from the door. He came in, and sat down beside me on the sofa. He took my cold hand and clasped it between his. He said "Hester—Hester—Hester!" every time more tenderly, till I could bear it no longer, and burst into tears.

"Oh, Harry! you might have told me," I exclaimed passionately, "you might have said that you cared for some one else before you cared for me!"

"It would have been false, if I had said so, Hester," he answered me, in a very low earnest tone.

"Oh, Harry, Harry! do not deceive me now," I said, making a great effort to keep down a sob.

He drew me close to him, and made me lean upon his shoulder. "In this I never have, nor ever will, deceive you," he said, bending over me—"I never knew what love was till I knew you, Hester. What I say is true. See—I have no fear that you can find me out in a moment's inconstancy. My thoughts have never wandered from you since I saw you first—and before I saw you, I was desolate and loved no one. You believe me?"

Could I refuse to believe him? I clung to him and cried, but my tears were not bitter any more. I could believe him surely better than a hundred strangers; but still I lifted my head and said, "What did the Professor mean?"

"I knew he would make mischief, this meddling fellow," said Harry. "Hester! do not distrust me, at least on this point, when I say I cannot tell you yet what he means. I have a confession to make, and a story to tell—it is so, indeed, I cannot deny it. But wait till we get to England—wait till we are at home—you will trust me for a few days longer—say you will?"

"I have trusted you implicitly, everything you have done and said until now," said I almost with a groan.

He kissed my hand with touching humility. "You have, Hester, I know you have," he said under his breath, but he said no more—not a word of explanation—not a single regret—not a hint of what I was to look for when he told me his story—his story! what could it be?

For some time we sat in silence side by side, listening to the wind without, and to the roaring and crackling of the wood in the stove. We did not look at each other. For the first time, we were embarrassed and uneasy. We had no quarrel—no disagreement, but there was something between us—something—one of those shadowy barriers that struck a sense of individual existence and separateness for the first time to our hearts. We were checked upon our course of cordial and perfect unity. We began an anxious endeavor to make conversation for each other—it did not flow freely as it had done, nor was this the charmed silence in which only last night we had been delighted to sit. The wind whistled drearily about the house, and rattled at the windows. "I hope we will have calm weather to cross the channel," said Harry, and then we began to discuss how and when we were to go home.

Yes—the charm of our rambling was gone, all my desire now was to get home to know what this confession was which Harry had to make to me. It was not the confession I had dreaded—it was not that somebody else had ever been as dear to him as I was now—what could it be? He spoke of it no more, but left it to my imagination without a word. My imagination, puzzled and bewildered, could make nothing of the mystery—could he, in his early youth, have done something very wrong? No, it was impossible, I could not credit that of Harry. I was entirely at fault, and I think before an hour was over I would gladly have undertaken to forgive him beforehand, and chase the nightmare away. But he did not seem able to forget it; it was a bigger nightmare to him than to me. He was very kind, very loving, and tender; but there was a deprecation in his manner which troubled me exceedingly. How I longed now that this Dutch professor had never broken in upon our happy, happy days. How annoyed I was at my own childish perversity, my opposition to Harry because I thought he was not cordial to the stranger. What concern had I with the stranger? and he had repaid me by bringing the first blank into our joyous intercourse—the first secret between our hearts.

Before evening was spent, we were a little better. It made me miserable to see Harry looking unhappy and constrained. We tacitly avoided all reference which could touch upon this mystery, and arranged and re-arranged our journey home, or to "England" as we said. I did not ask where we should go to, nor did he say, and so ended the first tedious evening of our married life.

THE SECOND DAY

It was the middle of October, stormy, cloudy, a searching chill disconsolate day. It had been wet in the morning, and the low lands near Calais were flooded with the previous rains. Everything on shore was as gloomy and uncomfortable as could be; and the decks of the little steamer were wet with sea water, as we stepped on board of her in the deceitful harbor of Calais, where the wild sea without was beyond our reach or ken. When we cleared the harbor and made our wild plunge amid the raging lions without, I never will forget what a shock it gave me. Crossing these wild little straits on our way to the Continent had been my first voyage—this was only my second, and I thought these monstrous waves which rolled up to us defiant and boastful like Goliath, were to swallow up in an instant our brave little David, the small stout straining seaboat, which bore our lives and our hopes within a hair's-breadth of destruction, as I thought. "Take the lady below, sir, she can't be no worse nor ill there," said a seaman pithily, as he rolled past us with a mop and bucket, with which they vainly attempted to dry the flooded deck. I was so much worse than ill here, that I was drenched with the dashing of the waves; but the man did not know with what a solemn expectation I waited—looked to be devoured and engulfed every moment by some invading wave.

Yet in spite of all, we reached the opposite shore in safety, and stood once more upon English ground— there we rested for a little and changed our wet dresses, and Harry pressed and entreated me to take refreshments. I made an effort, to please him; but he took nothing himself—he looked very much agitated, though he suppressed his feeling so anxiously. For a few days we had greatly regained our former happy freedom, and forgot that anything had ever come between us. I am sure it was not my fault that the feeling was revived to-day; I had made no allusion to what he was to tell me, I had even avoided speaking of the home to which we were going, lest he might think I was impatient for his secret. My mind was free, and I could forget it; but it lay on Harry's conscience, and he could not.

I think the storm had pleased him while we were on the water, it wailed and it chimed in with his own excitement; but when we landed, when we had to rest and refresh ourselves, and there was an hour or two to wait for a train, my heart ached for Harry. He looked so restless, so agitated, so unhappy. I kept by him constantly, yet I sometimes feared that I rather aggravated than soothed his emotion by any tenderness I showed him. He looked so grateful for it, that I felt almost injured by his thankfulness. He turned such wistful looks upon me, as if he doubted whether I ever would look upon him or speak to him as I did now after this day. The importance he seemed to attach to it, gave his mystery a new weight in my eyes. I had begun to grow familiar with it—to think it must be nothing and despise it; but it was impossible to do so when I saw this excitement under which Harry was laboring. What could it be? Nay, if it was indeed something very bad he had done in some former time—which was the most probable thing I could think of—that was nothing to me—that could never estrange us from each other. And when we set out again upon our journey, and rushed away with giant strides to London, I pleased myself thinking how I would laugh at his fears when I really heard his story—how I would upbraid him for believing that anything could ever come between us—how I would chase him back into his old self with tenderer words than I had ever spoken yet. We sat opposite each other, yet our eyes very seldom met— he was cogitating in doubt and trouble, I was thinking of him very lovingly—how good he was—how strange that he ever could do wrong—how impossible that either wrong or right should part him and me. My heart swelled when I recollected all his tender care of me—how, though I was his wife, I had never for a moment been divested of that delicate and reverent honor with which he surrounded me in the days of our betrothal. I felt that I could trust to him as a child trusts, and not even care to seek his secret; and I rejoiced in thinking how soon I could dissipate the cloud that was over him when the crisis really came.

We had another little interval of waiting in London, and then set out again for Cambridge, as I thought. It was now getting late, and the day declined rapidly. Harry did not seem able to speak to me; he sat by my side, so that I could no longer see his face, and we travelled on in silence, rushing through the gathering darkness; every moment Harry's excitement seemed to grow and increase. He took my hand and held it tight for a moment—then he released it to clasp and strain his own together. Sometimes he turned to me, as if just on the point of making his confession, whatever that confession might be, but immediately repented and turned from me again. I did all I could to soothe him, but vainly as it seemed; and had it not been for my perfect conviction that I had but to hear his story, to convince him that nothing horrible could stand between us, I could scarcely have endured those hours of rapid and silent travelling, full of expectation as they were. At length we stopped at a little unimportant station on the way. "We get out here, Hester," said Harry, in a stifled breathless voice, as he helped me to alight; his hand was burning as if with fever, and the light of the lamps showed me the white cloud of excitement on his face. Outside the station, a carriage was waiting for us. "You have found a house then, Harry; why did you not tell me?" I said, as he handed me into it. "Did you mean it for a surprise?" "Yes," he said hoarsely—he was not able to say any more. I saw, I was very sorry for him. I took his hand, which was now cold, and warmed it between my own. I could not help remonstrating with him. I could not bear it any longer.

"Harry," said I, "why are you so much troubled? have you no confidence at all in me? do you forget what I am—your wife? I cannot think anything would disturb you so much, but something wrong—but is it my place to sit in judgment upon any wrong you may have done? It will be hard for me to believe it. I would believe no one but yourself on such a subject, and whatever it is, it can make no difference with me. Harry! don't turn away from me—don't let us be separated; you make me very anxious; yet I would rather not know what it is that troubles you so. I am not going home to be a punishment or a judge upon you—you forget I am your wife, Harry."

But Harry only groaned; it was remorse, compunction, that was in his heart. He repeated my last words wildly with passionate exaggerated tones of fondness. His angel, he called me; much troubled as I was, I smiled at the name—but I was honest enough to know that there was very little even of the earthly angel about me.

And so we drove on—the gliding silent motion of the carriage seemed very subdued and gentle after the rush of the railway—on through dark silent hedgeless woods, over the wide level country, which stretched around us one vast dull plain under the shadow of the night. It was my own country, I saw; and I put out my hand from the carriage window to feel the fresh wind, which came over miles and miles of these broad flats, unbroken by any obstacle. Not a hedgerow, scarcely a tree, and neither passenger upon the way nor human habitation was to be seen in the darkness—nothing but the dark soil, the wide, wide indescribable distance, the fine breeze and the dim sky. The very road we were on was a level straightforward line, which seemed to have no turnings, but to go blindly forward, uninterrupted, as if it went to the end of the world. All the charm which I used to feel in my native locality returned upon me; space, and breadth, and freedom almost infinite, was in this land which people called monotonous and dreary. My spirit rose, my heart beat high. I felt my breast expand to the fresh wind—but when I turned to Harry—Harry seemed quite unmoved by it; he was still buried in his own dark thoughts.

The carriage was a private one, luxuriously fitted up, and I thought the servants recognised him as servants recognise their masters; but I had never been told that he was rich enough for this, and it joined with the greater mystery to puzzle me. When I looked out again, I began to think the way quite familiar to my eyes: that was not unlikely, being in Cambridgeshire, but now they grew strangely familiar, even in the darkness. Could the house Harry had taken be near Cottiswoode—my heart beat still louder at the thought—I scarcely knew whether it pleased or vexed me; yet I thought I would have pleasure in showing Edgar Southcote how independent of jealousy or any mean feeling Harry's wife could be. I looked out eagerly, recognising now a tree and now a cottage—we were surely near the hamlet. Harry, too, stirred in his course; I thought he watched me, but I was full of old thoughts and did not speak to him. Yes! there were the elm-trees—the old avenue. Then I drew back in my seat with tears in my eyes—eager as I was, I could not look out when we were passing so near my own old home.

The shadows of great trees were over us; but I had leaned back in my corner, and did not note them. Yes! I remembered that the public road crossed the very end of that stately grand old avenue—how slowly we were passing it! how long the overarching branches shadowed the carriage! and the air grew closer, as if something interrupted it very near. I did not look up, a strange fascination overpowered me—a moment more, and the carriage wheeled round into an open space and stopt. Almost before they drew up, Harry leaped from my side. Then he came round, threw the door open, held out his arm to me to lift me out—how his arms trembled—how hot his breath came upon my cheek—I could scarcely recognise his hurried, trembling, agitated voice, "Hester—welcome home."

Home! the great hall door stood open—the moon came out from behind a cloud to throw a momentary gleam upon the house. Home! I thrust him away, and sprang to the ground without his aid. He stood where I had left him, drawing back, following me with his eyes, and pale as marble. I stood alone, gazing up at the sculptured emblems upon the door. In a moment, in a flood of despair and bitterness, the truth rushed upon me—I had been trapped and betrayed—deceived like a fool—and every one had known the man but I—I saw it all at a glance—I was his wife! his wife! and he had brought me home.

In that wild moment, I cannot tell the impulses of frenzy which possessed me. To escape—to rush away from him, over the pathless, featureless country—through the darkness and the night—to be lost somewhere for ever and for ever, never to come to his knowledge more—to die upon this threshold and never enter it. It was vain! I was roused to a sense of my true circumstances when I saw a band of servants curtseying and gaping at me in the hall. My pride came to my aid, my very passion supported me. I went in with a firm deliberate step, bowing to them, and passed to the room which had been our dining-parlor, and from which there was a glimmer of light. I had not looked towards him, but I heard his step following me. I entered the room, it was very bright and cheerful, well-lighted with a ruddy fire, and tea upon the table. The glow of warmth and comfort in it struck me with an indignant sense of my own sudden misery. He had put me without the pale of enjoyment, I thought, for ever.

I did not take off my bonnet—I stood in the glow of the firelight, turning my face to him as he came eagerly up to me. I stopped him as he began to speak. "There is no need—no need!" said I, "I see your mystery—pray do not speak to me—do not drive me mad to-night."

He turned away from me, clasping his hands with a passionate exclamation—then he came back: "I deserve your reproaches, Hester, do not spare them! but think what you said to me not half an hour ago—you are my wife."

"Your wife—your wife—yes! there is the sting," I said with a wild outburst, "his wife, and it is for ever!"

He went away from me to the other end of the room, and threw himself down in a chair. I saw his suffering, but it did not move me. I thought of nothing but my own wrong—a hard, cold, desperate indifference to every one else seemed to come upon me. I saw myself tricked, cheated, despised. Mr. Osborne, Alice, my father, strange and impossible though the conjunction was, I almost thought I saw them all together smiling at me. I could have gnashed my teeth when I thought how conscious every one else was—how miserably blind was I—I could have thrown myself on the floor and dashed my hot brow against the hearth—his hearth—his house—his household sanctuary. But I rejected and hated it—it was not mine.

I cannot tell how long I stood thus, he sitting far apart from me saying nothing—it might have been hours—it might have been only moments, I cannot tell. I think it was the falling of some ashes from the fire upon the hearth which roused me; the trivial common sound brought a strange awakening to my misery. I went and rang the bell. As I did so, he looked up at me wistfully. "It is only for some one to show me my room," I said. "May not I do that, Hester?" he asked. I think, perhaps, though it is a strange, ungenerous thing to say so, that had he been less overpowered, less dejected, had he boldly entered upon the subject then, and compelled me to go over it, step by step, I would not have been so bitter against him; but he was disarmed and broken down, less by my reproaches than by his own feeling of guilt.

"Thank you, I will prefer a servant," said I, and when the woman came I followed her upstairs. She led me to my own old room, the last room I had left when we went away from Cottiswoode. My first glance at it showed me that it was furnished with the greatest care and elegance, and the door of a little room adjoining, which had been a lumber room in our time, was opened, and from it came a glimpse of firelight; in the bed-chamber, too, there was a fire, and everything in it looked so bright, so pure and cheerful, that I could not glance anywhere without an aggravation of bitterness—to place me here, was like placing a revolted and defying spirit in some peaceful bower of heaven.

The servant who conducted me, was a fresh young country woman, five or six years my senior. In the preoccupation of my own thoughts, I scarcely looked at her, but she seemed to linger as if for a recognition; at last she spoke. "I'm Amy Whitehead, please Miss—Madam," she said, confused and blushing, "and my old uncle, ma'am, that was at the Hall afore, he's been waiting, please, ever since we heard the news, to know when you was coming home."

"Another time—another time, Amy," said I, hurriedly, half-stifled with the sobs which I could restrain no longer. "Tell him I remember him very well and you too; but I am fatigued and want rest to-night; and tell your master, Amy, that I am about to go to rest, and will not come down stairs again."

She went away, looking surprised and a little discontented. I daresay this was strangely unlike Amy's simple notions of the homecoming of a bride. When I was alone, I went to the glass and looked in my own face. I was very pale, jaded, and wretched-looking; but it was myself—still myself and no other. This half hour's misery had made no volcanic sign upon my face. I tossed off my bonnet slowly, and all my wrappers—those shawls which he had arranged round me so carefully—I flung them on the floor where I stood. I did not know how to give some vent, to seek some expression for my wretchedness. It pressed upon my heart and my brain, with a close and terrible pressure; a great physical shock would have been a relief to me. I could have leaped over a precipice, or plunged into a river for ease to my crowding, thronging thoughts.

Then I threw myself down in a chair by the fire, and tried to be still. I could not be still. I rose and wandered through the rooms; they were furnished with the most careful regard to all my tastes and preferences. I saw that, but when I saw it, it only increased my bitterness; the dressing-room within, the little happy confidential room, scared me away with its look of home and comfort. At last, I opened a window and looked out upon the night; the same jessamine dropped its leaflets on the window-sills, the same moaning wandering winds came upon my face, as those I had known of old. It had begun to rain, and I listened to the heavy drops falling among the scanty autumnal foliage, and bearing down with them in their progress, showers of yellow leaves, and now and then the fitful blast dashed the rain into my face, as I looked out upon the dark trees—the dark indistinct country—the vast world of darkness and space before me. The chill air and the rain refreshed me, I leaned far out that the shower might beat upon my head, and then I thought I was able to return to my seat and to be calm.

Yes! I was in Cottiswoode. I was Edgar Southcote's wife; at this thought my heart burned. I cannot express the fiery glow of pain which overpowered me by any other words. Since I entered this fatal house, I seemed to have lost sight of Harry. Harry my tender wooer, my loving bridegroom, the nearest and dearest of all who were near and dear to me, had disappeared like a dream. In his place stood my scorned and rejected cousin, he whose compassion had sought me out to make amends to me for a lost inheritance. A hundred circumstances came upon my mind now to direct suspicion to him—his desire to take our name, oh! heaven protect my name! it was no suggestion of his love—it was a mean and paltry lie! and he had succeeded—there was the sting—and my father's words came back upon me with a strange significance, but only to place my father among the other conspirators against my peace. The bond of our marriage lay upon our hearts and souls, for ever and for ever—for ever and for ever—not even in thought or for a moment could I deliver myself from this bondage—even when I died I would belong to him, and the very name upon my grave-stone would be that of Edgar Southcote's wife.

I was passing up and down steadily, holding my hands clasped together. I could not be still and think of these things. I could not remember with composure where I was, and how I had been brought here. I went to the window again, and as I raised my hand to my face, I felt upon my neck the little chain with my mother's miniature—with a wild access of indignation I snatched it off; now I understood why it was that this connected him with my mother—that they found in my circumstances some resemblance to those of my father's shipwrecked life. I did not dash it now out of my hand as I was minded to do; with trembling fingers I put it away out of my reach, where the placid smile of that mild face could not drive me wild again. What could she or such as she understand of this misery which I was enduring now?

At this moment some one knocked lightly at the door. I went at once and opened it—it was himself. I looked full at him, to find out how I could have been deceived. This was not my Harry. Harry was nothing but an ideal, and he was gone. This was the boy, my cousin, whom I had met upon the road some years ago, with his stooping figure and his timid step. Once more in my injured and passionate strength, full of bitter resentment and proud scorn, I stood firm by Edgar Southcote, and he humbled, downcast, self-reproachful, stood like a culprit before me.

"May I come in, Hester?" he asked.

I gave way to him in a moment, but I could not do it without a bitter word. "You are the master of the house—I have no right to admit or to exclude any one here."

He held up his hands with a wild deprecating gesture. "Am I not sufficiently punished?" he said. "If I was wrong—criminal—think of what the circumstances were, Hester. Can your heart find no excuse for me? and see what my punishment is already. Instead of the natural joy which a man looks for, when he carries his bride home, I have anticipated this day with terror—and my fears are more than realized. Have I become a different person from him to whom you said this very night, 'I am your wife?' Am not I the same man you promised your heart and love to? the same with whom you left your father's house? Hester! I have deceived you—I do not try to make my fault less. Say it was a deliberate, premeditated fault—I do not deny it, but I am not changed. Condemn it, but be merciful to me."

"No, you are not the same man," I answered, "you are not Harry, you are Edgar Southcote. I never gave either hand or heart to you, I gave them to one who was not capable of fraud—who knew nothing of a lie—he is gone and dead, and I will never find him more either in heaven or earth. You have killed my Harry—you have killed my heart within me. I never molested you. I never appealed to you for pity. I had forgotten Cottiswoode; it was nothing to me. Why did you come with your false compassion to steal away my hopes, and my heart, and my youth?"

"Compassion, Hester? where is there any compassion in the matter?" he exclaimed; "you show none to me."

"No—I only want justice," said I; "oh! I know you have been generous—I know it was a kind meaning, a charitable impulse, to restore to me my father's land. Do not let us speak of it, if I am to keep my reason now—I fancied such a thing could never happen to me. I did not think I could have been so humiliated. I trusted you—I trusted you with all my heart—will you let me stay here, and leave me to myself? I want to collect myself—to think of what is all over and past, and of what remains."

"What remains? what will you do, Hester?" he cried, growing very pale.

But I could not tell—I looked round me with a dreary desolate search for something to support me. I had no one to flee to—not one in all the world. What a change since yesterday—since this morning, when I had everything in having him.

I remember that he came to me and kissed my hand—that he bent over it, and entreated me to forgive him; that I turned away and would not look at him, nor listen, with a hard and breathless obduracy, and that then he said, "Good-night—good-night!" and slowly went away.

When I was alone, my desolation, my wretchedness, my solitude burst upon me in an agony—he had gone away—he had granted my petition—I was alone! I stood for a long time quite silent, where he had left me, then I went back to my chair; I fancied the very foundations of the earth were breaking up. I had no longer any one to trust to; every one had deceived me, every creature I loved or cared for was in the conspiracy—even my father's suspicions must have come to certainty before I left him. Yet nobody had warned me—oh! it was cruel! cruel! for thus it came about that I had no one to go to in my distress, no one to seek refuge with, that my impulse was to turn away from all my friends, to seek a dreary shelter in this loneliness, which struck to my heart to-night, with such a terrible pang. What was I to do?

I could not think of that; my mind went back and back again to what was past. I began to follow out the evidences, the certainties which made it clear to Alice, and to my father, and which ought to have made it clear to me. I had no wish to go back to them. I was indifferent to everything; I only felt that in a moment a bitter antagonism had sprung up between him and me; that, according to our love, would be our enmity and opposition, and that even in our variance and strife, and with this unforgiven wrong between us, we were bound to each other for ever.

All this night, when I thought to have been so happy, I sat alone in that chair. At last, when it grew late, and the fire burned low, and I felt the chill of the night, my fatigue overpowered me, and I fell asleep. My dreams were of vague distress and tribulation, misfortune and misery, which I could not comprehend; but when I awoke, I found myself laid on the bed, carefully wrapped up, though still dressed, and the gray of dawn coming in through the windows. I could not recollect myself for the moment, nor how I had come to be here; but when I lifted my head, I saw him seated where I had seated myself last night, bending over a bright fire, with his arm supporting his head. When he heard me stir, he looked up; he had not been sleeping to-night, although I had, and then I recollected all that had passed, and that it was he who must have lifted me here, and covered me so carefully. His face was pale now, and his eyes dark and heavy; he seemed almost as listless and indifferent as I was—for though he looked up, he made no advance to me.

I sprang from my rest, and threw off from me the shawls I had been wrapped in; then he rose and offered me his chair. I did not take it—we stood looking at each other—then he took my hand and held it, and looked at me wistfully. I said a cold "Good-morning," and turned my head away. When I did that, he dropped my hand, and withdrew me a little—and then he seemed to make an effort to command himself, and spoke to me in a voice which I scarcely recognised—so clear it was, and calm. Ah! he could be something else than an ardent or a penitent lover; the voice of the man was new to me. I looked up at him instantly, with a respect which I could not help; but we had entered upon another day. These days of my life crowded on each other, and to this chill, real dawn, and not to the wild, passionate night which preceded it, belonged what he said.

THE THIRD DAY

The grey morning looked in chill and damp from the windows, the bough of jessamine fluttered upon the glass, the rain pattered on the leaves. It was the hour of night and day which is coldest, keenest, most ungenial, and we stood together, but apart—as pale, as chill, as heavy as the morning—quieted, yet still trembling with the agitation of the night.

"There is a messenger below from Cambridge. I sent on word of our arrival last night," he said; "your father is not well, and wishes to see you. I have ordered the carriage to be ready, and have been watching here till you awoke. It is very early, but I know you will not care for the discomfort—your father has expressed a strong desire to see you immediately, and he is very weak, they say."

"Do you mean he is dying?" I asked firmly, though I could not raise my voice above a whisper.

"I mean he is very ill. Yes, Hester! it does not become me to deceive you any more."

I turned abruptly from him, and went to put on my bonnet. He lingered, waiting for me—when I was ready, he took some of the wrappers I had worn on the journey over his arm, and went down stairs before me. The servants were astir already, and I saw breakfast prepared in the room which I had been in last night—he held the door open for me, and involuntarily I entered—I did not say anything. Indeed, what with the dreadful bewilderment and uncertainty of my own position, and the pang of foreboding that I was only called there when my father was in extremity, I had little power to say a word—I sat down passively on the chair he set for me by the fire, while he ordered the carriage to come round. I accepted without a word the coffee he brought me, and tried to drink it—I did not feel as if I had any will at all; but did everything mechanically, as though it was imposed upon me by a stronger will, which I could not resist. No longer the agitated youth of yesterday—the self-reproachful and unforgiven lover, whose happiness hung on my breath, and to whom I was ruthless, obdurate, and without pity, he was so different this morning that I could scarcely think him the same person. This was a man who had the sole right to think for me, to guard me, perhaps to control me, whether I would or no—I was not strong enough, at this moment, to resist his tacit and unexpressed authority. I only wondered at it vaguely in the languor and weariness which was upon me—I was worn out by last night's excitement, I had a dull terror of expostulation in my mind; but I had not heart enough to be impatient. My faculties were all benumbed and torpid. At another time, these few moments of waiting would have been agony to me— but they were not so now.

Then I heard the wheels at the door, and rose to go; he followed me closely—assisted me in, wrapped me round with the shawls he carried, and then took his place by my side. I made no remonstrance, I said nothing—I submitted to all he did with a dull acquiescence, and we drove off at a great pace. I think it did strike me for a moment how bitterly everything was changed since I stepped from that carriage on the previous night. Once more I leaned back and did not look at the noble old elms in the avenue; the shadow of their branches over us, made my heart sick, and I closed my eyes till we were once more dashing along the free unshadowed monotonous road. A dreary and sad monotony was on those fresh, broad plains this morning. The sky was nothing but one vast cloud—the fitful, chill breeze, brought dashes of rain against the windows—the country looked like an uninhabited desert. Distance, flight, an endless race, away, away, away, towards the skies; but it was not fleeing from my fate. My fate was here beside me, the companion of my journey—we could not escape from each other. I was his evil fortune, and he was mine.

We did not say a word all the time, though we were nearly three hours on the way. Then came the familiar Cambridge streets—then he rose and whispered something to the coachman on the box; we subdued our pace immediately, and quietly drew up at the well-known door. Our younger servant, Mary, was looking from it eagerly—when she saw us, she left it open and ran in—I suppose to say I had come. He helped me to alight, and I went in. I went slowly though I was so near. I wanted to see some one else first—some one else before I saw my father.

At the foot of the stairs, Alice met me; she came up to me, joy struggling with her gravity to kiss and bless me, as she had been used to do. I turned away from her with a harsh and forbidding gesture, and would not let her touch me. Her eyes filled with tears—her cheeks reddened and grew pale again. She muttered something in a confused and troubled undertone, of which I only heard the word "pardon!" and then she said in a voice which a great effort made steady and articulate—"Your father waits you, Miss Hester; will you come?"

I followed her in silence. I did not know what I was to say, or how to behave to my father. My heart swelled as though it would break, when I went along the familiar passages, where I had come and gone so lately in the gladness of my youth. I had a dull, heavy, throbbing pain in my forehead, over my eyes; but I followed her firmly, without a word. My father's bed-chamber looked only upon the ivy-covered wall of the close, and upon some gardens beyond it. The sun never came in there, and it was dim at all times; how much dimmer on this dreary morning, when there was no sunshine even on the open plains. There was a fire in the grate, but it burned dull like everything else. Before I looked at my father, I had taken in all the little accessories around him in one glance. The bottles upon the table, the drinks they were giving him, even the gleam of the wet ivy upon the top of the wall. My father himself lay, supported by pillows, breathing hard and painfully, and was very pale, but with a hectic spot burning on his cheek. He put out his thin white hand to me as I approached him. The diamond, a strange token of his former self, still shone upon his finger; it caught my eye in the strange torpor and dulness of my thoughts—and in this hour of extremity I remember wondering why he still chose to wear this favorite ring.

"You have come home in time, Hester," he said faintly.

I put off my bonnet, and sat down beside him. My face and my heart were still quite dull. I do not think I expressed any emotion. I spoke only to Alice, and to her as coldly as if she had been a perfect stranger. "Will you tell me what he must have—show me the things; and if you please, leave us alone."

Silently, as if she was not able to speak, she pointed out the medicines to me, and then went slowly away. I followed her to the door, for I saw that she beckoned me. How changed I must have been! for Alice seemed almost afraid to speak to me, whom she had been used to call her child.

"Miss Hester!" she whispered, with a faltering eager tone, and under her breath, "do not tell him—for pity's sake do not let him know what you have found out."

I made her no answer, but closed the door and came back to his bedside. There I sat down again in silence. I had nothing to say to him—nothing to say to him! neither of earth nor heaven!

"What have you to tell me, Hester?" said my father, at last. "I am about leaving you—are you aware of it?—do you know that this is the day which I looked forward to, when I asked you to place your fortune in my hands?"

"Yes, father!" I was stupid, sullen, dead. I could show no feeling, for indeed I felt none yet.

"I am glad that you decided as you did, Hester," continued my father; "I have now no weight upon my conscience—no dread that I have compromised your happiness; and you have a protector and a home. You are happy, my love?"

"Did you say happy? oh, yes!" I said with almost a laugh; "happy, very happy, papa."

Strange as it seemed to me, he appeared contented with what I said—he made no more reference to it; he lifted my hand gently up and down in his own.

"And I am going away," he said slowly, "going away, Hester—where?"

Where? the word struck me with a strange superstitious terror. For the first tune I was roused to look eagerly and inquiringly in his face.

"Not to the family grave, Hester!" he said with a smile of awful amusement—yes, amusement, there is no other word, "that is only a stage in the journey—where am I going beyond that? Have you nothing to say?"

"Father—father!" I said wildly, with a breathless horror.

"Ay, but you cannot pilot me!" said my father; "and by-and-bye my ears will be deaf, should all the voices in the world echo my name."

I bent over him, holding him with terror unspeakable. Little training in religion had fallen to my share; but I had the natural sentiment—the natural dread; and I forgot everything else in the deadly fear which made me cling to my father now.

"Why do you not tell me to be resigned?" said my father. "Do you know what I am setting out upon, Hester? Distance, distance, distance—vaster than anything in our moorland—a dark, solitary journey, where no one knows the way. Death! who believes in that? it is but an arbitrary word—one of the names we use for things we cannot comprehend; and no one tells me where is the end."

"Oh, father, father, it is in the Bible!" cried I.

"Yes, it is in the Bible. Are you afraid I do not believe it, child? I believe it—but I see no clearer for my faith," said my father. "I believe it as I believe that Columbus discovered a new world. But what is Columbus and his new world to me?"

"But, papa, the Saviour—" I said, timidly, and in an agony of terror.

"Ay, the Saviour—I believe in him, Hester, but I do not know Him!" said my father, in a hard and painful voice. "Yes—He has gone this road, they say. He might take one by the hand in this mysterious journey—but I know him not."

"Let me send for some one, father," I cried; "there are, surely, some who know. Let me send for a clergyman—papa, do not refuse me. He could tell us, and he could pray."

"Telling would do me little service, Hester," said my father, faintly, with again that strange, awful smile upon his mouth; "it is not information I want. It is—ah! breath—breath!"

A sudden spasm had seized him; he had been speaking too much, and he was worn out. I raised him up in my arms when I understood his gestures, that he might have air. How his breast heaved and panted with those terrible struggles! I supported him, but with nervous trembling arms. I feared the sight of this mortal suffering—it was dreadful to me—for I had never seen the anguish of the bodily frame before.

When he was eased, and the spasm wore off, I laid him down exhausted. He was no longer able to speak; but as I watched him, I saw his eyes, in which shone all his mind, as clear and full as ever, untouched and independent of his malady, passing with a considerate and steady gaze from one part of the room to another. I could not comprehend this mood. Not with disquietude, nor with anxiety, did he ask, "Where?" He was neither disturbed nor unhappy; he seemed to have no fear. That smile had returned to his face; he still could be amused; and no human emotions seemed to break up his deep, deep calm.

But I had no pleasure in seeing his composure. Horror, grief, distress, overpowered me as I sat watching him. Oh, that smile, that smile! Was this journey the only one in the world which a man should take composedly, without knowing where he was bound? I had the common youthful ideas about age, and deathbeds, and death. I gave the natural awe, the natural solemnity, to the wonderful termination, transition, change—the end of our life here—the beginning of the other world. It shocked and struck me with terror, to see him lie there upon the brink of it, asking "Where?" with a smile. I remembered all the common sayings about the death of good men. I remembered Addison's call to some one to come and see how a Christian could die. I wondered if there was ostentation in this, to set against the speculative amusement with which my father had spoken. Everything else was swept from my mind by this. I forgot the hard pressure of my own unhappiness, and it was only recalled to me for a moment when I thought of appealing to Harry, and with a shock and bitter pang recollected that I had no Harry now, but that only Edgar Southcote waited below—waited for the issue of this tragedy to take me home.

For an hour or two after my father lay dozing, taking no notice of me save when I gave him his medicine. He seemed, indeed, to sleep very often for a few minutes at a time; but if I chanced to look away, when my glance returned to him, I invariably saw those open, living eyes, full of strength and understanding, noting all they saw with a perfect intelligence which struck me strangely. His mind was not dying. I had never seen anything that gave me such a wonderful idea of life and vigor as those glances from my father's deathbed. He looked what was approaching in the face, and quailed not at it. Change was before him, not conclusion. With his living soul he looked into a vague, vast future, and knew not what it was; but Death, as he said, was but an arbitrary term—it meant nothing to that inquiring, speculative, active soul.

After a long interval he seemed to revive and strengthen, and turned his eyes upon me again.

"And you are happy, Hester—are you happy?" he said, looking closely in my face.

I turned my eyes away—I think it was the first lie I had ever told—and I said only, "Yes!"

But he was wandering once more among his own thoughts, and heeded not my looks, nor what they meant.

"Life is a strange problem," he said, with the sombre shadow which it used to wear, returning upon his face. "I am about to find the solution of it, Hester—all my existence centres in one event. I have suffered one act to overshadow my best years—that was my great error—what a fool I was! because I failed in one thing, I threw everything away."

"Because the failure in that one thing poisoned all your life!" I exclaimed, "oh! do not blame yourself, father! the blame did not lie with you."

"What was that to me if the penalty did?" said my father, in his old reasoning tone—a tone which contrasted so strangely with the feeble voice, and the great weakness in which he spoke. "One act should not poison life, Hester! not even for a woman, how much less for a man! There are greater things in this world than marrying, or giving in marriage."

He spoke with an emphasis of scorn, which made me tremble more and more. Alas! I saw that still in his very heart rankled this poisoned sorrow; and I shuddered to think that the same doom was mine. That I would carry to my death this same bitterness—that my life was already overshadowed as his had been, and that I was ready, like him, to throw everything away.

"If it should be that I am to find out the wherefore of these dark mysteries; if that is the congenial occupation in the place whither I go;" he paused suddenly when he had said so much—though I watched him eagerly, and listened, he did not continue. He fell into immediate silence, and again he began to sleep.

The confidence with which he spoke to me was strange. I scarcely could understand—perhaps his weakness had some share in it, perhaps my absence, and it was the first time I ever had been absent from home—had inclined his heart towards his only child, and perhaps he could not help those audible wanderings of his thoughts, as strength and life failed him, and he gathered all his powers to his heart to keep his identity—to be himself. When he was awake I saw his eyes, I scarcely could believe in what was coming; but when he slept, I thought I could see moment by moment how the current ebbed and ebbed away.

During one of these intervals of sleep, the doctor came in, and with him Mr. Osborne. With that practised scientific eye, which it is so dreadful to mark for our dearest ones, the doctor looked at him, and shook his head. He was lying so solemnly with his closed eyes, and not a movement in his frame, so pale now, so feeble, so perfectly at rest, that a pang of momentary terror struck to my heart; but he was not gone. He did not wake till the doctor had gone away, and Mr. Osborne was left standing beside me. I never raised my head, nor greeted him. I did not answer his whisper of satisfaction at finding me here— even by my father's bedside. I would not meet as a friend a man who had wilfully snared and betrayed me.

When my father opened his eyes, he saw his friend by his bedside; but his eyes were not so full nor so clear, nor so bright with life and intelligence as they had been—there was a change—he stirred nervously.

"Ha! Osborne, my good fellow!" he said, "I am just setting out—any messages, eh? any word to—to— Helen."

After he had said the name, a momentary color came to his cheek, he lifted his hand heavily, and drew it over his brow.

"What did I say? am I raving? no, no, I know you all! stay here, Helen," the diamond on his finger had caught his eye—it was I whom he was calling by that name, and already his faculties failed to distinguish it from mine, "here," he repeated, trying to draw off the ring, "here—take it from me—wear it—wear it—'tis a misfortune—keep it till you die."

I took it from him, and he seemed to sink into a stupor. I never withdrew my eyes from him. The day had come and gone while I had been watching, and now it was night. Lights were brought into the room. I felt some one come behind me, and stand there at my chair; but I did not look who it was. Oh! that silent dim death-room, with no sound in it but his breath! Mr. Osborne leaned, hiding his face upon the pillow of the bed. I heard one suppressed sob behind me, and knew it was Alice; and I knew, too, instinctively that though I did not see him, there was another in the room. But I never moved nor turned my head; not a tear came to my dry eye, my lips were parched and hot; but neither sobbing nor weeping were possible to me. I sat still by that bedside, in full possession of my mind and faculties. I never observed more keenly, more closely, more minutely in all my life—I felt no grief, I knew no emotion, I only watched and watched with intense attention and consciousness to see my father pass away.

And there lay he—his speech was gone from him—his voice was no more to be heard in mortal ears—his soul was within those dark closing eternal gates—he was almost away. Suddenly he opened his dim eyes, and looked about him wildly, and said, "Helen!" Mr. Osborne turned to me with a rapid gesture to seek the miniature on my neck. "Let him see her—let him see her, why have you left it behind?" he said, in a whisper, which had all the effort of a loud cry. How vain it would have been! my father's eyes closed once more in a moment—opened again to look round upon us with a scared bewildered glance—then were shut closely. I thought he had fallen asleep, but there was suddenly a movement and rustle among them all, a faint stir—I could not describe it, as if something had been accomplished. I understood what it meant, it went to my heart like a knife. Yes! it was so—it was so—I was standing among those who had wronged me, and he was gone.

I did not move, though they did. Mr. Osborne came and put his hand upon my head, and bade God bless me! and said, "All is well with him—all is well with him, dear child! go with Alice, this is no place for you;" and Alice stole to my side and put her arm round me, and entreated, "Miss Hester, darling, my own child, come and rest!"

I shook them both away—they were weeping, both of them—but not a tear came to me. I was the only one quite self-possessed. I did not say a word to either; I kept my seat, and shook them from me when they attempted to remonstrate. No! I could not yield to their false kindness, I would rather be alone—alone, as I was indeed alone in the world.

Then he came to me—when I saw him approaching, I rose. "Do not say anything," I said; "if I must leave my dear father, I will go to my own room; let no one come to me, I will not be interrupted to-night."

He followed me as I went to the door—he followed me along the passage, perhaps he thought I needed his support, but I was firmer in my step than he was. I knew that his heart was yearning over me in my new grief—I knew it better than if he had told me—but my heart was not softened to him. I turned when I reached my door. "Why do you follow me?" said I, "is it not enough that I have lost everything?—leave me in peace to-night."

He held out his hands to me, he caught mine. "Oh! Hester, Hester, weep, and weep with me," he cried, "do not condemn me to this outer darkness—let me be with you in your grief."

I drew myself away from him. "No one can be with me in my grief, I am desolate," I said, but I waited for no answer. I closed my door, and he went away from the threshold—this threshold to which he had come for me when I was a bride.

I went in and shut to my door. I shut the door of my heart, and closed myself up alone in this dreary, solitary place. I was not without a consciousness even now that I had left them all longing, anxious, miserable about me; but I felt as though they were all enemies—all enemies, as if I had not a friend in this wretched, forsaken world. I did not think what this real blow was which had struck upon me. I only felt my dreary, hopeless solitude, and the desire I had to be left here unmolested. I thought it would please me to see no more a human face again. I was in a wilderness more desolate than any Eastern waste—there were no hearers above me, and no human fellowship around. God and the Lord were words to me. I believed, but I did not know them—I could not seek refuge there, and here there was not one—not one of those I had loved so well, but had betrayed me.

My little room, my bower, my girlish sanctuary which I had left in my bride's dress, I had returned to now, worse than a widow. Quietly and mechanically I began to take off my dress—it was not grief but misery which filled my heart, and there is a great difference between them. My wretchedness stupified me, and when I laid down my head upon my pillow, I fell at once into a heavy, deep sleep.

THE FOURTH DAY

It was a clear, cold, sunshiny autumn morning, the atmosphere was full of sunshine, yet there was little warmth in the air, and there were thin misty clouds upon the sky, which looked like vapors which the earth had thrown off from her own still bosom, and the wind carried up unchanged. Yet out of doors it was a beautiful fresh day, and the sun beat in through our darkened windows with a full bright flash in mockery of our sombre shade. A dreary dull excitement was in the house—it was the funeral day.

I had been living a strange, miserable, solitary life. Every day Alice brought me some food, and I took it mechanically. Every day I went down stairs, and heard them speaking together. I listened when they addressed me, and answered them with perfect composure. I knew all the arrangements—by no pretext that I was not able, did I permit anything to be hid from me. I was quite able—my frame was strong—my heart was stunned—I could endure anything—there need have been no fears for me.

But my intercourse with them went no further. I heard what they had to say, and answered, but I suffered no approach towards friendship. Alice waited upon me with assiduous tenderness, but I never spoke to her. Mr. Osborne appealed to our long acquaintance—to my father's old, old friendship for him—to his love for mine and me. My heart was steeled. I made no response. I went and came among them alone—alone—as I was to be alone all my life.

And he—he was always there—always ready to interpose for me if I expressed a wish, or opposed any intention of Mr. Osborne, who managed everything. If I was likely to be annoyed by any importunity, I knew that he interposed and freed me from it. I seemed to see everything he did, present or absent, by some strange magic. He did not persecute me with vain endeavors after a reconciliation—he left me to myself—we scarcely spoke to each other; yet when he was away I chafed and fretted at his absence, and when he returned I knew how he looked—what he did—as well as if I had flown to meet him, or hung upon him with a young wife's foolish fondness. We were evermore parted, yet evermore united—this feud and antagonism between us was as strong a bond as love.

My father was to be laid in the family grave—this was at a little solitary church half way between Cambridge and Cottiswoode. Some haughty Southcote in the old time had desired to be laid at the boundary and extreme line of his own lands, and hence had arisen a little desolate church and graveyard, and the mausoleum of the race. They had arranged that Edgar Southcote was to be the chief mourner at this lonely funeral—that I could not bear—I could not see my father carried to his grave with only them two—Mr. Osborne and him, following up the last journey. I said nothing, but I prepared myself—I wrapped a great black cloak about me, over my mourning dress—black, black, black—it was very neat. I veiled my head and my face, and went out from these doors like something that belonged to the midnight, and not to the day. Alice stood and gazed at me aghast while I robed myself; and when I turned to go out, she fell down at my feet, and clasped her arms round me, and cried and pleaded: "Do not go—it will kill you," she cried. I drew my dress out of her hands and bade her rise. "It will not kill me," I said bitterly, "yet if it did, it would be well."

As I went down stairs I met Mr. Osborne. He stood before me in amazement. "Hester, Hester, you will not think of this!"

"Let me pass!" I said, "let some one who loved him go with him—let me pass—no one shall prevent me—he has none in the world of his own blood but me."

"My child, my child, you cannot bear it—all shall be done as you shall approve," he said anxiously. I did not answer, but passed him with an impatient gesture. In the close, I found yet another interruption—but he did not try to prevent me—he followed me into the carriage—he knew me better than they did.

And so we set out upon our dreary journey—once more I looked from the carriage windows, and wondered if this day was but a common day to the common people round. Once we met a marriage party—a gayer party than ours had been, five weeks ago, with young bright faces, and smiles and jests, and all the natural tokens of a time of joy. I looked at them with the strangest interest. I wondered which was the bride and what was appointed to come to her. Should she be so miserable as I, or was mine a solitary instance? You would fancy a mourner had little room for such thoughts—but I had room for every kind of thought—no wild fancy or speculation in that slow dreadful journey came amiss to me.

Everything looked different from what it had been when I came by this same road to my father's death-bed; now the people were at work in the fields; there were cries in the air—passengers on the road, everywhere, life and motion, sunshine and hope. I saw the rustic people pause at their labors to look at our solemn procession; I could fancy how they asked each other who it was that came this way to his last rest. My thoughts went back to that night seven years ago, when my father and I drove this way together, leaving our ancestral home. We had never been on the road again, so far as I knew, never till now, and now we were taking him to a home of which no man should ever dispossess him, to rest with his forefathers for ever.

A very low rude wall, one of those fences of the country, was round the church-yard, the church itself was small and poor—a humble little chapel, where only a few scattered worshippers ever came. I do not know why it had been permitted to fall so much into neglect, for the family tomb was in a little chapel closely adjoining and opening from it. This little shelter of our race was paved with old tombstones, every one bearing the name of a Southcote, and the walls were covered with tablets to the memory of the dead of our house. There were two raised tombs besides, with recumbent figures, memorials of some more distinguished or more ostentatious than the rest; and this house of the dead was lighted by a small Gothic window, filled with scraps of ancient glass; here, under the shelter of this groined roof, within these inscribed and monumental walls, and not where the free air of heaven should visit his grave, we were to lay my father. It was well—better for him than the green grass, the flowers, the sunshine, and the outer human world, was the little family chapel where, withdrawn from the common dust, his race and kindred waited till the end.

In silence and solitude I stood at the head while it was being laid in its place. I did not weep, nor cry, nor faint. I never faltered for an instant from my firmness. In my cold, cold composure I stood and looked on. The words of the service never woke me, yet I heard every one of them. I noticed the very tone of the clergyman's voice, and the habitual cadence of the words. I knew it was because he said them so often that they rang to that measure. I observed everything; not the smallest incident escaped my eye. By and bye all was silent again—it was over, and we had to go away.

Only then did I linger for a moment—I looked round upon this well frequented place, where so many had been brought and had been left before. I glanced over all the names, how full it was. This place was home. The house we were all born to inhabit—the permanent, lasting dwelling-place. The new comer was not alone here; he was gathered to his fathers; he was entered upon his last and sweet inheritance. I came away with a steady step—I think almost with a smile upon my face. My father had many friends around and beside him—only I was alone.

And then we set out to return to our life, and left the dead behind. Oh! life inexorable—cruel! how it sweeps upon the traces of the last slow journey, and beats out the mourner's footprints with its race and tumult! It was not hard to leave him, for he was well; but it was hard to note our quickened pace, to know that we were going back to every-day. No one spoke—I was thankful for that—even Mr. Osborne did not break upon the silence. Once more the people in the fields looked up to see us going back again, and the light came from the west, and the labors were almost over, and we had left our new inhabitant in the grave; that was all the world knew of us as we went home.

When we entered, I saw the table was spread, and it occurred to me, that at my father's table we ought to be represented, not by Edgar Southcote, nor by Mr. Osborne; and when I had taken off my mantle, I returned and took my place. I saw Mr. Osborne look at me with extreme and uncomprehending wonder. He could not understand my motive, nor what he called the rule of my conduct. He did everything very properly himself, and conformed to all the usual decorums, and he did not know how to judge me. I was aware of his wondering, and almost disapproving glance. I was aware that I ought not to have been able, on this day, to take my place here as I did; but I was not moved by knowing it; I only felt an indignant determination that neither of them two should rule at my father's board—this was his house still, and I was his heir.

When the meal was over, I returned to my room; but I could no longer rest there—there was a visible void in the house—a dull ache and vacancy in my heart. I wandered about from room to room, to his bed-chamber where he died, and where he had been lying like a king in state and rest; from thence I went to the library where his chair stood by the table, where his desk and his books seemed almost to have been used to-day.

There I sat down in my dull, vacant misery; the door was closed, the house was still—save for the branches waving in the evening wind across the window, there was neither sound nor motion near. I was quite alone. I sat looking at the diamond ring upon my finger, his last gift. I wondered what he meant by saying it was a misfortune. A misfortune—I had no need, yet no fear of such in my withered life. One great calamity, as I thought, had put me beyond the reach of fate. "No, no!" I repeated to myself unconsciously aloud, "fate has done its worst—I can suffer no more. I can lose no more—there is no misfortune left possible to me."

As I spoke I heard some motion in the room, and starting saw Mr. Osborne rise from behind the curtain where he had been reading. In proportion to my former confidence in him, was my resentment against him now, and I became very angry when I perceived he had been watching me.

"Then you have made up your mind to be miserable," he said, somewhat sharply, as he came up to me. "This is very foolish, Hester! it is worse than foolish—it is criminal, and it is weak—you forget your natural grief to nurse your wrath, and confirm yourself in a sense of injury. Where is your poor mother's miniature which I gave you for a charm to keep those evil thoughts away? It might have soothed your father's last hour, if you had not thus embittered your heart. Child! child! it is easier to make misery than to heal it—do not throw your life away."

"I have no life to throw away," said I, sullenly, "it has been taken from me and all its hopes. I do not care if I should die to-morrow."

"Do you think that those who make such speeches are in the best mind for dying?" said Mr. Osborne. "Dying is a solemn matter, Hester! and can only be done once. But at present, living is more in your way. Do you know that this revengeful passion of yours will estrange all sympathy from you? Men and women who have lived long in the world have generally known some real calamities, Hester! it is only boys and girls who can afford to indulge in despair, and say fate has done its worst. You do not know what you say—instead of fate and its curse, Providence has blessed you more greatly than you are able to perceive."

"Not Providence—Providence never works by falsehood," cried I.

Mr. Osborne's face flushed with displeasure. "You are very bitter, Hester, very harsh in your judgment," he said, "and I could not bear with this passion of yours so long if you had not been a dear child to me for many a year—for your father's and your mother's sake I overlook your resentment against myself, though I have not deserved it; but, Hester, beware—it is all very well now to be heroically miserable; but you are young—you have a long life before you; and, however long you may dwell upon your injury, some time or other you will begin to want and long for the happiness which now you despise. Hester! come, I will confess you have had a hard initiation into the cares of life; be a woman and a brave one, let us see no more of the girl's whims and humors. I can promise you all tenderness for your honest sorrow, Hester, but not for your wilful wretchedness."

"I ask no tenderness, no sympathy. I will not accept it," I cried, starting from my seat. "You know I have not a true friend in the world—who should sympathize with me? every one of you has deceived me!"

"If that is your conclusion, so be it," said Mr. Osborne, walking to his seat. "I can only hope that your true friends will not be lost, even before you have real need for them, and that when you come back to look for it, Hester, and find your right senses, your happiness will not be entirely out of your reach."

I did not wait to hear any more, but left the room, unable to speak with anger and indignation—the stupor of my misery was broken, I was roused almost to madness. It was not yet a week since I had fallen from my happy confidence into this dark abyss of falsehood and betrayal, and already they blamed me—already they called me resentful, revengeful, obdurate. I, the victim of their successful plots, I who stood alone and no one with me! I saw at once how I would be judged on all sides, how every one would condemn me—how light his offence would be in the eyes of the world—how unpardonable mine! If I had been like to yield before, I could not have yielded after that. I set myself fairly to meet it all. He should have justice! justice! and neither deceit nor pity from me.

In this tumult, my heart awoke. Its dead and sullen inaction gave way to a vivid feeling of reality—and as if I had known it now for the first time, there burst upon me the full sense of my father's death. Yes! for the first time I felt to my heart, how desolate I was, and with a bitter satisfaction I remembered that I had nothing to wean me from my grief, nothing to distract the mourning of my orphanhood—no wooing tender happiness to lead me away from the grave where I would build all my thoughts. Yet now, also, for the first time I remembered what he had said upon his death-bed—strange words for him, "one event should not poison a life." I thought I heard the echoing round me of his failing voice—the voice I should hear no more; and I threw myself down before the bed, kneeling and covering my face in passionate and bitter weeping. My father! my father! where was he? where?

When I rose from my knees, it was quite dark. I do not think any one can be in great or real grief without trying to pray. I prayed little in the stupor of my misery, but now broken wandering disconnected petitions came to my lips among my tears. When I appealed to God, though ever so feebly, and, alas! so little as I knew of him! it calmed me in some degree. I rose and bathed my face to put away the tears—I was subdued and melted—my eyes filled in spite of myself. I did not weep over the death-bed or the grave. I felt now as if I could weep continuously, and that it was impossible to stay my tears.

Then I heard a timid step without; I knew it was Alice, and by-and-bye she came softly knocking at the door—under the door crept in the light from her candle. I remembered with a bitter pang the last time she came to me in the darkness—the night of my betrothal. When I thought of that, I rose firmly and admitted her. How I was changed! Alice came in with a hesitating step, looking wistfully at me to see how far she might venture. Alice was greatly shaken with the events of these last few days. The bright look on her face was overclouded, she was humble and deprecating and uneasy. I had been her child, loving, confiding, almost depending upon her—and there was such a dreary difference in everything now.

She set the light upon the table, and lingered looking at me. I fancy she saw some encouragement in the glance of my wet eyes and the softening of my face. She came behind me under the pretence of doing something, and then she said timidly, "Miss Hester, may I speak?"

I could not say no. I did not answer at all, and she took this for permission.

"You think every one's deceived you, dear," said Alice humbly, "and in your great trouble you stand by yourself, and will let nobody help you. I don't deny, Miss Hester, every one's done wrong; but, darling, it was all for love of you."

"Do not say so, Alice," I exclaimed, eagerly, "you insult me when you speak thus."

"Oh! Miss Hester, think upon my meaning," cried Alice. "I thought I knew his look, his step, his voice, from the first time he came under this roof. I pondered and pondered in my mind if it could be him; but he never told me that I should know. You were as like to know as I was, dear—you had seen him all the same; and it was not my part to speak, or I thought so, Miss Hester. Then the night he spoke to you first, he brought the roses here, and said to me, 'Do you think she would like them, Alice?' and in my heart I knew where they came from; but never a word was spoken of them by either him or me. On your wedding-day I got more again, by a servant's hand. I never doubted they came from Cottiswoode, nor that he sent them: but, dear, he never told me, and I had no right to know. You were willing to marry him, Miss Hester, you were bound up in one another; was I to presume that I knew more than you did, darling! and what was it I knew? nothing at all, dear, but the thought in my heart—oh! Miss Hester, you're all I have in the world—don't turn away from Alice—don't think I've deceived you, I'm desolate without you."

"I am quite desolate, I have no one in the world to trust to," said I.

"Oh! don't say it—don't say it!" cried Alice, "he's been led into a snare once, Miss Hester, but truth is in his heart!"

"It is I who have been led into a snare," said I, bitterly, "he has wrecked all my expectations—he has plunged me out of happiness into misery; but that is not all, he has placed me so that I must either yield and be satisfied like a weak fool, or if I resist be known as a passionate ill-tempered woman, who makes him miserable. I see all that is before me. I am doomed like my father. My own life is robbed of every comfort, and the blame of making him unhappy will be added to me—oh, I see it all! I will be called a termagant, a household plague, a scorn to women. It is not enough that my life is wretched—my good name must go from me too."

"Oh! Miss Hester, not by his will," cried Alice.

As she spoke, a change came upon me. The pride of a wife came to my mind. I could blame him myself—but I could hear no one else blame him—I could not admit a third person to our domestic discord. My quarrel with Alice was for her own fault, and not for his. My bitterness against Mr. Osborne was because he had deceived me, and not because Edgar Southcote had. No one but himself had any right to speak of his error to me.

"I am not speaking of my husband," I said coldly; "what is between us can only be settled by ourselves; no one can interfere between him and me. I speak only of circumstances of my unfortunate and unhappy position; that is all I refer to."

Alice paused, chilled and overcast once more; it was difficult for her, a humble, simple woman, who rarely was offended, and who, when she was, forgave like a Christian, and never suffered the sun to go down upon her wrath, to understand or to deal with me; she stole round behind my chair, and bent down on the ground by my feet.

"Miss Hester, will you forgive me? you are used to me—you would not take to another for a long time, dear. I was your nurse, and I have been your maid, Miss Hester, all your life—don't cast off Alice. May be, I don't deserve that you ever should trust me more; but let me be beside you, darling; let me serve you, and wait on you, and comfort you if I can. Oh! Miss Hester, my dear sweet young lady trusted in me—and even your papa trusted in me—don't cast me off, for you are my own child."

I cried long and bitterly. I could not help it. The pleading of Alice recalled again to me how desolate and solitary I was. I had not a friend in the world, old or young, to whom I could confide my trouble; not one whom I could lean upon if I was ill or suffering; alas, not a woman in existence, except herself, whom I should have wished even to see again! and disappointed as I was in those hopes of perfect sympathy and union with my husband, which every one forms at some time or other; my heart yearned for the natural solace—the comfort of mother or of sister which providence had denied to me. I let my hand fall upon her shoulder—I leaned upon her. "Oh, Alice, Alice, why did you deceive me?" I cried with a great burst of tears.

She did not answer anything, she drew me close to her bosom, and caressed me, and soothed me. My heart beat calmer. I was subdued—I scarcely knew how, as I leant upon Alice. I seemed to have found some rest and comfort for which I had been seeking vainly. When she began to weep over me, my own tears stayed; my heart was eased because I had forgiven her, and then I raised myself up, and we sat together speaking of my father. I had never heard about his last days.

"He never was well after you went away, Miss Hester," said Alice; "all that day after Mr. Osborne left, he wandered up and down talking to himself. The most that he said, that I could hear, was, 'she will be well—she will be well;' for, dear, his heart was wrapped up in you, though he said little; and then sometimes he would take a turn, as if he was doubtful, and once I heard him say, like trying to persuade himself, 'She is not like me—she will not resent it as I would have done.' I was not spying on him to hear this, Miss Hester; but he wandered about so, wherever I was, or whatever we were doing, and never seemed to notice us, and Mary, if she had minded, might have heard as well as me. A week before you came home he took to his bed, and when I was staying in his room waiting on him, he sometimes spoke to me. God was good to him, dear, and gave him time to think, and he was not near so high, as he drew near his latter end; but, Miss Hester, you might not care to hear what your papa said to me."

"Oh! tell me everything—every word, Alice," I cried.

"Sometimes he would not say a word for hours—and then all at once would speak as if he thought I had been following all that was in his mind," said Alice. "In this way, all at once, he said to me, 'When she comes home, you will stay by her, Alice—let nothing persuade you to go away from her—she has no mother, no friend,' and then he did not say another word that night. Then it was again, 'She may have disappointment in her life—few are free of it—the simplest comfort is the best. Alice, you are a simple woman, you live in every day—do you bring fresh heart to comfort my child.' It looks presuming, Miss Hester, I know it does, dear. I never could have thought such things of myself; but that was what he said."

"Go on—go on, Alice," said I, as well as I was able, through my tears.

"Dear, there was not a great deal more; sometimes he said only your name, and 'My only child, my only child;' and then he would turn and say, 'Be sure you never leave her, Alice, she will have need of you.' I cannot think on much more; but when I went and told him you were come (it was in the night we got the news, and I was sitting up with him), he said I was to send away that moment to call you to him—and you came—and oh, darling! what a comfort all your life, that you were in time to see his latter end!"

I was weeping now without restraint, leaning upon Alice. My solitude was less desolate, less miserable, when she was beside me; and I who had always prized so much my father's few tokens of tenderness, it went to my heart to hear how he had remembered me when I was away. "Do you think he knew, Alice?" I whispered; it was an unnecessary question, for I was sure he did.

"He never said a word, dear; but it was not like he would tell me," said Alice. "Yes, Miss Hester, he had found it out—I knew it by his eye that very day."

And now, that I had the clue, so did I; but I no longer felt anger against my father, though all of them had suffered me to sink passively into this gulf and grave of all my hopes.

When I went to rest that night, it was Alice's kind hand that smoothed away my hair, and said good-night at my pillow. I wept myself to sleep, but my sleep was not haunted by the miserable visions of those nights which were past.

THE FIFTH DAY

October was over now, and sullen and dark winter weather had oppressed the skies, and settled down upon the country. I was still in Cambridge, living alone in my father's house. My husband came and went constantly, yet left me unmolested; I almost think he was afraid at once to enter upon the question of my return, and he respected the grief which would not be sympathized with. I believe, indeed, that to have an excuse for delaying any explanation or arrangements between us—to put off fixing that future which we both dreaded, there was a mutual pretence of business which claimed my attention after my father's death; but there was, indeed, no such thing. He had left one or two legacies, and desired that, except the books he bequeathed to Mr. Osborne, his library should be left intact, and even the house preserved, and a housekeeper placed in it when I returned to my own home—but he had neither debts nor debtors—there were no arrangements to make. I lived a dreary life in the drawing-room, when I was too sick at heart to go near the window, and never left my chair when I could help it. I read earnestly, yet eagerly, whatever books came to my hand—novels when I could get them—I was glad of anything to cheat me from my own brooding unhappy thoughts; yet I never thought of going away. Where could I go to? All the world was alike solitary—alike desolate to me. The heavy listlessness of grief came upon me—I cared for nothing, I scarcely desired anything. I had never had any visitors, and though one or two came to see me now because I was mistress of Cottiswoode, to offer their condolences and sympathy for my loss, I denied them admittance when I could, and when I could not, suffered their coming and their going so indifferently that they seldom came to trouble me again. Mr. Osborne came now and then, but his visits were only of duty, and there was little pleasure in them for either him or me. By degrees I was left entirely alone with Alice, and with my husband, when he came. People had begun already to speak of me with astonishment. I made Alice confess this was the case; and no one knew me or could take my part; but in my heart I was rather glad than otherwise, to have my first condemnation over so soon.

It was now a month since we had returned home, and save on the first evening and morning after our arrival at Cottiswoode, we had spoken to each other only on indifferent subjects. I knew this could not last. I had always in my mind a certain deadened and dull expectation of our next interview. I feared it, and would have put it off from day to day, yet it seemed the one thread of life in my languid existence. My heart beat when I heard his footsteps come along the close—that springy light rapid step; I knew its faintest echo, and equally well I knew it when duller and fainter it went away. The misery of our position was, that we were not, and could not be, indifferent to each other; when he came, this subdued restrained expectation animated me into temporary vigor; when he went away, I was aware of an aching disappointment, which mingled with a sense of relief. Involuntarily I watched and waited for him—if our meetings had all been joy, they scarcely could have been so breathlessly anticipated, for then we should have known each other's plans, and intentions, and wishes, and now we knew each other in perfect ignorance of what the other meant to do.

I myself was still worse than that—I did not know my own intentions; I had no plan for the future. I knew we must by-and-by decide upon something; but my mind seemed incapable of any action, save brooding over my own thoughts or speculating on his. Alice had brightened, I could not tell why, since our interview. I suspected she nourished vain hopes that I was weak, and would yield to him; none of them understood me, or if any one did, it was he.

Things were in this position to-day, when Alice came and told me that he had arrived, and wanted to see me. I told her to show Mr. Southcote upstairs. I was able to compose myself before he entered the room. I am sure he could see no sign of agitation. It was very different with him; his face had an excited, unsteady look, he was very pale, yet sometimes his cheek flushed with a deep faint color. I could not see that he either had any plan. I read in his whole manner that he had come to try once more what entreaty, and persuasion, and penitence would do. This hardened and strengthened me; I was ready to hear him with coolness and self-possession when I saw that he brought neither to his conference with me.

He sat down near to me, and leaned forward to me across my little table. His voice was dry and hoarse with emotion. "Hester," he said, "I have waited, and been patient. I have not hastened nor troubled you. Have you no comfort, no hope, no forgiveness for me now!"

"It is I that should have comfort—for it is only I that have been in sorrow," I said.

"Yes, and you have put me away from you. I have not been permitted to say that I grieved with my wife," he said, "yet I have grieved with you, Hester—you can shut out the man who has offended you, but you cannot shut out the heart—all these wrong nights and days—all this wretched time, I have been with you, Hester. You cannot exclude my thoughts or my love—you cannot make me forget that you are mine."

"I cannot make myself forget it," I said. "No, you do well to taunt me. I know that I belong to you. It has all come true—I feel what is upon me like a chain of iron. I remember your cruel words, when you said 'for ever and ever'—I remember what my father told us—you do not need to repeat my misery to me, I acknowledge it."

I saw him start and draw back when I said "my misery," as if it was a pang; but he recovered himself. "For ever and for ever," he repeated, "do you remember that night—Hester, there was no misery in our way that night, and how is it that we are changed? I have sinned against you, and you have punished me. For a whole month now, and it is only two months since our marriage-day, the meanest passenger in the streets has had as much kindness at your hands as I—is this not enough, Hester? can you not forget now this dark episode, and return to what we were? Let me suppose it is again that night—let us return to the time of our betrothal, and being anew. Will you speak to me, Hester?"

"We cannot return to the time of our betrothal," said I; "then I was deceived. Now I know, and it is impossible to restore the delusion again."

"Was there nothing but delusion?" he said hastily, "was it folly to suppose that you cared for me at all—or is vengeance and not mercy the companion of love?"

"I cannot tell," said I, "I am no poet; but if you think it is easier to be wounded to the heart—to be deceived and ruined, and put to shame, by one who is dear to you than by an enemy, I know you are mistaken. If I had not cared for you, I should have had only myself to mourn for, and would have been a light burden."

He sank back in his chair for a moment with a look of blank dismay and almost horror. "Deceived and ruined and put to shame!" he repeated. "Hester! what meaning do you put upon these words?"

I felt the blood rush to my face, with indignation and shame and nervous excitement. "It is quite true," I said, "you have taken the hope and strength out of my life—is not that ruin? and you have disgraced me in my own eyes—I did not leave my father's home with you—you know I did not give either heart or hand to you; but I awake and find that I am your wife—you have disgraced and shamed me to myself. I can only bear contempt and scorn for the deceived and foolish girl whom you have shown to me in her true weakness. I can never hold up my head any more—and by-and-by you will disgrace me to the world."

"How will I do that, Hester?" he asked; his voice rang sharp and harsh; he felt what I said deeply, and, in addition, I saw that at last I roused a kindred opposition and anger in his mind.

I found a certain pleasure in it. I was glad to rouse him to be like me, in bitterness and enmity; though I was much excited, I had command of myself; I could speak slowly and clearly as I thought. I had never been given to many words—but I appreciated the possession of them now.

"When your neighbors see the disappointed sullen woman who is called by your name, they will know what to think of her," I said. "I will be pointed at as one whose evil temper, whose bitter disposition makes every one round me miserable. All the hard tales of the old Southcotes will be revived in me— they will say I am a curse instead of a blessing—they will make an example of me, and tell how happy I might be—how miserable I am. No one will know of the secret poison that has come into my life; but they will know that I am bitter and harsh and unlovely, and they will judge from what they see; the very servants, poor Amy who could not leave me till she had told me who she was—they will think me an evil spirit—they will shrink out of my way, and all the world will give their sympathy to you."

While I spoke thus, though it moved him much, though he changed color, and sometimes for a moment his eye flashed upon me with indignation, I saw at once that I had relieved him in some point. When I thought of it, I perceived that all this speech of mine pointed to no separation; but almost told him that I was ready to follow him home. I had not intended this, indeed I did not know what I had intended—I had formed no plan, and I only spoke, as I so often acted, on the moment's impulse, without pausing to think what it might lead to. When I discovered his satisfaction, it startled me for a moment; but then I was occupied listening to what he said. He spoke in a softened and hopeful tone.

"This will not last, Hester! your own good heart will interpose for me. I have deceived you once, it is true; but neither I nor any one else will do you injustice."

I made no answer. I saw he had something more to say, and I waited sullenly to know what it was.

"Will you come home?" he asked. "There is nothing here but memories of sadness. Come, Hester! life and its duties wait upon us while we dally. If you cannot forgive me, still, come with me, Hester. If we do our duty, the blessing will come to us. At present we are paralysed, neither you nor I are good for anything, and our life was not made for our own caprice—come!"

"And what should I be good for?" I asked with some astonishment, for hitherto my life had been of the most complete and total uselessness, and I did not understand what was required from me. When he took this tone, I always acknowledged his influence—it was only when we came to personal matters— when I sat triumphant on the eminence of injury, that I got the better of him.

"What? anything!" he said. "I know what you are, Hester! you have life before you as I have; and happy or not happy, we have all its duties to do—not one thing, but a multitude. Come among your own people, to your own home—you have authority to exercise, charities and kindness to spread around you. You are no less yourself, because, if you will, you are disappointed and deceived in me—I will bear my burden as it is just I should; but, Hester, it becomes you to be no less brave; you must take up yours."

I gazed upon him with amazement; involuntarily my heart responded to this call he made upon me. No one had ever bidden me rise and work before; but when I heard his voice, I suddenly acknowledged that this was the want of my life. I was quite in the mood for it; I might have gone into a nunnery, or joined a sisterhood of mercy, had I been a Catholic, or in a country where such things were. I immediately leaped upon a wild imaginative vision of those things which he described so soberly as the duties of life. I took the heroic view of them at once; I had no eye for patience and meekness, and such tame virtues. My rapid glance sought out the great self-sacrifices, the privations of voluntary humility; I was ready to walk over the burning ploughshares, to be a martyr at once.

Yes! I began to be ashamed of my expectation that he would plead, and pray, and humble himself at my feet, and that I, injured and deceived, would spurn him from me. I was ashamed of resenting so bitterly my own unhappiness. In a moment I had reached the opposite extreme. What was happiness? a mere bubble on the surface. Duty and labor were the zest of life.

With the speed of lightning these thoughts passed through my mind, and all the time he sat gazing at me across the table. I think he was scarcely prepared for my answer; for he met the first words with a startled look of mingled embarrassment and joy.

"When do you wish to go home?" I said. "I am ready now."

"Ready now—to go home?" he exclaimed, with a flush of surprise and delight, rising to come to me; but he caught my abstracted, pre-occupied eye, and, with a deeper blush of mortification, sat down again. "You cannot come too soon, Hester," he continued, in a subdued and disappointed tone, "for everything is disorganized and out of order—there is the greatest want of you—though I will not say how I myself long to see you in your proper place—will you come to-morrow?"

"There are some things to do," I said, vacantly, delaying without any purpose in the delay. "Will Monday do?"

"Yes, yes!" he said, with eagerness. "I will come for you then; and now, I go away in hope."

I made no answer—my mind was busied with my own projects—already in my mind I had begun my life of heroism and martyrdom at Cottiswoode. Already I washed the feet of the poor, and watched by the bedside of the plague-stricken. I did not pause to consider possibilities, nor ordinary rules; but followed up my own wild idea, in my own eager fashion. He waited for something further from me; but I said nothing to him, and after a little interval he went away.

It was now Friday, and I had pledged myself to be ready on Monday to go to Cottiswoode. I went immediately to find Alice; I could perceive that she had been waiting with great anxiety the issue of our interview, though, absorbed as I was in my new thought, it did not immediately occur to me why—and when I went to her, Alice was quite nervous with expectation.

"Do you think some one could be got quickly to keep the house, Alice?" said I, "do you think you could find some one to-day or to-morrow?"

Her face lighted up suddenly.

"To be sure I could, Miss Hester," said Alice; "but, dear, why?"

"Because I have arranged to go home on Monday," said I, "to go home, Alice, to the duties of my life."

"Bless you, darling!" she cried; but her color changed when she saw my unresponsive face; "it's not against your will, dear," she said timidly, "you're not forced to go, Miss Hester?"

"Forced? no! unless by my duty, which is there," said I. "I begin to see what is the use of me, Alice, or what should be, rather; for I have never been of use to any one. I must go to begin my work, there is the proper field for me—and now, when I know what it is, unhappiness will never prevent me from doing my duty."

"Is that all, Miss Hester?" said Alice, with a wistful look—she was more disappointed than even he had been.

"Yes! that is all," said I, "what more should any one seek for? I wonder you never told me, Alice, how useless I was."

"Has any one told you now?" said Alice, drawing herself up with a little flush of simple anger; "or, dear, what has put such a thought in your mind to-day?"

"Not any one telling me," I answered; "but I see it very well, and clearly—perhaps, indeed, after all, I could not have done very much when I was a girl—it is different now; but, Alice, let us see what preparations we have to make, for there is very little time."

"Yes, Miss Hester, directly," said Alice, taking up her bonnet. "I'll go and see after the old woman—don't you be waiting about the library, dear, it's a dreary place for you. Wouldn't you come out now your own self, Miss Hester, and breathe the air—Cambridge streets are no great things, I dare say, to them that's been in foreign countries and in London, but better than always moping in the house—come, darling—come yourself and see."

I was persuaded, and went with her. The day was not so miserable out of doors as it looked within, and it was still scarcely past mid-day, and there were many people abroad. We had not gone far before we met Mr. Osborne, who had a clergyman with him—a tall, meagre, middle-aged man, in very precise clerical dress, about whom there was a certain look of asceticism and extreme devotion, which, as it happened, chimed in with my mood of the moment. Mr. Osborne and I met very drily after our late quarrel. I had not softened in my resentment towards him, and he was impatient and angry with me—so that I thought it was mere aggravation, and a desire to exasperate me, which tempted him to introduce his companion to "Mrs. Southcote of Cottiswoode;" it was the first time I had heard my name stated so, and I could not subdue the start and tremor with which I heard it—so that I did not at the instant notice the name of the person introduced to me, and it was only when I heard it repeated, that it struck upon me with a sound more startling than my own.

"Mr. Saville is rector of Cottiswoode—the clergyman of your parish—Hester," said Mr. Osborne—"when do you return home?"

"On Monday," I said; but my whole attention was fixed upon my new acquaintance—Mr. Saville—I could not think, for the first moment, what association I had with the name, but it was a painful one, and it had something to do with Edgar Southcote.

"I am glad to meet my young relative," said the clergyman with a stiff bow—his young relative! Could he mean me?

I gazed at him for a moment, but only with a dull astonishment, for it was quite beyond my comprehension what he could mean.

"The parish has been much neglected. I hope to bring its necessities before you soon," said the clergyman, in his measured, chanting tone. "I do not despair of making the desert rejoice, with your assistance, Mrs. Southcote; but at present it is in a deplorable condition. No church sentiments, no feeling for what is seemly and in order—there has been no resident on the estates for so many years."

"Ah! the young people will rectify that, no doubt," said Mr. Osborne, carelessly. "I am glad to see you out of doors, Hester, and glad to hear that you are going home—your own good sense—I always trusted to that."

"I will be glad to do all I can," I said, hurriedly answering the clergyman, and taking no notice of Mr. Osborne; "you will have to instruct me at first, for I am quite ignorant of work. Could I take anything with me that could be of service? pray let me know."

"I will make out a list of useful articles—no trouble, pray do not speak of it," said the Rev. Mr. Saville, with a wonderful bow.

Mr. Osborne groaned. "I am in some haste," he said sharply. "Good morning, Hester—I shall see you before you leave Cambridge," and as he turned away, I heard him mutter—"Poor, foolish child—is she to comfort herself after this fashion."

I turned away proudly—this worldly man might scorn these self-denying labors, which were to be all the pleasure of my life—but I only clasped them closer on that account. I called Alice to me again, and went on in silence. I persuaded myself how glad I was that I had encountered this clergyman; but in spite of my devotion to the work about which he seemed so anxious, I could not keep my mind from straying back to his name, and what he had said—Saville—Saville—it suddenly burst upon me—that was the name of the man who came with the boy Edgar to Cottiswoode, before we left it. I felt my face burn with indignation and displeasure—he called me his young relative—perhaps he was that man's son, and a relation of Edgar Southcote. I thought it a new insult, that by any chance such a person as the first Saville should be related to me. Yet so strongly was I moved by my new sentiments, that, I think I made the strongest effort which I ever recollect making to put down this feeling. Yes, I had become enamored of mortification and self-abasement. I had my work to begin too, and what did it matter if this clergyman was Saville's son—what did anything matter to me? Was I not about to court humiliation and offer sacrifices—to forget my worldly comforts and delicate breeding—to wash the feet of pilgrims? and I was glad to find at the very outset a great unexpected mortification in my way. I walked along very rapidly beside Alice. She was anxious to speak to me—very anxious about myself—but I did not think of beginning my labors by doing what I could to lighten the kind heart of Alice.

When we were returning, after visiting a woman whom Alice knew, and whom she arranged with—for though this might have been a very suitable beginning of my labors, I did not think of making it so, but was shy and stood aloof; we began at last to speak. Alice no longer understood or could deal with me; she hesitated and was timid, and never knew what to say in our conversations. I do not wonder at it—for when I look upon those days, I do not always find it easy to comprehend myself.

We had just passed a group of young ladies. Three handsome, tall, well-dressed girls, evidently sisters, and full of talk and eager interest in something they were discussing. "Dear," said Alice, with a sigh, "if you had but had a sister, Miss Hester, or some good young lady to be company for you at Cottiswoode."

"I want no company, Alice," said I.

"You never knew what it was, dear," said Alice; "a friend is a great blessing and comfort, more than you think for. Couldn't you now, Miss Hester, darling, think upon some one to keep you company this dull winter? You'll be lone in the country, and nothing to amuse you—do think upon it, dear."

"I do not want to be amused. I am going to work like a rational creature," said I; "do you think I am good for nothing but amusing myself, Alice? No, I have lived long enough for my own pleasure, and now that pleasure is out of the question, I want to live for others. I must have been very selfish all my life. I want to sacrifice myself now, and live for the good of the poor and the distressed."

"Dear, it's a blessed thing to hear a young lady like you speak such words," said Alice, with tears in her eyes; "and to serve God and to be good to his poor, is the way to be happy, darling; but you never need to live solitary, or give up a good friend for that."

"You do not understand me, Alice. I don't want to be happy," said I, sternly—"I want to do my duty— happiness is all over in this world for me. Do not say anything; you will only vex me; and you know I have no good friend to give up, even if I cared for it."

Alice paused again, disconcerted, eager, ready to say a great deal, but afraid of offending me, I fancy; at last she thought it best to let me have my own way.

"And what will you do, Miss Hester?" said Alice.

"I scarcely know," said I, "the clergyman will tell me, and I will learn, and I am sure you know, Alice, what ladies can do in the country. I could go to nurse the sick in the village—that is one thing."

"But, dear Miss Hester," said Alice, "if the Queen had come to nurse your papa, do you think she could have made up to him, poor gentleman, for the want of you?"

"No, no, no! why do you say such things?" said I.

"Because poor folks feel just the same," said Alice, with a little dignity; "a poor man would sooner have his own wife, and a poor woman her mother, or her child, to nurse her, than the greatest lady in the land."

I was slightly offended at what Alice said. "I will only go where I am of use, you may be sure," I said; "I will seek out the poor, and work for them. I will teach the children. I will take care of the old people. There is a great deal of misery everywhere—I can understand it now, and I will find plenty to do."

"Yes, dear, there's plenty of trouble," said Alice, with a heavy sigh: "plenty of God's own sending, and plenty of our own making, Miss Hester—and old folks like me, that have seen grief, it goes to our heart to see the young and the great that have happiness at their feet, and will not stoop down to lift it—and that's the truth."

"If you speak of me—I do not wish to hear of happiness. I have no longer anything to do with it," said I, angrily.

How I clung to this! how I closed myself up in a gloomy panoply, and defied their vain consolations. We went the rest of the way home in silence. I was displeased with Alice, and she was grieved for me. I do not know how she comforted herself; but I took refuge in my intended martyrdom. I did not wish it to be agreeable. I was impatient of being told that I could do all this, yet not diminish either my comforts or enjoyments. I was anxious to suffer, to scorn delights, to meet with trials—not the Lady Bountiful of a village, but the heroine of some dangerous mission, was it my desire to be. I had the true ascetic mood upon me. I was not disposed to "endure hardness" for the sake of doing good; but rather to endure doing good for the sake of the sacrifice and suffering which I anticipated so eagerly; and this was how I intended to act upon my husband's sober exhortation to come to my own home and my own people— to take up my burden and do the duties of my life.

THE SIXTH DAY

Monday dawned bright and genial; one of those rare November days, when summer seems to come back again to see how the world looks under the reign of winter. The air was not cold, but so clear that, on these wide plains of ours, you could see for miles around you. There was no wind; white clouds lay entranced upon the deep blue sky, which was mellowed and warmed with a flood of sunshine, and against it the few trees stood out with a distinctness which became almost ridiculous where it was a bristling pollard willow, which outlined all its bare twigs, like the hair of a frightened rustic standing on end, upon that wonderful background. The sandy path sparkled with minute crystals; the mosses on the low stone fences caught the eye like banks of flowers; here and there a little rivulet of water, bridged with a plank, came sparkling through a meadow with a line of trees on either side; and under this full sunshine, an occasional morsel of new-ploughed field gave diversity to the vast, level, and long lonely roads; while a single horseman or foot-passenger, coming clear out on the sky, broke through the sunburnt meadows, hedgeless and naked, raising up, now and then, another leafless affrighted willow— a far-seeing sentinel—scared by something coming which it could see, though you could not. The sky itself, falling out of its glorious full blue, into wonderful grays and olive tints deepening and deepening, yet everywhere breaking into streaks of light to the very edge of the horizon, gave a wonderful charm to everything below; and upon our faces came the fresh air, which was not wind, without violence, yet full of exhilaration, so fresh, so pure, so limitless—a world of sweet existence in itself. Though I closed my heart against its influence, I could not help but note the day—I could not help comparing it to that bright face of Alice opposite me from which youth had passed, which had little hope for this world, and on whom sorrow had fallen with its utmost weight, yet which was happy still. When I looked at my husband, there was the light and the hope of manhood upon his face, yet it was clouded; and what was I—a sullen spring-day, ungenial, ungladdened. So I carried out my involuntary metaphor.

Everything had been suitably arranged in Cambridge—a housekeeper was established in the house, and Mary remained with her—nothing was disturbed of all our old household arrangements. My father had left his income to me, of course; and I was able to maintain this for myself. It was equally a thing of course that Alice should accompany me—no one needed to speak on the subject, it was so clearly understood between us, and my husband, and Alice, and I travelled very silently to Cottiswoode. I had sent there the previous night, a large box full of things which Mr. Saville, in a very stiff polite note, had recommended me to bring. Among its contents were some prayer-books and catechisms, but I am afraid one of the most bulky items was dark cloth for a sort of uniform which Mr. Saville recommended to be worn by the lady visitors in his parish, for he had hopes, he said, of establishing a devout and energetic sisterhood to assist him in his work. I was much occupied with my own intentions and purposes in this respect. I saw myself in the gloomy mantle of the order, going about sternly, sadly, awing other people only to mortify and humiliate myself. I did not pause to ask whether, with my clouded face and obdurate, dull, determined breast, I would be an acceptable visitor anywhere. The poor were merely the passive objects of my own martyrdom. I never took them into account in the matter, nor paused to consider whether or not my ministrations would be a comfort to any one. My whole wild plan sprang entirely from thoughts of myself.

When we came to the great avenue of elms, I gazed up at it steadily. They were grand old trees. The free wide air about them had strengthened the noble life in these stout retainers of our house. They threw abroad their great branches with a glorious freedom. They had no bias nor stoop in one direction or another, but stood boldly upright, impartial, indifferent from what point of the compass the wind might blow; and behind the forest of boughs and twigs, at every countless crevice and opening, the sky looked through, marking the intertwining lines, great and small, like some grand lacework, upon the white rounded clouds poised upon its surface, and upon its own magnificent full hue. I saw how excited and nervous Alice became as we neared home—she gazed about her with eager glances—she folded her hands together, wrung them close, put them to her eyes. It was hard for her to keep still, harder still to be silent, as glimpse after glimpse of the familiar road burst upon us. My husband spoke to me once or twice in sympathy. I said nothing. When we passed the village, I saw the clergyman standing in the garden at the Rectory, looking at us as we passed by, and there were many little groups in the neighborhood of Cottiswoode, and the children set up a chill hurrah as we drove through the village; but I sat back in my corner, and cared for nothing. At last we drew up and alighted. This time I suffered his hand to help me, though the memory of that former night returned upon me, so that I scarcely could keep my composure. Once more I looked up at the arms of our house sculptured above the door—once more I saw the servants ranged within, and then I suffered him to lead me through them, and bowed, though I could not smile. I saw they looked at me now with a new and wondering curiosity. I saw that I was an object of more personal and eager interest than when they gathered with smiles to greet their master's bride. Yes! my reputation had come before me—they were prepared to wonder, to comment, to criticize—but I was not wounded at the thought, I only passed by them with a little additional haughtiness, and went to the room which was prepared for me—the same room where I spent that first dreadful night after our coming home.

When I had arranged my dress, I went down stairs to the room which now was the drawing-room, but which had been our dining-parlor in past days. It was a large long room, spacious but not bright, with one great window opening to the lawn, and a smaller one in the corner of the wall. When I entered, he was walking about with an expectant look upon his face—he started and made a step forward as if to advance to me as I came in, but though I saw him perfectly, I did not look at him, and he stopped and returned again. I went to the window to look out upon the lawn, and the great walnut tree, which I could only see imperfectly from this point—then I took a seat in silence. A painful interval followed. I sat quite still, vacantly looking out. He paced about the room with unequal steps—sometimes rapidly and with impatience. We were neither of us doing anything—we were like two enemies watching each other, ready to strike. I do not think that till that moment either of us realized what a frightful thing it was to live together, confined within the same walls, and with this feud between us.

"How are you pleased, Hester, with the new arrangements—the furniture—the house?" he said, throwing down a book upon the table, somewhat noisily, in his extreme agitation.

"I am quite pleased—it is all very well," I answered. I found it difficult to command my own voice. I suddenly was seized with a wild wonder, why we were placed here to torture each other. It might preserve appearances, but we surely would have been better with the whole world between us, than together as we were.

"When we were boy and girl we had a conversation here," he went on rapidly, now coming up to me: "do you recollect it, Hester?"

"Yes," I said, "then I believed in you, and pointed to my father the picture you resembled. My dear father! I thank God he does not see us to-day."

"What picture did I resemble, Hester?" he asked, with a good deal of emotion in his voice. I pointed to it with a quick gesture, I could not trust myself to speak.

"You took my part," he said, "you had compassion for me. You bore me witness that I was no deceiver; and, Hester, your face, your voice, your generous, brave, girlish frankness, have made my heart warm since that day."

I held up my hand in entreaty. I could not bear it.

"No, I will not persecute you," he said; "no, do not fear me. We will gain nothing by discussions of the old question. I bid you welcome home to your own house. I will say nothing else. I will now relieve you of my presence, and I am sure you will thank me for that, at least."

But I did not even thank him for that. What had been wretched, while he was with me, became intolerable when he was gone. I drew the chairs aside, and walked up and down the long apartment in restless misery. Day after day, year after year, were we to live thus?—together, yet with a world between us—with nothing to say to each other—nothing to do with each other—a sullen, dreary silence, or half-a-dozen forced words, making all our domestic intercourse. I had anticipated much vague misery, but the actual exceeded the ideal; and yet, though it was miserable to be together, I was impatient and jealous of his absence; and when I threw myself into a chair by the fire, and began to gaze into it, and to brood over our new life, my thoughts settled down upon a nearer object, and I only wondered where he had gone to, when he would come back again, and if he came again, what he would say.

It was so strange to raise my head, and look round, and see the familiar faces of those family portraits looking down upon me. Instinctively I turned to that portrait which I had said he resembled as a boy. I did not think it was like him now; his face was no longer the face of a student, with those downcast, thoughtful eyelids, and lines of visionary pensiveness. My husband was no visionary; he was not a man to be consumed of over-much thought; he loved the free, open air—he loved exertion and wholesome labor. With a strange perception I found out that this was the case. We seemed to have changed characters since the time of our youth. It was I, now, who lived the unwholesome inner life, who shut myself up with my thoughts. I, whose nature was not so—whose spirit was eager, and courageous, and enterprising—who all my life, till now, had loved adventure and freedom—I was paralysed. I was contented to sit still, brooding and wretched. I cared no longer for the healthful functions of life.

But I was glad when Alice came into the room, and interrupted my thoughts. I had still sufficient discretion to know that, at this moment at least, it was safer not to indulge them. I made Alice sit down by me, and talk to me, though she looked wistfully round the room, and into my face, as if to ask me where he had gone. Alice had learned caution now, and was silent about him. We began to speak of my father. The harsh tempest of my unhappiness had swallowed the tears, the tenderness, the complaints of grief. I had scarcely mourned at all for my father, as people call mourning. His loss added a perfect desolation to my other misfortunes, but I did not weep for it as for a great calamity. It shut up my heart in a closer seclusion—it did not soften and lay me prostrate. I was under a process of hardening, and not of subduing. Contact with death did not humble me—it only made me withdraw myself the more into my own disturbed and darkened world, my own desolated and solitary heart. But since I had been reconciled to her, I found a little refuge, a little comfort with Alice. I sat and wept when she spoke of him. I was glad to hear her do it. I felt myself lightened and eased by a conversation such as we were having now.

While we talked thus, my eye happened to fall upon my father's ring. I had to wear it on my forefinger, it was so much larger than the other; and I did not like to have profane hands touch it, or to give it away from me, even for an hour, to have it altered. A misfortune! I had no clue to what my father meant when he called it so.

"Did you ever hear any story of this, Alice?" I said, holding it up to her; "he said it was a misfortune. I cannot tell what he meant."

"Yes, Miss Hester! I've heard the story," said Alice; "it belongs to the family, dear. And there's a strange tale to it, and a prophecy, though whether it's just fancy, or true, or what trust you may put upon it, it's not for the like of me to tell. But I never believe myself, Miss Hester, that there's power in a bit of gold and a shining stone, even if it's as precious as that."

"I have never heard of it. Tell me, Alice," I said.

"It's called the Star of Misfortune, dear," said Alice, lowering her voice with some awe, though she had professed her scepticism, "and I've heard say it was a very grand diamond, and could buy up many a poor man's house; but this I know to be true, Miss Hester, that though it's been sold, and lost, and given away, the house of Cottiswoode never can keep it from them—it always comes back again—and it never can be lost till the time, let them do what they will."

"But I do not understand this. Tell me the story, Alice," said I.

"Well, Miss Hester, it belonged to the second son of Cottiswoode many a long year ago," said Alice; "it was in a time when there was little learning—far different from now. But them that were learned had great arts that are never heard of now-a-days. The story goes that he got it from a spirit—but you're not to think, dear, that I put faith in that—he had been a strange gentleman, given up to learning and caring for nothing else—though good to the poor and kind-hearted, as I have heard. There was but two sons of them, and the eldest, the Squire that was, a great gentleman at court, gave Cottiswoode to his brother to live in; and then he used to live all solitary, reading his books and studying everything in the earth and the skies, and was counted a great scholar in his day. And wherever he went and wherever he was seen, he wore that ring on his left hand."

Involuntarily, without thinking what I did, I removed my ring to my left hand as Alice spoke. In spite of her professions of unbelief, Alice spoke very reverentially, and impressed her hearer with a strong conviction of the truth of what she said.

"Yes, dear, there he is," said Alice, pointing suddenly to one of the portraits, "if you look close, you'll see the ring on his finger; and I don't doubt he was a fine young gentleman, and all the look of a scholar about his brow."

I started with great surprise—the portrait—the one which I thought like Edgar Southcote when he was a boy—was the very same one at which I had been looking before she came in. "I have heard of him often," I said—"but I never heard this story—and, Alice, my father never wore this diamond while we were in Cottiswoode."

"It was because of the tale, Miss Hester. Hush, dear, and I will tell you," said Alice. "His name was Mr. Edgar, and he was the Squire's only brother, as I said—and for long they were loving friends—the one was great at court and the other a great scholar, and Cottiswoode was a grander estate, and a grander Hall there than it is now. But Mr. Edgar chanced to see a young lady nigh and fell in love with her, Miss Hester—and the Squire came down on a visit, and he fell in love with her too—and strife came between the brothers, as it comes between many a generation of the name since—and the lady chose the Squire and cast off Mr. Edgar, and there was sad work in the house. But the end was that Mr. Edgar left all his books, and went away to foreign parts—to foreign parts—to the wars—and though his brother and the lady wanted to make friends, he would not, but held his left hand to them, and said he would leave their children an inheritance. Well, as the story goes, Miss Hester, no one thought more of that, except to be sorry for the poor gentleman, and the Squire and the lady settled down at Cottiswoode, and had two beautiful boys, and were as happy as a summer-day; but when ten years were gone, an old man from over the sea brought a letter to the Squire—and what was this but Mr. Edgar's ring, and a prophecy about the house and the name of Southcote—the ring was always to go to the second son, and it was to be called the Star of Misfortune; and trouble was never to depart from the race till it was lost."

"But you said it would not be lost," I said, eagerly.

"Neither it can, till its time," said Alice with solemnity; "when there is no second son born to the house of Cottiswoode, but only an heir, then the curse was to be over; and when it was worn upon a woman's finger it was to lose its power; if it had not been for that, dear—though I put no trust in such things—I could neither have told you the tale, nor seen that evil thing shining on your innocent finger. Well, it came to pass, Miss Hester, that when the poor lady at Cottiswoode read the words Mr. Edgar had written, and saw the diamond, she screamed out it was shining and looking at her like a living eye, and fell down in a fit, and was brought to bed of a dead baby, and died before the week's end, and the Squire's heart broke, and the two boys grew up with no one minding them. There was strife between them from that very day, the story goes, and when they came to be men—it was the time of the civil wars—and one took one side and one the other; and the youngest boy went off from the house by night with that jewel on his finger, and nothing else but his sword; and Cottiswoode was taken by the rebels, and blood shed upon the kindly threshold—brother's blood, Miss Hester, but neither of them was killed—and when that young man died, the ring came back to the hall by a strange messenger, though it had been sold to buy bread. And so it has been ever since. When there was more than two sons in Cottiswoode, there was less harm—but that has only been twice in all the history of the house. Brother has warred against brother, Miss Hester, from Edgar the scholar's time down to Mr. Brian and your papa; but one way or another, dear, the ring has come back to the house, and never gone to any but the second son of Cottiswoode till now. When your papa was master here, he put it away, and maybe he thought the curse was past; but them that knew the tale, knew well that the curse would not be past till there was a born heir, and only one son in the house. And when the present young squire came, your papa put on the ring again—it goes to my heart to see you wear it, Miss Hester. It never was but a token of evil. I think it put thoughts of strife into the mind of every one that ever wore it; thoughts and examples of ill, darling, and we're all too ready to follow iniquity, God help and preserve us! and that is the story of the ring."

"And, Alice, tell me again how it is to be lost?" I asked anxiously.

"When there is but one heir, and no second son; and when love and peace is in the house of Cottiswoode, and when those that are nearest in blood are dearest in heart; then the ring that never could be lost before, will fall from the hand of a born Southcote, and never be seen again—that is the prophecy, Miss Hester," said Alice, "and if I saw it come to pass, I would give thanks to God!"

I was much excited by this story—it threw a strange weird ghostly romance about us and our race. I fitted the ring closer upon the fore-finger of my left hand, and held it up sparkling with its living quivering radiance, in the firelight. For myself, I felt no desire to lose it—it had gained a superstitious importance in my eyes: I resolved to keep it sacred, and preserve for ever, as my father had bidden me, this strange inheritance. I was not pleased with my exemption, as a woman, from its magic power—women, as I had cause to know, were quite as accessible to passions of resentment, and even to the desire for revenge, as men were, and I should have been better satisfied had there been some place for me in this grand system of family vengeance. With a different, yet a stronger interest, I looked up at the picture of Edgar the scholar, with its contemplative student face and pensive eyes. How strange that this man should be the origin of such bitter retribution—for it was very bitter, pitiless, almost fiend-like, an inheritance of animosity to be borne by brother against brother. I wondered as I looked up at the regular calm features, the undisturbed refined face, I could see no cruelty in it, as it looked down upon me thoughtfully from the familiar wall.

"It should be called the star of strife, and not of misfortune, Alice," I said.

"It has been of misfortune, too," she answered; "never one has thriven with that ring upon his finger; there never is strife in a house, dear, but trouble comes. They say the lands are not half so great as when that diamond came to Cottiswoode, and though it is a precious stone itself, Miss Hester, it's never been reckoned in the wealth of this house. There's violent death, there's great grief and sin, there's losses and misfortunes among the Southcotes ever since it came; and the second son of Cottiswoode has never had children to leave it to. I never heard of one that gave it to his own child, but your papa."

Once more we relapsed into silence. I had a new subject for my thoughts in Alice's tale; and, perhaps, it may be thought strange that I should receive it with such entire faith. Family superstitions have always a great hold upon the imagination. It is hard to disbelieve stories that come to us on the voucher of our own ancestors, and which are part of the family creed, and concern the whole race; but even without these claims upon my attention, I should have at once believed and received this story. I was quite in the mood for it, and though I did not fear "ghosts," nor show any of the popular signs, I had a natural tinge of superstition in my mind.

But Alice warned me how late it was, and I had to go upstairs with her and dress. I cared nothing about my dress. I suffered her to adorn me as she would. But I would wear no ornaments—not that bracelet, nothing but the storied and fatal ring. Like a real star it glittered on my finger—catching the ruddy gleam of the firelight, and shining in the darkened air of the winter twilight. He could not know this story, and I could not tell him of it—it was very strange to be so near, yet so far apart.

When I went down to dinner, Mr. Saville was there. It was a relief, yet it piqued me that he should ask any one to come on the first day, though how we could have met alone at table in our sullen estrangement I cannot tell. The Rector was in a very precise clerical dress, his manners were a great deal too fine and careful for a man of breeding, and he seemed to be so much alive to his "position," and so careful to keep it up, that I perceived at once that he must have been raised to this, and that he was not a gentleman either by birth or early training. By some strange logic, I thought of this as an additional offence to me. I did not care to inquire what my husband's motives had been in giving the living to this person. I did not take time to think that probably he had been appointed before Edgar Southcote had conceived his plan for my deception. I thought he had meant to insult me by surrounding me thus with his mean relatives, and depriving me even of the comfort of a suitable neighbor; but I resolved to show him that I was above this mortification, and all the more freely, because I said nothing to him, did I converse with the Rector. He told me of the church which wanted repairs—he said restoration, but I was not acquainted with the ecclesiastical science so fashionable at the time; he told me that his sister had begun to embroider a cloth for the altar—that the very vestments, the sacred vessels for the altar— everything was falling into decay—that the last rector, "a worthy man, he believed, but lamentably lax in his church principles," had whitewashed the interior of the unfortunate church—had barbarously removed the remnants of an ancient screen of carved stonework—had taken up a mutilated brass in the chancel, and laid down a plain flag-stone in its stead; which things, Mr. Saville said pathetically, had so much disgusted the people, that there really had arisen a dissenting place of worship in this formerly orthodox village, and his people were led astray from the true path under his very eyes. Had Mr. Saville told me of an epidemic raging in Cottisbourne, of some deadly disease abroad, and no one bold enough to nurse the patients, I should have been more satisfied—but such things would arise, no doubt; and in the mean time, I should have been glad to have worked with my own hands at the restorations, if these were necessary, though, alas! I was disappointed, and could not feel that there was any martyrdom in making an altar-cloth.

All the conversation during dinner was carried on between the Rector and myself. My husband scarcely spoke; he looked at us eagerly, keenly, as if he would have read my thoughts. I could perceive what was passing in his mind; he had given up the Hester of his imagination, as I had given up the Harry of mine; and he was trying to make himself acquainted with what I was now.

When I returned alone to the drawing-room, and once more sat down by the fire, a pang of pain and self-reproach came over me for a moment, as I thought what a great change had indeed passed upon me; and how unlike I was my former self. But then I asked who caused this, and once more established myself on my old ground. When the gentlemen joined me again, I resumed my conversation with the Rector, and now at last he propounded something which suited my views.

"There were a number of old people in the village," he said, "some bed-ridden, some palsied, a burden upon their children, and imperfectly attended to in the midst of more clamorous claims. My sister, too, long had the idea of placing herself at the head of a sort of almshouse, where these poor creatures could be nursed and taken care of. My sister is an energetic person, Mrs. Southcote, and though, of course, like other ladies, accustomed to very different pursuits, has a natural love for work, and great tenderness to her fellow-creatures. She thinks, with the assistance of a few kind-hearted ladies, hired help might also be dispensed with—an apostolic work, Mrs. Southcote, washing the feet of the poor."

"Ah, yes! that is what I wanted to hear of," I said; "who is your sister, Mr. Saville—is she here?"

"I am surprised that Mr. Southcote has not informed you, Madam," said the clergyman, with momentary acrimony; "my sister, Miss Saville, resides with me, and as a near neighbor, naturally looked for an introduction to you—a relation too, I may say, by marriage," he concluded, with a ceremonious bow.

I felt my cheeks burn—but I subdued my pride of blood. "I will call on her to-morrow," I said.

"Nay, permit me," said Mr. Saville, with another bow. "Miss Saville is the oldest resident in the parish; she will have pleasure in calling on you."

Again my natural hauteur almost got the better of me. So! I was to be on ceremonious stately terms with Miss Saville, as though we were potentates of equal rank and importance—and relatives, too!

"She will have the greatest satisfaction in communicating all her plans to you," continued the clergyman. "Mr. Southcote would have had her come to-night; but my sister was too well aware how indecorous such an intrusion on your privacy would be. Ladies understand the regulations of society much better than we do."

In pure mockery, I bowed to Mr. Saville as ceremoniously as he bowed to me; but there was a great deal of bitterness in my satirical courtesy, which he, good man, took in perfect sincerity. My husband had been standing by a little table, where was a vase of beautiful hot-house flowers, which it must have been some trouble to get for me, and was pulling the costly blossoms to pieces, as if he did not know what he was about. When he saw the curl of my lip, as I bowed to his relation, he came forward hastily and began to converse with him.

How much indebted I was to Mr. Southcote! how much disappointed that Miss Saville had not come!

THE SEVENTH DAY

We had just set out together to begin our work. It was a raw winter day, damp and foggy, and the heavy haze fell white and stifling over our flat fields, but was not dense enough to hide the dreary line of road, nor the dull depths of distance round us. We were dressed in great cloaks and hoods of dark grey cloth, with small black bonnets under our hoods; and each of us carried a basket—while Miss Saville had a little leathern case, containing medicines, hanging from the girdle round her waist. She was a tall, stiff woman, with a frosty face, and angular, thin frame. I cannot tell how she looked in summer—very much out of place, I should think, for this dull, foggy, cold day seemed too gentle for her, and you could fancy a keen frosty wind constantly blowing in her face. Her manners were like her brother's, very fine and elaborate at first; but by-and-by she forgot, as he never did, that she was talking to Mrs. Southcote of Cottiswoode, and began to tell me of her plans, as she might have told any ignorant girl, and showed no special respect for me. When she came to her natural tone, I could not help being better pleased with her. She was much more in my way than the Reverend Mr. Saville was. She did not say a word about charity or benevolence; but she told me how she intended to manage the old people, and how, with one servant and a lady coming to help her every day, she could keep a home for them all together, and keep them comfortable, if the means were provided for her.

"Extremely disagreeable work, I don't doubt, for you dainty young folks," said Miss Saville, who no longer thought it necessary to pick her language; "but I had my own old father to mind for long enough, and it's nothing to me."

"Disagreeable!" said I, "what does it matter? I wonder what right we have to agreeable things!"

"Well—I am glad you think so!" said Miss Saville, with a grim smile. "You will be the more thankful for what has fallen to your share; for very few people, I can tell you, have to provide disagreeables for themselves, as you have. They are almost all ready-made, and not very well liked when they come."

I had nothing to say to this. Nor could I have expected that she would understand me. We were walking quickly, for it required no small exertion to keep up with Miss Saville, who strode along in her thick boots with a manly disregard of every obstacle—along the lane which led to the village. Just before we reached Cottisbourne, we passed the Rectory. Miss Saville looked up at it as she passed, and so did I. I was startled to see a face looking out from the window, which I recognised, or fancied I recognised. It was a weather-beaten face, unshaven and slovenly, and stooped forward with an inquisitive, sidelong glance. I tried to recollect where I had seen it. Could this be Saville—the Saville—the man who brought Edgar Southcote to Cottiswoode? I was disposed to think so. My companion gazed at him a moment, and then waved her hand impatiently, as if to bid the man go from the window. Yet I had been now three weeks at Cottiswoode, had frequently seen the clergyman and his sister, but had never heard of another. I wondered why they concealed him—I wondered if it was he; but Miss Saville never spoke.

We were close upon the village now. The first group of two or three houses stood by themselves upon the brown grass of the meadow-land around. They seemed to have no gardens, no trees, nothing to protect or shelter them; but stood apart among the grass, which pressed round their very walls and doorsteps, as if it grudged the little bit of ground they occupied. There were some plants in the window of almost every house, poor, shabby plants, crushed against the green gauze curtain suspended across the three lower panes, darkening the light; but doing little else by way of compensation. The want of gardens seemed to disconnect them strangely from the soil on which they stood. There was no beauty or sentiment about them; but only very poor, meagre, hungry poverty. Beyond them, a very small stream, which made no sound in the heavy, deadened atmosphere, wound through a field, with some low willows standing by, like a class of unkempt boys at school. A little further on, withdrawn into a grassy mass, was the village well, with its bucket and windlass; and then came Cottisbourne proper, a cluster of houses oddly placed, with strange little narrow lanes winding among them, as intricate as a child's puzzle: some brown and dingy, with the thatched roof clinging upon them like a growth of nature—some brilliantly whitewashed, with great patches of damp, from the rain, upon their walls. One or two carts tilted up, stood in a corner of the bit of common which belonged to the village. About them, and in them, were a number of children, whose voices scarcely woke the sullen air to cheerfulness. The houses stood about in genuine independence, every one faring as it pleased him, and the wealthy cottager's pig sniffed the same air as his master, and placidly meditated upon the doings of his master's next neighbor, whose open cottage door was opposite the piggery. There surely was no want of work to do, for any one who cared to take in hand the reformation of the little commonwealth of Cottisbourne.

Miss Saville proceeded to business, while I looked on. She went forward to the children in the cart, and lugged down the reckless urchins who came clambering into it, just in time to prevent an accident, as the heavy body of the cart, high in the air, where they had been climbing, was suddenly thrown off its balance, and came down heavily, doing no harm, thanks to her exertion. "You little foolish things," said the excited lady, "how often have I told you, you were not to go near these shocking things? you might all have been killed. I can't be always looking after you, and if Jemmie Mutton had been killed when that cart fell, what do you think you would have done then?"

Not one of the little culprits was able to reply to this solemn question, and the lady continued, as they gaped at her, clustering together, stealing their hands underneath their pinafores, or putting finger in mouth, with awe and astonishment: "Depend upon it I shall make examples," said Miss Saville, with solemnity. "Christmas is not so far off that I should forget what you are about now; and if I should hear of such a thing again, beware!"

Saying this in the tone of a Lord Chief-Justice, with an awful vagueness of expression, and penalties implied which only the threatened offenders knew the weight and import of, Miss Saville turned to enter a cottage. "I am obliged to keep them in awe of me, my dear," she said, turning to me with complacent satisfaction, "and even to threaten them about their Christmas things. Some of them get quite an outfit of things when they attend school well, and say their catechisms; but children are a deal of trouble—the little good-for-nothings, they're at it again!"

I was amused at Miss Saville's contest with the children, yet somewhat disgusted withal. Like other visionaries, I was horrified when I descended to practise, or to see practised, what I had been dreaming. Your sweet docile children would have been out of my way, and unwelcome substitutes for the harder labors on which I had set my heart. But stupid children—children who gaped and curtsied—who folded their hands under their pinafores, and played in carts, and were held in terror of losing their annual dole at Christmas! this was quite a different martyrdom from what I had dreamed of. I had no vocation at all for this.

However, we had now entered the cottage. It was very poor, and had a sort of sofa or settle near the fire, on which was laid an old paralytic woman, whose shaking head and hand proclaimed at once how she was afflicted. A stout tall woman, the mistress of the cottage, went and came about the poor room, preparing the dinner, I suppose, but taking no notice of the invalid, that I could see, though her feeble half-articulate voice seemed to run on nevertheless in an unfailing stream, and there was an eagerness in her gray bleared eye, which testified that this old woman, at least, though she had lost everything else, had not lost her interest in the world. She assailed us with a flood of imperfect words, which I could scarcely make out, but which seemed easy to Miss Saville, and a craving for news, and restless curiosity, which seemed very dreadful to me in this old, old woman. "So, she's com'd home!" she said, and I knew she referred to me, "does she know her own mind by this time? Ah, ah, ah! it do make poor folks laugh to see the ways of the quality, that never know when they're well."

"Hold your peace, Sally," said Miss Saville, imperatively, "the lady herself has taken the trouble to come from Cottiswoode to see you, you ungrateful old woman; and to see what she can do for you to make you comfortable; do you hear? You ought to thank her and show some feeling; but I am sure you poor folks in Cambridgeshire are the most ungrateful in the world."

"The old folks you mean, Miss," said the younger woman.

"You will call her Miss, ye unmannerly wench," said the mother-in-law, chuckling; "Madam Saville, I know you—I know naught of the young one. Make me comfortable! I'm an old poor crittur, past my work, and I've had a stroke; and I want rest to my old bones. But these young uns, that's able to stir about and help themselves, they think aught's good eno' for me."

She began to whimper as she spoke. Alas—alas! the heroism of my vocation had deserted me. I felt nothing but disgust for the miserable old woman. I could not endure to go near her or touch her—it sickened me to think of the proposed asylum, and of doing menial services with my own hands to such a creature as this.

But Miss Saville was unmoved. I suppose she had no elevated ideas of self-martyrdom.

"Well then, Sally, that is just what I came to speak about," she said; "you're in the way in your son's house; and you feel you're in the way."

"Who said it? was't Tilda there?" cried the old woman, firmly. "I'll make him wallop her—that I will, when the lad comes home. Where is an old woman to be welcome but with her children? Oh! you sarpent! it's all along o' you."

"Matilda never said a word about it," said the peremptory Miss Saville; "she has a great deal of patience with you, poor thing; for you're an ill-tempered old woman! Be quiet, Sally, and listen to me. How would you like to be taken to a new house, and have all your little comforts attended to, and a room to yourself, and ladies to take care of you, eh? I would have charge of you, you understand, and this good young lady from the Hall, and others like her, would come every day to help me. What would you say to that, Sally?"

The younger woman, with unequivocal tokens of interest, had drawn nearer to listen; and was standing leaning upon the table, with her face turned towards us. Sally did not answer at first, and I watched the eager gleam of her old bleared eyes, and the nodding of her palsied head in silence.

"I don't knaew," said the old woman, "she'd be glad, I dare say; but am I agwoin to be put out of my way, to please Tilda? I'll not have no prison as long as my Jim has a roof over his head. I'm not agwoin to die. I wants to hear the news and the talk, as well as another. I wants none o' your fine rooms to lie all by myself, and never see nought but ladies—ladies! You're grand, and you think poor folks worship you; but I'd rather see old Betty Higgins to come and tell me the news."

"If that is all you have to say, Sally, we had better leave you," said Miss Saville. "You shocking old woman, do you think you will live for ever? You'll soon get news from a worse place than this world, if you don't mind."

"I'll send for the parson when I've made up my mind to it, that I'm agwoin to die," said Sally; "but here, give it to me, lady; don't give it to Tilda—she'll spend it on her own, and never think on the old woman. Well, you've a soft hand: where's your white bonnet and your white veil, and all your grandeur? What's the good of coming to poor folks all muffled up like madam there? You're no show, you're not—you should have come like a picture. Now, Tilda, get me some brandy and a drop o' tea, and tell Betty Higgins to come and sit by me while you're gone."

I retreated with a shudder when she dropped my hand. Her cold touch sickened me, and I could not bear the sharp twinkling of those half-closed eyes, and the palsied motion of her head, as she looked into my face, and spoke to me. I was very glad to escape from the cottage when poor 'Tilda, a subdued, broken-hearted woman, not very tasty, went away to execute her commission. I was very much shocked on the borders of my new enterprise, very much disgusted, and almost staggered in my purpose. Yes! I had thought of nursing the sick and taking care of the aged; but I did not think of such sordid, selfish, wretched old age as this.

And yet, these were my own people—old retainers and dependants of the house. I had not been without acquaintances among the cottagers, when I was a girl at Cottiswoode; yet I recognised few of the blank faces which stared at me now. As we threaded the strange, narrow turnings, from cottage to cottage, I had to make no small effort to remind myself that it was clearly my business. Unpleasant! how I scorned the word and myself, for thinking of it—what was pleasant to me?

Miss Saville had not been silent all this time, though I paid no great attention to her. She was not disgusted; she had been accustomed to such scenes, and took them with perfect coolness; and I was astonished to find that she was not even displeased, nor inclined to shut out this wretched old Sally from the benefits of her asylum.

"You must not mind what that thankless old creature says," said Miss Saville. "I know how to deal with them; and poor Matilda would be a happy woman if that old tyrant was away. You may trust to me to manage her. I promise you, she'll not struggle long with me."

I only shuddered with disgust. I could not anticipate very heroically my own promised assistance to wait upon this old Sally.

We were now at another cottage, where the door was closed, and we had to knock for admittance. It was opened by an elderly woman, fresh-complexioned, yet careworn, with scissors and pincushion hanging by her side, and some work in her hand. The furniture of the little room was very scanty, and not very orderly, but clean enough; and from the cuttings and thread upon the floor, the litter on the little deal table, and the work in the woman's hand, I saw that she must be the village dressmaker. The lower part of the window, as usual, was screened by a coarse curtain of green gauze, and three flower-pots with dingy geraniums stood on the window-sill, with a prayer-book and a work-box, and a range of reels of cotton standing between. Here, as in the previous cottage, an old woman occupied the corner by the fire; but this one was placed in a large wooden elbow chair, gay with a cover of cotton print, which had been a gown before it came to its present preferment, and was tidily dressed, and had some knitting in her hands. A girl of twelve sat by the table helping her mother—a younger one was washing potatoes in a corner, while a little girl of three or four, sitting on the corner of the fender close to the fire, seemed to be exerting her powers for the general entertainment of the industrious family. When we entered, the mistress of the house, after her first greeting to Miss Saville, stepped aside to let us enter, and looked earnestly at me. The signs of her occupation helped me to a remembrance of her. I looked at her with a puzzled curiosity, trying to recall the changed face in its widow's cap.

"Miss Hester," she cried. "I humbly beg your pardon, ma'am, but I made sure it was you."

She curtsied again and again, and seemed so unaffectedly glad, that my heart warmed in spite of myself. Miss Saville was quite thrown into the shade. The children made their little curtsies, the old woman endeavored to rise, a chair was carefully wiped by poor Mary's apron, and placed between the window and the fire for me; and Granny made a moving explanation of "her rheumatiz, that made her unmannerly." I was restored to satisfaction. I do not think I had been so much pleased since I came to Cottiswoode. Yes! these were my own people.

"We've had a deal of trouble, Miss—ma'am—a deal of trouble," said Mary, putting the corner of her apron to her eyes. "There was first poor Tom fell ill and died, and all the little uns had the fever, and Granny took the rheumatiz so bad, that she never can move out of her chair. It's been hard to get the bit and the sup for them all, lady. But now Alice gets a big wench; and little Jane goes of errands, and Farmer Giles gives 'em a day's work now and again, weeding and gathering stones; and I'm a bit easier in my mind—but, oh! it's been hard days in Cottiswoode since you and the good old Squire went away."

I knew no reason Mary had to call my father the good old Squire: yet I was pleased with the appellation. "Come to the Hall, Mary, and Alice will see if there is anything for you," I said; "and you must tell me what poor old Granny wants, and what I can do for her. Granny, do you recollect me?"

"I rechlet your grandmama, Miss," said the old woman, "better than you—that was the lady, she stood for my Susan, next to Mary, that I buried fifty years come Whitsuntide. I kneawn all the family, I do. I rechlet the young gentlemen, and Mr. Brian, that never had his rights. This Squire is his son, they tell me. Well, you've com'd and married him, Miss, and I bless the day; everything's agwoin on right now. The Southcote blood's been kind to me and mine, and I wish well of it, wishing ye joy, Miss, and a welcome home."

I bowed my head in silent bitterness. Wishing me joy! what a satire it seemed.

"Are you very busy, Mary?" said Miss Saville. "Now do you think, if Alice had not come to school, and been taught her duty, she would have sat there so quietly helping her mother. I don't believe anything of the kind."

"Thank you all the same, Ma'am, it done her a deal of good gwoing to school," said Mary, with a submissive, yet resolute courtesy, "but she always was a good child."

"I don't say she's a good child now—she's doing no more than her duty," said Miss Saville, with a peremptory little nod; "there's nothing worse for children than to praise them to their faces. There's that boy of yours, not half an hour ago, if I had not been at hand, he might have broken his neck, clambering into the cart on the edge of the common. I am sure, how these children escape with their lives, with nobody to look after them, is a constant wonder to me."

"Providence is always a-minding after them," said Mary, "poor folks' children is not like rich folks; and my boy can take a knock as well as another—I'm not afraid."

"Well, now I have something to tell you of," said Miss Saville.

"Since Mrs. Southcote has come home, she wishes to do good to you all like a Christian lady; and I'm going to take a house, or have one built here at Cottisbourne, and live in it myself, and take care of the old people who are helpless, and a burden on their families. Mrs. Southcote, and other good ladies, will come to help me, and the old folks shall be well taken care of, and have comfortable rooms and beds, and be a burden to nobody. What do you say to that, Granny? Mary has plenty to do with her own family, and I dare say doesn't always get much time to mind you, and you'd be off her hands, and make her easier in her mind, for I'm sure you know very well how much she's got to do."

A shrill hoohoo of feeble, yet vehement sobbing interrupted this speech. "I'm a poor old soul," said the hysterical voice of Granny; "but I toiled for her and her children, when I had some strength left, and I do what I can in my old days—God help me! My poor bit o' bread and my tater—a baby 'ud eat as much as me. Lord help us! you don't go for to say my own child would grudge me that?"

"Folks had best not meddle with other folks' business," said Mary, with an angry glance towards Miss Saville. "You mind your knitting, mother, and don't mind what strangers say. You ladies is hard-hearted, that's the truth—though you mean kind—begging your pardon, Ma'am," she said, with a curtsey to me; "but I work cheerful for my mother—I kneaw I do. I no more grudge her nor I grudge little Polly, by the fire. She's been a good mother to me, and never spared her trouble; and ne'er a one of the childer but would want their supper sooner than miss Granny from the corner. And for all so feeble as she is, there's a deal of life in her," said Mary, once more putting up to her eyes the corner of her apron. "She'll tell the little uns' doins, it's wonderful to hear—and talks out o' the Bible of Sundays, that the parson himself might be the better—and knits at her stocking all the week through. They kneaws little that says my mother's a burden. Alice 'ud break her heart if she hadn't Granny to do for, every day."

"Well! I must say I think it very ungrateful of you," said Miss Saville, "when I undertake she should be well taken care of, and Mrs. Southcote would come to see her almost every day. You're a thankless set of people in Cottisbourne. You do not know when people try to do you good. There's old Sally—"

"You don't name my mother with old Sally there?" cried Mary, with indignation. "You wouldn't put the likes of her under a good roof! I won't have you speak, Ma'am—I won't indeed. My mother and old Sally! in one house!"

"I think it possible," said Miss Saville, with a little asperity, "that God might choose to take even old Sally to Heaven. She's a naughty old woman—a cross, miserable old creature—and what she'd do there, if she was as she is, I can't tell. But God has never said, so far as I know, 'Old Sally shan't come to Heaven.'"

This rebuke cast poor Mary into silence. She continued in a tremulous, half-defiant, half-convinced state for a few minutes, and then wiped her eyes again, and answered in a low tone:

"I wouldn't be unneighborly, nor uncharitable neither—and God knows the heart—but my mother and old Sally wouldn't agree, no ways—and I'd work my fingers to the bone sooner than let Granny go."

"You must take your own way, of course," said Miss Saville. "I only wanted to befriend you, my good woman. No—I'm not offended, and I don't suppose Mrs. Southcote is either. What we propose is real kindness both to Granny and you—but, oh no! don't fear—there are plenty who would be glad of it."

Mary turned to me with a troubled glance; she thought that perhaps her balked benefactor was angry with her too.

"Is there anything Granny would like—or you, Mary? Could I help you?" said I. "Is there anything I could do myself for you?"

Mary made a very humble, reverential curtsey.

"You're only too good, Ma'am," said Mary. "There's always a many things wanted in a small family. I'd be thankful of work, Miss, if you could trust it to me, and do my best to please—and Alice is very handy, and does plain hemming and seaming beautiful. Show the lady your work, Alice. If there were any plain things, Ma'am, to do—"

"But, Mary, I am sure you have too much to do already. I would rather help you to do what you have, than give you more work," said I.

Mary looked up at me with a startled glance, and then with a smile.

"Bless your kind heart, lady! work's nat'ral to me—pleasure is for the rich, and labor's for the poor, and I'm content, I'd sooner sit working than go pleasuring; but it's another thing with the likes of you."

Miss Saville was already at the door, and somewhat impatient of this delay, so I hurried after her, arranging with Mary that she was to come that afternoon to Alice at Cottiswoode. When we got out of the house, Miss Saville took me to task immediately.

"You don't understand the people, my dear," said Miss Saville. "Mary was very right about the work: it's far better to give employment than to give charity—and that's not to save your purse, but to keep up their honest feelings. They're independent when they're working for themselves, and they're bred up to work all their life; and for you to speak of going to help them, it would only make them uneasy, and be unsuitable for you."

"But I wish to help them—and giving work to Mary does not stand in the place of working myself," said I, with a little petulance.

"Oh, of course, if you want to do it for pleasure that's quite a different thing—but I really don't understand that," said Miss Saville, abruptly.

"I do not wish it for pleasure," said I, growing almost angry; but I did not choose to explain myself to her, and it was a good thing that she should confess that she did not understand me.

We visited a number of poor houses after this, but I found nothing encouraging in any of them. There were one or two old people found, who were quite willing to be received into Miss Saville's asylum— they were all poor stupid old rustics, all helpless with some infirmity, but I did not find that there was anything heroic now in the prospect of waiting upon and serving them. It was not courage nor daring, nor any high and lofty quality which would be required for such an undertaking, but patience—patience, pity, and indeed a certain degree of insensibility, qualities which I neither had nor coveted. I was much discontented with my day's experience—I was known and recognised latterly wherever we went, and though I had no recollection of the majority of the claimants of my former acquaintance, I was very ready to give them money, and did so to the great annoyance of Miss Saville. As we threaded our way through the muddy turnings, she lectured me on the evils of indiscriminate almsgiving, while I, for my part, painfully pondered what I had to do with these people, or what I could do for them. Though I had read a good deal, and thought a little, I was still very ignorant. I had a vague idea, even now in my disappointment, when I found I could not do what I wanted, that I ought to do something—that these people belonged to us, and had a right to attention at our hands. But I could not lift these cottages and place them in better order. I could not arrange those encumbered and narrow bits of path. Could I do nothing but give them money? I was much discomfited, puzzled, and distressed. Miss Saville plodded along methodically in her thick boots, perceiving what she had to do, and doing it as everyday work should be done—but there was no room here for martyrdom—and I could not tell what to do.

THE EIGHTH DAY

Visitors! I did not know how to receive them; and not only visitors but relatives of my own—of my mother's—her only remaining kindred. I went down with a flutter at my heart to see my unknown kin. He was with them, Alice told me, and I composed myself as well as I could before I entered the room; for by this time we had grown to a dull uncommunicating antagonism, and his presence stimulated me to command myself. It was past Christmas now, and we had spent more than two months in this system of mutual torment. We had been once or twice asked out, and we had gone and behaved ourselves so as not to betray the full extent of the breach between us; but we asked no one to our house—a house in which dwelt such a skeleton; and nobody can fancy how intolerable this dreary tête-a-tête, in which each of us watched the other, and no one spoke save the few necessary formalities of the table, became every day. Yet how every day we began in the same course, never seeking to separate—keeping together as pertinaciously as a couple of lovers, and with the strangest fascination in this silent contest. To look back upon this time is like a nightmare to me. I feel the heavy stifling shadow, the suppressed feverish excitement, the constant expectation and strain of self control when I think of it. I wonder one of us was not crazed by this prolonged ordeal; I think a few days of it would make me frantic now.

I stood for a moment at the door listening to their voices before I entered—they were cordial, sincere voices, pleasant to hear, and in spite of myself I brightened at the kindly sounds. There were three of them—father, mother, and daughter—and when I entered the room, the first thing I saw was a pretty sweet girlish face, very much like the portrait which Mr. Osborne gave me of my mother, looking up all smiles and dimples at my husband's. I cannot tell how it happened, but for the moment it struck me what a much more pleasant home this Cottiswoode would have been, had that sunny face presided over it—and what a dull sullen heavy countenance in comparison was that clouded and unhappy face which glanced back at me as I glanced at the mirror. I wondered what he thought on the subject, or if it had crossed his fancy; but I had no time to pursue the question, for suddenly I was overwhelmed in the shawl and embrace of a large kind smiling woman, the mother of this girl.

She held me by the hands after the first salutation, and looked at my mourning dress and my pale cheeks, and said, "poor dear!" She was herself very gay in an ample matronly finery, with satin skirts, and a great rich shawl, with a width and a warmth in her embrace, and a soft faint perfume about her which were quite new to me. Her fingers were soft, large, and pink and delicate; her touch was a positive pleasure. There are some people who make you conscious of your own appearance by the strange contrast which you feel it bears to theirs. Mrs. Ennerdale was one of those; I felt how cloudy, how dull, how unreal it was, living on imaginary rights and wrongs, and throwing my life away, when I felt myself within the warm pressure of these kindly human arms.

Mr. Ennerdale was a Squire like other Squires, a hearty comfortable country gentleman, with nothing much to distinguish him from his class—he shook hands with me very warmly, and looked still more closely in my face than his wife had done. "You're a little like your mother, Mrs. Southcote," he said in a disappointed tone, as he let me go. I might have been when I was happy; but I certainly was not now.

And then Flora came to me, shyly but frankly—holding my hand with a lingering light clasp, as if she expected a warmer salutation from her new found cousin. She was a year younger than I, very pretty, very fresh and sweet like a half-blown rose. She took her place upon a low chair close by me, and kept her sweet blue eyes on my face when I spoke, and looked at me with great interest and respectfulness. Poor young innocent Flora!—she did not wonder that I looked ill, or question what was the matter with me. She was not skilled, nor could discriminate between unhappiness and grief.

It was not jealousy that crossed my mind, nor anything approaching to it. I only could not help fancying to myself how different everything would have been had she been mistress of Cottiswoode—how bright the house—how happy the master. It was a pleasure to look at the innocent sweet face. I admired her as only women can admire each other. I was not shy of looking at her as a man might have been. I had a pure pleasure in the sweet bloom of her cheek, the pretty turn and rounding of its outline. I had a great love of beauty by nature, but I had seen few beautiful people. Many a time the sweet complexion of Alice, and her comely bright face, had charmed me unawares, and I was a great deal more delighted with Flora now.

Mrs. Ennerdale took me aside, after a few minutes, to talk to me after a matronly and confidential fashion, for I was not well, and did not look well. But her kindness and her sympathy confused me, and I was glad to come back to my old place. Flora followed me with her eyes as I followed her—my sad clouded looks woke Flora's young tender heart to respect and affectionate wistfulness. I don't think she ventured to talk much to me, standing apart as I did, to her young fancy, upon my eminence of grief, but she looked up with such an earnest regard in my face, that I was more soothed than by words. When Mrs. Ennerdale began to settle her plumage, and to express her hope to see us soon, a sudden idea seized upon me. I took no time to think of it, but acted on my impulse in a moment. I suddenly became energetic, and begged that Flora might stay a few days with me. Flora looked up with an eager seconding look, and said, "I should be so glad," in her youthful whispering tone. The papa and mamma took counsel together, and my husband started slightly and looked with a momentary wonder in my face; but I suppose he had almost ceased to wonder at anything I could do.

"Well, I am sure you must have need of company, my dear," said the sympathetic Mrs. Ennerdale, "and Flora is a good girl too, but must I send her things, or how shall we do? We thought of asking Mr. Southcote and yourself to come to Ennerdale, but I never dreamt of you keeping Flora. Well, dear, well, you shall have her, and I'll see about sending her things; and, Flora, love, try if you cannot get your poor dear cousin to look cheerful, and recollect exercise," said the experienced matron, turning aside to whisper to me, "remember, dear, it is of the greatest consequence, walk every day—be sure, every day."

There was some delay consequent on my request and the new arrangements, but in less than half an hour the elder pair drove off, and left Flora with me. I took her up-stairs with a genuine thrill of pleasure—I think the first I had felt since I entered the house, to show her her room, and help her to take off her cloak. "But come out first, do, and have a walk," said Flora. "Mamma says you ought to go out; and it is so pleasant to feel the wind in your face. It nearly blew me away this morning—do come!"

"Are you not tired?" said I.

"Tired!—oh no! I am a country girl," said Flora, with a low sweet laugh, as pretty and youthful as her face, "and when the boys are at home, they never let me rest. I always take a long time to settle down after the holidays. Dear Mrs. Southcote! I hope I will not be too noisy, nor too much of a hoyden for you—for you are not well I am sure."

"Oh, yes! I am well," I said, half displeased at this interpretation of the moody face which looked so black and clouded beside Flora's. "Will you wait for me, Miss Ennerdale, while I get ready?"

"Don't call me Miss Ennerdale, please don't," entreated the girl; "papa says we are as good as first cousins, for his father was your mamma's uncle, and his mother was her aunt. Do you not know, Mrs. Southcote? your grandpapa and mine were brothers, and they married two sisters—that is how it is— and we are as good as first cousins—and I think, you know, that we ought to call each other—at least, that you ought to call me by my own name."

"Very well, we will make a bargain," said I; "do you know my name, Flora?"

"Oh yes! very well—it is Hester," said Flora, with a blush and a little shyness. "I have no other cousins on papa's side—and I always liked so much to hear of you."

"Why?"

"Because—I can't tell, I am sure!" said Flora, laughing. "I always could see my other cousins, but never you—and so few people knew you; and do you know," she added quietly, lowering her tone, and drawing near to me, with that innocent pathos and mystery which young girls love, "I think my father, when he was young, was very fond of your mamma."

"Strange! he, too! everybody must have loved her," I said to myself, wonderingly.

"Yes, he says he never saw any one like her," said Flora, with her sweet girlish seriousness, and perfect sincerity.

"Did no one ever say you were like me?" I asked.

Her face flushed in a moment with a bright rosy color.

"Oh, dear Mrs. Southcote! do you think so? I should be so proud."

"I thought we were to call each other by our Christian names?" said I; "but you must wait for me till I get my bonnet."

"Let me fetch it—is not that your room?" said Flora, following; "oh! who is that with such a kind face? Is that your maid, Mrs.—cousin?"

"Come and you shall see her, Miss—cousin," said I, unable to arrest the happy and playful fascination of this girl; "she is my maid and my nurse, and my dearest friend, too, Flora—my very dearest friend— Alice, this is Miss Ennerdale, my cousin."

Alice started to her feet very hurriedly, made a confused curtsey, and looked at the young girl. It was too much for the self-control of Alice. I believe she had become nervous and unsettled, like the rest of us; and now she turned suddenly away, her lips quivered, her eyes filled. Flora gazed at her shyly, and kept apart, knowing nothing of the cause of her emotion.

"Is she very like, Alice?" said I, in an under tone.

"Very like, dear! God bless her! it's like herself again. Miss Hester, is her name Helen?" asked Alice with a sob.

"No."

The glance of disappointment on Alice's face was only momentary.

"It ought not to have been, either; I'm glad it is not, dear—ah, Miss Hester! if she had but been your sister!"

"No, Alice, you would have loved her best; and I could not have borne that," said I, still in a whisper; "but she is to stay with me. I will not let her go away again, till she is weary of Cottiswoode."

And Alice, dear, kind, faithful Alice, who had no thought but for me, was grateful to me for seeking my own pleasure thus. I felt as if I had done her a favor, when I heard her "bless you, my darling!" Ah, this humble love was very consolatory; but I am not sure that it was very good for me.

I was not very strong nor able to walk as I had been used to do. But I felt the sweet exhilaration of the wind upon my face, and looked with pleasure along the level road, to see the thatched houses of Cottisbourne clustering as if for a gossip under the sunshine, and the great sky descending in its vast cloudy parallels to the very edge of these boundless featureless fields. The hum in the air so different from the hum in summer; the sharp, far-away bark of that dog, which always does bark somewhere within your range of hearing in a winter landscape; the shriller harping of the leafless elms, a sound so distinct from the soft rustling of their summer foliage—everything had a clear, ringing, cheering sound— and Flora went on by my side, the embodiment and concentration of all the lesser happiness, with a gay light tripping pace like a bird's, and all her heart and mind in sweet harmonious motion with her young graceful frame. I had always, myself, been the youngest in our little household—it was a new pleasure to me, and yet a strange, unusual sensation, to find myself thrown into the elder, graver, superior place, and this young creature with me, whom I could not help but treat like a child, a younger sister, rich in possession of youth, which I had never known.

At fifteen, I think, I must have felt old beside Flora, and now at one-and-twenty—no great age, heaven knows!—I was struck with wonder and admiration at the beautiful youthfulness which was in every motion and every word of this simple pretty girl. My marriage, and my unhappiness, had increased the natural distance between us. I did not envy Flora; but I had a sort of reflective, half melancholy delight in looking at her—such as old people have, I fancy—which was strange enough at my years.

"Do you not like walking, cousin?" said Flora—"I think the fresh air is so sweet—I do not care whether it is summer or winter. I think I should like always to be out of doors. I always could dance when I feel the wind on my face like this."

"But I am older than you, Flora," said I.

Flora laughed, her sweet, low, ringing laugh—"I am sure you are not so much older than me, as I am older than Gus," she said; "but mamma says when they are all at home, that I am the wildest boy among them. Do you like riding, cousin?"

"I never ride," said I.

"Never ride?—oh! I am fond of horses!" cried Flora, "and a gallop along a delightful long road like this— why, it's almost as good as flying. Will you try?—I am quite sure you are not timid, cousin. Oh, do let Mr. Southcote find a horse for you and try to-morrow. But, oh, I forgot!" she said with a sudden blush, which brought a still deeper color to my cheek, as she glanced at me, "perhaps it would not be right for you."

There was a pause of momentary embarrassment, and Flora greatly distressed I could perceive, thinking she had annoyed me. At that moment, some children from the school at Cottisbourne passed us, going home, and made their clumsy bows and curtseys, which I only acknowledged very slightly as we went on. Flora, for her part, cast a wistful glance after the little rustics. "Will you not speak to them, cousin?" she asked with a little surprise—"have they not been good children?—I should so like you to see our school at Ennerdale. I always go there every day, and I am very fond of them. They are tidy pleasant children; and I believe, though it looks so vain to say it," said Flora, breaking off with a laugh, "that they all like me."

"I should not fancy that was so very extraordinary either," said I; "other people do that, I suppose, besides the children at Ennerdale."

"Yes, everybody is very good to me," said Flora, with a quiet seriousness; "but then, you know, cousin, I have sometimes to punish the children as well as to praise them. How do you do here? I am sure you know a great deal better how to manage than I do. Do you forgive them when they seem sorry, or do you keep up looking displeased at them? Mamma says I spoil them, because I only look angry for a moment; but you know I never am really angry, I only pretend, because it's right."

"Indeed, Flora, I do not know. I never visit the school; I have had so little to do with children," I answered hastily.

Once more Flora cast an annoyed glance at me. This was more wonderful still than never riding—I began to grow quite a puzzler to Flora.

"Mamma has so many things to do, she seldom gets any time to help me," continued the girl, rallying a little after a pause. "Do you know, cousin, mamma is a perfect Lady Bountiful; she is always busy about something—and when people tell her of it, she only laughs and says it is no credit to her—for she does it all for pleasure. Don't you think it is very silly for people to praise ladies like mamma, or to find fault with them either? She is only kind to the village people because she likes to see them pleased and getting on well; and we all like company, cousin Hester, and we know the village people best and longest, and they are our nearest neighbors; and don't you think it is right to be kind to them? But the Miss Oldhams, at Stockport House, say we are undermining their independence, and condescending to the poor."

"I am sure your mamma must be quite right, Flora—but here comes some rain—I think we must go home," said I.

Flora held up her fresh pretty face to it, and caught the first drops upon her cheeks.

"It is rather too cold," she said, shaking them off with a pretty graceful motion, and beginning to run like a young fawn. "I like to be caught in a spring shower; but oh, cousin Hester, what shall I do if I get my dress wet, I haven't another one till they send; and then, I am running and forgetting you. Don't run—I don't care for being wet, if I may come down stairs in this frock after all. Oh! there is Mr. Southcote with a mantle for you, and an umbrella, and now I'll run all the way home."

She passed him with a laughing exclamation as he came up. She could not guess that this brief walk alone would be irksome to the young husband and wife, not four months married. I suffered him to wrap the mantle around me. I wondered almost to feel with what undiminished care he did it; and then we walked on side by side, in dreary silence, looking at the flying figure before us, with her mantle streaming behind her, and her fair curls escaping from the edge of her bonnet, as she turned round her laughing, glowing, pretty face to call and nod to us as she ran on. We did not speak to each other; we only looked at her, and plodded on slowly, side by side; and again the thought came upon me—and now, with a gush of pity for both of us, which overpowered me so that I could have thrown myself down there on the rainy roadside and cried. What a happy man he would have been had he brought Flora Ennerdale, instead of Hester Southcote, to Cottiswoode, as his bride.

I suppose the sight of her, and her innocence and happiness had moved him, too; for just when he left me, after our silent walk, he leaned over me for a moment, taking off my mantle, and whispering in a tremulous tone—"Dear Hester! I hope you will have pleasure in this good little girl's society." As he spoke, I caught his eye; there were tears in it, and a tender anxious look, as if he was very solicitous about me. I had great difficulty at the moment in restraining a great burst of tears. I was shaken almost beyond my own power of control. If I had waited another moment, I think I must have gone to him; clung to him, forgetting everything but one thing, and wept out all the tears in my heart. I fled to save reply. I am sure he heard me sob as I ran up stairs; but he did not know how I was almost overpowered—how a new love and tenderness, almost too much for me, was swelling like a sea in my heart. I fled to my own room, and shut myself in, and sank down upon the floor and cried. Alice had been speaking to him: I read it in his eye—but I—I could say nothing. I could not go, as his wife should have gone, to share with him the delight, and awe, and wonder, of this approaching future. I lay down upon the floor prostrate, with my face buried in my hands. I tried to restrain my sobs, but I could not. Long afterwards, I knew that he was watching, longing without the door, while I went through this moment of agony within—afraid to enter. If he had entered, perhaps—yet, why should I say perhaps? when I know it is quite as likely that my perverse heart would have started up in indignant anger at his intrusion, as that my pride and revenge would have given way before my better feelings; it was best as it was. I see all now; and how every event was related to its neighbor. I see I could not have done without the long probation, and the hard lessons which remained for me still.

When I recovered myself, it is strange how soon I hardened down once more into my former state. I had no longer any fear of meeting him, or of yielding to my own weakness. I rose and bathed my face, though I could not take away the signs of tears entirely from my eyes, and then I remembered how I had neglected Flora, and went to seek her. I found her sitting on a stool before the fire in her own room, spreading out her dress round her to dry, and looking up in the face of Alice who stood beside her. What a pretty picture the two would have made! Flora's wide dress spread out around her upon the soft varicolored hearthrug; her hair hanging half out of curl, and slightly wetted; her pretty hand held up before her to shield her cheek from the fire, so that you could trace every delicate little vein in the pink, half-transparent fingers, and her sweet face turned towards Alice, looking up at her; while Alice, on her part, looked down, with her kind motherly looks and fresh complexion; her snowy cap, kerchief, and apron, basking in the firelight. I was reluctant to break in upon them with my red eyes and heavy face.

"Oh, cousin! what will you think of me!" said Flora, starting as I entered. "I ought to have come to see how you were after being so hurried; but Alice began to talk to me, and we forgot. It is so comfortable here, and there is such a delightful easy-chair. Dear cousin Hester! sit down and stay with me here a little, till my dress is quite dry. You were not angry with me for running away?"

She had drawn her delightful easy-chair to the fire, and coaxed me into it before I was aware. Once more I felt an involuntary relaxation and warming of my heart. This feminine and youthful pleasure— this pleasant gossiping over the fire, so natural and pleasant and unconstrained, was almost quite new to me. I did not know, indeed, what female society was. I had lived in ignorance of a hundred innocent and sweet delights which were very health and existence to Flora. My heart melted to my own mother when I looked at my new friend. I began to understand how hard it would be for such a creature to live at all under the shadow of a silent, passionate, uncommunicative man like my father, even if he had not distrusted her.

"I am afraid I was crying," said Flora, wiping something from her cheek, "for Alice was speaking of your mamma; and, cousin, Alice too thinks I am like her. I am so very glad to be like her; but papa said you were a little too, cousin Hester."

"No, I do not think it," said I. "I am not like her, I am like the gloomy Southcotes, Flora. I have missed the sweeter blood of your side of the house."

"Dear cousin Hester! I think you are very melancholy," said Flora, looking up at me affectionately. "Pray don't speak of the gloomy Southcotes, you are only sad, you are not gloomy; and I do not wonder—I am sure if it were I," the tears gathered heavily into her sweet blue eyes. No—Flora, like myself, six months ago, knew nothing of the course of time and nature. Flora could understand any degree of mourning for such a grief as mine.

Alice had met my eye with an inquiring and slightly troubled glance, and now she went away—we were left alone. Flora and I—for some time we sat in silence together, my eyes bent upon the fire, and hers on me. This sweet simple girl seemed to fancy that she had a sort of charge of me—to amuse and cheer me. After a short interval, she spoke again.

"I saw some beautiful flowers down stairs, are they from your green-house, cousin? Some one told me there was such a beautiful conservatory at Cottiswoode; do your plants thrive? Do you spend much time there? Are you fond of flowers, cousin Hester?"

"I used to like them very well," I said; "but I do not think I have been in the conservatory here more than half-a-dozen times. Would you like to go now, Flora?"

"Oh, yes—so much! if it would not tire you," said Flora, starting up; "we have only such a little shabby one at Ennerdale. Mamma used to say the nursery was her conservatory; but I am very fond of flowers. Oh, what a beautiful place! Did you use to have this when you were at Cottiswoode before? I think I could live here if this were mine!"

And she flew about, light-hearted and light-footed, through the pretty conservatory, which indeed looked a very suitable place for her. As I followed her languidly, Flora found flower after flower which she did not know, and came darting back to me to know the names, reckoning upon my knowledge, as it seemed, with the most perfect confidence. I did not know—I did not know—I had never observed it before. Her young bright face grew blank as she received always the same answer; and by-and-by she restrained her natural exuberance, and came and walked beside me soberly, and ceased to assail me with questions. I was not much satisfied with the change, but I caught Flora's grave, anxious, wondering look at me, and knew that this and everything else was laid to the source of my sorrow, and that the sincerest pity and affectionate anxiety for me had risen in this young girl's simple heart.

She brightened again into great but subdued delight, when I said that some of the flowers she admired most, should be put aside to go to Ennerdale, and when I plucked a few pretty blossoms for her to put in her hair—they were too good for that, she said, and received them in her hands with a renewal of her first pleasure. Then we went into the drawing-room, and sat down once more, looking at each other. "Do you work much, cousin Hester?" asked Flora, timidly, "for, of course, not thinking that you would wish me to stay, I brought nothing with me to do. Will you let me have something? I am sure you think so much, that you like working; but for me, I am always with mamma, and when we are busy, she says I do get through so much talk. Let me work, please, cousin Hester, it is so pleasant for two people to work together."

"I have got no work, Flora," said I, faltering a little. It was true enough, yet I had some little bits of embroideries in progress, which I did not like to show to her, or to any one, but only worked at in solitude and retirement, in my own room up-stairs.

This time Flora sighed as she looked at me, and then looked round the room in quest of something else. "Do you play, cousin Hester? are you fond of music? I know great musicians have to practise such a great deal," she said, looking at me interrogatively, as if perhaps this might be a sufficient reason for my unaccountable disregard of village schools, and hot-house flowers and embroidery. For the moment, with her simple eye upon me, I felt almost ashamed for myself.

"No, Flora, I never touch the piano," said I.

Flora rose and drew softly towards me with humility and boldness. "Dear cousin Hester," said the innocent young girl, kneeling down upon a footstool beside me, and putting her pretty arm around my waist, "you are grieving very much and breaking your heart—oh! I am so very sorry for you! and I am not surprised indeed at all, for it is dreadful to think what such a loss must be; and no mamma to comfort you. But, cousin, dear, won't you try and take comfort? Mamma says it will do you harm to be so very sad—though I know," said Flora, leaning back upon my knee to look up into my face, and blushing all over her own as she spoke, "that something will make you very happy when the summer comes, for Alice told me so."

This simple and unpremeditated appeal overpowered me. I leaned down my cheek upon hers, and put my arms round her, and no longer tried to control myself. She was alarmed at this outbreak, which was almost as violent as the former one in my own room, and when she had soothed me a little, she ran upstairs and came down breathless with some eau-de-cologne and water in a little china basin, and bathed my forehead with a dainty little handkerchief, and put back my hair and smoothed it as if she had been my nurse, and I a child. Then she wanted me to lie down, and conducted me tenderly upstairs for that purpose—when, however, I only put my dress in order for dinner, and went down again.

My husband encouraged her happy talk while we sat at table, and she told him, "Cousin Hester had been a little nervous, and was so very sad, and could he tell her what to do, to amuse her cousin?" For my own part, I did not dare to meet his eye. Not only my own agitation, but the natural and happy life interposed between us in the person of this simple girl, made it a very great struggle for me to maintain my composure and self-control.

When we returned to the drawing-room, Flora drew her footstool to the fireside again, and sat down at my feet and told me of all her pleasant ways and life at home. Then she rose suddenly. "Would you like me to sing, cousin Hester? I cannot sing very well, you know; but only simple songs, and papa likes to hear me, at this time, before the lights come. Shall I sing? would it amuse you, cousin Hester?"

"Yes, Flora," I said; she asked no more, but went away in her simplicity to the piano. Then while the evening darkened I sat by the fire which burned red and warm, but sent only a fitful variable glow into the corners of the room, listening to the young voice, as sweet and clear as a bird's, singing song after song for my pleasure. They went to my heart, these simple words, these simple melodies, the pure affectionate sincerity of the singer, who never once thought of herself. I bowed myself down by the fire and hid my face in my hands, and in perfect silence, and strangely subdued and softened, wept quiet tears out of a full heart. She was still going on, when I became aware in an instant of another step beside me, and some one stooped over me, and kissed the hands which hid my face, and kissed my hair. My heart leaped with a violent start and throb; I looked up and raised myself on my chair. My husband had joined us! Flora perceived him, and I had but time to dry my wet eyes, when lights were shining in the cheerful room; and the music, and the charm, and this touch which once more had nearly startled me back into the natural woman, had vanished like the wintry twilight, and I was once more calm, grave, languid, the resentful, cloudy, reserved Mrs. Southcote, such a one as I had been ever since the first night when I was brought to Cottiswoode.

THE NINTH DAY

It was February, a mild, pensive spring day—for the spring was early that year—and Flora still remained with me. As Flora lived with us day by day, and saw the reserve and restraint between my husband and me, innocent and unsuspicious as her mind was, it was impossible, I think, that she should fail to discover something of how it was with us. But she was wise in her simplicity; she never made the very slightest allusion to anything she had discovered. Sometimes, indeed, when she thought me occupied, I saw a puzzled, painful shade come upon her sweet young face, as she looked from me to him—from him to me. I could guess that she was very unwilling to blame either of us, yet could not quite keep herself from wondering who was to blame; but the girl had a nice and delicate perception of right and wrong, which prevented her from hinting either suspicion or sympathy to me.

The house was changed while she remained in it. It was not easy to resist the sweet voice singing in those dull rooms; the light step bounding about involuntarily, the light, unburdened heart smiling out of the fair, affectionate face. I became very fond of my young relative. She stole into my confidence, and sat with me in my room, a more zealous worker at my little embroideries than even I was. I was constantly sending to Cambridge for things which I thought would please her; for Flora's sake I began to collect a little aviary; for Flora's sake I sent far and near for rare flowers. If Flora's own good taste had not withheld me, I would have loaded her with jewels, which I never thought of wearing myself. All my happier thoughts became connected with her. She had all the charm of a young favorite sister, combined with the freedom of a chosen friend. We walked together daily, and my health improved, almost in spite of myself, and she drove me about in a little pony-carriage, which had never been used till she came. I think Flora was very happy herself, in spite of her wondering doubt about our happiness; and she made a great difference in the atmosphere of Cottiswoode.

While we were pursuing our usual walk to-day, we met Miss Saville. She was going to Cottisbourne, and went on with us, talking of her schemes of "usefulness." I had given up the visitor's uniform myself after a second trial, and had contented myself with sending money by the hands of Alice to Mary and Granny, and several other pensioners, whom, however, in my languor and listlessness, I never cared to visit myself. But I was surprised to find how much more easily Flora suited herself to Miss Saville, and even to the Rector, than I could do. She was deep in all their plans and purposes—she was continually asking advice about her own schemes at home from one or other of them. Their peculiarity of manners seemed scarcely at all to strike Flora. She said they were very good people—very active people—she was quite sure they would do a great deal for the village. I assented, because I did not care to oppose her; but I— poor vain fool that I was!—thought their benevolences trifling, and unworthy of me, who could find no excuse here for heroic deeds or martyrdom.

Miss Saville looked strangely annoyed and anxious to-day. I saw her brow contract at every bend of the road, and she cast searching glances about her, as if looking for somebody, and was not, I think, very well pleased to have encountered us. Sometimes she started, and turned to look back, and asked, "Did you hear anything?" as though some one was calling her. If Flora had observed her perturbation, I have no doubt we should have left her, for Flora's delicate regard for others never failed, when it was exerted, to influence me; but Flora was not so quick of sight as I was, nor so learned in the signs of discomfort, and my mind was so indolent and languid, that I should have gone on quietly in any circumstances, and would not willingly undertake the exertion of changing my course for any cause. So we continued our way, and as we proceeded, Miss Saville told me that old Sally had changed her mind, and that she and a few others were quite ready to become inmates of her asylum now.

"But you—you surely would never condemn yourself to keep house with that miserable old woman!" said I, with a shudder. "You will think I am capricious for changing my mind, but indeed I did not think what a penalty it was. Pray don't think of it, Miss Saville. Let me give her something every week to support her at home."

"You have, indeed, changed your mind," said Miss Saville, with a smile which was rather grim. "But, indeed, I don't wonder at it. I never expected anything else, and it was only a fancy with you. You have enough of natural duties at home. But here is how the case stands with me, my dears. The Rector may marry—I hope he will—indeed, I may say that there is great hope of it. I have enough to keep myself, but I have nothing to do. I should like to be near William—I mean the Rector; but what would become of me if I was idle, do you think? I did once think of gathering a few clever girls about me, and setting up an establishment for church embroidery; but William—the Rector, I mean—very justly says, that I could not afford to give such expensive things away, and to receive payment for them—though only for the materials—would be unbecoming a lady; so I think it was quite a providential suggestion when I thought of taking care of the aged poor at Cottisbourne. Hark! did you hear any one call me, my dear?"

"No, Miss Saville. Are you looking for any one?" said Flora, perceiving our companion's anxiety for the first time.

"No—no!—no!" said Miss Saville, hurriedly, "I cannot say I am. A friend who is visiting us, strayed out by himself—that is all. He does not know the country. I am afraid he might miss his way," she continued, in a very quick, conscious, apologetic tone.

And suddenly there came to my recollection, the face I had once seen at the Rectory window. Could this man be under surveillance by them? Could he be crazy, or in disgrace? Could he have escaped? I became suddenly very curious—almost excited. I looked into the corners of the hedges, henceforward, as carefully as Miss Saville did herself.

And in my exaggerated disinterestedness, and desire for pain rather than pleasure, I was offended with her plain and simple statement of what her design was in setting up this asylum of hers. I said, not without a little sarcasm:

"If it is only for occupation, Miss Saville, I think Sally herself could give you enough to do."

"Who is old Sally?" asked Flora, with a wondering glance at me.

"A wretched, ghastly, miserable old woman," said, I; "one who would disgust even you, with all your meekness, Flora."

"Mamma says we should never be disgusted with any one," said Flora, in an under-tone—in which, shy as it was, my quick ear could not fail to detect a slight mixture of disapprobation.

"But this is a selfish, discontented, unhappy creature, who looks as if she could curse every one happier than herself," said I.

"You give a hard judgment, Mrs. Southcote," said Miss Saville, roused even to a certain dignity. "Did you ever consider what she has to make her discontented—great age, weakness, disease, and poverty? Do even such as you, with youth, and wealth, and everything that heart can desire, make the best always of the good things God gives them? I am sure you should do so, before you give her such names as wretched and selfish. Look what a difference between old Sally and you—and she's had no education, poor old creature! to teach her to endure her evil things patiently. But I've seen thankless young folks take blessings as if they were curses—I have indeed."

"Oh! here we are, close upon the school," cried Flora, breathlessly eager to prevent a breach between us. "Are you able to be troubled, dear cousin Hester? Please do let us go in."

I was not offended. I am not sure that this assault upon me was disagreeable to me at all. At the moment, it rather increased my respect for Miss Saville, and gave her importance in my eyes; though I confess, when I thought of it after, I did not derive a great deal of satisfaction from comparing myself, my temper, and my hardships, with those of old Sally.

Without any more words we entered the school—the half of it appropriated to girls and infants. As the startled children stopped in their classes, or got up from their seats, where they were boring and bungling over their soiled pieces of sewing, and made their clumsy curtseys, I took a seat which Flora brought me, and she began to dance about among them, overlooking their work, and inquiring about their lessons, and making awkward smiles and giggles among the little rustics, every one of whom hung her head, turning her crown instead of her face to Flora as the young lady approached. Dull, listless, separate, I sat and looked on, while Miss Saville talked to the schoolmistress, and singled out some of the elder girls for admonition or encouragement, and Flora ran about from form to form. Miss Saville represented the constituted authorities. Flora—sweet, pretty Flora!—was only herself, young, happy, affectionate—a spring of delight to everybody. I cannot tell what any one thought of me. After a little interval, I became conscious of myself, with a dull pain. I never was like Flora; yet I once was Hester Southcote—once I dressed magnificent dolls for Alice's little niece, and enjoyed such innocent occupation, and had, among the very few who knew me, my own share of popularity—but what was I now?

"Cousin Hester!" said Flora, coming up to me, and bending down to whisper in my ear, "I should like to give them prizes, and have a little feast here—may I? they are always happy, and such a thing pleases everybody. May I tell Miss Saville and the teacher? Please do say yes—cousin Hester?"

"Surely, Flora, if you will like it," said I.

So Flora ran to intimate her purpose—and there was a great flutter, and stir, and brightening among the little faces. Then she chose to think, or at least to say, that I would like to hear them sing—and the children rose with blushing pleasure, and sang a loud shrill hymn at the top of their voices, led by the schoolmistress, while Flora shook her head, and smiled, and frowned, and nodded, keeping time, which the singers were nobly indifferent to. She did not like it the less, because it was sung badly—she laughed and clapped her hands when a few stray voices fell behind the others and prolonged the strain, to the discomfiture of the schoolmistress. If there was not much melody, there was enough fun in the performance, and enough goodwill and satisfaction on the part of the performers to please Flora—and she concluded by begging a half-holiday for them, after she had first come and asked my permission, like a dutiful girl as she was. Though Flora was so ready to take care of me, she never forgot that, for the moment, I represented mamma, and was an authority over her; for to be dutiful and obedient was in the very nature of this sweet simple-hearted girl.

When we left the school we went with Miss Saville, at her especial desire, to look at two empty cottages, which she thought might be made into a house for her. I stood and listened with no great edification as she explained how doors could be opened in the wall between them, and the homely arrangements of the interior altered to suit her. A bit of waste ground behind, she proposed to enclose for a yard. "The friends of the old people will willingly give me a day's labor now and then, and the gardener at the Rectory will see everything kept in order," she said. "Here, Mrs. Southcote, I propose building a sitting-room and bed-chamber for myself at my own expense, which will leave abundant accommodation for my patients. May I expect you now and then to see how we are getting on? I don't expect anything more. No! my dear; I knew you would change your mind—make no apologies—I felt sure of it all along."

I was not much flattered by thinking that Miss Saville was quite sure of it all along—but I thought it most prudent to say nothing on this now. Flora was extremely interested in all the arrangements. "I will come whenever I am at Cottiswoode, Miss Saville," she said, eagerly; "for, of course, my cousin is not strong, and it would be quite wrong for her to fatigue herself. I shall like so much to come. May we not go and see old Sally, now, cousin Hester! and the other old people? They are such famous story-tellers. I like old people for that; but, oh dear, how selfish I am! You are looking quite pale and tired out. Will you lean upon me, cousin? or may I run and tell them to get out the pony carriage? I am sure you are hardly able to walk home."

But I was able, in spite of Flora's fears. Miss Saville returned with us, looking jealously about her, and seeming to have a certain terror of us, and of encountering her strayed friend. We stopped at the Rectory gate to take leave of her, but she did not seem inclined to leave us then. "I am at leisure this morning—I will walk on with you;" but I could see very well that it was not any particular degree of leisure, but something much more important which made her accompany us. She grew more and more agitated as we approached Cottiswoode—still no one was in sight; but I thought I had caught a glimpse of the Rector himself, telegraphing at a window as we passed, shaking his head and saying "no," and it was not possible to avoid perceiving Miss Saville's anxiety, and her anxious looks around her. At last, as Flora clambered over a low stone fence in search of a plant, which she thought she recognised among the grass, Miss Saville addressed herself to me.

"I think it best to mention it, Mrs. Southcote, connected as our families are," she said in an agitated tone, "though being an only child, you can scarcely know what family anxieties are, we have a brother with us—I am sure you have a right to be surprised—but really his state of mind is such that we could not introduce him into society. He has been a gay man in his day—and he has—oh! such a grief, my dear, to William and me!—fallen into ways—well, that we can't approve of. He was bred an attorney—a lawyer, and was in very good practice till he got into misfortune. I am sorry to say poor Richard has not been able to bear misfortune, and he came down here for his health; and we have tried to keep him very quiet, the only thing to do him good—but this morning, you see, he has stolen out, and we can't tell where he is gone. My dear, don't look alarmed—he is not insane. Dear me! how could I imply such a thing—far different from that—he is very clever—but, you know, we don't want him to trouble Mr. Southcote—or—or any one—and when he takes anything into his head he is very firm, and will not be persuaded out of it. He has taken a violent fancy since ever he came of speaking to Mr. Southcote or yourself—and we have done all we could to prevent him—for you know, we don't like to show our family troubles any more than other people—especially as William is a clergyman; but I must tell you— hush! here is the young lady coming back—and if you meet my poor brother, Mrs. Southcote, do not be afraid."

Miss Saville ended this very long speech, out of breath with hurry and agitation, as Flora reappeared. If he was not a madman, why should I be afraid of him? and madman or not, what could Saville want with me? On my husband, of course, he had the claim of gratitude, and I could not resist my impulse to mention that.

"I think I saw him over at the Rectory window," I said quietly, and in a tone which must have jarred dreadfully on Miss Saville's excited ears. "Was not he the man who brought Mr. Southcote first to Cottiswoode? I recollect him; I trust my husband has not forgotten the claims his friend has upon him."

I had scarcely spoken the words, when I was bitterly ashamed of them; and I felt my face burn under my companion's eye. She was startled by my tone, and she had evidently forgotten, if, indeed, she ever clearly knew, that my husband's possession of Cottiswoode had been any injury to me, who now shared it with him. When she answered, she spoke in a tone of pique—she saw a certain disrespect, but she did not see the bitterness in my tone.

"He is not what he once was, Mrs. Southcote," said Miss Saville; "but I think poor dear Richard does deserve something better than to be spoken of as 'the man.' I am not proud, but I know Edgar Southcote has reason to reckon a friend in Richard Saville. It was he who brought the poor boy over from Jamaica, when he had not a friend in the world to care for him—and he got him his rights. I am sorry for what has happened to my brother, and grieved for him; and I was foolish to think I might get sympathy from a stranger—but I'm not ashamed of Richard, Mrs. Southcote, and never will be."

"I beg your pardon, Miss Saville," said I—for the moment I felt very much ashamed of myself.

Flora had not succeeded, and was tired with her scramble, and momentarily silenced by the fatigue; while neither Miss Saville nor I had much to say to her, or to each other. We walked on quietly, till we came to the little private gate which entered directly into the grounds surrounding Cottiswoode; for this favorite lane which led to the village, was much nearer to the house itself than to the great gate at the end of the avenue. When we arrived there, I invited Miss Saville to come in, but she would not; though, as we passed through the garden ourselves, I could see that she still stood by the little wicket watching us anxiously—no doubt, to see if we encountered her brother even here. I was no less on the watch myself, but we saw no one till we had entered the hall. Flora, as usual, tripped on before me. I followed after, slow and languidly; she was already in the drawing-room, when I had scarcely crossed the threshold, and when the wide hall-door, still held fully open, admitted the entire flood of noon-day light into the hall. At that moment, the library door was opened suddenly, and the very man I had been looking for stood before me. I could see that he was heated and flushed, as if with some recent argument; and his stealthy, sidelong, cunning look, which I could remember, had given way to an air of coarse dissipation; that state in which everything is surrendered, and when even appearance and dress and personal neatness are lost in the universal bankruptcy. Behind him, within the library, appeared my husband, pale, haughty; holding the door in his hand, and dismissing his visitor with a formal solemnity, such as I had never seen in him before. When Saville perceived me, he stood still for a moment, and made me a swaggering bow, and then advanced a step as though to address me. I bowed slightly to him, and hastened my steps to get out of his way. "Stay an instant, madam—stay an instant," he said, with a little excitement, while my husband still remained behind, looking on. I only hurried in the more quickly. "Very well," he said, with a loud exclamation—"surely, there is no reason, if you will not hear what concerns you, that I should trouble myself about you."

I was strangely disturbed when, at last, I got into the quiet shelter of the drawing-room. I took refuge upon a sofa, and lay down there to recover my breath. The sight of this man, and the sound of his voice, which I almost thought I could remember in the over-excitement of my feelings, overpowered me with recollections. I remembered how we were when he came—how I was disgusted with the familiarity of his first address to me—how my father, for the moment, resisted Edgar Southcote's claims; and how I endeavored to convince him that they were true. In this room, where we had conversed together— looking at the very portrait to which I had pointed, I scarcely could persuade myself that all was real, and that this was not a dream.

Flora took my bonnet from me, and loosed my mantle, and bade me be still and rest. "I am always so thoughtless. I am sure we ought not to have walked so far, cousin Hester," said the penitent Flora. "I will come down immediately, and read to you, shall I? you ought to have a good rest." But when Flora left me, I rose from the sofa to walk about the room. When I am disturbed in mind I cannot be still, unless, indeed, I am very greatly disturbed, when I can do anything.

I had only been a few moments alone, when my husband came to me. I retired to my usual seat immediately, and he came to my side. He still looked as I had seen him at the door of his library—almost like my father for a time—resolute, pale, stately, a man of invincible determination, on whom words would be wasted, and whose mind no persuasions could change. A little indignation and a little scorn united in his look. I cannot describe how very different from his usual appearance he was to-day.

"I have been having a visitor, Hester," he said. "I fancied you recognised him, and I think it right you should know what he had to say. He is—"

"Pray, do not tell me," said I hurriedly; "I know who he is—but, indeed, I do not desire to hear his name, or anything he may have had to say."

"You know who he is—did you know he was here, Hester?" said my husband, looking at me.

"Yes—I saw and recognised him at a window of the rectory some time since," I said, "and Miss Saville has been telling me of him to-day—of course, you did not suppose that I had forgotten his name, or failed to suspect that the rector and his sister were relations of the man who brought you to Cottiswoode."

"I have very few ways of knowing what you suspect, Hester," he said, with some sadness, "but this you must permit me to tell you without delay—he thinks he has found—"

"Will you do me one kindness?" I asked. "Flora is coming, and I do not wish to hear anything he said. I can have nothing to do with it one way or another, and it is irksome and painful to me. Indeed, I am tired and not well, and might be excused on that score. Here is my young cousin. I would rather you would not tell me."

He drew back with a slight haughty bow, and retired from me. "As you will!" he said; and when Flora entered, which she did instantly, he left the room without another word.

What a perverse miserable creature I was! Though I had refused to hear him when he wished to speak to me, I was wretched when he was gone. When Flora came to me book in hand to read, I permitted her, that I might have a little uninterrupted leisure; and while she, poor girl, labored thus for my entertainment, my mind was wandering after my husband, and what he would have said—what could it be? Whatever it was, he was displeased at it, and in spite of the wide and constant difference between us, I could not forgive myself for rejecting his confidence—though, indeed, had he returned at that moment, I cannot answer for myself that I would not have done it again.

I could not bring my attention to Flora's book; she appealed to me for admiration and sympathy at her own favorite passages; but the blank look with which I met her appeal, pained, though it did not offend, the affectionate girl. She excused me to herself as she always did, and quietly put the book away, pretending she saw the gardener going to the conservatory, and wanted to beg a flower from him. Thus I was once more left alone with my unreasonable and vexing thoughts. I might have heard what he had to say, my conscience whispered me, and I recalled the haughty withdrawal from me which marked his displeasure, with a pang which I wondered at. It was all Saville's fault—Saville! this miserable man, who brought disgrace and unhappiness home to his brother and sister. I felt almost a positive hatred in my mind as I recalled him.

Feeling heated with my recent excitement, and very nervous and unhappy, I drew the little hood of my mantle over my head, and went out into the grounds before the house to subdue myself a little. The day was still at its height, sunny and warm, almost like summer, and every twig of all the trees and hedges was bursting with the young life of spring. Rich golden and purple crocuses spotted the dark soil in all the flower borders; and the pale little pensive snowdrop, instead of looking precocious as it usually does, looked late, feeble, and all unlike the sunshine. Waving their numberless boughs far up across the blue depths of the sky, I thought I could see the buds bursting on the elm-trees, and life was rising and swelling in everything like a great tide. I was refreshed by the cool breeze on my brow, and calmed with the sounds and breath of the fresh air out of doors. I cannot tell what induced me to turn my steps to the little wicket-gate, at which this morning we had left Miss Saville, and which opened on the lane leading to the rectory. I went to it, and leaned my arm upon it, looking down the road. I had not been there a minute when I heard a murmur of voices—"Don't, Richard, pray, don't!—I won't have you frighten the poor child," remonstrated the voice of Miss Saville. "It's for her good," answered another voice, and before I could leave my place, Saville had sprung across the low fence into the lane, and was close beside me.

For the first moment I did not move, but stood looking full at him with a gaze which subdued the man, though I cannot tell how. "Young lady! let me have half an hour's conversation," he said, in a humble tone; "I know a great deal which you would be very glad to know. Come, don't be proud, I know you're not over pleased to be only Queen Consort—if you'll be ruled by me"—

"I will not be ruled by you—be so good as to leave me," said I, drawing back—"I will hear nothing you have got to say—not a word."

"If you will not hear me, you will repent it," said the man. "I warrant Edgar has not told you a word—no, trust him for that."

At this moment, I do not deny that my curiosity was very greatly roused, but strange emotions were roused with it; I could not bear to hear my husband's name in this fellow's lips.

"If my husband did not tell me, it was because I would not hear him," said I, "and I will not hear you. I do not care what you have got to say. Miss Saville, I hope, will not think I mean any unkindness to her—but I have not a word to say to you."

And I hastened away into the house, up-stairs to my own room. How my heart throbbed! how wearied, and bewildered, and sick at heart I felt! What could he mean? What could it be? Out of the temporary quietude I had fallen into, I was raised again into an eager consuming excitement, and I think for the first time that day, in the preoccupation and strain of my own mind, I wished Flora Ennerdale at home; for her sweet natural life, so great a contrast to mine at all times, was almost unendurable now.

THE TENTH DAY

Those lingering, uneventful days, though they looked so long and tedious as they passed, how they seemed to have flown when I look back upon their silent progress—for it was now April, the trees were rich with young spring leaves; the sky and the air were as bright as summer; the flowers were waking everywhere, peeping among the herbage on the road-side, looking out from the tufts of meadow grass, filling the breeze with a whisper of primroses and violets, and all the nameless favorites of spring. But spring had not come to Cottiswoode—we were as we had been since my first coming here; only that the estrangement between us daily became wider, more sullen and hopeless. We were as little as possible together; yet if his thoughts were as full of me as mine were of him, it mattered little that we sat in different rooms, and pursued alone our separate occupations. The consuming and silent excitement of this life of ours, when, though I never addressed him voluntarily, I watched for his coming and going, and anxiously expected, and sought a hidden meaning in every word he said, I cannot describe to any one—it was terrible. I could fancy that a demoniac in the old times must have felt something as I did—I was possessed—I had, in reality, no will of my own, but was overborne by a succession of frantic impulses, which must have looked like a deliberate system to a looker-on. I can neither understand nor explain the rules of my conduct—or rather, it had no rules. The wild suggestion of the moment, and no better principle, was the rule which guided me.

Flora had just left us after a second visit; she had been one day gone, and I felt her absence greatly. Even Alice did not make up to me now for this younger companion; for Alice was dull, and disturbed, and sad. I felt her every look a reproach to me, and I did not seek her to be with me as I had once done. I lay down on my sofa doing nothing; cogitating vain impressions of injury and wrong; going over imaginary conversations with my husband—turning my face away from the sweet daylight, and all the joyous life out of doors. As I rested thus, I heard my husband's step approaching, and raised myself hurriedly; my heart began to beat, and the color came back to my cheek—why was he coming here now?

He came in—he advanced to my side—he stood before me! I turned over a book nervously—glanced once at him—tried to command my voice to speak, but could not. Then he sat down beside me on my sofa. I drew away from him as far as I could, and waited for what he had to say.

"Hester," he said, "this has lasted long enough. If we are to preserve our senses—if one of us at least— some period must be put to this torture. Are you satisfied yet with the penance you have exacted? Or how much more do you wish me to suffer? For I declare to you, I have almost passed the bounds of endurance—you will make me mad!"

"I wish you to suffer nothing," said I. "I will keep my room; I will keep out of your sight, if it makes you mad to see me. I will go away, or else confine myself to my own apartments; I exact nothing; I only desire you to leave me at peace."

"You will keep out of my sight if I will leave you at peace? That is a sweet compact, is it not?" he said, with vehemence and bitterness, and I could see that, at last, his patience had quite given way. "What do you mean, Hester? Have you any recollection how it is that we are related to each other—do you know what is the bond between us?"

"Yes! we are in slavery," I said; "we belong to each other—we are united for ever. It is no use deceiving ourselves; we never can be any better—that is all I know."

"And why can we never be any better?" he said, softening and growing gentle in his tone. "Unhappy and disturbed as I am, my fears do not go the length of that. I will not do you the injustice to suppose, that you will keep this delusion all your life. If you will retain it now, I appeal to your better judgment afterwards. But why should you retain it now, Hester? You are no happier for your revenge—I am no better for my punishment. It is now a long time since the offence was committed; look at it again, and see if it is equal to the penalty. Tell me, Hester, what have I done?"

"You have deceived me," I said.

"I told you nothing untrue of myself," he said, quietly. "I did not tell you all the truth. See how you have changed me already—a man cannot be at the bar so long without trying to justify himself. At first I was a penitent offender—but nothing but mercy can make repentance, Hester, and you have shown no mercy to me. What have I done to deserve all that you have inflicted upon me?"

"You have deceived me," I repeated sullenly.

He started up and made a few rapid strides through the room as if going away—but then he returned again. His temper, his self-command, his patience, could not bear any more—I saw that I had fairly roused him to strive with me.

"Is this all you have to say, Hester?" he asked almost sternly. "Am I to hear this and only this rung in my ears continually—have you nothing but my first offence to urge against me—is this all?"

"Yes," I said, "it is all, and I have nothing more to say."

He could not trust himself to speak, but went away from me again, and rapidly returned once more. "Grant it so," he said, with a quick and breathless voice, "if I have deceived you, I have been myself deceived—we are on equal terms."

I could not understand what he meant—when it dawned upon me, I rose slowly, and we stood, confronting each other, looking into each other's eyes. "Have I deceived you?" I asked—it cost me an effort to preserve my calmness, but I did it.

"Yes," he said vehemently, "you were a sweet and tender woman when you left your father's house. I thought you one of those whose very presence makes a home—your high spirit, your rapid mind, only gave a noble charm to your generous loving heart—I thought so, Hester—I delighted in believing it. I thought the key of my joy in this world was given to me when they put your hand in mine. Look at me now—I am bankrupt, shipwrecked—from the first hour I brought you home, happiness was ended for me. This house is wretched—the very sunshine and daylight that God has made are no longer blessings to me. My life is a burden. My duties are intolerable. My hopes have departed one by one. I tell you that more bitterly, more grievously than you have been deceived, have you deceived me."

I was stung and wounded to the heart. A dreadful passion took possession of me. I could have killed myself as I stood, that he might have seen me do it, and repented when it was too late. Even then, when these bitter words were said, I believe he repented.

"Why did you seek me then?" I cried passionately. "Why did you come out of your way to make us both so wretched? I am not a sweet or a tender woman. I never was so. I never pretended to be. Why did you not seek Flora Ennerdale? She was fit for you. She might have made you happy. Why did you not leave me in my solitude? I never came to seek you."

"You insult me," he said, turning away with renewed anger. I think he said something else. I did not hear it. I made no answer. I sat down to wait till he was gone. I cannot even tell how long it was till he went away, but when he did, I rose, and, guiding myself by my hands, went slowly up-stairs. I know my step was quite firm, but I held by the banisters and took pains to guide myself, for there was a darkness over my eyes, and I could not see plainly where I went. It seemed a long time before I could reach my own room, and when I entered it, Alice started, and came towards me with an exclamation of fright. This restored me a little to myself. I said I was faint—told her to bring me some wine, and lay down upon the couch till she returned. "Are you ill, my darling?" said Alice, bending over me with a pale face, as she gave me the wine. "No, no!" I said, "only faint—I must not be ill, for we have a good deal to do. I should like to take a drive—will you order the carriage to be ready in an hour, and then, Alice, come back to me."

I lay quite still, recovering myself till she returned. I felt that to command and compose myself sufficiently to be able for all I wanted to do, required all my powers. Exerting all the resolution I had, I lay upon the couch, refusing to think, resting with a determined purpose and resolution to rest, such as seemed very strange when I thought of it afterwards—but I thought to do it then—slowly my eyes cleared, the beating of my heart subsided. I cannot tell what crisis I might have come to, had I given way to the dreadful agitation which had possession of me for a time; but as I lay here, silently looking round upon the familiar room, I felt both mind and body obeying me, and rejoiced to find that I was mistress of myself, as I had not been for many a day.

When Alice returned, I rose. I foresaw Alice's remonstrances, her tears and entreaties, and I had intentionally left very little room for them by ordering the carriage so soon. When she came in, I sat up, refreshed and strong. I could not try to "prepare" her for it, I said abruptly, "Alice, I am going away."

"Where, Miss Hester?" said Alice.

"I cannot tell where," I said; "all that I know is, that I must go away from Cottiswoode. Alice, come near me—I will not constrain you. I will not be offended if you stay; but you must tell me at once what you will do, for I have very little time."

Alice looked with great and pathetic earnestness in my face, but she did not cry or entreat me against it, as I feared she would do.

"Has it come to this?—are you sure it has come to this?" she asked, anxiously clasping her hands and gazing at me. "Oh! Miss Hester, consider what it is—consider how you are—and tell me solemnly has it come to this?"

"Yes, Alice," I said, "we cannot remain any longer under the same roof—it would kill us both. He says he is wretched, and that I have deceived him. I did not try to deceive him. I did not wish to make him wretched, Alice!" I cried with a sob which I could not restrain, "but now I must go away."

"Oh! Miss Hester, see him once more first," pleaded Alice. I suppose she had been struck with sudden hope from my tone.

"No," I said, "it is all over. I am very glad it is all over. Put the things together, Alice—they are all in that drawer, and take what I will need—nothing more than what I will need, and what you require yourself, and we will go away together. We have no one now but each other, Alice. You will go with me. You will not desert me. I have not a friend but you."

"God help us! and clear all this trouble away in His own time!" said Alice solemnly, "but it will be a strange day when I desert you, my darling. Brighter times will come for you, dear—happiness will come yet, Miss Hester: but come joy or sorrow, I will never leave you, till God takes me away."

She kissed my cheek silently as I stooped to her—and then she began her sorrowful packing. I could see the tears dropping on the things as she put them in; but she did not make a complaint or a remonstrance. She did not even seem startled. I was surprised that she should acquiesce so easily. While I helped her to gather everything together, I said, "Alice, you are not surprised—are you content that this is best?"

"I'm content that nothing can be worse, Miss Hester," she said sorrowfully. "God will show what's for the best in his time, but to aggravate and torment each other as you two are doing is not to be called good any way; and maybe if you were far off, your hearts would yearn to one another. I'm waiting for the light out of the darkness, though I see none now."

And she went on patiently with her work, in a resigned and melancholy fashion, which subdued me strangely. I had put on my own bonnet and cloak, and sat waiting ready to go away. The house was unusually quiet, yet every far-off sound roused me to renewed excitement. Would he do anything to prevent me going? should we have any further personal encounter? I sat shivering, wrapped in the cloak, which at any other moment would have overpowered me with its great warmth, listening eagerly to hear something. At length, my heart leaped when I caught the roll of the carriage wheels coming to the door. Now everything was ready for our going away. Alice had locked the trunk, which carried all our necessary things, and stood before me, dressed for her journey, waiting my pleasure. Now, for the first time, I began to tremble and give way.

"Will you not write a note, Miss Hester—a few words to tell him you are gone? Do not leave him in such dreadful suspense!" said the melancholy voice of Alice.

"Go down and see if he is in the library," said I under my breath, and trembling painfully. I did not want to speak to him, but my heart yearned to see him, to look at him once again. I sat with quivering lips and a colorless face, waiting till she came back again. I could see myself in the mirror; how I trembled, and what a ghastly look I had. I thought she would never come again, as I sat there waiting for her, hearing nothing but my own quick, short breathing, and the rustle of my dress. At last, Alice returned. He was not in the house. The Rector had called about a quarter of an hour ago, and Mr. Southcote had gone out with him. "That is very well, Alice, very fortunate," I said, with my blanched dry lips; but it almost was the last stroke—the utmost blow, and I was stunned with the great momentary anguish which it woke in my heart.

Alice drew a table to my side, and put my blotting-book before me. I took my pen in my hand almost unconsciously, and began to write. While I was thus occupied, she had the trunk carried down stairs, thinking I did not perceive her. But even while I tried to write, my eye mechanically followed her movements. What should I say to him? how I was losing time!

At last I completed the note, and carried it in my hand down stairs. This was what I said:—

"I do not ask you to pardon me for going away, because it is all I can do to relieve you now. If I have deceived you, as you have deceived me, then we are equals, and have nothing to say to each other in reproach or indignation. I am content that it should be so—and as we cannot restore the delusion—you to my eyes, or I to yours, it is best that we should part. I will not continue to make you wretched; and the only one thing which is in my power, to relieve us both, I will do. I cannot tell where I am going—to some quiet place where I may find shelter and rest, till I can die. I wish you only good, and no evil; and I wish you this blessing first of all—to be relieved of me.

"H. S."

I went down stairs with it softly, with a noiseless step, as if I were a thief, and feared detection; and it was only when I saw Amy and another servant lingering with scared faces in the hall, as if they suspected something about to happen, that I recovered myself. They went away when they saw me coming down firmly, in my usual dress, and with, I suppose, something like my usual looks; and when I saw that they were gone, and that Alice waited for me at the door, I went softly into the library for a moment. He was constantly now in the room where my father had spent so many years—but I did not think of my father, when I stole tremulously into it, and placed myself in his seat, and bowed my head upon the desk at which he had been writing. Who was I thinking of?—not of the man who had deceived me, and whom I had deceived—I could not tell. I was conscious of nothing but of the flood of tender affection—of longing—of forlorn and hopeless desolateness which came over me. I cried under my breath, a name which had not passed my lips for months; the name of my bridegroom—my betrothed. I laid my cheek close down upon his desk; I prayed in my heart, "God bless him!" and then I rose, pallid and exhausted, to leave his house for ever. Yes, there was the bright mocking daylight, the walnut rustling at the great window; the horses pawing impatiently at the door. I left my letter where my cheek had rested a moment since, and went steadily away.

Alice helped me, and came beside me; once more I saw the face of Amy at the door, and of the housekeeper at the window above, looking out with wonder and dismay; and then we drove through the grand old avenue of elms, and the tender fresh spring foliage, which, for many a year, had brought to these old hoary giants a renewal of their youth. I now looked back; I threw myself into my corner, and drew my veil over my face. Now, at last, I could surely rest. We had only driven about half a mile past the Rectory and Cottisbourne, when Alice suddenly touched my hand and pointed out. I raised myself to look: he was standing in the road, speaking to a farmer, or rather listening; and I saw his look quicken into sudden wonder and curiosity when we dashed past. He did not see me, for the windows were closed, and my veil down; but I saw him as I had wished; the excitement of the morning partially remained on his face, but he was listening patiently to what the man had to say to him, and did not neglect anything, as I could see, by a strange intuition, because he had been so strongly moved and agitated. It was strange to notice what a difference there was between him and me. These passionate emotions of mine ruled and swayed me. He—did he feel less acutely than I did? I could not persuade myself so; but he did his endeavor, at least, to rule and restrain his own heart.

Yes! I should have been strongest at this moment—I never before had taken so decided a step; I had burst the natural bonds asunder. I had rent the veil of domestic privacy, and told all the world of the skeleton in our house. I ought to have been more resolute now than at any previous time of all my life. But I was not. Instead of reposing on what I was doing, the wildest conflict arose within me. I began to doubt the justice of everything I had ever done. I began to see myself in darker colors than I had ever been represented—a capricious, irritable, revengeful trifler—a fool!—a fool!—I stood aside like a terrified child who has set in motion some frightful machinery. I remembered what Mr. Osborne said—it was easy to make misery; but who should heal it when it was made? and while I bade Alice tell them to drive faster, my heart sank within me with a desperate hopelessness. I was going away—going away—I would never see him again.

It seemed a very short time to me when we arrived at the railway. As it happened, a train was to start immediately, and within a few minutes more we were rushing along this mighty highway, hurrying to the universal centre—going to London. Alice had never travelled in her primitive life. Grieved and full of anxiety as she was for me, Alice was too natural a woman not to show a faint glimmer of expectation when I spoke of London; and while she folded my mantle round me, and wrapped a shawl about my feet, she looked out at the strange road-side stations and unfamiliar country through which we dashed, with an excited yet half dizzy curiosity; for Alice was disposed to think we were rushing upon some catastrophe at this frightful, headlong speed. For me, I doubled my veil over my face, and withdrew into the corner, and was thankful for the kindly shade of night, when it fell at last. I could not bear to recall my last journey hither, if I could in reality recall it—if I could go back and change the past; but, no—I would not have done that even now.

When we arrived, Alice was helpless—the bustle, the speed, the lights and noise of the great terminus we had come to, made her sick and giddy. She could only stand helplessly among the crowd, pushed about by the active people round her, looking to me for directions—which, weak and overcome as I was, I was not only able to give, and scarcely less a novice than she was in the art of taking care of myself; however, we managed to extricate ourselves at last, and drove away, a long fatiguing course, to the hotel where I had been with my husband immediately after our marriage. I remembered its name. It was scarcely less strange to me than to Alice, to pass through those continuous never-ending streets, sparkling with light and full of noise, and what seemed tumult to us. I grasped her hand instinctively, and she clung to me. We were both helpless women alone in the midst of this busy crowd, no one protecting, no—no one knowing where we went, I began to have a glimpse of what was before me now, as well as of what was behind—and self-protection and self-support do not show in their proper heroic colors, when you have to exercise them first upon a journey, and when your frame is weakened and your mind disturbed. I felt to myself something like a suicide. I had succeeded. I had put a barrier between my former and my future life. I had new habits to learn; new faculties to cultivate. I was no longer to be taken care of—everything was new.

When we arrived and rested, at last, in a comfortable room of the inn, I did not go to rest as Alice bade me; but sat down to write to my agent in Cambridge, who managed the little property which my father had left me. I paused and hesitated a moment, whether I should not also write to Mr. Osborne, to explain to him what I had done. But I decided upon leaving that to my husband. My other letter was half written, and I had come to an abrupt pause, remembering that I had fixed upon no place to go to, and could not yet tell the agent where he was to send my remittances, when Alice, who had been standing by the window within the curtains, looking with wonder, admiration, and dismay upon the lighted street without, and its many passengers, suddenly turned round to me with the same question.

"Miss Hester, are we to stay here?"

"No, surely not," I said, "but indeed I do not know where to go to," and I paused to recollect plans I had read about, for I had seen nothing out of our own country. I thought of the lakes, and the beautiful North country for a moment; but though I had turned my back upon it for ever, I could not bear the idea of going far away from home. The railway guide, the renowned and mysterious Bradshaw, lay on the table near my hand; I took it up and began to look over it. So vacant and destitute were we of attractions and likings, after we left our own lawful dwelling-place, that the only way of selecting a new home which occurred to me, was to look over their bald list of names till some one should strike my wandering fancy—it was a dreary method of choice.

I put aside my letter, half written. I roamed over these dull lists; and both of us, solitary women as we were, shrunk at the sounds of steps and voices in the great passages without, and drew close to each other to preserve some resemblance of security and privacy, in this public place where we almost fancied we might be exposed to intrusion any moment. At last, I found a name which caught my eye, in Essex, not very far from London, in consequence not very far from Cambridgeshire—I decided that we should go there to-morrow, and try to find a house, and so, very dreary, very solitary—startled and frightened by the strange sounds in the great strange house—shutting ourselves into our bed-chamber, feeling ourselves so desolate, so unprotected, among strangers, we went to our rest.

BOOK III

THE FIRST DAY

It was a peaceful solitary village; a cluster of houses gathered round one simple church, the tower of which was the central point in the quiet landscape. Behind it at some distance was a low hill—a very low hill—not much more than a mound, but with some dark Scotch firs upon it, which gave solidity to the thick plantation of lighter trees, not yet fully clothed. Behind the hill ran a railway, upon which a train appeared, which we watched, flaunting its white plume into the air, as it shrieked and rushed into the shadow. The village itself was quite upon the water's edge, standing close by the shore of a blue quiet bay, looking over to the trees and green fields on the other side of the broad Thames. The place was a little below Gravesend, quite out of the fret and bustle of the narrower river, and there was not even a steamboat pier to disturb the quiet of this cluster of harmless houses, though they watched upon their beach the passage of great navies down the greatest thoroughfare of England. It looked so quiet, so primitive, so retired, with its few boats in its little bay, that you could not have fancied it so near the Babel of the world. The spring day was bright and calm; the river was stirred only by the great ripples of its current; the white sails of passing ships were dazzling in the sunshine, and you could even catch a glimpse of the dancing motes of foam on the rougher sea-water, as it widened and widened downward to the ocean. Though there were few striking features in the landscape, it charmed me with its new and unaccustomed beauty. It won my thoughts out of myself; I was pleased to think of living here.

There was scarcely anything to be called an inn in Elith,—but as we had no other where to go to, we went to the little humble house which bore the name, and were shown into a faded little parlor, where such visitors as we were seldom made their appearance, I suppose, and which was certainly adapted for very different guests. Alice was much more annoyed and disturbed than I was at coming here; I am afraid she almost thought her respectability compromised by the glimpse we caught of the aborigines of the place, smoking long pipes and drinking beer as we came in, and she was nervous and reluctant to be seen at the window, whither I had gone immediately, to look out upon this wonderful elysium of water and sunshine; then occurred to me the strangest silent ecstasy in these ships, their sails rounded with the slight wind, and shining with such an intense whiteness in the sunshine against the blue river and the bluer sky. They seemed to be gliding on in a dream—in a rapture—and my mind glided on with them, for the moment satisfied and at rest.

But I had now everything to think of—everything to arrange. Alice had lived at home so long, and had been so undisturbed in her daily duties, that she was not at all fit for this emergency—she was quite ready to do everything, but she depended entirely on me to be told what she should do; so I asked the country girl who attended us, if there were any houses to be let in the village, and she answered me eagerly and immediately in a somewhat lengthy speech, intimating that this was scarce the season yet, but that "a many families" came from town for the beautiful air here, and that she knew of a widow lady who had a furnished house to let, and wanted badly to have it off her hands. The girl was quite anxious to be the negotiator in the possible bargain—should she run and let the lady know?—would I have her come to me? or would I please go to the cottage? And we immediately had an inventory of its furniture and decorations, of which Alice, I could perceive, was somewhat contemptuous. But I had a fancy, newly acquired, about our mode of living here; I determined on making no pretence or attempt to live such a life as I had hitherto done. I had separated myself from my rank and my home; I still wanted hardships, privations, toils, if they were possible, and I had made up my mind; so I took Alice's arm to support me, for I was very much fatigued, and we went out together, conducted by our zealous attendant, to see the house.

It was a little, square, two-storied house, standing by itself on a little grassy knoll, at one side of the village; the small inclosure in front was but two stripes of bare grass, with fantastic flower-beds cut in the turf, divided by a paved path leading to the door. There were no flowers, but only a shabby little evergreen in each of the mounds of soil, and the front of the house was festooned with ragged garlands of the "traveller's joy," a favorite creeper, as it seemed, in this neighborhood. The door opened into a little narrow passage, terminating in a steep flight of stairs, and with a door on either side—the little parlor and the little kitchen of this "genteel" little house. The "widow lady" made her appearance somewhat fluttered, for we had disturbed her at dinner and I do not think she was quite pleased with her zealous friend, the maid at the inn, for revealing to strangers the table spread in the kitchen, and the careless morning toilette, which was only intended for the sanctity of her own retirement. The parlor, into which she ushered us with pride, was a little stifling apartment, with Venetian blinds closed over its little window, so as scarcely to leave one row of panes uncovered; it was very fine with a red and blue carpet, an elaborate composition of colored paper in the grate, and little flower vases filled with immortelles and dried grass, reflecting themselves in the little dark-complexioned mirror. There was a small cheffonier in one corner, a haircloth sofa, and a round table, with sundry books displayed upon it, and the "widow lady" exhibited her pride and crowning glory with evident satisfaction. Alice looked upon all with a discontented eye—this homely finery made no impression upon her—for Alice could not be persuaded that I was a voluntary exile and outcast; she could be reconciled to my leaving home, but she could not reconcile herself to any descent in rank. I was still Mrs. Southcote of Cottiswoode, to Alice.

Upstairs there were two bed-rooms, and no more; one very white and in good order, with dimity hangings, and carefully polished furniture; the other with no hangings at all, and not much furnishing to boast of; and these, with the kitchen, made all the house.

Alice looked in my face anxiously. "You never can live in this little place, dear? What could you do here?" cried Alice. "Miss Hester, you won't think of it; there's no accommodation for a lady here."

"There is quite enough for us two," I said. "I do not wish to live as we lived at home; I want to help myself with my own hands; I want to live as your daughter might live, Alice; I think this is very good—we do not want any more."

Alice, for the moment, was almost impatient with me. "So you mean to think you can live and sit all day in this little place," she said, looking round upon the fine parlor; "it's sinful, Miss Hester, it is. I'll not give in to it. Do you think upon what's coming, dear? Well-a-day, that it should be coming now! Do you think you can lie down upon that hard sofa, and put up with this place, after what you've been used to?—it goes against my conscience—it's sinful, Miss Hester."

"And why, Alice?" said I.

Alice found it difficult to answer why, but was not less positive on that account. "I don't like it myself," said Alice; "I've not been used to it this many a day, but, darling, you!"

"Alice, let us be humble—let us be quiet—let me have something to do," I said earnestly. "We will have nobody in the house but you and I. We will serve each other. We will do everything with our own hands. Do not try to resist me, Alice. I think I have a great deal to learn yet. I am not so proud as I was. Let me try what life is among poorer people. Let me have my will, Alice."

Alice made no further resistance. Her face was not so contracted as usual—that was all—but now she made me sit down, and went to the kitchen herself to bargain with the landlady. I heard their voices immediately in audible parley. The widow was anxious to have her house taken for some fixed time; while Alice, I could hear, was rather mysterious and lofty, and did not know how long her lady might be able to stay. Then there came an inquiry about my name, and something which sounded like a request for a reference, and Alice came abruptly back to me. I was sitting where she had left me, listening to their conversation, and she came close to my side, and stooped to whisper in my ear, and said, "What name will I say, Miss Hester?"

"What name?" Did Alice mean to insult me? "My own proper name, of course," I said, with a little anger. "Why do you ask? Do you think I wish to conceal myself because I have left home? No, no, my own name."

"But the squire will be sure to find you, darling," said Alice, still whispering; "you don't think he'll be content and never make any search, and he'll soon find you if you always go by your own name?"

"I will do nothing clandestine," I said, with displeasure; "nothing shall ever make me deny my name. No, Alice, we are not fugitives—we are not guilty—I fear no one finding me."

She went away after this without a word, and then the dialogue in the kitchen was resumed. Her lady was Mrs. Southcote, a lady from Cambridgeshire, Alice said, and wanted quiet and fresh air for a term, though she could not tell how long; and then there were many curious questions about my health, and many inquiring hints as to my motive in coming here; but to all this Alice turned a deaf ear, and answered nothing. One thing she insisted upon earnestly, and that was that we should have immediate possession. The widow demurred, but Alice carried her point, and came back to me triumphant, to tell me that we were to remain here, and have the house entirely to ourselves to-morrow. She commenced operations immediately to improve the appearance of the little parlor. She drew up the blinds, removed the lower one, opened the window, for the day was very warm, and began to tug the reluctant sofa out of its corner, to place it at the window for me. While she was so occupied, and while this crazy piece of furniture creaked and jolted on its way to its new position, I caught the anxious eye of the mistress of the house looking in at the door watching her proceedings. This good woman did not understand the shifting of her much-beloved and cherished furniture. The sofa was the true inhabitant of the room, while we were only strangers and sojourners; she came in with a half courtesy to hint a remonstrance; she hoped I would not be offended; she had seen better days, and never thought to be in her present position, and her furniture, would I please to have it taken care of? and then she went to offer her services to help Alice to lift the sofa, for it would tear her good carpet, she was most sure.

Alice did not receive this obliging offer with a very good grace; I for my part looked on with quiet amusement; I was astonished to find how much the novelty of all this lightened my mind, and relieved me from myself. I could not have believed when I left home twenty-four hours ago that anything would have brought a smile to my lips so soon; yet so it was; and when the widow went away, I took my place in a corner of the hard sofa, and looked out upon the river, with a dreamy ease and leisure at my heart which astonished me still more. Ship after ship, great and small—I could not tell one from another, nor had the slightest conception of any distinctions of class or name between them—went gliding downward, majestic with their full white sails and lofty masts, upon the current, which was flowing strongly to the sea. Little steamers fumed and fretted upon the peaceful river, going up and down and across. Great ones came in, making a solemn rustle in the water with their unseen footsteps. Little shadowy skiffs shot along like sea-birds on the top of the stream, and more substantial wherries, laden with parties of pleasure, now and then went by, keeping cautiously to the side of the river. The tide had ebbed a little from the stony beach of our small bay. A boat which had been floating an hour since, was now stranded on the shore. This was altogether new to me. I knew nothing, except words, of those mysterious ocean tides, nor of where they penetrated and where they strayed. I watched the water gleaming further back at every ripple with a strange delight, watching and wondering how far back it would go, almost counting the soft peaceful waves. I looked anxiously out upon the course of the river, where those far away white specks were dancing on the roughened edge of the sea. I speculated on the voyages which these stately wayfarers were bound upon. I thought with a shudder of the storm at sea which I had myself seen, and I was only roused from my pleasant occupation by the voice of Alice, as she stood beside me looking out also, but with different thoughts. "I warrant there's many a pretty boy and many a child's father in such great ships," said Alice, with a sigh; "they're beautiful to look at, Miss Hester, but I had a deal rather see them coming home. Many a house will be dreary to-day for want of them that's sailing there."

I know well she did not mean to grieve me, but even while she spoke my burden came back upon me; I looked after the ships with a wistful glance; yes, many a home had given its best blood to these frail gallant ships, to risk the storms and the sea. Why? for duty and necessity, for daily bread, for honest labor; but what pretence had I for making my home desolate, or launching my poor boat upon this unknown sea of life? I had no answer to make; I had no resource but to turn my back upon the question, and ignore it. I turned from the window suddenly, and laid my head down upon the hard, prickly, hair-cloth cushion, and said I would rest a little. I was not quite so miserable even now as I had been yesterday, but my thoughts had returned to the same channel again.

As I thus reclined, sometimes watching her, sometimes seeing visions of Cottiswoode, and of all the agitation and tumult which must be there, Alice came and went between this little room and the kitchen, and began to spread the table, and to prepare our early, humble dinner. It soothed me to see her making all those little simple arrangements; everything was so far removed from the more stately regulations of home, and there seemed to me such a comfort and privacy in thus being able to do without the intervention of servants, to do everything "for ourselves," as I flattered myself. What a rest and deliverance to my constrained mind would be the constant occupation which I must have had, had I really been the daughter of Alice! I thought of Amy's cheerful bustle, of our simple maid Mary, singing at her work in my father's house at Cambridge,—with tangible and real things in their hands and their thoughts all day long, what leisure would they have for the broodings of the mind diseased? What time for unprofitable self-communion? Ah, now I thought of it, that sickening doubt of myself came over me again; I was shaken in my false position; and now, when I wanted the fullest confidence in myself and in my course of action, my perverse heart began to glance back with dreadful suspicions of every step I had ever taken. I could no longer rest when this most ingenious process of self-torment began again. I had to rise and walk about, hurrying, as if to escape from it; and I was glad and thankful when Alice came in again with our simple meal.

After we had dined, I went with her, glad to be kept in any way from my own sole company, to unpack our trunk upstairs. I took out the things I had been working at, and my materials, and when she was ready to go with me, I carried them down stairs. I would not go without Alice. I made her sit by me, and take her own work, and be constantly at my side. By this time we had drawn a little table to the window for our sewing-things, and Alice sat opposite to me in a hard mahogany arm-chair, while I, half reclining on my sofa, went on slowly with my occupation. I was still busy with those delicate bits of embroidery; and I think almost the only pleasure I recollect in that dark time of my life, was the progress I made with these. I was putting some of them together now—"making them up," as we call it in our woman's language. I had a great pride in my needlework, and I have always had a singular pleasure in construction—so I was almost comfortable once more, and sometimes had such a thrill of strange delight at my heart, that it almost was a pang mingled of pain and joy, to see the definite shape these fine delicate bits of cambric took under my fingers. All this while Alice sat by working at similar work, and telling me tales of young wives like myself, and of mothers and children, and of all the natural experiences of womanhood. Like myself! with a shudder I wondered within myself whether there was one other in the world like me.

After a while, when I wearied of this—as, indeed, in my present mood of mind and weakness of frame, I soon wearied of anything, I made Alice get her bonnet and come out with me. It was now getting towards evening, and the usual hum of play and of rest, which always is about a comfortable village after the day's work is over, was pleasantly audible here. At some distance from our house, behind it, some lads were playing cricket in a field, and women were gossiping at the cottage doors, and men lounging about, many of them in their blue woollen shirts and glazed hats—sailors, as we fancied in our ignorance, though they were, in reality, only watermen, who went a fishing sometimes, after a somewhat ignoble fashion, to the mouth of the river, and managed these pleasure-boats when they were at home. We wandered down close to the river, where the water now came rustling up to our feet, creeping closer and closer in every wave. "It is the tide," said I, with involuntary reverence. Alice did not know much about the tide, but her heart, like every other natural heart, was charmed by that liquid soft-ringing music, the ripple of the water, as it rose and fell upon the beach, and Alice was reverential too. I bent down myself like a child, to put my hand upon the pebbly wet line, and feel the soft water heaving up upon it higher and higher. Ships were still passing down the beautiful calm river, gliding away silently into the night and the sea—the soft hum of the village was behind us, the musical cadence of these gentle waves filled the quiet air, yet soothed it, and we stood together saying nothing, strangers and solitary, knowing Nature, only one of us knowing God, but strangers to all the human people here.

As we went back, many of the cottage doors were closed, and through some of the half-curtained windows we saw the humble little families gathered together for the night. From the church, as we passed, there came some sounds of music; the organist had been practising, I suppose, and the "linked sweetness long drawn out," the "dying fall," which commands the imagination more entirely than anything perfect and completed can, was stealing into the darkening twilight as we passed by the half-open door. I cannot tell why all those sweet influences make even the happy pensive; but I know they brought such heaviness to my heart, and such tears to my eyes, as I would not like to feel again. Alice did not say anything, perhaps she saw that I was crying; but I was very glad to get home, and lay myself down upon my bed, and seek the sleep which always mercifully came to me. How glad I was always to fall asleep; no other way could I get rid of myself and my troubles; they looked in upon me with my first waking in the unwelcome light of the morning, but I had oblivion in my sleep.

THE SECOND DAY

We were now in complete possession of our little solitary house; our humble neighbors had become accustomed to us, and no longer clustered about their doors and talked in whispers when we came out for our daily walk. I have no doubt that there was still much gossip, and even some suspicion about Alice and me; but we were inoffensive, and were not without means, so we were annoyed by no great investigations into our history.

We had no one in the house with us. Alice did everything; and though I made a pretence of helping her, I did her little service. Sometimes I put my own bedchamber in order, with a childish satisfaction, but no small degree of fatigue; and with so small a house, and so little trouble necessary, there was not much to do. I could not bear Alice to be out of my presence; we ate together, sat together, walked together; I was quite dependent upon her; altogether a great change had come upon me. I never had been what people call intellectual, but now in the day of my weakness how I clung to the womanly occupations, the womanly society, aye, to such a poor thing as gossip, which was only redeemed from being the very vulgarest of amusements, because it was gossip of the past. When I sat at my sewing, with Alice talking to me; when I listened to tales of this one and the other one, whom she had known in her youth,— everything about them; their dress, their habits, their marriages, their children, their misfortunes; when I cut, and sewed, and contrived these pretty things I still was making, sometimes I was almost happy. Yes, if it was in reality a descent from more elevated and elevating occupations, I still must confess to it, a woman after all is but a woman, and there are times when the greatest book, or the grandest imaginations in the world, have no attractions compared with those of a piece of muslin, a needle and a thread. I felt it so, at least. I remember the little parlor gratefully, with its round table and overflowing work-basket, the beautiful river and the passing boats without, and Alice recalling the experiences of her youth within.

For all this time my only safeguard lay in trying to forget, or to turn my back upon the great question of my life. I no longer brooded over the injury my husband had done me; it seemed to have floated away from my sight, and become an imagination, a vision, a dream. I could not even recall our life at Cottiswoode; when I attempted to return to it a veil fell upon my eyes, and a dull remorse at my heart made the very attempt at recollection intolerable to me. Instead of that, the bright days before our marriage, the bright days after it, continually, and even against my will, came to my mind. I went over and over again the course of our happy journey; I recalled all our hopes, all our conversations, all our plans for the future; and this was all over, all gone, vanished like a tale that is told! It is not wonderful that I should try with all my might to keep myself from thinking. It was dreadful to fall into such a reverie as this, and then to awaken from it, and recollect how everything really was.

I had heard from my agent in Cambridge, and had received money from him. We were plentifully supplied, yet needed very little. We lived as simply as any peasant women could have lived; and though we had now a few flowers in the little fantastic flower-pots before the window, and had dismissed the shabby evergreens, and pruned the "traveller's joy," we had made no other alteration in the house. It was now May, nearly the middle of the month, and perfect summer, for, as I have said, everything was unusually early this year. No letters except the agent's had come to me. I thought my husband was content that I should be lost, and have my own will. When I was quite alone, I sometimes thought that he was eased and relieved by my absence, and the thought cost me some bitter tears. I could not bear to be of no importance to him; and then I fretted myself with vain speculations. Why was he so angry when I spoke of Flora Ennerdale? If he had but married Flora Ennerdale, how happy she would have made him; and I—I would have pined and died in secret, and never done him wrong. So I thought in my fond, wretched, desolate musings. Fond!—yes, my heart had escaped from me, and flown back to him. I would not for the world have whispered it to any one—I refused to acknowledge it to myself, yet it was true.

I was alone in the house, and these thoughts had come strongly upon me. Alice was very reluctant to leave me alone, and only when she was compelled by some household necessity went out without me; but she had wanted something this afternoon before the time of our usual walk, and I was sitting by myself in the silent little house. Though I avoided solitude by every means in my power, I yet prized the moment when it came to me—and I had been indulging myself in dreary longings, in silent prayers, and weeping, when Alice returned. She came in to me very hastily, with a good deal of agitation in her face, and when she saw my eyes, where I suppose there were signs that I had been crying, she started, and cried, "Have you seen him? have you seen him already?"

"I seen him—whom?" I cried with a great shiver of excitement. What a useless question it was! as well as if I had seen him, I knew he must be him.

She came and took my hand and bent over me, soothing and caressing. "Darling, don't be startled," said Alice; "oh, how foolish I am! I thought you had seen him when I saw the water in your eyes. Dear Miss Hester, keep a good heart, and don't tremble, there's a dear. I've seen him indeed—he's here, come to see you, looking wan and worn, and very anxious, poor young gentleman. Oh, take thought of what you will say to him, Miss Hester; every minute I expect to hear him at the door."

It was a great shock to me; I felt that there was a deadly pallor on my face. I felt my heart beat with a stifled rapid pulsation. I could not think of anything. I could not fancy what I would say. I was about to see him, to hear his voice again. I felt a wild delight, a wild reluctance; I could have risen and fled from him—yet it seemed to lift me into a sudden Elysium, this hope of seeing him again. Strange, inconsistent, perverse—I could not be sure for a moment what impulse I would follow. I sat breathless, holding my hand upon my heart, listening with all my powers. I seemed for the instant to be capable of nothing but of listening for his footstep; my physical strength and my mental were alike engrossed. I could neither move nor think.

I do not know how long it was; I know there was a terrible interval during which Alice talked to me words which I paid no attention to, and did not know, and then it came—that well-known footstep; I heard the little gate swing behind him—I heard the gravel crushed beneath his quick step, and then Alice opened the door, and a sudden lull of intense emotion came over me. He was before me, standing there, yes, there—but a dizzy, blinding haze came over my eyes—after the first glimpse I did not see him, till I had recovered again.

And he was not more composed than I was; not so much so in appearance, I believe. He came up and held out his hand, and when I did not move, he took mine and held it tightly—tightly between his own, and gazed full into my face, with his own all quivering and eloquent with emotion. At this moment the impulse for which I had been waiting came to me, and steadied my tremulous expectation once more into resolve—once more the bitterness which had perished in his absence returned with double force—his own words began to ring in my ears, and my cheek tingled with the fiery flush of returning resentment. I had deceived him; he had married a sweet and tender woman, and when his eyes were opened, he had found by his side only me. I thought no longer of my bridegroom, my yearnings for affection were turned into a passionate desire for freedom; it was not Harry, but Edgar Southcote on whom I looked with steady eyes.

He, I am sure, did not and could not notice any change of expression; he saw my color vary, that was all, but his own feelings were sufficiently tumultuous to occupy him.

"Hester," he said, "Hester, Hester!" He did not seem able to say any more, he only stood before me holding my hand very close, looking into my face with eyes in which everything else was veiled by his joy in seeing me again. I saw it was so—heaven help me—what a miserable torturer I was! my heart gave a bound of wild delight to feel my power over him still.

When I made no response, he forced me at last; already he was chilled, but he did not change his position—he held out both his hands, his arms rather, tears came to his eyes, and with a longing, wistful, entreating gaze he fixed them upon me. "Hester, Hester!" he said, "come, I have the only right to support you. In absence and solitude we have found out how it is that we are bound to each other, not by promise and vow alone, but by heart and soul. In strife or in peace we have but one existence. Hester, come back to me, come, let us not be sending our hearts over the world after each other; we cannot be separated, come back to me."

How true it was, how true it was! but the heart that had been yearning for him, oh, so drearily, oh, so sadly, half an hour ago, was beating against my bosom now with miserable excitement, resisting him bitterly and to the death.

"Why should I come back?" I said; "has anything changed? are our circumstances different from what they were?"

"Yes," he cried eagerly; "we have been apart, we have found out our true union, we have learned what it is to pine for a look, the very slightest, of the face most dear in the world to us. We have found how transitory, how poor all offences and resentments are, and how the original outlives and outlasts them. Hester, do I not speak the truth?"

I dared not contradict my own heart and say no, I dared not do it, everything he said was true.

"I do not mean you to suppose that it is self-denial on my part and a desire to test this, which has made me so slow of following you," he continued, growing heated and breathless as he found that I did not answer; "I have but newly found out your retreat, Hester—found it out after long and diligent searching, which has given me many a sick heart for a month past. I need not describe the misery into which your flight plunged me; when you passed me on the road I was struck with a pang of fear, but I refused to entertain it. Think how I felt when I went home, and saw the pitying looks of the servants, and found your pitiless note upon my table. They told me you placed it there yourself Hester; and when I enter that fatal room, I sit idly thinking of you, trying to fancy where you stood, wondering, wondering if there was no truth nor mercy in your heart."

The recollection of that moment rushed back on me as he spoke; he saw the convulsive trembling which came upon me; he heard the sob which I could not restrain; thus far I betrayed myself. I could not remember that unmoved; but when he bent over me with eager anxiety, I drew my hand away, and said I was quite well, quite well, I needed no support.

"Hester," he said, in a tone of such tenderness that it almost overpowered me, "I know I am trying your strength severely, I know I am. I may be inexcusable, I may be hazarding your health with my vehemence; tell me if it is so, I will not speak another word, I will rather give up all my own hopes. God forbid that you should suffer for my violence; speak to me, say a word, Hester, tell me what I am to do."

"I can bear to hear all you have to say to me," I said, with a burning blush upon my cheek. The exertion I made to maintain my own calmness was exhausting me dreadfully, but I could bear it better when he spoke, and when my natural spirit of resistance was roused by his words, than when he went away or was silent, when I would be left to the consuming remorseful persecution of my own thoughts.

When I said this he looked at me steadily and sadly;—"Was it hopeless then? would I receive him in no fashion but this?" I met his gaze with the blank look of sullen resentment; he turned away from me with a heavy sigh, and wrung his hands with impatience and suffering; then he came back, took the chair which Alice had been using, and sat down opposite to me.

"Then it is to be so," he said with suppressed bitterness; "neither time nor solitude, neither tenderness nor absence, says a gentle word for me in your heart; you are resolved that we shall be miserable, Hester; you will leave me to the pity of the servants, you will show none; you will condemn me to frightful anxiety, anxiety which I dare not venture to anticipate; you will shut me out from every right; I must not be near; I must not try to support you; is this what you quietly doom me to, Hester?"

"You use strange words; I doom you to nothing," said I; "we were very wretched when we were together; you told me you were deceived in me, and I also was deceived in you; all that I have done is to come away, to free each of us from a galling and perpetual slavery. If I give no pity, I ask none; let justice be done between us, and it is justice surely to permit me to take care for myself when I do not encumber you. You have not more to suffer or to complain of than I have; we are on equal terms, and so long as we are apart we cannot drive each other mad, as you said I would do to you; I beseech you to be content, let us remain as we are; it will be best for us both."

If I was agitated when I began to speak, I had become quite calm before I ended. He never withdrew his eye from me—he followed my motions, almost my breath—and when I moved my hands and clasped them together, as I did to support myself, his gaze turned to them—my hands were thin and worn, and very white—they looked like an invalid's. Before I was aware, he bent over and kissed them, saying, "Poor Hester! poor Hester!" Ah, it was very hard for me to keep up to my resolution, reading his thoughts as I did with an instinctive certainty. He was not thinking of my unkind and bitter words—he was thinking only of me.

But when he spoke after this pause, I saw clearly enough that my words had not escaped him; he did not entreat any longer; he saw it was vain; but the kindness of his tone was undiminished. I fancied I could perceive the resolution he had taken now; that he had made up his mind not to strive with me, but to leave me to myself. I would rather he had persecuted me with the most violent and perpetual persecution; that I could have met with courage; but I knew what a longing, yearning, remorseful misery would come upon me when I was left to the sole company of my own heart.

"I will wait till you come to think of something else than justice," he said kindly, but sadly. "To have my rights yielded to me only because they are rights, will never satisfy me, Hester. I warn you of this now; you are not doing justice. I know that you can have no doubt what are my feelings to you; you know what my love is, but not how much it can bear, and you treat me with cruel injustice, Hester. Enough of this. I will plead my own cause no more. I will leave everything to yourself. By-and-bye, I do not doubt you will see my rights in a different aspect; but I will not be content with my rights," he continued, growing unconsciously vehement; "when you are willing to do me justice, I will still be dissatisfied. It is not justice I want from you, and the time of our reunion will never come till you reject justice as I do. I know that I am right."

"It will never come," said I, under my breath.

"The most wretched criminal has hope, Hester," he said, rising with impatience which he could not control, and coming to the window, "and I am not so much wiser than my kind as to be able to live without it. I have read of humility and patience, I grant you, and these are difficult qualities; but I will quarrel no more on my own account, and it is hard to maintain a feud on one side only, Hester? Will you permit me to live near you, since you insist on leaving me? Will you let me see you now and then? will you let me be near at hand, if by any chance you should relent and wish for me? In your present circumstances, this is no great boon to yield to your husband, Hester?"

"What end would it answer?" I said, though my heart leaped with a strange mixture of joy and pain at his words; "I am sure we are better quite apart."

"Be it so," he said, and then he came forward to me very gravely; "I wait your time, Hester," he said, taking my hand once more, with a face of serious and compassionate kindness, "we have, both of us, much grief to go through yet, but I will wait and be patient; I consent to what you say; I will not intrude into your presence again till you bid me come—you smile—you will never bid me come? that is in God's hands, Hester, and so are you, my bride, my solitary suffering wife. I leave you to Him who will support you better than I could. Farewell. It is a bitter word to say, but I obey you. Hester—Hester—not a word for me! farewell."

He stooped over me, kissed my forehead, wrung my hand, and then he was gone.

He was gone;—I gazed with aching eyes into the place where he had been; here this moment; gone perhaps for ever; I cried aloud in wild anguish; I thought my heart would burst; it required no long process, no time nor thought to change my mad rebellious heart again; I could struggle with him, resist him, use him cruelly while he was here before me; but when he was gone; oh, when he was gone!

When Alice came in I was sobbing aloud and convulsively; I had no power of self-restraint; all my pride and strength were broken down. "He is gone," I repeated to myself; "he is gone!" I could think of nothing else. Alice spoke to me, but I did not hear; she tried to lift me from the sofa, where I lay burying my face in my hands, but I would not let her touch me; no one had ever seen such violence and such a wild outbreak of passion and misery in me before.

It was all my own doing, there was the sting of it. I could ask sympathy from no one, confess my distress to no one. My own heart stung me, upbraided me, made malicious thrusts and wounds at my weakness. I had done it all myself—what did I think of my miserable handiwork? I had made my own life, and this was the result of it. I had cast him away—cast him away! I could not tell why, I could remember nothing cruel that he had ever done to me, and he would come back no more.

"Miss Hester, you will kill yourself," cried Alice indignantly. I heard these words as if they were the first she had said, and with an immediate and powerful effort I controlled myself. No, I would not endanger the future, I would not lose everything. I raised myself up and returned to my work; I tried to forget what had happened,—that he had actually stood there before me, that this little room had held him, that his voice was still ringing in the dim subdued atmosphere. Every time I thought of it I trembled with agitation. The day was the same, yet it was different; the hours went on as usual, yet how totally changed they were. It was over,—the event I had been unconsciously, involuntarily, looking forward to. This dimmed, dulled life was to go on now with no new expectation in it, it was all over; he had promised to let me alone.

And there was Alice, looking at me with eager, solicitous, inquiring eyes, anxious to know what had been said, what had happened, wondering at my strange mood, trying to find out, with her own thoughts and looks, how I felt. Alice could not comprehend me. When her first belief, that I did not care for him, was shaken, she could find no reason for my conduct, no cause for all I had done; she did not understand my perversity; in the motives of her own simple Christian heart she found no clue to the problem of mine. She put no questions to me, but sat, where he had been sitting, sad, disapproving, full of wonder; her hope disappointed and her love grieved, aware I was wrong, yet so reluctant to think so. Poor Alice! I was a great charge to her, and a perplexing one; she did not know how to deal with me.

When I was able to command my voice, I spoke to her. "Alice, Mr. Southcote has been here," I said; "but he has promised not to come back again. He will never intrude into my presence again, he says, till I call him, and I am not likely to do that. When anything happens, Alice—I intended to have said so before— you will write to him without delay; remember, I told you so; he has a right to that."

The words struck me strangely as I repeated them. Had I already begun, according to his own proposing, to calculate what his rights were? but he had warned me that he would find no satisfaction in that.

"And is this all, Miss Hester?" said Alice, looking at me wistfully; "oh, darling, well you know I've never said a word. I've never dared to take part with him that never should have needed help from a poor woman like me, but I can't keep silent—Miss Hester—I can't now; what's in my heart I must say, for you're my own dear child. Miss Hester, dear, I can't help if you're angry. But what do you think a true friend can pray for you? one that loves you dear above all the world; what do you think she would be obliged to pray, the first thing of all that was in her heart?"

I was much startled by the question, for it was at once perfectly unexpected, and very solemnly and seriously put. I did not answer, but looked at her with earnestness as great as her own.

"First of all, before even the safety, and the blessing, and the joy, oh, Miss Hester," cried Alice, with strange emotion, "that you may be made to see which is good and which is evil, and to choose the right way. I dare not ask the blessing first, darling, I dare not! I'd lay down my life for an hour's comfort to you, Miss Hester; you know it's not boasting, you know it's true; but you're following a wrong way, and sorrow is the right thing to come to that rather than joy. I cannot help it—I cannot help it—you may put me away from you, as you've put a better love than mine, but I must say what is in my heart."

I could not be angry, I could not be indignant; I could not meet Alice's unexpected severity as she thought I would. I was no heroine, I was only a woman, a poor, young, foolish, solitary woman. I cried: it was all I could do. I was almost glad she reproved me—glad that she thought God must punish and forsake me for my sin. I could not excuse or justify myself. I had no heart to say anything; all my powers were exhausted. I could only lie upon my sofa, silent, not venturing to look at Alice, and doing what I could to restrain my tears. But they would not be restrained; gentler and gentler, yet more abundant they fell from under the cover of my clasped hands, and, little as I intended it, this was indeed the only way in which I could have vanquished Alice. She kept her own place for a few moments, trembling and irresolute, and then she came humbly towards me and drew my head to her bosom. "Oh, darling, forgive me, forgive me," cried Alice, and her tears fell as fast as mine.

When I found that I could not put an end to my own weeping-fit, Alice grew very much alarmed. She brought an armful of pillows, and arranged them on the sofa, and made me lie down to sleep. I obeyed her like a child. I took some wine when she gave it me, and closed my eyes at her bidding. She sat by my side watching me, and when my eyelids unclosed a little, I saw her soft white apron close by my cheek, and almost thought I was sleeping with my head on her knee as I used to do when I was a little girl. At last I did fall asleep, but I never was conscious that I had done so. I did not change the scene in my dreams. I was still here, still in this room, and he was beside me again, but we did not speak of parting now, all that was over; that was the dream, and it was past. I do not recollect that there were any words to make our reunion sure, but there did not need any, for I was completely persuaded of it in that strange real dream. When I woke, Alice was still sitting by me, and there was the strangest ease and satisfaction in my heart. I looked past her eagerly, and round the room, and asked, "Where is he? where is he?" she did not speak, and then I knew it was all a dream.

But I would not break down again. I sat erect and took up my work, and told her I was quite well now, but my head was aching violently, and my heart sank with such a dreary heaviness. A cup of tea would do me good, Alice said, and she left me to prepare it. When I was alone I went to the window and opened it to let in the fresh sweet air upon my hot brow. Yes, it was the happiness and the reconciliation that were a dream; the wretched solitude, the remorse, the hopelessness were real things; and what was the future? I could not help a shudder of expectation and terror. My truest, dearest, most indulgent friend Alice herself was almost afraid to ask a blessing for me. Hitherto I had always asked it myself, but her words arrested me; I only wondered what kind of judgment God would send to mark my sin—would it be only death? and once more a few tears fell from my eyes; I began to think of the letter I would write to my husband to be given him when I was gone away for ever; of perhaps the precious legacy I would leave him; the gift that would pay him tenfold for all his grief and trouble with me. These thoughts soothed me. When Alice returned, I withdrew from the window, and came to the table and took the tea she poured out for me. I was subdued and exhausted. I was not now so miserable as I had been. I pleased myself with the idea of making this last atonement, of putting an end to the misery of our wedded life, and to the problem which I did not know how to solve otherwise, by the early death which every one would shed a natural tear for. Once more I wiped a few tears from my own cheek, and then I went up-stairs very quietly in my exhaustion to prepare for our walk.

When we went out, I was less composed. I remembered then that he had trod this same path only a few hours ago; that, perhaps, he still was here. I hurried Alice on, I looked back and around with a stealthy eagerness, my heart began to beat and my breath to fail as this occurred to me. He might be here, he might even see me now with my lingering feeble footsteps, and read in my face traces of the wild and strong emotion which had visited me since he came. I drew my veil over my face, I hastened to the very margin of the water where no one could see me closely. Wherever I turned I was possessed with the idea that from some eminence—some visionary height—he was watching me, and interpreting my very movements. I did not desire to escape. I hurried about restlessly, but I did not wish to go in again; and it was only when the darkness fell that Alice persuaded me to go home. Alice did not know what was passing in my vexed and troubled mind. I think now my physical weakness must have had a great deal to do with it—what a dreadful chaos it was!

THE THIRD DAY

A little low cry—what was it?—I never heard it before, yet it went to my heart almost with a pang of delight. Alice, bring it—bring it. I cannot wait for all those snowy robes, and all the joyful, tearful importance of my dear, dear, kind nurse, my almost mother. Here in its little flannel wrapper—a little moving bundle, thrusting about its little limbs, turning round its little downy head with the first instincts of life to that kind bosom, crying its little wailing cry—oh, kindest heaven!—oh, God most wonderful!—it is mine, mine, my own child!

I felt neither pain nor weakness. I consented to lie still, because they said I must, and because I was happy beyond expression, and neither rebellion nor disobedience was in me. I lay quite still, pulling back the curtains to look at Alice as she put on those dainty little garments, one by one—to look at the moving thing upon her knee, the little hand thrust up into the air, the vigorous kicks and thrusts with which it struggled. It! a spark of sudden anger woke in me when some one said it—that was correct enough half an hour ago—but this was he, an individual being, my baby, my own, mine! I cannot tell to any one the rapture in which I lay watching Alice as she put upon him his first little robes. I was in a woman's paradise—a moment which can come but once in a lifetime. What mother does not remember, after all her dread, her awe, her suffering, the heavenly rest in which she lay looking at her firstborn? I think there is no such ecstasy either before or after—it is all over—all over—the ordeal which frame and spirit have been trembling at, is past like a dream, and who remembers it?—and in that strange delicious luxury of ease and weakness, there seems no longer anything to desire. I do not know,—perhaps it is not an elevated idea at all,—but my best realization of unspeakable happiness was in that hour after my little boy was born.

When that most important toilet was finished, Alice brought him to me in the long white robe, rich with my own needlework, and the pretty close cap covering his little downy head. She laid him down on my arm, and drew a step apart, and looked at us both, crying for joy. "Bless you, my darling!" cried Alice, and then she fairly ran away with her bright glistening face, and I knew very well it was to relieve her full heart, and spend her tears.

And I lay here with my baby on my arm alone. He did not mind who watched him, as he knitted his baby brows, and twisted his baby mouth, and clenched his harmless fists, till I laughed and cried together in indescribable delight. Then a change came over me. I wanted some one to share my happiness—to show my treasure to. Some one—oh, what cold words these were! I wanted one—only one—to make my joy perfect. My heart expanded over my baby, with such a sense of want, of incompleteness. I cried aloud, "Oh, Harry, Harry, Harry!" Where was the father to see and bless this child? This blessing which every other mother had, I had cast away from me.

I could not put his infant into his arms—I could not watch the joy on his face to brighten the light upon my own. I wept now after another fashion. I turned my head aside that my tears might not fall upon my baby. "Oh, Harry, Harry!" I was content you should be away from me in the evil time, but it broke my heart to be alone in my deep great joy.

Alice could not see how I had been moved when she returned. I took care to conceal my tearful eyes from her, and indeed it was not hard to return to gladness, looking upon the face of my child. She brought me a cup of tea, and pretended she had only gone away to fetch it. "I did, indeed, Miss Hester," she said, with a tearful smile that belied her; "though, to tell the truth, I had a good cry when I got down-stairs. Dear, do but look at him, with his sweet little fist doubled. Will you beat your mamma already, baby boy, and a son too? Darling, I'm sure you don't know what to say for joy."

"Oh, Alice, it is all beyond saying," said I; "I don't know why this should have come to me, when even you yourself—you who are always kindest, did not dare to ask a blessing for me; and after you said that, Alice, I never dared to ask one for myself."

"I never meant that, Miss Hester," said Alice, humbly; "I did crave for the blessing night and day, and here it is, bless his dear little heart; the sight of him brings back my pleasant days to me, dear. A woman never has such a joy as a baby. Do you shake your head at that, Miss Hester? My darling, you'll come to know."

"I do know, Alice," I said under my breath; "I never was so happy before, nor so thankful, nor—so sad. If I do not die he will have nobody but me, and what can I do for him? Alice, did you think of what I told you to do? Do you remember, you were to write when all was over? I thought then I was sure to die."

"Every one does, dear," said Alice, cheerfully; "but there's nothing about dying now, darling. We can't have that, and, Miss Hester, have you ever thought what was to be the baby's name?" Once more I was taken by surprise. Once more I turned my face away from him, that his sweet cheek might not be fretted by tears. I could say only one word—"Harry"—but that was enough for Alice. Her face brightened again, and she stooped over baby to give me time to recover myself. Alice was a wise nurse, and would not even notice my agitation; so I made an effort to subdue it, and was calm once more.

"Alice, you will be sure to write," I whispered; "and—well, you have seen other babies—do you really think he is very pretty, or is it only because he is our own?"

Alice satisfied me by a great many assurances. "Babies are not always pretty, darling," said the impartial Alice; "I have seen the oddest little things, though their mothers were always pleased; but Master Harry is a noble boy! Look how big he is; why he's quite a weight to lift already, and such a head of hair," she continued, gently pushing back his cap to show the silky down beneath; "and look here, Miss Hester, what arms, he might be a month old, bless him, instead of half a day. Do I really think it? My darling, I never, all my days, was called a flatterer before."

Nor had I the least inclination to call Alice a flatterer now, for, without any partiality, he really was a very beautiful boy, though he lay there winking, frowning, and making such pugilistic use of his little hands. I thought they were miracles, these little hands, when it pleased him to unfold them; such beautiful little miniatures, with their delicious soft touch, and tapered tender little fingers. I bent down my cheek to put it into the way of those natural weapons of his as he fenced about with them. I could have cried again with delight at those small blows. Then Alice pretended he was too much for me, and that she could not permit me to get excited; but I knew very well this was only an excuse to get him into her own arms; but I was as glad of Alice's joy as of my own. I had given her much to grieve her kind faithful heart, it was time I gave her something to make her glad; and what could do that so well as my baby boy? I watched her walking softly up and down the room, holding him so daintily, so prettily upon both her hands, and then she removed him to one arm, and made a reclining couch of it, when he seemed to lie so easy, so securely with his head upon her bosom. I looked, and wondered, and envied. Only study and experience could give that facility, and I had a strong impression that I would be afraid to handle that little precious frame as Alice did. Somehow or other it seemed to complete Alice, and make her a perfect picture. The baby, with its long streaming white robes, nestled so sweetly into her breast, looked a necessary adjunct to her now. I wondered how I should never have perceived the want of it before. I called her to me, and told her what I thought. Alice smiled with real gratification. "I was thinking so myself, dear," she said; "I am ten years younger since this morning. But it goes to my heart, Miss Hester, for it reminds me of old times."

She put up her hand to her eyes softly, though she still smiled; but those sweet tears of Alice's would never have chafed a baby's cheek. Sweet resignation, pure love, the breath of a subdued and chastened heart was in them. She was thinking of those whom God had taken away, whom God would one day restore her to—they were different tears from mine.

When he fell asleep Alice brought him back to me, and laid him down upon my arm once more. I watched for a while his sweet breath, his closed eyes, his baby face in its first repose, and then a drowsiness crept over me, and I, too, fell asleep—it was such a sleep as I had slept once before, the day when my husband came. I knew I was lying here with my baby in my arms. I realized all the joy that was in my heart, but I dreamed that I was presenting his child to Harry, that I was telling him how I had named the baby already, that I was pouring out all my thoughts and all my desires into the only ear in the world that could hear everything that was in my heart, and there was not a care or a cloud upon me. Again they seemed only dreams. And this happiness was the truth.

When I awoke it was with a slight start, and I was strangely bewildered to see that Alice had lifted baby from my arms, had wrapped him in a great shawl, and was carrying him away. "Where, where are you going, Alice?" I cried in alarm. She was confused when she saw me awake, and hesitated for a moment. "My darling, I am only going to let little Master see the house he has come home to," she said, with an attempt to be playful, which only called my attention to the tremble in her voice; "we'll come back again this moment, dear," and she carried him away down stairs. A suspicion of what it was came to me, and I listened eagerly. I heard her slow careful step descending; then I heard a suppressed exclamation. Neither my prudence nor my regard for my own health could restrain me; I was not able to subdue the wild beating of my heart, my breathless agitation. Did they think they could deceive me?—did they think his voice or his step could be in the house and I not know it? I raised myself up a little, and listened with my whole heart and might. Yes, he had come to see his child, and it was Alice who showed my beautiful boy to him—it was not I. I could hear his whisper; I thought myself that I could have heard and known it at any distance. I could imagine the scene; I could imagine his silent delight, his thanksgiving, his words of joy. I could almost fancy myself a clandestine spectator, a stealthy looker-on, beholding from behind a curtain the joy in which I had no share. Oh, it was bitter! dreadful!—he rejoicing over our baby below—I lying alone in my misery and weakness here. I did not think of him watching without the door, shut out from the house, while I was tasting first this exquisite and sacred joy. I thought but of myself, deserted, desolate, no one approving of me, no one commending me, my own very heart rising up in judgment, my every thought an accuser, alone and solitary, my husband only caring to know that I was safe, and desiring nothing more. I think I had such anguish in that moment as only comes to many, diluted through a whole life. How breathlessly I watched and listened—how conscious I seemed to be of every movement and every word; how I started at the faint sound of Baby's voice, and had almost sprung from my bed to snatch him at least to my arms. I who was the only one who could still him, his mother, his nurse, the being upon whom his little life depended by nature. Why, even for a moment, did they take him away from me?

When Alice returned I did not say a word of my suspicions or discoveries. My heart sank when I heard the door close upon my husband, when I heard the step whose faintest echo I knew so well passing through the gravel path of our little garden. Till then I still retained an involuntary hope that at least he would request to see me. But he did not; he was gone, and his steps rang upon my heart with a dull echo as he passed out of hearing. I felt like one suddenly struck dumb—I could not speak, I could not shake off the weight and oppression upon my brain, and the bitter pang in my spirit. Already I felt a fever growing on me, but I did not complain of it. My lips were sealed; I could not say I was ill—I could not speak a word. The little one was laid in my bosom once more, and I held him with passionate tenderness; but even while I did so, I felt the sickness at my heart, and the cold dew on my forehead, and the fainting, failing sensation over all my frame. I did not speak; I seemed to be bound up within myself with a strange, terrible wakefulness and consciousness, like one in a nightmare. I felt as one might feel who saw a murderer slowly advancing towards him when there was help at hand, yet who was paralysed, and could neither move nor cry for deliverance. I held my baby close, till he cried and struggled, then I suffered Alice to take him away. I heard her questioning and calling me; she came and wiped my forehead, and stooped down to me, and begged me to speak to her. "Are you ill, darling? are you ill?" cried Alice. At last I said faintly, "I suppose so;" and she rang the bell in great haste to summon a woman who waited below, and send her for the doctor. I was growing almost unconscious; the only clear thing I recollect in the chaos of indefinite pain and trouble which overwhelmed me, was Baby's little plaintive cry, and my anxiety to get him back into my arms. Faintly and dimly I could perceive Alice feeding him; and I did not feel quite sure whether my husband was or was not in the room in my strange, half-delirious state. I was not sure of anything; I heard strange noises in my ears—sometimes I thought I was lying in some danger, and something from which I could not escape was hurrying upon me to crush me to atoms; and then again I was at Cottiswoode—yet always here, always conscious of Baby and of Alice. Hitherto the many and great agitations to which I had been subject, or which I had brought upon myself, had done me no harm. As safely as though I had been living the most placid life had this great trial been surmounted; but it was different now. The cause was different; always before my husband had been but too anxious to change my mind towards him himself. It was a new and dreadful experience, this leaving me alone; and I was exhausted and weak, though I had not expected it; the long arrears of past suffering came back upon me now.

I suppose I must have been very ill for a few hours. I cannot tell; I remember only a vague and feverish wretchedness, an aching, longing desire to complain to some one, and a burning consciousness that I had no one on earth to complain to; I saw visions, too, in my illness; unhappy momentary dreams; glimpses of my husband rejoicing with strangers; placing my baby in the arms of another; always deserting and forsaking me. My heart was shocked and wounded; it was not an ordinary stroke, but a blow unexpected, which struck beyond all my poor defences, and laid me prostrate. Yet I could not have been long thus, for when I came to myself it was still the twilight of the same day. The room was darkened, and the candle burned faintly on the table at the extreme end of the little apartment, and there was a faint perfume in the room of some essence they had been using for me. It was June, a soft mild summer night, yet a little fire was burning in the grate, for baby's sake, and by it sat the woman who had come to assist Alice, holding my child in her lap. The first sign I perceived in myself of recovery was the indignant start with which I observed that this woman, I suppose overcome by the heat and doing nothing, was nodding and dozing at her post. I was not aware at the moment of having had anything the matter with me. I looked up with a startled, indignant glance at Alice, who was bending over me anxiously. "Bring him to me, Alice," I cried eagerly; "or, if I must not have my baby, do you keep him at least. She is a stranger; she does not care for him. Look, look, she has fallen asleep!" I saw the woman start and open her eyes with a guilty look as I spoke, and Alice said, "Yes, darling, yes," as she bent over me and continued bathing my forehead. I put away her hand impatiently. "Take him yourself, Alice, or bring him to me," I cried again. I had a shuddering which I could not restrain at my seeing him in the stranger's arms.

"Do what she tells you," said the doctor, who was standing by the side of Alice, in a low tone of authority; "she is better, bring the child to her, she will be well now, if she can sleep."

Then Alice brought my baby and laid him in my arms; my dear, sweet, innocent, sleeping child! what horrible desert had I been wandering in since he was taken from my arms? He was sleeping so quietly, so softly, nothing knew he of the subdued, yet still existing pain, in the bosom his little head was pillowed on. "Sleeping like a child!" I knew now what the common saying meant. My cap and nightdress were wet with the perfumed cool waters Alice had been bathing my brow with, and I had a confused pain and ringing in my head, and the most complete exhaustion over me; but I was better, and felt almost easy in my weakness in mind as well as in body. When the doctor had given me a draught, I suppose to make me sleep, he went away, and I was so much disturbed by the stranger in the room, that Alice sent her downstairs, and herself began to prepare for the night. I remember now, like a picture, the aspect of that little dim room; the single candle burning faintly far away from me; the summer night, scarcely dark; the pale, blue sky, looking in at the edge of the narrow blind; the bright sparkle of the little fire midway in the room, burning with a subdued, quiet glee, as if in triumph over the summer warmth which needed this auxiliary. Beside me was a large, old-fashioned elbow-chair, in which Alice was to watch, or sleep, as she said, and a round table with some eau-de-cologne and phials of medicine, a small flower vase containing some roses, and a book. It was deep twilight here in this corner, but my eyes were accustomed to it, and I could see everything; most clearly of all, I could see my baby's sweet, slumbering face, and feel his breath like balm, rising and falling upon my cheek.

And then my eye, I cannot tell how, was caught by the book upon the table; when Alice came to her chair beside me, I told her to read me something. Alice was very tremulous and afraid, and feared I could not bear it, but I knew better; as she brought the candle nearer and began to read some chapters from the Gospel of John, I cannot tell how it was that after that terrible fit of illness and anguish I should, have felt my mind so clear and so much at leisure, it was like the fresh dewy interval after a thunderstorm when the air is lightened and the earth refreshed. As Alice read, I lay perfectly calm, holding my child in my arms, grave, composed, thoughtful, as if I had reached a new stage in my life. There seemed a certain novelty and freshness in these divine words; I was not listening to them mechanically, my imagination went back to the speaker, and realized what individual voice this was, addressing me as it addressed all the world. What wonderful words these were, what strange meanings: Justice, justice, God's meaning of the word, not man's; that He should bear it Himself,—the grand original, universal penalty. He, the offended one; no, not a weak, poor, benevolent forgiveness, not that, but justice, justice; divinest word! Justice, which blinds the very eyes of this poor humanity with that glorious interpretation which only the Lord could give, that he should bear the punishment, and not the criminal. Strange, strange, most strange! the word read differently when men translated it, but this was how God declared the unchangeable might and power it had, to a wavering, disquieted human heart, straggling with its poor wrongs and injuries, rejecting pity, demanding justice; how wonderful was all this! Alice stopped in her reading after a while, but my thoughts did not pause. I lay quite still, quite still, looking with my open eyes into the dim atmosphere with its faint rays of light, and fainter perfume. How my coward fancies slunk and stole away out of sight, out of hearing, of Him who spoke. My justice and His justice, how different they are; did the same name belong to them? I was not excited, I was not afraid; I thought of it all with a strange composure, an extraordinary calm conviction. I had no desire to sleep, yet I was quite at rest, I did not even feel guilty, only dolefully mistaken, wrong, as unlike Him as anything could be, and only able to wonder at His sublime and wonderful justice, and at the arrogant, presumptuous offence, which had taken the place of justice with me.

And then at last, I fancy I must have fallen asleep, for I had strange sights of bars and judgment-seats, of criminals receiving sentence, and a terrible impression on my mind that I was the next who should be condemned, but that always a bright figure stepped in before me, and the Judge perceived me not. When I woke again it was deep in the night,—Alice was lulling baby, the moon was shining into the room, and I was lying as quiet and as easy as if no such thing as pain had been in the world.

"You are better, dear?" said Alice in a whisper of hesitating joy, as she came to me with some cool pleasant drink she had made. My heart was light; I was almost playful. "I think I am quite well," I said. "I ought to get up, and let you lie down, Alice; have you had a great deal of trouble with me to-day?"

"Hush, darling, no trouble," said Alice, hurriedly, "but you've had a bad turn; go to sleep, dear, go to sleep."

I said "Yes, Alice," as a child might have said it, and I clasped my hands and said the same prayers I had said on the morning of my wedding day. I fell asleep in the middle of them, and ended this day in the deepest peacefulness,—I knew not why.

THE FOURTH DAY

I was now quite well, and it was July, the very flush and prime of summer. After that first day I had progressed steadily and was well, before I had any right to be well, according to the established order of things—for though I was not robust, my health was of the strongest, and I had a vigorous elastic frame, which never long succumbed. I would not listen to Alice's proposal to have a nurse for baby. As soon as I was able I took entire possession of him myself, and did everything for my boy. I had no other cares or occupations; he was my sole business, and he filled all my time with his requirements. What a happiness it was! If I had been at Cottiswoode, and had a proper, well-appointed nursery, how much of the purest delight, how many of the sweetest influences I must have lost! He was very rarely out of my arms, except when he slept through the day, in the luxurious, beautiful cradle—an odd contrast to the other equipments of the house—which we had got for him. I often smile at my own wilful, voluntary poverty now. We had by no means changed the simplicity of our living, and I was my baby's sole attendant, and was perfectly contented with this little, mean, limited house; but I sent Alice to London with the widest license to buy the prettiest baby's cloak, the richest robes, the most delicate equipments for little Harry; and Alice, nothing loath, came back again with a wardrobe fit for a young prince. Sitting by the morsel of fire in the small bed-room up-stairs, with its white dimity hangings, and its clean scanty furniture, I dressed my baby in embroidered robes more costly than a month's housekeeping, and wrapping his rich cloak about him, and tying on, over his rich laced cap, the soft luxurious hat of quilted white satin which Alice had chosen to declare to every chance spectator the proud pre-eminence of his sex—a boy! I put on my own simple straw bonnet and went out with him, straying along the quiet roads, up and down the bank of the river, perfectly indifferent of what all the world might think, and smiling when I passed some genteel young mother of the village, with her little maid trudging behind, carrying her baby. I trust my precious Harry in indifferent hands!—No—I only laughed at Alice's oratory as to what became my station. I had no station here, and wanted none. The curate's wife might lose caste if she wandered about, a volunteer nursemaid, with her child—but I was entirely free to follow my own will, and follow it I did, as, alas! I had always done all my days.

I do not wonder that the people were bewildered what to think of me, and that gossip almost came to an end out of sheer amazement. I was always dressed with the most extreme simplicity and plainness, but I always wore upon my finger that splendid hereditary diamond which was the curse of our house. It was to be supposed that I could not afford a nurse, yet there never had been seen such a magnificent baby wardrobe—very strange, nobody could make it out; and even the rector's wife, who paid me the extraordinary honor of a visit, after baby's baptism—though why she came I could not conceive, for she was a great lady, and chary of her patronage—looked round with an odd, amused, bewildered smile at the luxurious cradle, standing beside the hard hair-cloth sofa, and seemed slightly disposed to speak to me as she might have spoken to a capricious child; but I was wonderfully little moved by anything said to me, or of me; I went upon my own way undisturbed. All those bright summer forenoons I walked about with my baby watching my sweet flowers grow and flourish in the sunshine, myself enjoying the glory and the beauty of those summer days, as I never had enjoyed them before; sometimes I sat down upon a sunny bank near the river, when little Harry was asleep, and watched the ecstasy and rapture of the ships, as they flowed down entranced towards the struggles and tempests of the sea. I never wearied of my sweet burden, though I was so proud to say he grew heavier every day, and made boastful complaints of his weight, as mothers use. Often my thoughts were grave enough; sometimes I wept over my beautiful boy, but I could not resist the influences round me, the supreme delight of looking at his slumbering face—the sweet air that refreshed my own—the beautiful scene that still had power to charm me out of my heavy thoughts. Many doubts and many questions had agitated my mind since the day of my baby's birth, that day so full of joy, yet of humiliation and anguish. I had never recovered entirely from the depression which my husband's stolen visit to see his child had occasioned me. At the very time my heart was softening to former yearning for him, at that very time it seemed his heart was closed against me. I had never since mentioned him to Alice. I did not pretend to ask her if she had written, nor to take any notice of his visit; and amid all the happiness I had with my child in my own heart, there was the most dreary doubtfulness as to what I should do. My heart was not sufficiently humbled to forget entirely its former mood. I could not subdue myself to call him back, even if I had not had so clear in my remembrance that last visit of his, which was not to me. It seemed a strange dreary retribution for all my offences against him, that now he himself was content to let me alone—that he had granted at last, when I no longer desired it, my often-repeated request, and left me unmolested; was it at peace? Alas, at peace was a very different matter! sometimes the words, "'Tis better in pure hate to let her have her will," came over me with almost a ludicrous sense of my downfall and humiliation, but the smile was very bitter and tremulous with which I acknowledged the caricature and satire on myself.

So here I was content to stay, unsettled, doubtful, knowing nothing of what my life, or more than my life, my boy's, was to be, waiting if perhaps he would come or send, or make some appeal to me. Perhaps, I cannot tell—perhaps if he had, my old perversity might have still returned, and I rejected it; but he did not try me, and I could form neither plan nor purpose for the vague, dim future. I persuaded myself that I left it in God's hands, but I was searching its dull horizon with my wistful eyes, day by day.

And then another thing, a fanciful yet not light dread, weighed upon me. When I sat in the sunshine on the bank of the river adjusting my baby's veil, laying it back from his sweet face, as he lay sleeping on my knee, with my ungloved hand, I shuddered at the sinister gleam of the diamond upon his innocent brow. My imagination was excited and restless; it did seem a sinister gleam as it flashed upon the innocent sleeper, and all the curse of the story returned to my mind, no more as a mere visionary legend, or a tale half believed, half smiled at, but as a real hereditary curse. Suppose I should die, and my husband marry some sweet loving wife, who would make up to him for all he had suffered with me—once I used to persuade myself that I would be glad of that—and my boy should have another brother, who was not his mother's son? When I took this possibility into my mind and pondered it, I almost thought, like the unhappy lady to whom it came first, that this fatal jewel blazed at me with malignant splendor like the eye of an evil spirit. No reasonings of mine could shake my terror of it. I was not wise enough, nor sufficiently courageous to banish this fanciful apprehension from my mind, and I trembled, and a cold dew of pain came upon my face as I thought of the lifelong enmity and strife which might be perpetuated in this child, doubly a Southcote as he was, and born in an atmosphere disturbed and clouded by the ceaseless discord of this race.

This day I was seated at my usual post on a grassy bank near the river. Baby lay in my lap asleep, his rich veil laid back round the edge of his hat, showing his sweet innocent face in a nest of lace and ribbons, warm with the subdued sunshine which fell intensely on his white cloak and robes and upon me, but which I carefully held a little parasol to shield from his head. There was a slight fantastic breeze about, crisping the water, and blowing in small warm capricious gusts, now from one quarter, now from another. As usual, the river was bright with many passengers, and some pleasure-boats were setting out from our little bay, for there were now some London people in the village, which was a tiny watering-place in its quiet way. I had newly taken my seat, after a considerable walk, and was just drawing my glove from my hand to put back a stray morsel of the down which we called hair from baby's forehead. My hands were still thin, and my ring had always been loose on my finger; this time, as it happened, it came off with the glove, and a little gust of wind coming at the moment, my glove blew away from me as I pulled it off, and the ring fell and rolled glistening down over the knoll to the edge of the beach, where it lay among the pebbles, gleaming and sparkling like a living thing.

I never paused to lift my glove. I snatched up my baby hurriedly and almost ran away. I would not look back, lest I should see some one find it, and be obliged to acknowledge it as mine. I hastened along as if I had been stealing instead of only losing this precious ornament. I am sure I felt as guilty, for this was not an innocent and bonâ-fide loss, and I trembled between hope and terror. I had been out for some time, and, truth to speak, Master Harry had momentarily fatigued the arms of his mamma. Then the capricious wind chose this time of all others to loose my hair from under my bonnet, and catch a wild half-curled lock to sport with, and I had no glove upon my right hand; the only one which baby's ample vestments permitted to be visible. In this case I hurried on, meeting a London nursemaid with some wild pretty children, who drew herself up in conscious superiority; meeting the Rector's pony carriage, with Mrs. Rector in it, who nodded to me with her usual amused disapproving look, and, I was very certain, laughed when I was past. Somehow or other, I almost enjoyed these interruptions, and hastened homeward with my gloveless hand and my face flushed with haste and exercise. I certainly could not have looked much like a miserable forsaken wife, or a self-consuming passionate misanthrope, when I reached our cottage door.

The brightest face in the world was looking out for me at the window—Flora! Flora Ennerdale! what could bring her here? But I had scarcely time to ask the question when she ran out to meet me, as eager and joyful as her sweet, affectionate nature could be. Flora seized upon my ungloved hand, and stood looking at me in her pretty shy way to see if I would kiss her. I did, this time, with real love and pleasure; and Baby!—she took him, though I only half consented, out of my arms, with a natural instinct for it, yet not with the perfect skill which I flattered myself I had attained to, and insisted upon carrying him in, very proud and delighted, to the little parlor, where she had already made herself quite at home, but where her mother's elderly maid, who had come with her, sat very dainty and frigid, much more disgusted with our penurious appointments than Flora was. For the first moment I was conscious of nothing but pleasure in seeing her, but now I began to inquire within myself and to wonder—who had told her? who had sent her? was she the investigating dove, the messenger to tell if the floods had abated?—a momentary pang of pique and jealous pride made me look gravely at Flora; but it was impossible to look at her sweet, innocent face, and think of any hidden design. No, she would tell me honestly why she came—I was sure of that.

When Alice came in, Flora's respectable attendant condescended to withdraw with her, and we were left alone. Flora had thrown down her bonnet and shawl upon the haircloth sofa, where she now hastily placed mine, after disrobing me with her own hands. I took my low nursing-chair, for I had now regained Baby, but Flora was standing before the window in her wide floating, pretty muslin gown, so summerlike and girl-like; she was not disposed even to stand still, much less to sit down for a reasonable conference, and all this while was running on with her pleasant voice and happy words, as light of heart as ever.

"Oh, cousin Hester, how beautiful it is," she cried; "how did you find out such a lovely quiet place? and such ships? I have heard the boys speak of ships, but I thought there was always something nasty and noisy about where they are. I could look at these all day—how they float! what beautiful round sails—is that the wind in them that fills them out so?—and how they seem to enjoy it, cousin Hester!"

"How did you find me out, Flora?" I asked.

Flora hesitated for a moment, and then suddenly came and knelt down beside me. "Dear cousin Hester, Mr. Southcote came and told Mamma all about it. You will not be angry, cousin? Mamma thought it was not right of you, and Mr. Southcote came and explained it to her, and said it was he that had been wrong, and that you had a right to be angry with him. Then he let us know when Baby was born—oh, what a sweet rogue he is, cousin Hester!—do you think there ever was such a pretty baby? and then we had to come to London—about—about—some business, and I teased Mamma till she let me come to see you. I did so want to see you, and I had something to tell you too."

"What had you to tell me, Flora?" I asked, stiffening into pride again. This of course was some message from my husband, and I could not explain why I felt aggrieved that he should choose her for his messenger.

Flora looked up wistfully into my face—"Have I said anything wrong—are you angry, cousin?"

"No, no; why should I be angry?" I answered, almost with impatience. "Tell me what message you have."

"Message! It is no message," said Flora, her whole pretty face waking into blushes and dimples; "it was all about myself, cousin Hester—I am so selfish; it was something that happened to me."

I saw how it was at once, and was relieved. "Well, tell me what has happened, Flora," I said.

But Flora buried her pretty face and her fair curls in Baby's long robes, and laughed a little tremulous laugh, and made me no answer.

"Must I guess?" I asked, smiling at the girlish, sweet confusion. "I suppose, as people say, somebody has fallen in love with you: is that what has happened?"

She looked up for a moment with a glance of delighted astonishment—"How could you find it out, cousin Hester?" said Flora; "it looks very vain even to believe it; but, indeed—indeed, he says so, and I think it is the strangest thing in the world."

Her innocent surprise and joy brought tears to my eyes. I remembered myself the humility of a young heart wondering, wondering if this strange gift of gifts, the love of romance and poetry, could really have fallen to its own share; yet Flora was so unlike me—and my eyes, worn with tears and watching, were they disenchanted now?

I stooped to kiss her sweet blushing cheek. "I must hear who he is now, and all that you have to tell me," said I. "Are they pleased at home, and is he a hero and a paladin? It was very good of you to come and tell me, Flora."

"No, he is not a hero," said Flora, and then she paused and looked up in my face, and made a breathless appeal to me, clasping baby's little soft hand within both her own; "Oh, cousin Hester, will you come home? it must be so dreadful to be parted; I can understand it now," said Flora, with her sweet blush. "Please, cousin Hester, dear cousin, what matter is it if Mr. Southcote was wrong, he is so fond of you, he thinks there is no one like you; oh, will you come home?"

I was taken by surprise. I could not help crying as the eager young face looked up in mine. I was not in the least angry; but alas! she did not know,—how could she know?

"Hush, Flora, hush," I said, when I could speak; "hush, hush;" I could not find another word to say.

"You would be a great deal happier, cousin Hester," said Flora, kissing my hand, and clasping it with baby's between her own.

I only repeated that one word "Hush." If my child himself had appealed to me, I do not think I could have been more strangely moved.

She said no more, but sighed as she gave up her guileless endeavor; and now again the smiles and blushes came beaming back, and she told me of her own happiness. He was a young landed gentleman in their immediate neighborhood, only five miles from Ennerdale, and if neither a hero nor a paladin, had managed to make Flora very well contented with him, that was certain. And everything was so suitable, she said, and mamma and papa were so much pleased, and the boys were wild about it, and they had come up to London to supply the bride's wardrobe, and it was from this delightful occupation that Flora had spared a day to visit me.

"And he has three sisters, cousin Hester," said Flora, "such pretty, good, nice girls, and they all live at the hall; and we have always been such friends, especially Mary and I, and they will be such pleasant company. Oh! if you were only at Cottiswoode, I think I should have nothing more to wish for; I can see mamma almost every day, and Annie is almost old enough to take my place, and when Gus and the rest of the boys come home for the holidays, of course they will be as much at the hall as they are at Ennerdale, and he is as fond of them all as I am, and if you were at home, cousin Hester, I think I should be almost too happy."

The only thing I could do was to draw my hand caressingly over this happy, pretty head before me. Flora could go on in her pleasant talk without any help from me.

"So that will be one thing to hope for," said Flora; "you might come and see me, cousin Hester. Mamma is so busy getting everything, that she could not come down with me to-day; such quantities of things, I cannot think what I shall do with them, and you know I never had a great many dresses before; just look what a child I am," cried Flora, springing up with a burst of laughter at herself and opening a dainty little basket on the table, to bring out sundry bits of bright rich glistening silk. "I brought them to show them to you, cousin; I know you don't care for such things, but—but—you were always so kind to me."

I was not so philosophical as Flora supposed. I think myself that however universal the feminine love of dress may be, it is never so perfectly developed as in a happy young wife who has her babies to adorn and decorate as well as herself. Though I was far from happy, I felt the germ of this within me, and was not at all indifferent to Flora's pretty specimens. We were soon deep in a discussion of laces and satins, and modes, matters in which Flora was so delighted to have my advice, and I so willing to give it; the forenoon went on very pleasantly while we were thus occupied. I was pleased and drawn out of myself, and I had always been very fond of Flora; the sight of her happiness was quite a delight to me.

When baby had taken his refreshment and been laid to sleep in his cradle—he was not much more than a month old, and slept a great deal, as I suppose healthy, vigorous children generally do—Flora went up to my room with me, for I wanted to give her some little present, such as I had; Flora was somewhat amused at the bare little room, the scanty white dimity hangings, and clean poverty of everything, and at baby's little bath, and the pretty basket which at present held his night things only. "Do you do everything for him yourself?" she asked, wonderingly. "Do you know, cousin Hester, I should think that was so very pleasant, and to carry him about out of doors, as you were doing; oh, I should so like to be your nursemaid, cousin!"

"Well, Flora?" I said, inquiringly, for she had stopped with hesitation, as if she wanted to ask something of me.

"Perhaps you would not like it, dear," said Flora, in her caressing way; "but I should not be at all hurt if you said so. Oh, I should like so much to come here for a few days. Cousin Hester, I could sleep on the sofa, I could help Alice, I always was handy, and I know you would let me carry baby sometimes when you went out. Will you write to mamma now, and ask her to let me come? Oh, cousin Hester, do!"

"But, Flora, your mamma does not approve of me," said I, with an involuntary blush.

Her countenance fell a little. "Indeed I did not say so, cousin Hester," she explained, though with an embarrassment which made it very evident to me that I was right. "She thought it wrong of you to go away, but it was different after Mr. Southcote told her, and she is so very sorry for you, dear cousin, and says she is sure you are not happy. Oh, indeed it was not at all hard to persuade her to let me come to-day. I am very bold to beg so for an invitation, but I do so wish to come, cousin; you will write?"

"It would do me good to have you with me, Flora," I said, sadly; "but I think I have grown very foolish and nervous. I am almost afraid to write to your mamma. I fancy she cannot see anything to excuse me. Happy people are sometimes not the best judges, Flora, and she has never been very wretched, I am sure. And then, what would he say? Nobody can think well of me in Cambridgeshire; and he would not like to have his young bride staying with me. I am sure he would not, Flora."

"Say you would rather I did not come, cousin Hester," said Flora, who was nearly crying; "don't say such cruel things as that."

"Yet they are true," I said; "I know what I have lost, and that few people can think well of me. It will be better not, dear Flora, though it would be a great happiness to me. Now, come here. This was my mother's, and I have sometimes worn it myself. You like to be called like her, Flora. Will you wear it for her sake?"

As I spoke I clasped upon her pretty neck the little gold chain, with its diamond pendant, which I had been so proud to wear on that first fated night when I met Harry. She had not yet dried her few bright tears of disappointment and sympathy, and one fell upon the gems, making them all the brighter. She still cried a little as she thanked me. I knew it was a gift to please her greatly, for pretty as it was itself, and valuable, it had an additional charm to her affectionate heart.

"And for your sake, cousin—am I not to like it for your sake?" cried Flora; "I love to hear of her—but I love you, your very own self—may I wear it for your sake?"

I answered her gratefully, as I felt; but as I opened the case which held my mother's jewels, the same case which my father had given me in Cambridge, and which I had always carried about with me since my eye fell upon Mr. Osborne's present, the little chain with my mother's miniature, my heart was softened; I was a mother myself, and knew now the love above all loves which a mother bears to her child, and I was terribly shaken on my own original standing-ground, and at the bottom of my heart knew myself bitterly, cruelly wrong. My father, it was possible to fancy, might have been even more wrong than I was; and Flora's sweet face, like hers, yet wanting something of the perfect repose and sweetness which this little picture showed, was the last touch that softened me. When I put my mother's diamond ornament on Flora's neck, I clasped the miniature on my own. With my plain dress and total want of ornament—for I had not even a ring except my wedding-ring—the simple little chain and the circle of pearls round the miniature, made a great show. Flora came eagerly to look at it, I had never shown it to her before; she thought it so beautiful—so sweet—she never could be so vain as to let any one say she was like my mother after seeing that.

And then we returned downstairs to the early homely dinner which Alice had been at considerable trouble with. Alice was much disturbed and humbled by the invasion of these visitors; she did not like the idea of any one finding us in our new circumstances, and Flora's maid was a great affliction to Alice. "She could have borne the young lady," she said, "but all the servants at Ennerdale and all the servants at Cottiswoode, everybody would know that Mrs. Southcote kept no nurse for her baby, and lived in a house of four apartments, and waited on herself." It was very galling to Alice, but she forgot it in the secret glow of delight with which she observed the miniature I wore.

Flora did not leave me till it was quite evening, and even then not without another petition that I would "ask Mamma" to let her come for a longer visit. It was a great piece of self-denial, but I steadily resisted her entreaties. I knew Mrs. Ennerdale—a placid, unawakened woman, who knew nothing of me nor of my struggles—could have no sympathy for me, and I rather would want the solace of Flora's company than expose her to her mother's disapprobation. I had voluntarily left my husband and my own house, perhaps with no sufficient cause, and I sternly doomed myself to a recluse's life, and determined to involve no one in any blame that belonged to me.

In the early evening, when the sun had just set—baby, by this time, having had his full share of attendance, and Flora herself, by especial favor, having been permitted to place him in his cradle—I set out with her to the railway, which was at a considerable distance from the village. But when we were ready to go, I suddenly remembered I had but one glove, and Alice as suddenly perceived the want upon my finger. "Do you not wear your ring to-day, dear?" whispered Alice, looking at me anxiously as she put my shawl round me. In the same whispering tone, but with guilt at heart, I answered, "I lost it by the waterside this morning," and Alice uttered a subdued cry of joy. I had happily forgotten it all this day, but when it occurred to me I felt considerably disturbed and timid. I could not persuade myself I had lost it honestly. I fancied I could still see it gleaming among the pebbles at the water's edge when I could so easily have picked it up, and if it did come back to me after this, I fancied I would, more than ever, think it a fate.

We had a long pleasant walk in the peaceful sweet evening. Flora's influence over me had always been good; to-night she made me almost as light of heart as herself, and we parted with a great many hopes on her part of seeing me again before she left London, and with a good deal of sadness on mine. When I turned back alone, I found even a tear hanging upon my eye-lash. Her young, sweet, unshadowed hope was a great contrast to mine, but that was not what made me sad; I liked Flora, she seemed to connect me at once with the bright girlhood and young womanhood of which, in my solitary life, I had known so little, and it grieved me to think that for a long time, perhaps for ever, I might not see her again. Natural likings and desires came upon me so strangely in that unnatural position: I should have liked to go to Flora's marriage, to help her in her preparations, to do all which young people, friends to each other, delight to do on such occasions; and the thought that her mother now, and, most likely, her husband hereafter, would rather discourage Flora's affection for me, was rather a hard thought. As I turned my face homeward, the peaceful evening light was falling into shadow over these quiet houses; from the church there once again came that faint inarticulate sound of music, solitary chords, struck at intervals, vibrating through the lonely building, and through the harmonious quiet of the air, and everything, except the passing ships, was at rest and at home. I turned my wistful eyes to them, perpetual voyagers! my overladen heart followed them as they glided out to the sea—distance, space, blank, and void and far. I thought of the wilds of my own country, and of the endless, breathless travel, the constant journey on and on to the very end of the world, which my girlish fancies had thought upon so often. It seemed for a moment as though that, and that only, could ease the restless disquiet in my breast.

"Mrs. Southcote, I beg your pardon for interrupting you so abruptly," said our village doctor, coming up hastily to me, and perceiving how I started at the sound of his voice recalling me to myself, "but did you lose a ring to-day? My wife picked up this on the beach. It is yours, I think."

I looked at him with blank dismay, though I did not look at the glittering jewel in his hand; of course I knew at once that it was mine—that it must be mine—and that malicious fate returned the curse to me. It was no use trying to deny or disown this fatal gem. Malicious fate! What words these were! I sickened at the passion and rebellious force that still was in my heart.

"Yes," I said, almost with resentment; "yes, thank you, it is mine," but I did not hold out my hand for it. The doctor looked amazed, almost distrustful of me. I was not comprehensible to him.

"It seems of great value," he said, with a slight, half-indignant emphasis; "and even in the village, I dare say, it might have fallen into hands less safe than my wife's. The river would have made small account of your diamond had the water come an inch or two higher. Ladies are seldom so careless of their pretty things, Mrs. Southcote."

He was an old man, and had been very kind to me. I did not wish to offend him now that I recollected myself. "It has very unpleasant recollections to me, doctor," I said, as I put it on my finger; "I almost was glad to think I had lost it: but I thank you very much for taking the trouble, and will you thank Mrs. Lister for me; it was very kind of her to pick it up."

The old doctor left me, more than ever bewildered as to my true character and position. I heard afterwards from the rector's wife, who was not above caricaturing and observing the village oddities, that he went home to the little house, which had been cast into great excitement half the day by finding this prize, completely dismayed by my indifference. "I was almost glad to think I had lost it!" Who could I be who thought so little of such a valuable ornament? The doctor and his household could not understand what it meant.

As for me, when I left him, my impulse was to tear it from my finger, and fling it with all my force into the middle of the river. To what purpose? it would not be safe, I believed, even there. Wilful losing would not do, as I had experienced already. With secret passion I pressed it upon my finger, as if extra precautions to secure it might, perhaps, answer my purpose. What a fiendish, malignant glare it had to my excited eyes as I looked at it in the soft twilight: it seemed to gather the lingering light into itself, and turn upon me with a glow of defiance. When I reached home, where Alice had already lighted candles and put our little parlor in order, I held it up to her as I entered. I believe I was quite pale with fright and passion. "See, it has come back to me," I said; "it will not be lost."

Alice was not so much dismayed as I was. "I feared it would be found," she said; "but patience, dear; there is but one heir to Cottiswoode, and it's worn on a woman's hand."

I had to content myself, of course; but I scarcely liked to put up my hand, with that ring upon it, to my neck, where hung my mother's miniature. Alice's eye followed me, as I did it once, and her face lighted up. "If the ring is the sign of strife, the picture is peace itself, Miss Hester," she said with a faltering voice. I almost thought so myself. How strange it was to wear these two things together!

THE FIFTH DAY

My baby was very ill. He had been seized a week before, but we had not apprehended anything. Now we were closely shut up in my bed-room, trying to shield every breath of air from him; keeping up the fire though it was only September, while I sat by the fireside holding him on my knee, watching the changes of his face, his breathing, his movements, with frightful anxiety, and reproaching myself, oh, so bitterly, for that one last walk, which had brought this illness upon him. He had taken a violent cold, and I could not but see, by the anxiety of the doctor, by the gravity of Alice, and the pitying tender look which she cast upon me, how they thought it would end. When I awoke from my security to think of this, I dare not describe the misery that came upon me. Oh, I had talked of misery and hopelessness before, but what were all the griefs in the world to this one! To look at him, and think he might be taken from me—to look upon those sweet features, which might be by-and-by removed from my eyes for ever; oh, heaven, that agony! that was the bitterness of death.

He had rallied two or three times and relapsed again, so that we were even afraid to trust the appearance of recovery when such appeared, but there was no sign of recovery now. It was just dawn, very early in the morning, and we had been watching all night. I had made Alice lie down, and baby was in a disturbed and painful slumber. As I sat watching him, restraining my very breath lest it should make him uneasy as he lay upon my lap, my eye wandered to the cold gray sky, over which the morning light was flushing faintly, and it came to my mind how I had watched the dawn upon this day twelvemonth, my wedding-day. The sweet serenity of that morning came back to my recollection, the agitation of my own mind, which, great as it was, was happy agitation still, and my trust, my hope unbounded; my perfect confidence in Harry, my fearlessness of any evil—yet, that was the beginning of sorrows; now the fear in my heart shook the very foundations of the earth; if such a calamity came, there was no light, no hope beyond it. I had come to love life for my baby's sake, and even now I know I made a great painful effort to say I would be resigned and content with God's will, whatever it—but I felt in my heart that life would be only a loathing and disgust to me; oh, heaven have pity upon me! What would I have in all the world if my baby were taken away!

Every fleeting change that there was—every momentary alteration, I wanted to have the doctor, or to call Alice, to ask what they thought now. Then I remembered vaguely the name, the Great Physician—and that however far others might be, he was near at all times; oh, if I only could have got to his feet, as they did in Palestine in those blessed days when He was there, if I could but have thrown myself on the earth before him, and cried, "my child! my child!" I said, as in my prayer, from my very despair, I caught boldness. I cried with my heart, till it was bursting with that agony of asking,—praying for your child's life, do you know what it is?

There was no difference, no difference! and the pallid light was growing on the sky, and the first sounds of life began to break upon the stillness; then I was stayed in my prayers as by an invisible hand. I cannot tell how or why these words came to my mind, but they came with a terrible force, making me silent, shutting my mouth in an instant: "If I regard sin in my heart, the Lord will not hear me." I was appalled by the sudden sentence; was there no hope, then? No hope? Did I not even dare to appeal to Him who never before cast any applicant away?

I was struck dumb; I sat still in a breathless, hopeless pause of dismay, my heart suddenly yielding to this dreary calamity. In a moment there came upon me a fearful vision of what might be my life bereaved, my hope lost. Heaven and the ear of God shut upon me; I knew what was right, and I had not done it. I was self-convicted of wrong, but I did not change my course. I was crying wildly to God for the blessing which he alone could grant, but I was still regarding sin in my heart.

At this moment Alice woke and hastily rose; she saw no change in baby, he was just the same, just the same; oh, these dreadful hopeless words! But I consented she should take him upon her lap, and myself went downstairs, though not to rest myself, as she said; I went with a faint desperate hope that perhaps if I were absent a few minutes I might perceive a favorable change when I returned. I went into the cold deserted parlor, which already looked so uninhabited, so miserable, and where baby's unused cradle stood in the chill morning light, reminding me, if I had needed to be reminded, of the sweet days that were past, and of the frightful shadow which was upon us now. I knelt down upon the floor beside it. I did more than kneel; I bent down my very head upon the ground. I could not find a position low enough, humble enough. I tried to persuade myself that He was here indeed, that I was at His feet, where the woman which was a sinner came; but my cry was balked and my words stayed by that great unchangeable barrier; ah, the woman which was a sinner was not then regarding sin in her heart.

I could not bear this intolerable oppression; my prayers and cries must have outlet one way or another. I raised up my head, almost as if I was addressing some mortal enemy who had whispered these words into my mind. "I will go home—I will humble myself to my husband," I cried aloud. "I do not care for pride—I will humble myself—I will humble myself!" While I was speaking my tears came in a flood, my troubled brain was lightened, and when I laid down my head again and covered my face with my hands, I felt at least that I could pray.

I am not sure that I could have been five minutes absent altogether, but when I went back I was sick with the eager breathless hope which had risen in my mind. There was no ground for it; he was no better; but I took him in my lap again with patience, trying to put the dreadful shadow off from me. The dawn brightened into the full morning; then came the dreadful noon with all its brightness; the doctor came and went; the hours passed on, and the baby lived—that was all.

And now I could not pray any longer; my mind had sunk into a feverish stupidity; I was alive to nothing but the looks of my child; yes, and to one thing besides. I had a strange, helpless feeling of clinging to "the Great Physician;" the name was in my mind, if nothing more; it was not prayer, it was not faith; I could not say it was anything natural or spiritual at all; I rather felt as if something held me, as if I were clinging to a cord or to the skirts of a robe; as if I was only thus prevented from plunging into some dreadful abyss of despair and ruin, and my dumb, strange, almost stupid dependence was upon Him solely—only upon Him.

I was waiting, waiting; I did not dare to say to myself that baby lay more quietly; I dared not look up at Alice, or ask her what she thought; but when the doctor came again it was nearly evening, and as I watched his face my heart grew sick. Oh, yes, it was hope—hope! I scarcely could bear it; and when the old man said real words—real true words, not fancies, that he was a great deal better, I think I had very nearly fainted.

But it was quite true; he improved gradually all that afternoon; he began to look like himself again; rapidly as he had grown ill, he grew better; I suppose it always is so with young children; and when I sat by the fire in the evening with him, he put up his dear little hand again to catch at my mother's miniature, as he had done before his illness. "Oh, my darling, give God thanks," said Alice, as she sat on a stool by me, not able to control her tears. I had, indeed, an unspeakable thankfulness in my heart, but I could not give expression to it—words would not come. "Lips say God be pitiful, that ne'er said God be praised!" Is that true, I wonder; I was very, very grateful, but I could not find words as I did in the agony of my prayers.

And now I returned to the resolution I had come to when baby fell asleep. Oh, that sweet, hopeful sleep; it was delight enough to look at it! I sat over the fire pondering on what I had to do. Then it occurred to me how unjust I had been. This dear, precious child, without whom my life would be a blank and hateful; this little creature, who had been to me a fountain of every sweet and tender influence; who had made my days joyful, burdened though they were,—was my husband's child, and by as close and dear a tie as he was mine. I had no right to keep for myself, and for my own enjoyment, this sweetest gift of Providence, which was not bestowed on one of us more than another, but which was given to both. If he had wronged me, he had not wronged his child; and I bowed my head in shame to think how I had broken even my own rules of justice—how I could restore my husband to his rights. Without being conscious that this was still another salve to my own pride, I took up eagerly this view of the matter. I would humble myself to say that I was wrong—to return to Cottiswoode—to acknowledge how unjust I had been, and to share with my husband the care of our child; and then, when my heart ached with thinking that right and wrong were not the only things to build household peace upon, imagination came in to charm me with dreams of what he would do and say. How he would once more seek the heart which once was given to him so freely; how he would come to my feet again as he had done a year ago. Ah, this was our very marriage-day!

I wondered how he was spending it—where—if he was all by himself at Cottiswoode—perhaps in that library in the chair where I had placed myself leaning upon the desk, where I leant the day I came away, perhaps writing to me—surely thinking of me; yes, I did not think he could let this day pass without wishing for me over again, and I wondered if I could get home before his appeal should reach me, for already I could imagine him writing a loving, anxious letter, full of the memories of to-day.

What a strange difference! a pleasant excitement of plans and hopes was busy in the mind which only this morning had been lost in such despairing supplications. I think I had only risen the higher in the rebound for the depth of suffering to which I fell before. The idea of the journey, the return, the joyful surprise to my husband, the joy to myself of perceiving his delight in little Harry, the satisfaction of Alice, and my own content in being once more at home, and carrying with me the heir of Cottiswoode, woke pleasure new and unaccustomed in my heart. I did not question myself about it, I did not pause to think of any humiliation, I permitted the tide of natural gladness to rise at its own sweet will; I thought any degree of joy, and every degree, was possible, when I had thus regained, from the very shadow of death, my beautiful boy.

"I won't have you sit up to-night, Miss Hester," said Alice, who had returned to sit beside me, and gaze at him, but who did not disturb my thoughts; "you must lie down, darling; he'll have a good night, I'm sure, and I'll sleep in the big chair, it's very comfortable; now, dear, lie down, you're wearied out."

"No, indeed, I am not even tired," I said; "I want nothing but to sit and look at him, Alice. Oh, is it not a delight to see him now?"

"Ay, dear," said Alice slowly and sadly; "ay, Miss Hester, especially for them that have seen the like of him pass to heaven out of their own arms."

I knew now what the griefs of Alice's life must have been. I, who had often thought lightly of them in comparison with the griefs which I had brought upon myself, I knew better now. I took her hand into my own, and pressed it close, and kissed that dear, kind, careful hand.

"Don't, darling, don't," cried Alice, in a voice choked with tears; "Oh, Miss Hester, have you given thanks to God?"

"I am very thankful, very thankful, Alice," said I kindly, and there was another pause. "Alice, when do you think he would be able to travel?" I asked at last; "perhaps a change might do him good, do you think so? how soon do you think we could go?"

"Are we to go to another strange place, Miss Hester?" said Alice, with a little dismay: "Dear, I think you should rather stay here; we're known here now, and nobody takes particular note of us; but to see a young lady like you with a baby, and all by yourself, makes people talk, and I wouldn't go to a strange place, darling; it's very pleasant here."

"I did not think of going to a strange place, Alice," said I.

"Then you thought of Cambridge, Miss Hester," continued Alice, rapidly; "for my part, I've no heart to go back to Cambridge, I'd rather go anywhere than there; they'd say it was to vex Mr. Southcote you went; they say a deal of malicious things, and everybody knows us there, and it's a dreary house for you to go back to, dear; you'd be sure to feel it so, even with baby. My darling, don't go there; I've come to like this little place, we have it all to ourselves, and now it's like home."

"Then do you think there is no other home I have a right to, Alice?" I asked. I felt very much cast down and humbled because she never seemed to think of that. Perhaps, indeed, I had no right to go back to the home I had left.

"If you mean that, if you can think of that, Miss Hester," cried Alice, in a tremulous voice.

"Should I not think of it? will he not permit me to live there again?" said I, not without some pride, though with more sadness. "I suppose you know my husband's purposes better than I do; Alice, it is a sad state of matters; but I have been very wrong, and even though he should refuse to admit me, I must go; I have been very unjust to him; my baby belongs as much to him as to me. I have deprived my husband of his rights, and now I must restore them to him."

"I do not understand you, Miss Hester," said Alice, looking almost frightened.

"Baby has a father as well as a mother, Alice," I repeated; "and I am wronging my husband. I know he has seen little Harry, but he ought to be able to see him every day as I do. I have no right to keep my darling all to myself; he belongs to his father as much as to me, so I have made a vow to go home."

"Only because it is right, Miss Hester?" asked Alice.

"Do you think anything else would conquer me?" I cried, keeping back my tears with an effort. "I could die by myself without murmuring. I don't ask to be happy, as people call it; but I will not do him injustice—he has a right to his child."

After this petulant speech, which, indeed, excited and unsettled as I was by the sudden idea that my husband might not desire to receive me, I could not restrain, I settled myself in my chair, and half from pure wilfulness, half because my mind was so much occupied that I had no great inclination to rest, I made Alice lie down, and continued in the chair myself. Hushed and nestling close to my breast, Baby slept so sweet a sleep that it was a delight to see him; and my thoughts were free to speculate on my plans. Could it be possible that bringing his son, his heir, with me—or, indeed, coming myself in any guise—I would be unwelcome at Cottiswoode? The thought was overwhelming. I was almost seized again with the same dreadful spasm of heartache and weakness which had attacked me on the day of Baby's birth. Was it possible—was it complete alienation, and not mere separation?—had I estranged his heart entirely from me? More than that, the fiend began to whisper—it was all deception—it was all a generous impulse; he never did love me at all—he was only anxious to restore to me my lost inheritance, to make up to me for all he had deprived me of.

I tried to fly from the evil suggestion; I put up my hand to feel for my mother's miniature, as if it could help me. This hurried, anxious motion awoke Baby. Oh, I was well punished. He cried a great deal, and woke up thoroughly, and his crying brought on a coughing fit. It was nearly an hour before we had composed and lulled him to sleep, for Alice had started up instantly on hearing his voice. All my terrors were roused by this, though it was rather a little infantine temper and fretfulness than anything else. I fancied I had brought it all upon myself; I trembled with a superstitious dread before the wise, and kind, and pitiful Providence which guided me, as if my own constant transgressions were being followed by a strict eye, and quick retribution. Oh, pity, pity!—what was justice to such as me? and what would become of me who dared to judge others, if God dealt with myself only as I deserved?

Then I made up my mind firmly and steadily once more, however I was received there, to go to Cottiswoode, and if my husband did not object, to remain there, that neither of us might lose our child. One wild impulse of giving up my baby to him, and fleeing myself to the end of the earth, was too dreadful to be more than momentary. No, I would go to Cottiswoode; I would tell him that I had wronged him—I would offer him all the justice it was in my power to give. It was now past midnight, and baby was once more fast asleep. Alice was sleeping—everything was perfectly still, except the faint crackling of the fire. Once or twice I had already dropped asleep myself for a few moments, when there was no urgent claim upon my attention, carrying my restless thoughts into dreams as restless. Now I suppose I must have fallen into the deep slumber of exhaustion, holding my baby fast in my arms, for I remember no more of that day.

And that was how I spent the first anniversary of my bridal day.

THE SIXTH DAY

It was now late in September, a true autumnal day, just such a day as one of those which had carried us joyfully over foreign rivers and highways a year ago, when Alice and I made our final preparations and set out on our journey home. The owner of the house—the widow lady, had returned on the previous evening, and she was very well satisfied with the rent I paid her in place of the "notice" to which she was entitled. Baby was perfectly well, I think even stronger and more beautiful than ever; and though I trembled with nervous excitement, anticipating this new step I was about to take, I was tolerably composed, considering everything that was involved. It was very early, I think not much after six o'clock, when we sat down at our homely breakfast-table. I with baby on my lap, fully equipped and well wrapped up for his journey, and Alice with an odd variety of little parcels about her, and far too much agitated to take anything now, though she had carefully provided herself with a basket of "refreshments" to present me withal upon the way. The sunshine slanted with its golden gleam upon the river, and the half-awakened houses on the water's edge. There were no ships, but only a vacant pleasure-boat, flapping its loose sail idly on the morning wind, and rocking on the rising water as the morning tide came in upon the beach. The air was slightly chill and fresh, as it only is at that hour, and the sun, slanting down upon house after house, shining upon curtained windows and closed doors, seemed calling almost with a playful mocking upon the sleepers. Our little bustle and commotion, the excitement in our pale faces, and the eventful journey before us, though they were not unsuitable for the opening of a common laborious day, bore yet a strange contrast to this charmed house, which was almost as sweet and full of peace as the evening. I stood by the window for a moment, looked out wistfully on the landscape which had grown so familiar to my eyes—how sweet it was! how the water rose and glistened, dilating with the full tide! I suppose we have all picture-galleries of our own, almost surpassing, with their ideal truth, the accomplished works of art; and I know that there is no more vivid scene in mine than that morning landscape on the Thames.

We had but one trunk when we came, but baby's overflowing wardrobe, and that pretty cradle of his which it had cost us so much trouble to pack, added considerably to our encumbrances; but I was glad to think Alice was not quite so helpless now as when I hurried her, stunned and frightened, away from the peaceful home which she had never left before. It was so strange to go over these rooms, and think it was for the last time; these little humble rooms, where so much had happened to us, where baby had been born!

Stranger still it was to find ourselves travelling, rushing away from our quiet habitation and our banished life. Then, London—Alice was upon terms of moderate acquaintanceship with London now, she had been here all by herself to provide baby's pretty dresses; so that this was now her third time of visiting it. I was very anxious to lose no time, for there was a long drive between the railway and Cottiswoode, and I wished to arrive before night. In spite of myself new and pleasant emotions fluttered within me, uncertain as I was how my husband would receive me; painful as it was, on many accounts, to ask him to admit me once more to my proper place. I still could not help contriving, with a mother's anxious vanity, and with a deeper feeling than that, that baby should look well, and not be fretful or tired when his father, for the first time, saw him in my arms—so we scarcely waited at all in London. My heart began to beat more wildly when we were once more seated in the railway carriage, and proceeding on our way to Cambridge; for a little while I was speechless with the tumult of agitation into which I fell. Was it real, possible? unasked and uncalled for—was I going home?

We had arranged to stop at a little town where we were quite unknown, and where we were sure to be able to get a chaise to Cottiswoode; I do not think half-a-dozen words passed between us while we dashed along through this peaceful country at express speed; baby slept nearly all the way, the motion overpowered him, and I was very thankful that he made so little claim upon my attention; when he did wake up we were nearly at the station, and Alice took him and held him up at the window. When he was out of my arms, I bowed down my head into my hands and cried, and tried to pray; how my heart was beating! I scarcely saw anything about me, and the din of opening and shutting the carriage doors, the porter shrieking the name of the station, and the bustle of alighting, came to me like sounds in a dream. I stirred myself mechanically and gathered up our parcels, while Alice carefully descended from the carriage bearing baby in her arms. Alice, with careful forethought, considered my dignity in this matter, and for myself I was not displeased at this moment to be relieved from the charge of my child.

How pretty he looked, holding up his sweet little face, looking round him with those bright eyes of his!— even in my pre-occupation I heard passing countrywomen point him out to each other; my heart swelled when I thought of taking him home, and placing him in his father's arms. Alas, alas! that father, how would he look at me?

We had come to a very small town, scarcely more than a village, save for one good inn in it; it had once been on the high-road to London, but the railway had made sad failure of its pretensions. Here, however, we did not find it difficult to get a post-chaise, and I made Alice take some refreshments while we waited for it; I could not take anything myself; I could not rest nor sit still; I took baby in my arms, and paced about the long, large, deserted room we were waiting in. Alice did not say anything to me, and as soon as she could, she got little Harry from me again; I was very impatient; I could not understand why they took so long to get ready. It was now nearly two o'clock, but they told me they could drive in two hours to Cottiswoode.

At last we set off. I gave up baby entirely to Alice; I sat with my hand upon the open window looking intently out; I do not think I changed my position once during that entire two hours. My eyes devoured the way as we drove on; my sole impulse all the time was, to watch how fast we went, to see how we drew nearer step by step and mile by mile, my own country! I leant out my head once and drew in a long breath of that wide, free air, coming full and fresh upon us from the far horizon. It seemed to be years instead of months since I had last been here.

When we began to draw very near, when once more we passed Cottisbourne and the Rectory, and made a circuit to reach the entrance of the avenue, my heart beat so fast that I could scarcely breathe; I held out my arms silently to Alice, and she placed baby within them; I held him very close to me for an instant, and bent over him to gain courage; oh! my beautiful, innocent, fearless baby!—nothing knew he of wrong or punishment, of a guilty conscience or a doubtful welcome. He lay looking up in my face smiling, as if to give me courage; but his smile did not give me courage. I must indeed compose and collect myself; or instead of telling my husband that I came to do him justice, I would make a mere appeal to his pity with my weakness and my tears; and that was what, even now, I could not do.

Down that noble avenue under the elm trees; and now we drew up at the door of Cottiswoode. I trembled exceedingly as I descended the steps, though I maintained an outer appearance of firmness. Mr. Southcote was not at home, the man said, gazing at me in astonishment; I was struck with utter dismay by this; I had never calculated on such a chance. I turned round to Alice with stunned and stupid perplexity to ask what we were to do.

But there was a rush from the hall, and the housekeeper and Amy and another woman-servant came forward, the younger ones hanging on the skirts of Mrs. Templeton: "Master will be home immediately, ma'am," cried the housekeeper; "it's a new boy, he don't know who he's a-speaking to. Please to let me take the dear baby; oh, what a darling it is! and such rejoicings as we had when we heard of its being a son and heir. Master's but gone to the Rectory. I'll send off the chaise. Dear heart, Alice, show the way; my lady likes none so well as you."

I went in faintly. I would not give up my boy to any one of them. I had not a word or a look for the kind, eager women who followed me with anxious eyes. I would not even go into the drawing-room, but turned hastily to the library. When I sat down at last in his chair, I felt as if a few moments would have overpowered me. I was here at home, under the kindly roof where I had been born, holding the heir of Cottiswoode in my arms, waiting for my husband; but my heart was dumb and faint with dismay, and I scarcely knew what I expected as I sat motionless before his table, looking at the materials and the scene of his daily occupations. I could not see a thing there which suggested a single thought of me. No—the desk on which I had laid my note was removed, modern books and papers lay on the table; I could almost fancy he had studiously removed everything which could remind him that I once was here.

My heart sank, my courage gradually ebbed away from me; but baby began to stir and murmur, he was not content to sit so quietly; and I was obliged to rise and walk about with him, though my limbs trembled under me. Then, indeed, could it be in recollection of me? I saw a little table placed as mine had used to be in the little windowed recess where I had spent so much of my time when I was a girl, and on it a little vase with roses, those sweet pale roses from my favorite tree. I remembered in a moment how this room had looked on the autumn night when Edgar Southcote first came to Cottiswoode. Could this be in remembrance of that, and of me?

I cannot tell how long I walked about with baby, acquiring some degree of composure amid my agitation, as my trial was delayed, though I was faint, exhausted, and weary in frame more than I could have fancied possible. I heard the chaise rumble heavily away, and the noise of carrying our luggage up-stairs. I thought I could detect a whispering sound in the next room, as if Alice was being questioned; and in the large lofty house, with its wide staircases and passages, so different from the little refuge we had been lately accustomed to, the opening and closing of distant doors, and steps coming and going, echoed upon my heart. Once Alice entered to beg that she might have baby, while behind came the housekeeper entreating, with tears in her eyes, that I would take something. It cost me a great effort to ask them to leave me, for my lips were parched and dry, and I scarcely could speak; and they had given me a great shock, little as they intended, for I thought it was my husband when I heard some one at the door.

So thus I continued walking about the room, doing what I could to amuse baby. I had neither removed my bonnet nor relieved him of his out-of-doors dress, but it almost seemed as though my sweet little darling knew that to cry would aggravate my distress—how good he was! springing and crowing in my arms, encumbered as he was.

At last I saw a shadow cross the window—my heart fluttered, bounded, was still, as I thought, for a moment—and then my husband was in the room.

I could not speak at first, my lips were so dry. I came to a sudden standstill in the middle of the room, gazing blankly at him, and holding up the child. I saw nothing but astonishment in his face at my first glance; he came rapidly towards me, crying, "Hester! Hester!" but that was all—he never bade me welcome home.

"I have been very wrong," I said, at last; "I have done you great injustice. I have prided myself on doing right, and yet I have been wrong in everything. I have come back to you to humble myself—he belongs to you as much as to me—he is your son, and I have been unjust and cruel in keeping him away from you; will you let me stay here, that we may both have our boy?"

When I began to speak of wrong and of injustice, he turned away with an impatient gesture and exclamation, but, by this time, had returned and was standing by me, listening, with his head bent, his eyes cast down, and a smile of some bitterness upon his mouth. When I stopped, he looked up at me—strange!—he looked at me—not at my baby—not at his child!

"You have come to do me justice," he said.

What did he mean? the tone was new to me, I did not comprehend. I said, "Yes," humbly. I was overpowered with exhaustion, and could scarcely stand, but I suppose he thought me quite composed.

"This house is yours, Hester," he said, with some emphasis: "it is unjust, since that is to be the word, to ask me such a question. You have come to do me justice, to restore to me some of my rights. I thank you, Hester—though I warned you once that I should not be satisfied, with justice," he continued hurriedly, once more turning away from me, and making a few rapid strides through the room.

I should have been so relieved if I durst have cried; I was so worn out—so much weakened by fatigue and excitement; but I only stood still in my passive mechanical way, able to do no more than to hold baby fast lest he should leap out of my arms.

In a minute after he came back again and stood by me, but not looking at me, leaning his hand on the table, as if he were preparing to say something; for myself, I was exhausted beyond the power of making speeches, or reasoning or explaining, or carrying on any sort of warfare; I was reduced to the barest simplicity; I put out my hand and touched his arm; "Will you not take him?" I said, holding out baby; "Edgar, he is your son."

He glanced at me a moment with the strangest mingling of emotions in his face. After that glance I no longer thought him cold and calm; but then he suddenly snatched baby from me, and kissed and caressed him till I feared he would frighten the child; but he was not frightened, though he was only an infant, my bold, beautiful boy! For myself, I sank into the nearest chair, and let my tired arms fall by my side. I almost felt as if I had not strength enough to rise again, and a dull disappointment was in my heart; was it only to be justice after all? Oh, if he would but come back to me; if he would but forget his dignity, and my right and wrong, and make one more appeal to my true self, to my heart, which yearned for something more than justice! But he did not; oh, and I knew in my heart he was very right; it was I who ought to be thoroughly humbled, it was I who ought to appeal to him; but I was different in my notions now; instinctively I looked for pity, pity, nothing better; and almost hoped that he would remember I was weak and fatigued, a woman, and the mother of his child.

By and by he returned, carrying baby fondly in his arms, his face flushed with undoubted delight and joy. As he drew nearer to me he became graver, and asked me suddenly, "Why did you call me Edgar, Hester?"

"Because it is your proper name," I said.

I felt that he looked at me anxiously to discover my meaning, but I had not energy enough to raise my head to give him a clearer insight into what I thought. Then I fancied he gradually came to some understanding of what I meant. I never addressed him by any name since our coming home. I would not. I could not call him Harry, and I had so little desire to make peace or to establish any convenient or natural intercourse, that I never tried to adopt the name by which I had always designated my cousin. Now, matters were different; I wanted to begin upon a new foundation; I wanted to put all the past, its dream of happiness and its nightmare of misery, alike out of my mind,—and this was why I called him Edgar, not unkindly, rather with a sad effort at friendship. I think he partly understood me before he spoke again.

"Yes, it is my proper name, but so was the other; and the child? you have called your boy?"

"Harry," I said, in a faltering tone.

He must have known it, but his eye flashed brightly from baby to me, once more with a gleam of delight. "Hester," he said, bending over me as he placed my child in my arms again; "when you call me once more by that name, I will know that I have regained my bride."

I bowed my head, partly in assent, partly to conceal the tears which stole out from under my eyelids even when I closed them. I enclosed my child in my arms, but I sat still. I had scarcely power or heart enough to raise myself from that chair.

"Are you ill, Hester?" he asked, anxiously.

"No, only very tired," I said faintly. His lip quivered. I did not know how it was that the simplest common words seemed to move him so. He ran to the door of the room and called Alice, who was not far distant, to take baby, and then he offered me his arm very gently and kindly, and led me upstairs.

Mrs. Templeton, the housekeeper, stood without, waiting. "Mrs. Southcote has not taken a thing since she came, sir," she said in an aggrieved tone; "please to tell her, sir, it's very wrong; it's not fit for a young lady, and nursing the darling baby herself, too."

"Mrs. Southcote is fatigued," said my husband, kindly, sheltering me from this good woman's importunities. "Will you have something sent upstairs, or shall you be able to come down to dinner, Hester? Nay, not for me," he added, lowering his voice, "I will be sufficiently happy to know you are at home; and you are sadly worn out, I see. Little Harry has been too much for you, Hester."

"Oh, no, I have him always," I said quickly. Alice was carrying him upstairs before us, and he laughed and crowed to me from her arms. When I tried to make some answer to his baby signals, I saw his father look at me with strange tenderness. His father, yes; and I was leaning as I had not leant since the first month of our marriage upon my husband's arm.

Every face I saw was full of suppressed jubilee; they were almost afraid to show their joy openly, knowing that I—and, indeed, I suspect both of us—were too proud to accept of public sympathy either in our variance or our reconciliation, if reconciliation it was. The face of Alice was the most wondering, and the least joyous of all—she could not quite understand what this return was, or what it portended; she did not accept it as her uninstructed neighbors did, merely as a runaway wife coming home, asking pardon and having forgiveness; and though her eyes shone with sudden brightness when she saw my husband supporting me, and some appearance of conversation between us, she was still perplexed and far from satisfied. My husband left me when we reached my room, and I gladly loosed off my bonnet and mantle, and laid myself down upon the sofa. It was evening again, and the sunshine was coming full in at the west window; the jessamine boughs were hanging half across it with their white stars, and the rich foliage beyond, just touched with the first tints of autumn, rose into the beautiful sky above. My own familiar room, where Alice's pretty muslin draperies had been, and where, a year ago, my husband had decked a bower for his unthankful bride. I saw all its graceful appointments now in strange contrast with the small white dimity bedroom in which I awoke this morning. How pleasant, I thought, that little house when first we went to it! What an agreeable relief from the etiquettes and services of this statelier dwelling-place! I had become accustomed to the ways and manners of our homely life by this time, and the charm of novelty was gone from them. I found a greater charm on this particular evening, in looking about, while I lay overpowered with the languor of weariness on my sofa, upon the costly and graceful articles round me in "my lady's chamber." The second change was quite as pleasant as the first.

"So this is Cottiswoode, Alice," I said, in a half reverie, "and we are at home."

"Oh, never to leave it again, Miss Hester—never to leave it till God calls," cried Alice, anxiously. "I don't ask for a word, not a word, more than you're ready to give; but, tell me, you've made up your mind to that, dear, and I'm content?"

"I will never go away of my own will—no, happy or unhappy, it is right I should be here," I said. "Does that satisfy you, Alice?"

"Miss Hester, I'd rather hear less of right and more of kindly wish and will," said Alice, with most unlooked-for petulance. "You oughtn't to be unhappy—God has never sent it, and it's time enough when He sends to seek grief."

I looked at her with a little astonishment, but took no notice of her momentary impatience—I had given her cause enough, one time and another; and now Amy came in with a tray, and something that Mrs. Templeton was sure I would like, and another maid came with her to light a fire for the comfort of Master Harry. When the fire began to blaze, Alice undressed him, while I partook—and I was almost ashamed to feel, with some appetite—of the housekeeper's good things. Then I had a low easy chair drawn to the chimney corner, and a footstool, and had my baby back again. I think he looked even prettier in his nightgown and close cap, for his evening refreshment. The dormant ambition to have him admired, sprung up very strongly within me; and I think but that poor little Harry was very hungry and sleepy, I would have summoned courage to send him down stairs, as Alice suggested, to bid his papa good-night.

"What did they all say of him, Alice?" I asked.

"What could they say, dear?" said the impartial and candid Alice, appealing to my honor; "Mrs. Templeton thought he was the sweetest little angel that ever was born; and as for the maids!—it's like bringing light into a house to bring a baby, Miss Hester. Blessings on his dear, sweet face! and he's the heir of Cottiswoode."

"Did any one say who he was like?" I asked, timidly. This was a question I had never attempted to settle even in my own mind; though, like every other mother, I saw mind, and intelligence, and expression in the sweet little features, I never could make out any resemblance—I could not persuade myself that he was like his father.

"Well, he's very like the Southcotes, dear," said Alice, pronouncing an unhesitating yet ambiguous judgment; "there's a deal about his little mouth and his eyes; and, Miss Hester, dear, what did his papa think of him?"

"I think he was very glad, Alice," I said, with a sigh. Why were we so far from what we should be?—why, why could we not discuss the beauty of our child as other young fathers and mothers did? I only had seen the joy in Edgar's face—he had not said a word to me on this subject, though it was the only subject in which there could be no pain.

After baby was laid to sleep in the cradle, I sat still by the fireside, musing by myself, while Alice went down stairs. I was left alone for a long time quite without interruption, but I did not make use of the interval as I might have done, to form my plans for our new life. I could not project anything; a fit of ease and idleness had come upon me—wandering, disconnected fancies rather than thoughts, were in my mind; the exhaustion of the day had worn me out, and I was resting, reposing almost, more completely than if I had been asleep.

I almost thought that he would have come upstairs to see me once more and look at baby's sleep. I thought he ought to have come, for I was a stranger here. And my heart beat when I heard the step of Alice corning along the great roomy corridor—but it was only Alice; and when she had set candles upon the table, she came to me with the look of a petitioner—"Dear heart, the Squire's all by himself; won't you go down and sit an hour, Miss Hester?—maybe he thinks he must not come here."

I rose when Alice spoke to me, without once thinking of disobeying her. I was glad to be told to do it, though I scarcely should have moved of my own will. I was still in the very plain dress in which I had travelled, which was, indeed, the only kind of dress which I had worn since leaving Cottiswoode, with my mother's miniature at my neck, and that fatal hereditary ring upon my hand. I paused nervously before the mirror a moment to see if my hair was in order. I looked pale, and somewhat worn-out, I thought, and I wondered what he would think of my wearied, thoughtful face, so unlike what it used to be. Alice would fain have had me change my dress, which, indeed, was not very suitable for Cottiswoode, but I would not do that to-night.

When I went into the drawing-room, he was sitting moodily by himself, bending down with his arms upon the table, and his head resting upon them. He started when he heard me, lifted a thoughtful, clouded face, which made me think he had been fighting some battle with himself, and rose hurriedly to place a chair for me. We sat opposite to each other for a little time in awkward silence; a hundred things rushed to my lips, but I had not courage to say them, and I waited vainly till he should address me. At last I made a faint attempt at conversation; "What did you think of baby?" I asked, scarcely above my breath.

"Think of him, think of him—opinion is out of the question," he cried in great haste and eagerness, as if I had broken a charm of silence, and set him free. "He is your baby and mine, Hester, there is nothing more to be said. Let us understand each other," he continued, hurriedly drawing his chair close to the table with nervous agitation; "are we to endeavor to do our duty by each other—to live under the same roof, to fulfil our relative duties as justice and right demand? Is this the foundation we are to build upon, and is this all? Tell me, Hester, let me know what it is."

"It is so, yes, I suppose so," I answered, faltering with confusion and almost fear; for he was almost more excited now than I had ever seen him. I could not have given any answer but assent. I could not, though my heart had broken for it.

For a long time after that nothing was said between us. I saw that he struggled and struggled vainly to subdue himself, and I, a strange new task to me, tried to do what I could to soothe him. I spoke of baby, told of his illness, of our journey; I seemed to myself another person, and almost felt as if I were playing a part, while I made this desperate attempt to get up a quiet conversation with my husband, while this whole ocean of unsettled principles lay still between us—indifferent conversation! for I tried to direct him to the books upon the table, but I saw very well how little I made by my efforts, and how impossible it was that he could fully control and master himself till I went away.

When I had stayed long enough—it was hard to remain, it was hard to go away, I did not know which to choose—I went forward and held out my hand to him to say good-night. He took it and detained it, and looked up at me with again that doubtful impulse on his face; would he speak? No. He grasped my hand closely again, and let it fall.

"I am poor company to-night, Hester, very poor company," he said, turning hastily away; "but I thank you for your generous efforts, I will be able to respond to them better to-morrow."

And though he rose and opened the door for me, and attended me with the delicate respectfulness of old, that was all the good-night I received from him. It cost me some tears when I reached the shelter of my own room; yet my heart was strangely at ease, and would not be dismayed, and when I took my baby to my breast and went to sleep, I gave God thanks that we had come home.

THE SEVENTH DAY

It was now October, and the weather was still very bright and pleasant. I had become quite settled and established once more at Cottiswoode; had resumed my former use and wont, and more than that, for though my life was still sadly meagre and deficient in one point, it still was life, and that was something. I might no longer wander everywhere with my baby in my arms, but I had elected the sweet-tempered and kind-hearted Amy to be his maid, and he was growing a great boy now, and soon fatigued me; though in our own rooms I kept possession of him still. But I had begun with better understanding and more discreetness to help the poor people at Cottisbourne. I had ceased to spend my days in a dream. I was active and full of occupation. The nightmare had passed off from me, though some of its influences remained.

For in the most vital point of all we made little progress; my husband and I were no nearer each other, had come to no better understanding. I studied his comfort now with the eagerest attention. I grew punctilious, formal in my excess of care for him. I saw that he was served with devotion and humility as a prince might have been. I could not forgive any piece of neglect or forgetfulness in the household which touched upon his comfort. I almost think he knew how anxious I was, and attributed it—alas, were we never to know each other! to my extreme desire to "do my duty," to do him justice. He was, and yet he was not right in judging me so. I was shut out from all the ordinary modes of showing my regard; we were on ceremonious terms with each other, and I wanted to prove to him that whatever barriers there might be between us, there was always affection. What do I say—I did not want to prove anything—I only did all I could, eagerly, timidly, and with anxious devotion, everything that I could for him. And he received them as my father might have received my mother's regard to his comfort, as kindnesses, things to thank me for, exertions of duty for which he was obliged to me. Oh, how his thanks galled me! It sometimes was very hard ado to keep my composure, to hide how my heart and my feelings were wounded, or to keep the old bitterness from rushing back. In these days I behaved better than he did; we had changed positions; it was he who was restless, thoughtless, and self-reproachful now; it was he who thought of being right, and adhering to his resolution. He had promised not to molest me, to accept what I yielded to him, to leave it all in my own hands—and he was keeping his word.

Immediately after our arrival at Cottiswoode I had written a very brief note to Flora, telling her I was here, and begging her to come if mamma would permit. I was almost anxious for the judgment of mamma. I did not know how I should be received by the country ladies, who, doubtless, had already sat in judgment on me—whether they had pronounced me without the pale, or if my return had covered the sin of my flight. It was nearly a week, and I had received no answer from Flora. I was somewhat nervous about it. I did not feel that it would be at all agreeable to be excommunicated by the little society which was the world at Cottiswoode; and everything made me see more plainly how ill-advised and foolish I was to go away. Even Miss Saville patronized me grimly with a tacit disapprobation. It was not so much because I had done wrong, as because I had exposed my own affairs, and thrown off the privacy which belongs alike to family feuds and family happiness. I tried to persuade myself that I never had cared for society,—and that was very true; but rejecting society is a much easier thing than being rejected by it,—and I by no means liked the latter alternative.

This morning, I was sitting by myself in the drawing-room. My husband spent a great deal of time out of doors, and was seldom with me except at table, and for a short time in the evening. Baby was out with Amy, his maid. The external circumstances did not differ much from those in which Flora Ennerdale found me last winter, on her first visit to Cottiswoode; but there was, in reality, a great change. I no longer sat in listless indolence, neither doing, nor caring to do anything. I was working busily at some little frocks for baby. The flowers on my table were no longer without interest to me. I was not ignorant now of the management of the Cottiswoode School, and the wants of the old women at Cottisbourne. I had begun to use all the natural and innocent means of occupation that lay around me; and if I was not yet quite a Lady Bountiful, I had already made my peace with the clamorous villagers, who did not quite smile upon me at my first return.

I was singing softly to myself as I sat at work—not because my heart was light—but Alice was not near me to talk to, and, truth to tell, I no longer wished for too much commerce with my own thoughts. The sound was a great deal more cheerful than the meaning was; but when I was thus occupied, I heard the sound of some arrival, and immediately, not Flora only, but Mrs. Ennerdale, were ushered into the room.

I was so much surprised that it made me nervous, especially as I was at once enfolded in the wide, warm, odorous embrace of Mrs. Ennerdale: here, at least, there was no lack of cordiality. I breathed more freely when I emerged from under the shadow of her great shawl and ample draperies, and Flora was so bright, so happy in what she supposed to be my happiness, that my heart melted under the sunny gleam of kindred and kindness. I was grateful to Mrs. Ennerdale for acknowledging my presence in her own person. I was glad to be relieved thus from one phase of anxiety; at least, thus far, I was not tutored.

"And how well you are looking!" cried Mrs. Ennerdale; "Flora told me you were quite pale and thin when she saw you—ah, there's nothing like native air, my dear—you've got quite a bloom—you look better than ever I saw you look, though that is quite natural—where is baby?—not asleep or out of doors, I hope. Do you know you ought not to let me see him, for I shall begin to envy you immediately—I envy every woman I see with a baby in her arms. Ah, my dear, it's the very happiest time of your life."

I could very well understand how it should be so, and though I could not help sighing, I liked Mrs. Ennerdale the better for what she had said.

"May I run and look for him, cousin Hester?" cried Flora, eagerly. "I have been telling Mamma what a sweet baby he is, and I do so want to see him again; oh, I see Alice in the garden; there he is, I will run and bring him in myself to show Mamma."

"My dear, I wish you would tell Flora that she ought to be a little more sober now," said Mrs. Ennerdale, appealing to me with motherly consequence, and a look half of raillery, half of anxiety; "she will mind you when she will not mind me, and she ought to be sober, and think of what's before her now; do you not think so, Mrs. Southcote?"

"Oh, Mamma!" cried Flora, springing out from the window; we both looked after her light, bounding figure as she ran across the lawn towards Alice. "I know she told you all about it," said the good-humored Mrs. Ennerdale; "don't you think she is too young to be married? to fancy that such a child would even think of it! but indeed I've taken great pains with Flora, and she is the eldest of the family, and knows a great deal about housekeeping, and I really believe will make a very good little wife; though marriage is a sad lottery, my dear," said the good lady sympathetically, shaking her head and looking into my face.

I turned away my head, and felt my cheeks burn; first I was almost disposed to resent this lottery as an insult, but nothing was further from the thoughts of the speaker than any unkindness to me. It was the first indication I had of what "sympathy" was in such a case as mine, and it stung me bitterly.

"My dear," continued Mrs. Ennerdale, drawing close to me, laying her hand upon my shoulder, and lowering her tone; "I am glad that Flora is gone, just that I may say a word to you; I was grieved, of course all your friends must have been, though I don't doubt you thought you had good reason; but, dear, it's far best to make up your mind to everything, and do your duty where Providence has placed you. We are relations, you know, in a way, and you've no mother to advise you; if you ever should have such a plan again, my dear, will you come and speak to me about it? I'm no great wise woman, but I know what life is; will you ask my opinion, dear?"

"But I never can, nor will, have such a plan again," I answered rapidly.

"That's all the better, my love, all the better," said Mrs. Ennerdale, "but if you should, I'll rely upon your coming to me. Hush, here's Flora, and is that baby? Now are you not proud of him? What a great boy! What a true Southcote! I can't tell whether he's like his papa or you? but I can see he's got the family face."

Mrs. Ennerdale bustled out from the window to meet the advancing couple—Flora and little Harry—who, I think, without any vanity, would indeed have made as pretty a picture as could be imagined. I lingered behind a little to get over the pain and irritation of this first probing of my wound. It was kindly done, and I might have looked for it; but no one had ever ventured to speak to me in such a plain and matter-of-fact way before, and I felt both shocked and wounded. My own act it was, too, which had exposed me to this, which had made it possible for any one to speak so to me! Well, well! there was baby and Flora laughing, calling to me, inviting me. I smoothed my disturbed brow as well as I could, and went out to them. I had no reason to be offended with Mrs. Ennerdale, but I certainly was not grateful to her.

But her raptures were so real over my boy, her admiration so sincere and so ample, that I was gradually mollified. She "knew about babies," too; that experience which a young mother prizes so highly; and knowing about them still pronounced my little Harry almost unrivalled—"almost like what Gus was when he was a baby, Flo," said Mrs. Ennerdale, with a sweet sigh, which I knew by instinctive sympathy was to the memory of some one sweeter than all others, who was only a name now, even to the fond remembrance of the mother. After that, I could remember no offence. I began to tell her of little Harry's illness, to all the symptoms of which she listened with profound attention; now and then suggesting something, and wishing, with great fervor, that she had but been near at hand. "And if anything should happen again, my dear," said Mrs. Ennerdale, taking hold of my hand in her earnestness, "be sure you send for me; send for me with as little hesitation as you send for the doctor. I've nursed all my own through all their little troubles—all but one—and I have experience. My dear, whatever hour it is, don't hesitate to send for me!"

I promised most heartily and cordially; I forgot she had ever said a word disagreeable to me; I only thought how kind she was, and how much interested in my boy.

Yes, Mrs. Ennerdale had several motives for coming to see me; a lurking kindness for myself, fond regard for Flora's wishes, a half intent to lecture and warn, and establish herself as my prudent adviser; but, above all, the crowning inducement was, baby; nothing either whole or half grown up had anything like the same charm as a baby had to Mrs. Ennerdale; she might have resisted all the other motives, but baby was irresistible; and so she had fairly won over and vanquished me.

I made them stay till Edgar came in, and they had lunch with us; but my husband, to my surprise, did not relax the state of his manners towards me in their presence. I could see that both mother and daughter were amazed at his elaborate politeness; he thanked me for everything I did for him; he feared he gave me trouble; and Flora and Mrs. Ennerdale glanced at us with troubled looks, as if to ask, "Is there still something wrong; are you at variance still." My own heart sank within me; I had scarcely been prepared for this; I thought, for my honor and for his own, that he would have made an effort to be like himself to-day.

"Flora ought not to be away from home; she ought not, indeed, at such a time as this," said Mrs. Ennerdale, "but she wishes very much to stay till to-morrow. Will you keep her, my dear? not if it is to inconvenience you; but she says you would not let her come again when you were,—ah!—in the country, and that you owe her an invitation now. We have spoiled her. She is quite rude, asking for an invitation; but if you like, my dear, I will leave her with you till to-morrow. She has a great deal to tell you, she says."

"What, a great deal more, Flora?" I asked; "I will keep her very gladly, longer than to-morrow, if you will let me, and I should like so much to help if I could. Is there anything you can trust me with, Mrs. Ennerdale?"

"My dear, you have plenty to do with your baby," said Mrs. Ennerdale, conclusively. "What a beautiful present that was you gave her—far too valuable, indeed; but her papa says he has seen your mamma wear it, and she is so proud of being called like your mamma. Is that the miniature you told me of? May I see it? Well, indeed, Flora, though it is a great compliment to you, I do think there is a resemblance—ah, she was a pretty creature; but of course you cannot recollect her, my dear?"

I said, "No," briefly, and there was a momentary pause, which, however, Mrs. Ennerdale soon interrupted; she was very full of kind counsels to me concerning my baby, and of motherly importance in her own person, full of care and bustle as she was on the eve of the "first marriage in the family." After luncheon, Mrs. Ennerdale went away, leaving strict injunctions with Flora to be ready to return on the next day; my husband returned to his own constant occupations, and I was left alone with my sweet young cousin.

Flora made no investigations, asked no questions, yet even she looked up wistfully into my eyes as she exclaimed, "How glad I am you are at home—oh! are you not pleased, cousin Hester, to have baby at home?"

"Yes, Flora, very glad," I said, though I could not help sighing. She, sweet simple heart, knew nothing of my troubles; she never could know how far astray I had gone, nor what very poor compromise, in real truth, was my position now.

"And you will come," Flora said, blushing all over her pretty face. "It is to be in a month. You will be sure to come, cousin Hester? though I am afraid you will think it noisy and a great bustle, for there are to be a great many—six bridesmaids. Do you think it is wrong to be gay at such a time?—but indeed I could not help it, cousin Hester?"

"And, indeed, I do not think it wrong, cousin Flora," said I, smiling at her seriousness; "and I only wish I could do something to show how very right I think it to do honor to a bride. Is there nothing you would like yourself that Mamma is indifferent about? Not anything at all that I could do for you, Flora?"

By dint of close questioning, it turned out that there were two or three things which Flora had set her heart upon, and which Mamma was not remarkably favorable to; and the result of our conference was, that I was seized with a strong desire to drive to Cambridge immediately with my young guest, and make some certain purchases. There was time enough yet to do it, and Flora was in great delight at the proposal, which gave me also no small degree of pleasure. After the usual fears that it was troubling me, Flora ran up stairs very willingly to get ready, and I, with a little tremor, knocked softly at the door of the library. My husband was seated as usual at his table—busy, or seeming so. When I entered he looked up, as he always did now when I went to him, with a startled look of expectation. I told him we were going to Cambridge, but hoped to be back in time for dinner. It always confused and disturbed me, this look of his.

"And am I to go with you, Hester?" he said, rising with some alacrity.

"Oh, no!" I said, confused and hesitating, "I did not mean to trouble you. I—of course, if you pleased, we would be very glad; but I only wanted to tell you—I did not think—"

"Very well," he said, sitting down, and interrupting my tremulous explanation. "I thank you for letting me know. Perhaps Mrs. Templeton had better delay dinner to give you full time. I hope you will have a pleasant drive. Ah, there is the carriage—you should lose no time, Hester."

Thus dismissed, I hastened away—always, alas!—always bringing with me when I left him a sore heart. Would he have been pleased to go?—should I have asked him? How I tormented myself with these questions. If we had been living in full mutual love and confidence, I would have said to him, gaily—"We do not want you; this is quite a confidential woman's expedition—a thing with which you have nothing to do;" but now I went away pondering whether I should not spoil our little piece of impromptu business, and making the drive and the afternoon alike miserable by returning once more, and entreating him to go.

When we came to the hall door—Flora so bright and smiling, I so careworn and disturbed—he was waiting to put us in the carriage; and my heart rose again when he held my hand a moment, and asked if I was sufficiently wrapped up. It was impossible to resist the influence of the rapid motion, and of Flora's pleasant company. I recovered my spirits in spite of myself. We had a very quick drive to Cambridge; a round of calls at the principal shops, to the great satisfaction and delight of Flora; and then it suddenly occurred to me that I would like to see, if only for a moment, our old house.

But when we came to the door my heart failed me. I had never been there since I left it after my father's death, and one glance at the familiar place was enough to fill my eyes with tears, and to bring back the pang of parting to my mind. It was now about a year since my father died. I had not mourned for him with the heavy, lasting, languid sorrow that wears out a mind at peace. I had mourned him with pangs of bitter grief, with brief agonies, more severe but less permanent, and looking again at this retired and quiet dwelling-place as associated with him, and from which it was so impossible to believe him departed. I felt as if I had been stricken down at the threshold and could not enter. It looked something mysterious, awful, withdrawing thus in its perfect stillness—the past was dwelling in that deserted place.

While I sat hesitating, gazing at the closed door, I saw Mr. Osborne's familiar cap and gown approaching. I saw it was Mr. Osborne at the first glance, and, yearning for the sight of a familiar face, I looked out from the window, and almost beckoned to him. He came forward with a ceremonious bow, and greeted me very statelily. But my heart was touched, and in spite of this I began to tell him that I had intended to alight but dared not. He saw the tears in my eyes, and his manner, too, was softened. "No," he said, "you are quite right, you could not bear it. I, myself, find it hard enough, passing by this familiar door."

He paused a moment, looked at me keenly and then said, "Will you take me with you, Hester?—are you in haste?—I have an old engagement with Harry—where are you going?—ah, then I will join you in half an hour, and in the meantime don't stay here. There now, close the window. I will tell them to drive on, and join you in half an hour."

When I found Mr. Osborne sitting opposite to me as we set out again homeward, I cannot tell how strangely I felt. My cheeks were tingling still with the name he had used—Harry—and I was overpowered with all the recollections which his presence brought to me. The last time we had been together in the same carriage was at my father's funeral, and all the recollections of that most eventful time—my betrothal, my marriage, my father's illness and death—came rushing back upon me in the sound of his voice. I had hard ado to preserve my composure outwardly. I was scarcely able to do more than introduce him to Flora, to whom he began to talk with pleasure and surprise, as I thought, pleased with her for her name's sake, though, in the twilight, he could scarcely see her sweet face, and then I sank back into my corner, and gave all my strength to subdue the tumult of memories and emotions which rose in my mind. That I should be taking him home to Cottiswoode—that he should still speak of my husband as Harry—that he should come to see my defeat and anxious struggle to do my duty—how strange it was!

I remember that night as people remember a dream—our rapid progress through the dark—the gleam of the carriage lamps—the sound of the horses' feet—the conversation going on between Mr. Osborne and Flora, and the long sigh of the wind over the bare expanse of country. We went at a great rate, and reached home sooner than I expected. It looked so home-like; so bright; so full of welcome; the hall-door wide open; the warm light streaming out; and my husband standing on the threshold waiting for us. Oh, if these were but real tokens, and not false presentiments! It was bitter to see all this aspect of happiness, and to know how little happiness there was.

My husband greeted Mr. Osborne with surprise and pleasure. Flora ran up-stairs, and I went into the drawing-room with our new guest, though, in my heart, I longed to be with baby, from whom I never had been so long absent before. My husband came with us, though he and I scarcely said anything to each other. I could see how Mr. Osborne's acute eye watched what terms we were on. Then Edgar left us to make some arrangements for our visitor's comfort, and my old friend turned his full attention upon me.

I had taken off my mantle, and he saw the miniature at my neck. In a kindly, fatherly fashion he caught the little chain with his finger, and drew me nearer to him, and looked into my face. I could not meet his eye. I drooped my head under his gaze, and, in spite of myself, the tears came.

"Well, Hester," he said gently, and in his old kind, half-sarcastic tone, "now that you have experience of it, what do you think of life?"

"It is very hard," said I, under my breath.

"Ay, that is the first lesson we all learn," he said; "have you not got beyond this alphabet—is it only hard, and nothing more?"

I heard baby's voice outside. Alice was looking for me. I ran from him, opened the door, took my beautiful boy out of the arms of Alice and brought him in, and held him out to Mr. Osborne—his face brightened into the pleasantest smiles I had ever seen upon it.

"Ah, this is your bitter lesson, is it, young mother?" he said, laying his hand caressingly on my head, while he bent to look at my boy; "this life is something more than hard which yields such blossoms, Hester—is that what this famous argument of yours would say? and this irresistible piece of logic is a boy, is he? God bless you, little man, and make you the happiest of your race."

"I must go away, Mr. Osborne, baby wants me," said I.

"Yes, go away; I am quite contented, Hester," said Mr. Osborne, once more patting my head; "go away, my dear child—you are going to cheat me once more into entire approval, I can see."

I was pleased; yet went away with a heavy heart, under my first flush of gratification. I could not help remembering again and again what he had said—it was easy to make misery, but who should mend it when it was made!

Oh, my boy, my baby! what a disturbed and troubled heart you laid your little head upon! but its wild and painful beating never woke or startled you.

After dinner, when Flora and I were by ourselves in the drawing-room, we had our parcels in and examined them once more—such quantities of bright ribbons and pretty cotton frocks! Flora, though much delighted, was not quite confident that she had been right—she was afraid mamma would think it was a great shame to let cousin Hester put herself to all this trouble, "and expense too," said Flora, looking doubtfully up at me, "and all for my school-children at Ennerdale. I am so much afraid I was very wrong to tell you of it, and what will mamma say?"

"Who can we get to make them, Flora?" said I.

"That is just what I was thinking of," said Flora, immediately diverted from her self-reproaches; "Mamma's maid is a famous dressmaker, and I can cut out things very well myself, and they might have a holiday and meet in the schoolroom, and all of us work at them together; there is Mary and Janna and Lettie from the hall, and our own Annie and Edie, and myself; and oh, cousin Hester, would you come?"

"I should like to come," said I, "but what shall I do with baby? and I am too old, Flora, for you and your bridesmaidens; I am more fit to stay beside mamma."

Flora threw her arms round me caressingly, and a voice behind me said, "Does Hester say she is old? Do not believe her, Miss Ennerdale, she is a true girl at heart and nothing better—growing younger every day—though you never were very mature nor experienced, Hester, I must say that for you," and Mr. Osborne came forward very affectionately and stood by my side.

My husband entered the room after him; had they been talking, I wonder—talking of me? I could not tell, but I was learned now in all the changes of his face, and I saw that something had excited him. All this evening Mr. Osborne continued to speak of me so, in a tone of fatherly affectionateness, praise, and blame, of which it was impossible to say that one was kinder than the other. He told little simple stories of my girlish days—things that I had forgotten long ago—which made Flora laugh and clap her hands, but which embarrassed me dreadfully, and brought tears of real distress to my eyes. What was my husband thinking?—how did he receive all this? I scarcely dared lift my eyes to him, and then Mr. Osborne touched upon the time of our wooing, and of our marriage. What could he mean?—this could not be mere inadvertence. I sat trembling, bending down my head over the work in my hand, my eyes full of tears, afraid to move lest I should betray myself, and even Flora grew grave and smiled no longer, while Mr. Osborne went on unmoved. Oh, my husband, what was he thinking? I was glad to say faintly that I heard baby crying, and to escape from the room—it was more than I could bear.

Baby was not crying, but sleeping sweetly in his pretty cradle. I bent over him to get calmness and courage from his sleeping face. Alice was sitting by the fire, covering a soft ball with scraps of bright-colored cloth; just one of those occupations which give the last touch of permanence and security to the appearance of home. It was for baby, of course—he had already one or two toys of the simplest baby kind, and we had been delighted to perceive the other day how he observed something thrown up into the air like a ball. Alice looked up when I came to her, and saw at once my disturbed face—she guessed what it was, though only imperfectly—and she drew my chair into the corner, and made me sit down and rest—"I thought it would be too much for you, Miss Hester," said Alice, tenderly, "it brings back everything—I know it does—but it's only the first, dear."

I was content to wait beside her, and recover myself; though all the time my thoughts were busy downstairs, wondering what he might be saying now; and I am not sure that I was not more eager to return than I had been to make my escape. When I went back, I entered the room very quietly, for I was considerably excited; and in my anxiety to appear calm, overdid my part. My husband was seated nearer Mr. Osborne than he had been, and was bending down with his arms resting upon his knees, supporting his head in his hands, and gazing into the fire—while Mr. Osborne talked after his lively fashion to Flora as if he was not aware of having any other auditor—he was speaking when I came in.

"I flatter myself, I am Hester's oldest friend," he said, "and we have quarrelled in our day. She had many disadvantages in her childhood. She wanted a mother's hand; but I always did justice to her noble qualities. Hester is—well, she is more my own child than any one else ever can be. I feel as if I had found her again—and she is—"

"I am here, Mr. Osborne," cried I—"oh, don't, don't; you only humiliate me when you praise me!"

For there was he sitting silent while I was commended, hearing about my youth, and perhaps smiling at it bitterly in his heart. It struck me down to the very dust to be commended before him; I would rather have been blamed, for then the unconscious comparison which I always supposed him making between what he knew and what he heard would have been less to my disadvantage. Mr. Osborne did not know how his kind word and the affectionate tone which even now touched my heart, and would have made me very grateful under any other circumstances, wounded and abased me now.

When I spoke, my husband raised his head, and threw a furtive glance at me—what could he be thinking? I shrank before his eye, as if I had been practising some guilty act, as if I had conspired with Mr. Osborne to insinuate to him that he had not sufficient regard for me.

"I praise you, Hester! did you ever hear me?" said Mr. Osborne, smiling; "I was but telling Miss Ennerdale how you exhibited your baby to-day; and your young cousin, Hester, is not to be moved out of the opinion that your boy is the beau-ideal of boys—my dear child," he said, suddenly lowering his voice, and coming to take a seat beside me, "she is very like your mother."

"Will you sing to Mr. Osborne, Flora?" said I. "I think she is very like my mother, indeed, and she is very happy, and will be very happy; there is no cloud coming to her."

He shook his head, but was silent, as Flora began to sing. My husband took a book, but I know he did not read a word of it. He sat listening as I did to some of those velvety drawing-room love-songs, which Flora had purely because they were "the fashion," and some others of a better kind, which the girl's own better taste had chosen. Mr. Osborne did not admire them as I did. He shook his head again slightly, and said, "A very good girl—a very good girl," as Flora's sweet young voice ran over verse after verse to please him. "That is not like your mother, Hester," he said; but it was Mr. Osborne that was changed, it was not the music. He had been no connoisseur in the old days.

When Flora closed the piano it was nearly time to go to rest—and I was very glad to find it so. My husband and I were left last in the room when our visitors had retired—and when I went to bid him good night, he took my hand in both of his and put it to his forehead and his lips. I was very much agitated—I faltered out, "Have you anything to say to me?" I could find no other words, and he said, "No—no, nothing but good night."

THE EIGHTH DAY

Mr. Osborne was gone—Flora was gone—and we had relapsed into our former quietness. The neighboring ladies called upon me, and I called upon them in return; but I had no heart either to give or to accept invitations, for our personal relations to each other were unchanged; and though there was peace, entire dead peace, never broken by an impatient word or a hasty exclamation, there was no comfort in this gloomy house of ours. We were so courteous to each other, so afraid to give trouble, so full of thanks for any little piece of service! To my vehement temper strife itself was even better than this, and many times I almost fled out of the house, hurried, at least as much as I could decorously, to refresh my fevered mind in the fresh air, and ponder over our position again and again.

Why did he not make an end of this?—but then the question would come, why did not I make an end of it? I had come home to do him justice, but he had warned me long beforehand that justice would not satisfy him, and had promised solemnly to leave it all in my hands. Had I all the responsibility?—what could I say?—what could I do?—and it was not always easy to keep down a spark of the former bitterness, a momentary resentment against him who would not step in to assist me, but who left all the guilt and all the burden of this unnatural state upon me. For my own part, I persuaded myself that I had done everything I could do—I had made my submission—I had brought him justice;—what more could be done by me?

Every time he made his thanks to me, I was on the point of breaking forth in a passionate protest against being so addressed, but I know not what failing of the heart prevented me. I never did it; I learned to thank him myself after the same fashion, to try if that would sting him into giving up this obnoxious practice. I could see it did sting him, but not so far as this; and we were still polite—oh, so dreadfully courteous, grateful, indebted to each other!

Upon this day I had burst out after my usual fashion, in desperation, able to bear no more. Had Mrs. Ennerdale or any other prudent adviser been able to see into my heart, and to take me to task for it, I could have given no proper reason for my perturbation. My husband had not been unkind, but perfectly the reverse—he was considerate, careful, attentive in the highest degree; I had no reasonable cause to find fault with him—but—I could not be patient to-day. I had suffered a great deal, and permitted no sign of it to appear in my behavior. I had tried to learn the true secret of wifely forbearance, mildness, gentleness; but I was of an impetuous character by nature, and had never been taught to rule or restrain myself. My endurance was worn out—it was in my mind to make an appeal to him, to tell him he was unjust—unjust!—here was I using the term again, when I had wished so often that there was not such a word in the world.

I had my mantle on, and the hood drawn over my head. It was not unusual for me to wander along this quiet country lane in such a simple dress, for there were no passengers here, except the rectory people or villagers from Cottisbourne, and I was close by home. It was late in the afternoon the first day of November, and the weather was dark and cloudy. My husband was in the library, where he always sat; baby was in his cosy nursery up-stairs, in the careful hands of Alice. He, dear little fellow, always wanted me, and I was never unhappy while with him—but darkness and discontent had settled on me now. I realized to myself vividly that gloomy picture of a household—two dull large rooms closely adjoining each other, the young husband shut up in one, the wife in another. Why was it?—he was the first to blame;—why did he fail to yield me now what was due to a woman? Would it not have been generous to take the explanation on himself, and disperse this dreadful stifling mist which every day grew closer around us;—to say—"we have been wrong; let us forget it all, and begin our life again." He ought to say it—it was my part to wait for him, not he for me; he owed me this, as the last and only reparation he could make for the first deceit which I had forgiven. So I reasoned to myself as I wandered along this solitary road; there was more resentment, more displeasure in my mind than there had been for many a day. It was unnatural, it was shocking, the state of things which now existed. I began to grow indignant at him for not doing what it so clearly seemed his part to do. At this moment I saw Miss Saville advancing very slowly and dully along the road. She was so active and brisk a person at all times, that I was surprised to see the heaviness of her look and face to-day. She came forward reluctantly, as if every step she took added to her burden. Her mind was evidently oppressed and ill at ease, for she looked round her on every side, and started at trivial sounds as if in fear. When she saw me she suddenly stopped, and a red color came to her face. She was not young, and had never been at all pretty. I cannot call this a flush, but only a painful burning red which came to her cheeks—shame, and distress, and fear. I did not want to embarrass and distress her—I knew how much good lay under her formality and her pretensions now.

"Do not let me disturb you," I said eagerly; "do not mind me at all, pray, Miss Saville; I see you are engaged."

She waited till I came up to her, looking at me all the time. "I was coming to seek you," she said; "where were you going, Mrs. Southcote? are you at leisure? I have something to say to you."

"I was going nowhere," I said. "I am quite at your service—what is it?"

She looked at me again for a moment; "I can't tell you what it is—I don't know—I want you to come with me to the rectory; but, my dear," she continued, her "sense of propriety" coming to her aid, even in the midst of her agitation, "had you not better go back and get your bonnet? it is not becoming to walk so far in such a dress."

"No one will see me," I said briefly; "but what am I to do at the rectory—can you not tell me here?"

"It is not I, Mrs. Southcote," said Miss Saville, with suppressed agitation; "I told you once before that we had trouble in our family, and that there was one among us who gave great sorrow to William and me; but you did not mind my story, for you were like other young people, and thought no trouble so bad as your own. But my poor brother Richard is back again here, and he has not improved his ways, and he is always raving about you. He says he wants to see you. We won't let him go up to Cottiswoode, for when he sees Mr. Southcote I know he constantly seeks money from him, and we cannot bear that; so to pacify him, I promised to come out to-day, and try to persuade you to come to the rectory with me. Now, my dear, will you do it! You would not speak to him before, and I could not blame you; but he speaks as if something lay upon his conscience—oh, Mrs. Southcote, will you see him and hear what it is?"

"If you wish it, I will go," said I; "I do not want to hear anything he has got to say myself; but if it will please you, Miss Saville—I know you must have thought me very heartless once—if it pleases you, I will go."

She said, "thank you, my dear," breathlessly, and hurried me on—though, even now, not without a lament for my bonnet. As we came near, I saw once more the face of the Rector peering out from the corner window. Miss Saville saw it too, and burst into a hurried involuntary recital of their troubles. "William is miserable!" she cried with excitement, "you don't know what William is, all you people who look at the appearance, and not at the heart—he is the best brother—the kindest friend!—and now, when he had come to the station he was entitled to, and was in the way of doing his duty and being respected as he deserves, here comes Richard to wring our hearts and expose us to disgrace!—If we had money to give him he would not stay long with us, but William would rather sacrifice everything in the world than refuse a kind home to his brother—and then he is taking care of him—and the rector's study smelling of brandy and water, and bits of cigars upon his mantel-shelf and his writing-table—and he as patient as an angel—oh, Mrs. Southcote, it's very hard!"

As we entered at the trim gate, and went up through the orderly, neat garden, where not a weed was to be seen, I could understand this small aspect of Miss Saville's affliction, the ends of cigars, and the smell of brandy and water, as well as her greater and sorer sorrow over the fallen brother, who still was dear to her—but the idea of an interview with him was not more agreeable on this account—I waited while she hurriedly dried her eyes, and went in with her very reluctantly. What could this man want with me! and all my old abhorrence of him returned upon me as I prepared for this unpleasant meeting. He was the first messenger of misfortune to us, and I had never tried to surmount my first disgust and aversion to him.

The Rev. Mr. Saville's trim, snug study, was indeed sadly desecrated. He himself, the good Rector, was coughing in the atmosphere of smoke which hovered round the fire where Saville sat, with his legs upon a chair, in insolent ease and luxury. There was no brandy and water visible, but the heated look in the man's face, and the close, disagreeable air of the room, was quite enough to justify what his sister said. I suppose it was in the haste of her agitation that she ushered me immediately into the room, where we did not seem to be expected, and where I scarcely could breathe.

"You should not have brought Mrs. Southcote here, Martha," said the Rector, who was no less stiff and formal than of old, though a painful embarrassment mingled with elaborate courtesies; "this is not a fit place for a lady; we will join you in the drawing-room, Martha."

"Any place will do to tell good news in," said Saville, withdrawing his feet from the chair, and sitting erect. "Give the lady a seat, Martha, and leave us. Glad to see you, Mrs. Southcote; glad to have an opportunity of making my statement to you; had you heard it sooner it might have saved you trouble. Now, good people, why are you waiting? This piece of news does not concern you. William, take Martha away."

"Oh, don't leave me, Miss Saville," I said, retreating a little, and grasping her hand.

"What, afraid!" said the man with a sneer; "you had more spirit when I saw you first, young lady; but as this that I have to say to you," he continued, gravely, "is of the greatest importance to your family, I leave it with yourself to judge whether it would not be best to keep it for your ears alone."

What could it be? I looked earnestly at him and he at me. I was no coward; and here, when I had only dislike, and no other feeling which could betray me, I was brave enough after the first moment. I turned to the Rector and Miss Saville, who stood behind, half-frightened, half-displeased, and full of anxious curiosity. "Pray leave us, as he says," said I. "If it is anything worth your hearing, I will tell you what it is; but in the meantime he will not speak till you are gone."

The Rector made a bow to me, and withdrew slowly, much agitated, and very nervous, as I could see. Miss Saville went more reluctantly. "It was a very strange thing to turn the Rector out of his own study for a secret conference," she muttered, as she went away. Saville laughed—"Though it will be worth their hearing, I'll warrant you do not tell them a word of it," he said, with the same coarse insinuation of something wrong or untruthful, which I remembered so well on that first day when he came to Cottiswoode. "They are very curious, the fools!—as if they had anything to do with it. Now, Mrs. Southcote, of Cottiswoode, are you ready to hear me?"

I had drawn my chair away to the window, out of reach of his smoky atmosphere and his immediate presence—an artifice at which he laughed again. I bowed slightly in assent; and now he rose, and coming towards me, stood leaning upon the corner of the recess which inclosed the window, looking down into my face.

"I hear that my friend Edgar and you don't get on together," said the man, with rude familiarity; "pity when such things arise in families—and generally very bad policy, too. But, however, that can't be helped in the present case. He's disposed to be master, I suppose; and, after all, though you've humbled your pride to marry him, you've not got Cottiswoode."

"If you wish only to insult me," I said, starting from my chair, "not even for your good brother and sister's sake can I endure this wretched impertinence. How do you dare to speak in such a tone to me?"

"I dare worse things than facing a pretty young lady," said Saville, with his insolent laugh, "but that is not the question, and you shall have none of my impertinence if you like it so little; but I thought you were too honest to sham a reason for this marriage of yours: however, as I have said, that is not the question. As for your family happiness, every clown in the district knows what that is, as, of course, you are aware. And if I had been you, I'd have stayed away, and not made a fool of myself by coming back."

I said nothing. I felt my face burn, and there was an impulse of fury in my heart—fury, blind wild rage, murderous passion. I could have struck him down when he stood before me, with his odious sneer upon his face, but I did not move. I compressed my lip and clasped my hands together till the pressure was painful, but I made no other indication of how I felt the insult of his words. Yes, this was justice—I acknowledged it—my fitting punishment.

"Well, things being so," continued Saville, drawing a chair towards him and sitting down upon it, after he had gazed at me maliciously to see the effect of his words, and had been disappointed—"I think you are a very fit client for me: Edgar has done me more than one shabby trick—I give him up—I do as I am done by—that's my principle—and a very honest one, I maintain; so if you choose to make it worth my while, I'll put you in possession of all I know, and give you my zealous assistance to recover your rights. These fools, here," he said, waving his hand contemptuously to indicate his brother and his sister, "will tell you, perhaps, what a dissipated fellow I am, in this wretched hole of a place—give me excitement, and I don't care a straw how it's come by; I owe Edgar Southcote a hard hit yet—and hang me, but he shall have it, one way or another."

This speech awoke me at once out of anger, mortification, every personal feeling; I no longer feared or hated him—I was roused to a cool and keen observation, a self-possession and firmness which I did not know I possessed. I felt the stirring of strength and spirit in me like a new life. I was on the verge of a dangerous secret—a conspiracy—a plot against Edgar! the fool! the fool! to betray his evil counsels to Edgar's wife. My heart beat quicker, my courage rose; I was like one inspired; a little caution, a little prudence, and I might save my husband! How warmly the blood came to my heart.

I looked at him eagerly; I did not care to suppress the sparkle of excitement in my eyes: I knew his evil imagination would interpret it very differently from the truth; his evil intent and my own conscious purpose gave me perfect confidence in addressing him, for he had no perception of truth, or love, or honor, and would not suspect what lay beneath my eager willingness to hear him now.

"There is some secret, then," said I—"what is it? what are the rights that you will help me to regain? Such a startling speech makes me anxious of course—what do you mean?"

"I suppose," said Saville, very slowly to pique my curiosity, "that before you can be expected to put any dependence on me, I must tell you my story: first, let me collect my evidences," and he took a pocket-book from his pocket, and collected several papers out of it with great care and deliberation, now and then glancing at me under his eye-brows to see if I was impatient. I was not impatient—I watched him keenly—coolly—not a movement or a glance escaped my notice; I was Edgar's advocate, and I was watching his enemy.

"Mr. Brian Southcote," said Saville, going on slowly, and now and then looking up at me as he sorted his papers, "was an extremely benevolent person—so much so, that ill-natured people said he had no will of his own, and that he did not care how wrong or how foolish anything was, so long as it was generous; perhaps you object to such plain speaking when your respectable relation is the subject," he said, stopping short with a low bow.

"Pray, go on, go on," said I impatiently.

I suppose he thought now that he had tantalized and irritated me sufficiently, for he proceeded at a less deliberate pace.

"It is said that his younger brother, Mr. Howard, had married the lady to whom they were both attached, and lived in his father's house, in possession of all the ordinary privileges of an heir, while the elder brother was self-banished in Jamaica, on pretence of looking after an estate, which he knew nothing about, and had not activity enough to have done anything for, even if he had been informed. Now, Mrs. Southcote, under these circumstances, your uncle being still a young man, of course, married the first woman who made herself agreeable to him—and this woman happened to be my cousin, the widow of a young naval officer, a young penniless widow with one boy."

I started involuntarily—I could see already where the serpent was winding—was this the secret?

"With one boy," he continued significantly, "called Harry Southern—you see there is not much difference even in the name; this child, as I will show you by a paper executed by your uncle some time before his marriage, he had already chosen for his heir, directing that he should take his name, and, after his death, be called Harry Southcote. It is not to be supposed that after Mr. Southcote married Mrs. Southern, his partiality for the boy should diminish, and this boy I have every reason to suppose is your husband, whom, by politeness, I will still call Edgar Southcote of Cottiswoode."

I was stunned for the moment—the story looked reasonable, true—it was no exaggerated malicious lie coined on the spot. I looked up with dismay into the hard exultation of this man's face, but when I caught his cunning, evil eye, my heart revived.

"Had you always reason to suppose this?" I said, keeping my eyes fixed upon him.

For a moment, only a moment, his confident glance fell. "Of course not, of course not," he said, with a little bustle and swagger, which I could see was to conceal some embarrassment. "When I took steps in the matter, you may be sure I thought I had got hold of the right person; it is only lately that I have found my error out."

"And how did you find it out?" I asked perseveringly.

"Upon my word, young lady, you try a man's patience," cried my respectable adviser—"I did find it out— what concern have you with the how? If you are disposed to take advantage of my information, it is at your service—but I will not be badgered by the person for whose sole benefit I have taken so much trouble. Will that convince you, look?"

He almost threw at me one of the papers in his hand—I lifted it up mechanically—I was so sure what it would say from his description, that I almost fancied I had read it before. It was a will, bequeathing all the personal property of the writer to Harry Southern, the son of the late George Southern, Lieutenant R.N., on condition of his assuming the name of Southcote; I read it over twice, and it struck me strongly enough, that after the first words of the bequest there was a parenthesis, "(if he survives me)," which was repeated every time the name of Harry Southern occurred. I held it out—holding it fast, however—to Saville, and asked him what it meant.

"A mere point of law," he answered indifferently, "what could it be else! Ladies, I know, never understand business; but these trifling matters have nothing to do with the main question—you see very clearly who this child was, there can be no mistake about that."

"I see nothing to identify him with Edgar Southcote," I said.

"You are sceptical," said Saville—"let me see if I can convince you there are some papers which throw light upon the matter."

These papers were letters—three of them bearing dates very near each other—all referring in terms of tender fondness to some little Harry; the first was signed "Maria Southern," the other two "Maria Southcote," but little Harry had quite as much part in the former as in the latter, and these documents were evidently true. I was greatly disturbed;—could it be so? could it be so? Was my husband only the heir, and not the son of Brian Southcote? The evidence was very startling to my unused and ignorant eyes. I kept the papers closely in my hand, resolved not to give them up again. I did not know what arguments to use to myself to cast off this fear;—at last I cried abruptly—"If this was the case he could not be like the Southcotes, he would be like your family—but he is like Edgar the Scholar; I found out the resemblance at once."

"It is easy to find resemblances when your mind is turned to it," said Saville. "Is he as like now?—and suppose he had been introduced to you as Harry Southern, would you ever have cared to examine who he was like?"

Harry Southern! the idea was intolerable. I started from my seat—I could not bear it any longer. "I will think over this, and let you know what I will do," I said hurriedly. "It is very startling news—I must have some time to accustom myself to it, and then I will be able to tell you what I can do."

"Be so good as to return me my papers then," said Saville; "by all means think it over—it is no joke—you had best be prudent; but, in the meantime, let me have my papers—they are my property, not yours."

"I will not give them back—they concern me too nearly," said I. "Stay—if you try to take them I shall call your brother. I will not endure your touch, sir;—stand back—these letters are Miss Saville's—I will undertake that no harm shall happen to them, that you shall come to no loss—but I will not give them back."

I did not move, but stood within the reach of his arm, fixing my eyes full upon him as I spoke. He could not bear an honest gaze; he stared at me with impotent fury, but he dared not resist me. I saw his terror at the thought of summoning his brother, and how he lowered his voice and drew back his hand at the very mention of the Rector's name.

"You are a bold young lady—but I like your spirit," he said, with a scowl which belied his words. "Well, I consent that you shall keep the papers—that is to say, I trust them to your honor;—shall I have your decision to-morrow?"

"I cannot tell—I must have time," I said, growing nervous at last, and drawing nearer the door; "have you ever mentioned this?—does Mr. Southcote know?"

"You will not tell him?" cried Saville fiercely, starting and following me, "you will not be so foolish as to show him your hand before the play begins? I knew women were fools in business, but I did not expect this from you—from you, Mrs. Southcote! you do not mean to pretend you are so loving and true a wife. No, I am not a likely person to have mentioned it—I know my man too well; small evidence I should have had, if it had ever come to his knowledge—I will not permit you to risk my papers in Edgar South— in Harry Southern's hands."

As he advanced upon me, I retreated—as he grew vehement, I threw the door open and walked hastily away—he followed me with great strides, yet restrained by a strange cowardice which I knew how to take advantage of—and when his sister suddenly appeared from the next room, he stopped short, and threw a look of cowardly threatening, and yet entreaty upon me. "Do not let him follow me," I whispered to her—but I knew they would take care of that—and though I managed to leave the house at a decorous pace, whenever I got into the lane I began to run. I had always been swift-footed from a child—now I flew along the solitary lane, scarcely feeling that I touched the ground, holding the papers close under my mantle. When I came to Cottiswoode, flushed, and eager, and breathless, I did not pause even to throw back my hood, but hastened to the library. There was no one there—I hurried out disappointed, and asked for Mr. Southcote. He had gone out some time ago, I was told, and had left a message for me with Alice. I ran upstairs—the message was that he was suddenly called to Cambridge, and could not expect to return till late at night—and he hoped I would not think of waiting up for him— it was sure to be very late when he came home.

I cannot tell, indeed, whether I was most relieved or disappointed to hear this; though I think the latter—yet now, at least, I would have time to think over this tale, to try if it was a fable, a monstrous invention, or if it could be true. It was late, and I got little leisure till baby was asleep, but when he was laid down to his rest, and Alice left the room, I sat down by her little table and unfolded my papers. My heart beat loud while I read them over—my fears sickened me. I had no longer the presence of Saville before me, strengthening me in disbelief and opposition. Alas, poor perverse fool! this was a fit conclusion to all the misery I had made; this long year of troubles ever since my marriage I had been bitterly and cruelly resenting the discovery that my husband was Edgar Southcote—now how gladly would I have hailed, how wildly rejoiced in, an assurance that he had indeed a title to that name. The more I examined, the more I pondered, the more my fears grew upon me. If Edgar was an unwitting, involuntary impostor—the thought was terrible—and still more terrible it was to think that Cottiswoode would then be mine. I thought I could have borne to leave a wrongful inheritance with him, had it been pure loss to both of us; but that I should be "righted" by his downfall—ah, that was a justice I had not dreamed of! I could not rest—I wanted to do something immediately to settle this question; but that it was so late, I think I would have followed him to Cambridge—but that was not to be thought of now; so I wandered up and down from the library to my own room, always returning to the letters—and tried to conceal from myself how the hours went on, and how the household was going to rest. I still hoped that I might have gone to him at once on his return, and it was only when Alice, with a sleepy face, came calling me to baby, that I yielded at last, and went to bed, but not to sleep. Through all the dreary midnight hours after that I lay still and listened, hearing every sound, and supposing a hundred times over that I heard him return. Now and then I started up after a few moments' sleep, and went to the door to look out and listen—but there was still the dull light burning in the hall, the silence in the house, the drowsy stir of the man who waited for his master below—then my restlessness made my baby restless also, and I had to occupy myself with him, and subdue my anxiety for his sake. It was a dreary night; but I had nothing for it but to submit—lying still, sleeping in snatches, dreaming, thinking— thoughts that ran into dreams, and longing, as only watchers long, for the morning light.

THE NINTH DAY

I was astir by dawn; but before even Alice came to me I was aware that my husband had not returned. The sleepy light in the hall still burned through the early morning darkness, and the watcher still stirred the fire, which had not gone out all night. When I made sure of this I hastened down to relieve the man from his uncomfortable vigil, and on my way met Mrs. Templeton, newly roused, who began immediately to assure me that "something very particular must have detained master—it was a thing he had never done before all his life,—but she hoped I would not be uneasy, for he'd be sure not to stay from home an hour longer than he could help." I do not know how it was, but this speech of the housekeeper's roused me into unreasonable anger. I was offended that any one should suppose my husband's conduct wanted defence to me; or worse still, that any one should presume to know him better than I did. I answered briefly, that I was aware Mr. Southcote had business to detain him, and hastened to my room to complete my dress. Almost unconsciously to myself, I put on a dark, warm travelling dress; the morning was brisk, frosty, and cheerful, and for the moment I was roused with the stimulus of having something to do. Somehow, even his absence and the long watch of the night did not dismay me—all at once it occurred to me, not how miserable, but how foolish our discords were; the ordinary view—the common sense of the matter flashed upon me with a sudden light. I blushed for myself, yet I was roused; half-a-dozen frank words on either side, I suddenly thought, would set us right at once. I moved about my room with a quickened step, a sentiment of freedom; Saville's papers, my own fears, all the dismay and anxiety of the night, united, I cannot tell how, to give an impulse of hearty and courageous resistance to my mind. There was something to do; I forgot my own guilt in the matter, and all the deeper feelings which were concerned. I thought of it all with impatience, as I have sometimes thought of the entanglements of a novel, which a spark of good sense would dispel in a moment—I forgot—though I was about the last person in the world to whom such a forgetfulness should have been possible—that good sense could not restore love, nor heal the bitterness of wounded affection. I determined for my own part not to lose a moment, not even to think it over, but to go direct to my husband at once, and say those same half-dozen sensible, frank, good-humored words which should put an end to it all; strange enough, my mind never misgave me as to the result.

I breakfasted in tolerably good spirits. I made no account of the anxious looks of Alice; I was occupied with thinking of everything we could do, of the world of possibilities which lay before us, if we were but right with one another; how I could have lulled myself into ease so long, I cannot tell. I awoke out of it all with a start and cry when I heard the great clock strike twelve, and looking out—out of my lonely chamber window, out of my new dreams—saw the broad country lying under the broad, full, truthful sunshine; the morning mists dispersed and broken, and the day come to its noon.

Noon! my bright figments perished in a moment: he had not come home, he had not written nor sent any message; had he forsaken me, as I forsook him?

I got up from my seat at once, feeling nevertheless as if some one had stunned me by a sudden blow. Though Alice was in the room, I did not make her my messenger, as it was my custom to do, but rang the bell myself, ordered the carriage instantly, and put on my bonnet. Alice came to help me without saying anything; my fears caught double confirmation from her silence. Something must have happened! she never asked where I was going, nor if she should accompany me, yet helped me to get ready as if I had told her all my thoughts.

"Where did he say he was to go?" I asked under my breath.

She told me; he had gone to a lawyer's in Cambridge, about some justice business—nothing that could detain him; I said nothing more, except to bid her be careful of baby, whom I had never before left so long as I most likely should leave him now. Then I hastened away. The winter noon was bright, the road crisp and white with frost, the air exhilarating and joyous. I leaned forward at the carriage window, looking out eagerly, if perhaps I might meet him returning; but the only person I saw was Saville, his enemy, pacing up and down the lane between the rectory and Cottiswoode, waiting, as I supposed, to see me. The sight of this man brought my emotion to a climax. Any one who knows what anxiety is, will readily know that I had already leaped the depths of a dozen calamities—accident, illness, death itself— which might have happened to my husband—and when it occurred to me now, that I might be going to his sick-bed or his death-bed, with these papers which pretended to prove that he was not what he seemed, folded into my hand, I scarcely could bear the intolerable thought. I could not venture to anticipate how he would receive me if downfall came to him. I had deprived myself of all that generous joy of helping and lightening which might have given a certain pleasure to a good wife even in her husband's misfortune. I!—I dared not be generous to Edgar—dared not appear to come closer to him in his humiliation, if humiliation there was. I went on blindly in a kind of agony, scarcely venturing to think how I should speak, or what I should do. If anything had happened to Edgar—any of those physical misfortunes which people speak of, as calling forth the disinterested and unselfish devotion of women, what could I do, who, all these weary months, had been resenting so bitterly his disinterested affection for me? And if Saville was right—if I, and not Edgar, was the true heir after all, how would it become me to rejoice as any other wife could have done, in the certainty that all that was mine, was his as well. In a moment our positions were changed. I thought of my husband—Edgar—Harry! as a poor man, having no title to anything save through his wife. I thought of him solitary and in suffering, able to make no exertion for himself, depending for all care and tenderness upon me. Heaven help me! this was the recompense I had labored to secure for myself; our positions were changed; and how could I dare to offer to him the same love and benefits which I had rejected so bitterly when he offered them to me?

Yet we still went on at full speed to Cambridge. When we came to our destination I alighted breathlessly, half expecting to encounter him at once, and without the faintest notion of what I was to say, or how to account for my errand. But he was not there—he had left this house, and, indeed, had left the town, early in the previous evening. I turned away from the door, sick to the heart. I asked no more questions. I would not betray my ignorance of his movements to strangers. He had left Cambridge to go home, but he had not come—had he left me?—had something happened to him?—what could I do?

And there stood Joseph at the carriage door asking where we were to go next. How could I tell? When I recollected myself, I bade him go to our old house, my father's house, and to drive slowly. I do not know why I wished to go slowly—perhaps with some unreasonable idea of meeting Edgar on the way.

When I reached the house this time, I alighted and went in; for the first time since my father's death. That strange old, dreary, silent house where dwelt the past—what had I to do there? I went wandering about the rooms, up and down, in a kind of stupor, looking at everything with dull curiosity,—noticing the decay of the furniture, and some spots of damp on the walls, as if I had nothing more important on my mind. I cannot account for the strange pause I made in my agony of anxiety, fear, and bewilderment. I did not know what to do—I could not even think—there seemed a physical necessity for standing still somewhere, and recovering the power of myself.

I was in the library, looking round, seeing everything, yet only half aware where I was—when I started almost with superstitious terror to hear in the passage behind a well-known alert footstep, and the rustle of Mr. Osborne's gown. He had seen the carriage at the door as he passed—for he lived so near that he could not go anywhere without passing this way—and came to me in haste when he heard I was here. He came up anxiously, took my hand, and asked me what was the matter? I looked ill, I suppose.

And my heart yearned to have somebody to trust to—the sound of his voice restored me to myself. "I am in great trouble," I said; "have you seen Edgar, Mr. Osborne?—is he here?"

"Here! it would indeed have been a strange place to find him."

"I do not mean in this house," said I, with a little impatience; "is he in Cambridge? have you seen him?—I want to know where he is."

"It is a strange question, Hester, yet I am glad to hear you ask it," said Mr. Osborne; "I presume, now, you are both coming to your right mind."

"No—soon I shall not care for anything, right or wrong," said I. "Edgar—he is a man—he should have known better—he has gone away."

Then immediately I contradicted myself in my heart. He could not have gone away! And yet—and yet!—"Where is he?" I cried. "I have to speak to him: I have a great deal to say. Mr. Osborne!—he had better not do what I did; he is not a fool like me; he was not brought up like me, among ghosts in this house: he ought to know better than I!"

Mr. Osborne took my hand again, made me sit down, and tried to soothe me. Then I told him of Edgar's absence. It was only one night; it was no such great matter; he smiled at my terror. But, at the same time, he bade me wait for him here, and went out to make inquiries. I remained for some time alone in the house—alone, with recollections of my father—of myself—of Harry—of all those young thoughts without wisdom, hopes without fear! I started up with renewed impatience. I could not, would not, suffer this unnatural folly to continue. Ah! it was very well to say that; but what could I do?

When Mr. Osborne came back, he looked a little grave. I penetrated his thoughts in a moment;—he thought some accident had befallen Edgar. He advised me to go home immediately and see if there was any word—if I did not hear before to-morrow he would come out and advise with me, he said. So I went away again, alarmed, unsatisfied—reluctant that Mr. Osborne should come, yet clinging to the idea, and full of the dreariest anxiety to know what news there might be at home. As I drove along in the twilight of the sharp winter night, I tried to settle upon what I should do. Saville! If Edgar had left me, what could I do with this man? for I made up my mind to destroy the papers, and that my husband should never know of the doubt thrown upon him, if he had really gone away.

We were very near Cottisbourne on the Cambridge side, driving rapidly, and it was now quite dark. The first sharp sparkles of light from the village windows were just becoming visible along the dreary length of road, and a few cold stars had come into the sky. My heart was beating fast enough already, quickening with every step we advanced on the road home, when some one shouted to us to stop. We did stop after a moment's confused parley, in which I could only distinguish that it was the Rector's name which induced the coachman to draw up. Mr. Saville! It was his office to communicate calamities—to tell widows and orphans when a sudden stroke made them desolate. A sudden horror overpowered me. I leaned out of the window speechless, gazing into the darkness; and when I saw the light of the carriage lamps falling upon the Rector's troubled face, I waved my hand to him imperiously, almost fierce in my terror. "Tell me!" I cried; "I can bear it. I can bear the very worst. Tell me!" He drew near with a fluttered, agitated air, while I tried to open the carriage door. With a sudden pang of joy and relief I saw that he did not understand me—that he had no worst to tell; but was holding back by the arm the other Saville, the enemy of our house.

"Here! I have something to tell you," cried this man, struggling forward. "Do you call this keeping your word, young lady? What do you mean by keeping my papers, and then running away?"

"Mr. Saville," I said, hastily appealing to the Rector, "I have nothing to say to him yet. The papers are not his, but Miss Saville's. When I have anything to say to him I will come to the Rectory. Just now I am very anxious to get home. Oh, I beg of you, bid them drive home!"

"Don't do anything of the sort, William," said Saville. "Stop, you fellow! So your precious husband's run away; I thought as much. Stop, do you hear! I've something to say to the lady. Why, Mrs. Southcote, have you forgotten the appointment you made with me to-day?"

"Is he mad?" cried I—for he had jumped upon the step, and stood peering in at me through the open window. I was not frightened now, but I was very angry. I shrank back to the other side of the carriage, disgusted by his near vicinity, and called to Joseph. "No, ma'am, he's not mad, he's only drunk," said Joseph. While they struggled together, the coachman drove on again, and Saville was thrown to the ground. The poor Rector! he stood by, looking on with dismay and fright and horror—thinking of the disgrace, and of his "position," and of what people would say; but the only way to save him as well as myself, was to hasten on.

And there was Cottiswoode at last—the open door, the ruddy light; but Edgar was not standing by to help me—my husband had not come home! I had begun to hope that he had—I stepped into the hall with the heaviest disappointment; I could have thrown myself down on the floor before the servants in an agony of self-humiliation. It was all my own doing, he had gone away.

Just then, Mrs. Templeton made her appearance in considerable state, holding a letter. No doubt she, as well as myself, concluded what it was—a leave-taking—a final explanation—such a wretched letter as I had once left for him. "This came immediately you were gone, ma'am," said Mrs. Templeton, who looked as if she had been crying. "It ought to have come last night; but I gave the fellow such a talking to as he won't forget yet awhile. Please to remember, ma'am, it wasn't master's fault."

I took no notice of this—my whole mind was on the letter. I hastened in with it, without a word, and closed upon myself the door of the library. With trembling hands I tore it open—after that I think I must have fallen down on my knees in the extreme thankfulness which, finding no words, tried to say by attitude and outward expression what it could not say with the lips—for this was all that Edgar said:—

"MY DEAR HESTER,—I have met with an old friend unexpectedly, and have engaged to go with him to look after some business of importance. I am grieved to be absent without letting you know, and I have no time now to explain. I shall endeavor to be home to-morrow night. Affectionately,

"HARRY E. SOUTHCOTE."

I remained on my knees, holding by a chair, trembling, looking at the name; did he always sign himself so? I—I knew nothing at all about my husband;—since he was my husband I had never got a letter from him before. Harry!—was he Harry and not Edgar to every one but me?

Then I sprang up in the quick revulsion and change of all my thoughts; I ran out to call for Alice—to call for Mrs. Templeton—to make preparations for his return, as if he had been years away. They were all glad, but amazed, and did not understand me. No; I was far too unreasonable for any one to understand. I was in wild, high spirits now—singing to myself as I ran up-stairs for baby. I said to myself—Life was coming—life was beginning—and that our old misery should not go on longer—not for a day!

And then the evening stole on by gentle touches—growing late before I knew. I went myself to see everything prepared: I watched the fires, which would not keep at the climax point of brightness, but constantly faded and had to be renewed again. I exhausted myself in assiduous attention to all the lesser comforts which might refresh a traveller on this wintry night. I went out to the avenue to see what a cheerful glow the windows of the library threw out into the darkness; and within, it was pleasant to see how the whole house warmed and brightened under my unusual energy. The servants contemplated all this with evident surprise and bewilderment. From Joseph, who came to tell me that he had seen Saville safely housed in the Rectory, though with great trouble to the Rector, who scarcely could keep his brother from following me to Cottiswoode—and Mrs. Templeton, whose manners towards me all the day had been very stately and disapproving—up to Alice, who never asked a question, but looked on—a most anxious spectator—only able to veil her interest by entire silence; every one watched me and wondered. I knew, as if by intuition, how these lookers-on waited for the crisis of the story which had progressed before their eyes so long. Yes, my pride had need to have been humbled—it was I that had made of our household life a drama of passion and misery for the amusement of this humble audience—and I had my reward.

The evening grew late, but still no one came—I could not help growing very anxious once more;—then, stirred into excitement by the sound of some arrival, I was bitterly disappointed to see only Miss Saville, coming, as anxious as I, though after a different fashion, to find out if she could what the subject was, which had been discussed between her brother and myself. I was grieved for her distress, but I could not answer her—my own trouble was full occupation for me—and I said only, "To-morrow, to-morrow!"—that to-morrow which, one way or other, would be another era—a new time.

All this day I had avoided even looking at the papers which were Saville's evidence against Edgar. I kept them safe as I might have kept a loaded pistol, afraid of meddling with them. But after Miss Saville left me, I did what I could to compose myself, and endeavored to examine them again. When I read them I grew faint with the terror of ignorance. I knew nothing about laws of evidence; and worse than that, I knew nothing of my husband's early history, and could not tell whether there might not be some other explanation of these letters. One thing in them struck me with a gleam of hope; there was a strange scarcely explainable shade of difference between the first letter and the other two. I could not define it; but the impression left on my mind was, that the little Harry of the former paper was a child a few years old, while the expressions in the other letters were such as I myself used when speaking of my little Harry, and seemed to point so clearly to a baby that I was quite puzzled and disconcerted. It was a woman's discovery—I do not suppose any man would have observed it; but I did not at all know what to do with it, after I had found it out.

I put them away again—I waited, waited, far into the night; I would not be persuaded that it was near midnight, nor even permit the servants to go to rest. I kept the whole household up, the whole house alight and glowing. If he had been years instead of hours away, I could not have made a greater preparation for him. At length, very late, or rather very early, in the deep, cold gloom of the winter morning, about two o'clock, I heard horses' hoofs ringing down the avenue. I heard the sound before any one else did. I was at the door waiting when they came up—they! for I saw with a momentary impulse of passionate anger and resentment that my husband was not alone.

The person with him was a grave, plain, middle-aged man, whom I had never seen before. Edgar sprang from his horse and came to me quickly—came with an exclamation of surprise, a look half of pain, half of pleasure; but began immediately to apologize and to thank me for waiting till he came—thanks! I hastened in, I almost ran from him to restrain myself; it seemed an insult, after all I had been thinking, all I had been suffering, to meet my new-born humbleness with those thanks, which always wounded me to the heart.

And then he brought in his companion to the bright room where I had been trimming the fire, and spreading the table for him, meaning to open all my mind and thoughts, to confess my sins against him, to make of this once cold abiding-place a genial household hearth—he brought in here the stranger whom I had never seen before. The new comer took the very chair I had placed for Edgar, and spread out his hands over the cheerful fire. I am afraid to say how I felt towards him, and how his evident comfort and commonplace satisfaction excited me. They sat down together to the table—they began to talk of their business, which I knew nothing of. I was rather an unexpected embarrassment to my husband—he had no need then of me.

So I withdrew to my room, sick at heart—mortified, disappointed, wounded—feeling all my efforts thrown away. I could have borne it better, I think, but for the comfortable aspect of that stranger seated in my husband's chair. I think I could have done him an injury with satisfaction and pleasure. I felt a ludicrous grudge against him mingle with my serious trouble. And this was how this strange day of trial, hope, and resolution came to an end.

THE TENTH DAY

I had been asleep—this was a privilege which seemed to belong to my perfect health and vigor of frame—for even in the midst of my troubles I could sleep. I woke up suddenly in the grey and feeble daylight of the winter morning to remember, in a moment, everything that had occurred last night. My own great vexation and disappointment were far enough off now to bear a calmer contemplation, and I started up suddenly inspired with the growing purpose in my heart. I could not see how it was to be done, nor what my first step should be, but I felt, as if by an inspiration, that somehow, however hard it was, the wall of division between us must be broken down to-day.

I hastened my simple morning toilette, and went immediately down stairs. Breakfast was on the table—breakfast! how strange, in the midst of agitation and excitement like mine, seemed these common necessities of life. And there was the same chair standing in the same position as I had placed it for Edgar last night. Patience! but the recollection of the stranger in the house came over me like a cold shadow—what if he should come to interrupt us again?

I had Saville's papers in my hand, and was putting them away in a drawer of the old carved cabinet which I had brought back to Cottiswoode from Cambridge, when I heard the door open and some one come in. Some one! I began to tremble so much that I scarcely could turn my head—but I knew it was my husband—that he was alone—and that the crisis had come. He came up to me at once, but with no apparent agitation to counterbalance mine. Scarcely knowing what I did, I took the letters again from the drawer, and stood waiting for him. Yes, he was a little excited—with curiosity at least, if nothing more—he looked keenly at me and at the papers which trembled in my hand—and I waited helplessly, unable to say a word, my heart fluttering to my lips. He could not help but see the extreme agitation which overpowered me.

"Hester," he said slowly, his own voice faltering a little, "I heard you were seeking me yesterday in Cambridge."

"Yes"—

"Yes?—had you anything to say?—I heard you were disturbed and anxious—I see you are troubled now—can I help you, Hester? It distressed me greatly to leave home-without letting you know—but when you hear the circumstances, I am sure you will pardon"—

"Edgar! never mind," I cried, unable to bear his explanation, "don't speak of that—don't—oh, pray, don't speak to me like this to-day!"

I put up my hand—I almost grasped his arm—but he—he only went to bring me a chair—to draw another for himself near me, and to take his place there with what seemed a painful but serious preparation for some renewal of our past contests. It was a significant action—we were to treat—to discuss—even to advise with each other, after a solemn and separate fashion; nothing violent or passionate was to come between us. But I, who had neither calmness nor moderation to bring to this interview, what was I to do? So many words came rushing to my lips that I could not find one reasonable enough and calm enough to say.

And glad to divert me from the personal subject, he took the initiative again. He looked at the papers in my hand—"Is it some business matter that troubles you, Hester—are these the cause of your distress?—will you show them to me?"

"By and bye," I said, "after—afterwards—first I have something else to say. Edgar! I want to tell you that I have been wrong all this time since ever we were married. I want you to know that I feel I have been wrong—very, very, miserably wrong. I want you to know; I cannot tell how you feel now, nor what is to happen to us—but I have been wrong—I want you to know."

A violent color came to his face, rising high to his very hair. He rose up from his seat and went away from me the whole length of the room, with hasty and agitated steps. As for me I rose also, and stood trembling and breathless, looking after him. I could say nothing more—my future was in his hands.

Then he came back trying to be calm and self-possessed. "Hester," he said, "you told me the same when you came home, but I do not see any difference it has made. We are no better than we were."

I was growing sick, sick to the very heart—but it was not in my nature to throw myself at his feet. "Yes," I exclaimed, "but it is not my fault now—it is not my fault! Why do you leave everything to me?"

Once more he started, and made a desperate effort to be calm. He saw the crisis had come as well as I did, and like me had no moderation, no composure, to bring to it. He tried hard again to return to an indifferent subject, to put the passion and the earnestness away. "I will leave nothing to you, Hester, in which I can help you," he said, with a voice which faltered in spite of himself; "Why do you agitate yourself and me with these vain discussions? you know very well that I shall thank you heartily for asking my assistance."

"Yes," I cried, "you thank me a great many times—you thank me always—you make everything bitter to me by your gratitude. Thanks, thanks! you should keep them for strangers. Why do you thank me?"

I had meant to humble myself—to the very dust if that was needful—and now in bitterness, feeling my repentance rejected, I was only falling into an angry despair instead,—but the two things were not so different after all. He was roused at least,—at last—out of all further possibility of self-control. He paced about the room, keeping himself down, keeping back the words from his lips. Then he paused for an instant before me. "I thank you because you are kind," he said abruptly; "because—do you think I am so blind that I cannot see all the pains you take for me? I know very well the efforts you make—am I wrong to thank you for that?"

"Kind!" what a word! I echoed it sharply, with a positive cry of pain and injury. I was kind to him! It was come to that.

He turned upon me sharply, too; he also exclaimed with impatience. "What can I say?—what would you have me to say? Other standing-ground seems lost between us—how am I to speak to you? What do you want?"

I felt the air darkening round me as if I was about to faint; but, with a great effort, recovered myself. "I want to speak to you," I said low and quick, with a feeling that it was not I that spoke, but only my voice. "I have not rested since you left home. I have been waiting for you, longing for you, ever since you went away. I have something to say to you, Edgar! No—Oh, Harry, Harry, Harry!" I cried, carried on far before my thoughts by a passion not to be repressed, "it is not a stranger I have come to. I want to consult my husband. I want you, Harry,—you whom I have lost so long!"

I know he did not come to me at once, for the darkness gathered close, and I threw out my arms to support myself in that terrible, blind, falling faintness. I do not know what he did, nor what he said, nor how long a time it was before I came to myself. When I came to myself I was seated in his chair, trembling and shaken as if by some great convulsion, with Harry at my side, chafing my hands and kneeling down to look into my face. Was it all a dream? had we never been married? never been parted? I could not tell. There was a ringing in my ears, and my eyes were dim—I saw nothing but him, close by me, and not even him distinctly, and what this new thing was, which had happened to us, I could not tell.

At this time I do not think I even knew that his heart was melted as well as mine; and whether our terrible life of separation was to end or to continue, I did not ask and could not tell. For myself, I sat quite still, trembling, exhausted, yet at ease, like one who has just passed the crisis of a fever; and even when he spoke, I scarcely knew what words he said.

I came to understand them at last—he was praising me in the quick revulsion of his generous heart—he had been hard to win, hard to move—he had shut himself up as obstinately as I did at first—and now that it was all over, he was giving me the praise.

The praise! but I was humbled to the depths of my heart—I did not even feel it a mockery—I went back to my old, natural humbleness, and gave him all the merit for seeing any good in me. I bent my head before him like a forgiven child. "Harry," I said, "Harry! is it all over?" When he caught my look, wistful and beseeching as I know it was, Harry's composure failed him as mine had done. He was as weak as I! as glad as I! as little able to receive it quietly—for it was all over!—all over! vanished like a dream.

"But you are right, Hester—I should not have left it to you—you have punished me nobly!" cried Harry, "had I done what you have done now, it might have been all over when you came home."

"This is best," I said, under my breath. I knew myself better than he did—I was glad of it all now—glad of everything—glad that I had been driven desperate, and compelled to put myself right at last. I kissed my husband's hand humbly and thanked God. I had been very wrong—I had nearly cast away my own life—nearly ruined his—nearly thrown aside the best and holiest influences from my boy; but God had saved me again and again on the very edge of the stream, and now I was delivered for ever. Yes, I might fall into other follies, other sins; but at once and for ever I was delivered from the power of this.

But as I withdrew my hand from Harry's I remembered Saville's papers which were crushed together in my grasp; I started with an exclamation of pain when I saw them. Personal misfortune falling on her lover may do very well to awake into action the shy affections of a girl—but I could not bear to be supposed generous to my husband—I trembled lest he should think so; a violent heat and color came to my face—I shut my hand again with an instinct of concealment. Another time! another time would surely do—I dared not disturb our new-found happiness so soon.

But Harry saw my sudden confusion, pain, and embarrassment. He took my hand again half anxiously, half playfully. "What are these?—what were you going to consult me about—must I not be your adviser now, Hester?" he said with a smile. I put them away out of my hand upon the table with momentary terror. "Not now," I said eagerly, "not now; I got them from your enemy, Saville, that man—do not look at them now."

His face darkened, his brow knit—once more, once more! it was such a look as women love to see upon the faces of their husbands, but it made him for the moment like my father as I had once fancied him before. "So!" he said, "he has fulfilled his threat—the miserable rascal! he thought to involve my wife in it. Hester, is it because of these papers that you have come to me to-day?"

"Oh, no, no—do not think it!" I cried, anxiously. "I am not escaped long enough from my own delusions to have no fear of them; do not fancy it was any secondary motive—do not, Harry! I could not bear the life we were living; and whenever I really had to speak to you, all that was lying in my heart burst forth. It was so, indeed;—do not take up my sin where I leave it, Harry; do not suspect me—oh, we have had enough of that!"

The tears were shining in his kind eyes I could see—he looked as he used to look in the brief charmed days before our marriage;—no, better than that—for through sorrow, and bitterness, and estrangement—strange lessons!—I knew him now, as then I had no chance to know him. "Do not fear, Hester," he said; "I am not afraid of your generosity. I told you long ago I could bear to be pitied—the only thing I could not bear was justice;—and so long as what you give me is not barely my 'rights,' I will permit you to be as generous as even your nature can be. Now, Hester, at last may I speak of that long ago—that day when I came to Cottiswoode? and of the brave girl who brought me here, and her bit of briony? Not yet?—do you say not yet?"

"Harry, there are graver matters first," I said; "there is a plot against you—they want to say—he wants to say—that—that—you are only Brian Southcote's heir—you are not his son. I suppose he thought it would give me pleasure;—he told me—it is horrible! that Cottiswoode would be mine. Harry! think, if this should be true, what a frightful punishment to me! I should never have believed it for a moment, had it not looked so just a penalty for all my sins against you. Tell me, Harry—say it is impossible that such a fatal mistake should be."

The color rose upon my husband's face, and he raised his head with an involuntary gesture of pride and defiance. It was a Southcote face! I could not be mistaken—all around were the portraits of our race, and I read them with a quick inspection as my anxious eye glanced from him for a moment. He was not like Edgar the Scholar now—my Harry could never have planned a demon's revenge upon unborn children—he was not like any one of them perhaps—but in his face I saw, as in a glass, reflections, momentary glances, of all the pictured faces round us. And when I turned to gaze upon himself again, once more I was overwhelmed with that shadow of my father in his resolute expression. Oh, monstrous invention!—how could any one have found all these shadowy likenesses in the face of a stranger?

"Hester," he said gravely, "when Saville came to me last winter with some vague threats of his power to prove me an impostor, I almost wished at first that I could have yielded to him, and so restored to you the rights you were born to. But a man must be very wretched and debased indeed, when he can make up his mind to deprive himself of his name. Do you remember that you forbade me telling you what he had come to say? I carefully went over then, both by myself and with my lawyer, the proofs which were thought conclusive at a former time. I found no reason to doubt them, Hester—there was neither break nor weakness in the chain. You look at me doubtfully, wistfully—what do you wish me to say?"

"That you are quite sure—quite sure," I said, "I am speaking folly, I know—but that you remember your father—that you are sure you are my uncle Brian's son."

"That is easily done—I am quite sure," he said with perfect calmness; "but now, Hester, let me know what the fiction is. What does the fellow call me? I do not think his imagination is very brilliant—let me see."

He took the papers—smoothed them out, and read them—at first with interest, then, as I thought, with surprise and amazement. "What does it mean?" he exclaimed, at last, turning to me; "I suppose you have the interpretation, Hester. What is all this about my poor little brother?—what does it mean?"

I made no answer, but only looked closely at him. As he caught my eye, the color flushed to his face and he started up. "Do you mean to say that he tries to identify me with my mother's eldest son?" he cried, with considerable excitement; "is this the story?—and her own letters—how are they pressed into the service?—is this what you have heard, Hester? Why do you not speak?—this is what you have heard!"

"Yes," I said, under my breath, feeling something like a culprit under his eye.

And Harry began to stride about the room, in considerable excitement, muttering words which I am afraid were not very commendatory to Saville. "The rascal!—the villain!—and only to deceive her—only to make my wife a party against me?" he exclaimed, as he paced through the apartment—then gradually subduing himself he came back and resumed his place by my side.

"If it were not that the results of his scheming have blessed me beyond my hopes, I am afraid I should lack power to restrain myself," he said, "and all the more because this invention could only have been to deceive you, Hester, for it could not stand a moment's examination. I see what his abominable purpose was—to show to the world husband and wife contending with each other over this disputed inheritance. He must have trusted to your ignorance of the world—to your own truthful and open nature, which was beyond suspicion—and, good Heavens, Hester, think of it! to your hatred of me."

To the very depths of my heart I was humiliated; it was a palpable fraud then, a trick, which could only have been tried upon a credulous fool, a woman, or a child. My last eminence sank beneath my feet; I had no longer even discrimination enough to judge between the false and the true.

"Harry," I said faltering, "it may be only that I cannot bear you to think me so foolish: but I think indeed it might have deceived even a wiser person than I. I was prepared to think it a lie, but it looked very like truth, Harry; indeed it is difficult to consent to it that I have been so very easily deceived."

"Ah, Hester, it all comes of our past circumstances," said my husband, "you were deceived because you did not know my story; shall I tell it to you now?"

I said "yes," eagerly—then my eye caught the forsaken breakfast table, the poor kettle subsided into noiseless quietness, all its cheerful boiling over. "But you have had no breakfast!" I exclaimed. How Harry laughed, how his face shone, and the tears came to his eyes! Strange that it was always some simplest word that moved him most. He threw the papers down, and caught me in his kind arms, and rejoiced over me. These common things put him in mind of what had happened to us, of the life that lay before us now, the union that began to-day.

And when I began to arrange the breakfast once more, to put the kettle on the fire, and ring for hot coffee, and arrange his neglected meal for him, he sat looking at me, not caring to do anything else, I thought—and it was strange what a pleasure I found in these housewifely matters. I believe when one comes to the very truth, when youth and its first romances are over, that there is no such pleasure for a woman as in these little domestic services, which are natural to her. How gladly and lightly I went about them! and my heart was full. I could not be content without the third little member of our family; I ran up-stairs and brought down in my arms our beautiful boy. I think we were happy enough at that moment to make up for a whole year's trouble; and when Amy came into the room for baby, some time after, I saw her joyous, astonished glance from one to another, for Harry was dancing his son in his arms, and I was standing close by looking on, talking and clapping my hands to him. Amy did not like to be inquisitive or "unmannerly," but in the simplicity of her heart she gave me such a wistful, questioning, delighted look when I put baby into her arms. Poor Amy! involuntarily I patted her stout shoulder with my hand as she went away, and I knew very well she went immediately to tell her tale of a new era to Alice—I saw it in her face.

And then Harry gathered up these scattered papers and drew my arm within his, and led me to the library. How strangely this room was connected with the principal events in my life! We went to the pretty recessed corner where my hours of girlish study used to be spent, and there my husband told me, for the first time, the story of his young life.

"I remember that I could once recollect my father, Hester," he said; "but I think that is all. My mother I remember well enough; and I have the most perfect recollection of the stone in memory of Brian Southcote, to which she used to lead me; and the little grave close by, where I have seen her prostrate herself in passionate sorrow, and where my little brother, Harry Southern, lay. This little brother fills up a great part of my earliest memory. He was a blight and shadow upon my life, though I was full of vague, childish sympathy and admiration for him. He had died just before my mother's second marriage, and when I was born I was named after him, and my mother's greatest desire seemed to be to make me a sort of shadow of her best-beloved child. I recollect quite well her frequent exclamation: 'Your father calls you Edgar, but you are Harry to me—always Harry to me—not my lost Harry, but, at least, his name—oh! I cannot give up his name.' I suppose I was precocious, as lonely children are so often; and I do not think I was quite satisfied even then to be only the reflection of another. However, that time was followed by a dismal one of friendlessness and solitude. And then a sailor brother of the Savilles came by chance with his ship to Jamaica. My poor mother had been in regular correspondence with her cousin, Miss Saville, and the brother was commissioned to find me out. I came home to England with him. All that my father had left in Jamaica had got into very uncertain hands by that time; and, though the amount sounded well, it was, I am afraid, only a fabulous inheritance; and I was a very poor child, indeed, when our good Rector here, then a poor curate, took me in and gave me shelter. I owed everything to their kindness, Hester. They were humble people, and I had 'no claim upon them,' as people say; but they were angels of charity to me.

"A year or two after I came to England, the attorney brother came down from London to visit them. He was not then what he is now: he was unscrupulous, and not very respectable, perhaps, but he had a good deal of acuteness, and was prudent enough to restrain his evil appetites. In mere idleness, at first, he began investigating who I belonged to, as he called it. There had been a rumor in the family that my poor mother had made a great match; and Saville soon discovered what his simple relatives never could have discovered—who Brian Southcote was, and what his heir was entitled to. My father had been a man of foolish benevolence. He had taken no precautions for me; done nothing that he could help; so that it required no small research, and perseverance, and industry, to get proofs of my identity together. I always disliked the man, but I was indebted to him; and during the whole time of my minority he restricted my means greatly. Then, when I came of age, I pensioned him; but he has not been satisfied with this: he has gradually fallen in character and habits into the miserable reprobate, who is nothing but disgrace to his kind kindred who will not disown him. I have been obliged to resist his exactions again and again; and after he threatened me, of course my honor was concerned, and I could not permit myself to be bullied into further concessions. These letters, you see, are addressed to Miss Saville. Are you able to go to the Rectory with me, Hester, and hear her account of her cousin's children? and we will see this man together. The facts are very simple, plausible as this fiction is; but Harry Southern was five or six years old before my father's marriage: did not that occur to you, my timid wife?"

"Yes—yes," I said eagerly; "a great many things occurred to me. I felt almost sure that the first of these letters referred to an older child than the others; but I had no clue—nothing to guide me; and the thought that it might be true was enough to make me miserable. I am quite able: I promised to let him know what I would do. Come, come; let us go at once, Harry."

He smiled at my eagerness now; but went first to his desk, unlocked it, and a concealed drawer in it, and drew from thence a little bundle of papers. One was a certificate of his parents' marriage, the other of the birth of Harry Edgar Southcote; and the others corroborative documents. I returned them to him hastily. I was almost offended. "Why do you offer me these?" I said, impatiently; "is your word not enough for me?" "You must consider what is enough for law and the world, Hester," said my husband; "enough to secure to our boy an unblemished name—he is the principal person to be considered in this argument; though there is no fear of his inheritance between us, we must take care to establish his perfect right to be called Southcote. My family pride is all of your teaching—but I have caught it fully now. Shall you get ready, then? Ah, Hester, is all this nightmare that is past only a dream?"

"Only a dream, Harry, only a dream!" I cried, as we stood together hand in hand; so much a dream that I scarcely could suppose now how it had been with us yesterday—and when at last I left him to get my bonnet, I ran upstairs almost with a lighter foot than Flora's; the cloud was gone—gone—absolutely gone; and instead of being sceptical of my own happiness, it was the misery now that I was sceptical of—I could scarcely believe it, scarcely understand how I could have defied and rejected all these blessings of Providence so long.

When I went into my room, Alice was there, looking excited, heated, full of anxiety and trouble. How hastily she tied the ribbons of baby's cloak, and sent Amy away with him! How impatient she looked while I bent over him, and kissed the sweet face which brightened every day into more beautiful intelligence! Then she waited to know what I wanted, and when I told her what it was, she came behind me, arranging my cloak upon my shoulders with tremulous hands—and I caught a glimpse of her wistful agitated face looking at me in the glass, trying to read in my eyes what had happened to me. As she did this, I turned round upon her suddenly, and looked full in her face; she faltered, retired a little, and I saw was almost crying with extreme agitation and anxiety. I took both her hands and drew her very close to me.

"Alice, can you believe it?" said I; "God has cured me by great blessings, and not by great calamities, as you once feared He would. It is all over—it is all over, there will never be any more misery in this house. Have you been praying for it, Alice? Is it through you?"

"Oh, my darling, my precious child!" cried Alice, suddenly clasping me in her arms as if I had been a child indeed; "it's through His mercy! I'd be glad to die now!"

"Hush, hush, hush! there would be little joy then," said I, when I was able to draw myself from her arms, "we are all to be very happy now, Alice, like a fairy tale."

"Like them that love God," said Alice solemnly.

I bowed my head; these words overpowered me. Was it He who had guided me through all those dark and wilful ways? He who had filled me with the fruit of my own doings; given me my own will, till I knew what a miserable inheritance that was? He who had saved my baby; at whose feet I had prostrated myself, vowing to sacrifice the sin which I regarded in my heart? I bent my head into my hands and wept. I think every tear was a thanksgiving, for they relieved my heart.

That rectory lane! how dull it used to be—how full of beautiful life it was to-day. We did not look much as if we were going about a serious piece of business—we were so occupied and absorbed with ourselves—and it never once occurred to me what should be said to Saville till we were entering at the rectory gate. On the road my husband told me—a very strange coincidence too—that the stranger who accompanied him last night, and for whom he had left a message, had sought him out about the lost West Indian property, which still might be recovered. When we came at last to the rectory, I asked, "What will you say to Saville, Harry?" But there was no time to answer my question. Miss Saville met us in the hall—she looked disturbed, alarmed, anxious—she knew our visit must have some reference to my yesterday's conference with her brother, and she was very anxious for him. I ran to her eagerly, took her hand, and kissed her. I was very little given to this species of affectionateness, and she was completely taken by surprise. "Mrs. Southcote, my dear, what is it?" she said, sinking down upon one of the stiff hall chairs, and doing what she could to keep herself from crying. "Hester never knew before how much I owed to you," said Harry, coming to my help, for indeed I was nothing loth to cry too! "Come, dear friend, we want your kind assistance. Where is the Rector—and Richard—but, Miss Saville, let us first speak to you."

She led the way into a little housekeeping parlor, which was her own special sanctuary, and there sat down trembling to hear what we had to say. Then Harry told her the entire story; she was grievously distressed. She could not bear to blame her brother, yet the way in which he had taken advantage of her, wounded her to the heart. "My letters!" she said faintly. "Dear boy, dear Harry, you don't think I ever meant to do harm to you? He made me give him poor Maria's letters to amuse him, he said—he's got them all—can they do you any harm? can they? Tell me!—for he's got them all."

"They can do me no harm—they have done me the greatest good," said Harry, "they have restored to me my wife; but I must see him in your presence, and have this matter set at rest. He must be mad to think of injuring me by such an expedient as this."

"Hush! I sometimes think," said Miss Saville, under her breath, "that it is telling on his mind—I do, indeed. He raves of nights; and whatever William and I can say, he won't give up that dreadful drinking; he'll kill himself, Harry dear—that's what he'll do—and such a man as he was once—oh! such a man as he might have been!"

And tears of love and anguish—love, most undeserved, most long-suffering—fell slowly and bitterly from this good woman's eyes. I had scorned her once, but I felt very poor and mean beside her now.

When she had sufficiently composed herself, she took us into another room, and left us to bring her brothers. The Rector came immediately, the other refused. Miss Saville returned in great distress to say, that he would not come—that he refused to see us—that I had broken faith with him.

"We must go to him, then," said my husband, steadily; "the Rector will give you his arm, Hester. Do not be nervous, Miss Saville—this must be settled—but he shall be spared, be sure. Come, lean upon me— my kind, old friend, can you not trust me?"

"Oh, yes, yes!" she said, but her distress was so great and evident, that I scarcely could bear it. We went in this solemn order—the Rector, in great perturbation, giving me his arm, but looking afraid of me, to the study. Saville was sitting smoking by the fire; he started up, and dashed his cigar to the ground as we entered: he turned fiercely round upon us like a wild beast at bay, and asked, with an oath, what was the meaning of this?—was he never to be left alone?

"Yes, in half-an-hour," said my husband; "but first I must speak to you. Saville, you have been a very good friend to me—I acknowledge it; you know I have always been glad to say as much. What motive could you have to tell this false story—this story you know so well to be false—to my wife?"

"Motive?—I had motive enough, you may be sure," answered Saville, shortly—"that is my concern—it is yours to prove the story false, as you call it—false! What do you know about it?—there's not a man qualified to speak on the subject but me."

"Oh! Richard! Richard!" cried Miss Saville; "poor Maria's letters—was that the use you wanted to make of them? But you know very well it is not true. William and I know it is not true; and, to tell it to his wife!—oh, for shame, for shame!"

"Give me back the papers," said the man, hoarsely, holding out his hand to me.

I was surprised to see Harry take them out at once and hand them to him. I would have kept possession of them, for they were still important and dangerous to me.

He held them in his hands a moment as if undecided, and then tossed them on the table, where they fluttered about like scraps of useless paper, as they were. "I thought you had a serpent in your house," he said, looking at Harry—"I owed her a grudge as well as you; but if you are in league, I had as well give up the contest. I'll tell you what—give me cash enough to take me somewhere—America—Australia—I don't care where it is. I don't want to see one of you again, and you'll be rid of me."

Miss Saville started as if about to speak, but restrained herself—glanced at her better brother, and closed her eyes, growing very pale; bad as he was, she could not bear the thought of an everlasting parting—he was her brother still.

"I will do this," said Harry, quietly, "but it must not be done so that your perverse ingenuity can make it look like a bribe. Will you come to Cottiswoode to-morrow? the Rector will come with you—come as a man should come who dares look other men in the face—on my part, I will have a friend fit to cope with you, and settle this business once and for ever;—do you consent?"

He did not speak for a moment—he was hemmed in and saw no way of escape; he searched about with his cunning eyes in the vacant air, but saw no expedient. "I consent!" he said, sullenly, "anything for peace. Leave me alone, for heaven's sake—there, there, Martha, take your remonstrances away!"

We left him so—and Harry did not even take the trouble of gathering up these pieces of paper. "They are quite harmless, Hester," he said to me with a smile when I spoke of them, and I was obliged to be satisfied with that.

Then we went into Miss Saville's little parlor again—the Rector and she were consulting anxiously together. The Rector was sadly clouded and cast down—he was a good man, but he was weaker than his sister.

"Yes, it is much better I should go," she said; "I will go with Richard. Mr. Southcote—Harry!—if you are to have a stranger present let me come instead of the Rector—it might be awkward for William—he might meet the gentleman again; and consider he is a clergyman, and must not do anything unbecoming his station. I will come with poor Richard—it will do as well, will it not?"

"Quite as well," said my husband; "better indeed, except that it will grieve you."

"It will not grieve me so much as it would grieve William," she said quickly; and that point was settled.

"Dear Miss Saville, it is through me this distress has come upon you," I said, as she went out with us to the door. I looked up to her anxiously, now that I had come to esteem her so much. I was afraid she must think very little of me.

"My dear, it will be all settled through you," said Miss Saville, "and that will be a blessing—I am glad it has come to this—very glad in my spirit, though it's hard to the flesh. William will have peace at last!"

She went in abruptly as we left the door; she could not keep her composure any longer. With a woman's sympathetic instinct, I knew she was gone away with her burden, to try if she could lighten it by tears.

"Harry," I said gravely, when we went away, "she is not young nor pretty, nor clever, nor interesting—people don't love her even when they only see her as I used to do. What has such a woman to reward her for the neglects and slights that are her portion now?"

"Patience and hope here, nothing more, Hester," said Harry, "not even William loves her as she loves him—nothing but hope and patience—poor Martha!—and in the world to come, life everlasting. That is enough for her."

Enough for any one, surely, surely! but God had made a difference between her life and ours.

ANOTHER DAY

It was little Harry's birthday.

He was standing before me in the little fanciful dress of blue velvet which Alice and Amy, no less than myself, thought so particularly becoming to his beautiful complexion, and in which he had already made a grand appearance, and stood at full length in a wonderful gilt frame, upon the wall of the dining-room down-stairs, for the admiration of all the visitors at Cottiswoode, and the instruction of future ages. I was seated in the nursery proper, a large room, which communicated with my dressing-room, with "something else" upon my knee—something which was a maze of fine muslin, of lace, and embroidery, almost richer, if that were possible, than Harry's baby robes had been—and of which the only legible token of humanity was a pair of blue eyes shining through the maze of the pretty veil; blue eyes, the "sweetest eyes that e'er were seen" to my husband and to me.

I had been so very anxious about this little one—so overwhelmed with superstitious awe and terror lest this should be the fated second boy, the inheritor of that weird and ghostly jewel; but I was suffering Harry now to turn round and round upon my finger the hereditary diamond. Thus far, at least, the spell was broken. The blue eyes belonged to a little girl—a little Helen Ennerdale, a sweet representative of her whose sweet and peaceful face was always with me. I feared my ring no longer. I had even placed it sportively on baby's little finger, and promised Alice in the lightness of my heart that this was the woman, the Southcote born, from whose finger this pledge of family misfortune was to fall.

For I was now a happy young matron—a thrice happy mother; yes, Mr. Osborne was right—I was a girl at heart—I grew younger every day. Since my little girl was born, Alice herself, who would not have thought the crown jewels too fine for me, had looked on with amazement at the additions which I made to my wardrobe. The love of all these pretty things—the feminine pleasure in them, for their own sake— had grown and blossomed in me ever since I became a happy wife. Do you say that was no very great result to have arrived at? No, neither it was, if it had been a result, but it was only an indication. I was no longer indifferent to any thing—I had a liking, a choice, an opinion, in every daily matter of my life. I lived these bright days heartily, caring for everything, doing everything with a will—my heart was no longer dwelling abstracted in some course of private thoughts, of recollections or broodings. My heart was in my work and in my pleasure, and had to do with all I was engaged in. All those blessings that came fresh to me from God's hands—should I have taken them grudgingly? No, I received them with all my heart.

It was Harry's birthday—he was three years old; and we were just about setting out with his little sister to the church, to add her to the number of those on whom the name of the Lord is named. Alice, in the silk gown she had worn at my marriage, was standing by me, ready to carry the little neophyte downstairs, while Amy waited behind with her bright good-humored face and holiday dress, to follow in our train. It was a beautiful day of June, warm and sunny; the windows were open; the sweet air, rich with the breath of flowers, blew from window to window, stirring the veil about this sweet new face. There were flowers every where, sweet bouquets of roses—it was a double holiday, a day of family joy. I could not have the house sufficiently bright nor sufficiently adorned.

And there was Harry—the elder Harry—looking in at the door, making a pretence of chiding us for delay, but, in reality, looking at the group which belonged to him, with joy which was too great for words. And then we set out in our joyful solemn procession, Alice going first that we might not lose sight of the young newcomer. My pretty Flora, now quite an experienced young wife, was standing beside Miss Saville, waiting for us downstairs—these were to be my little Helen's god-mothers; the one a beautiful, happy young woman, rich in all the gifts of this world; the other, drawing near the frost of age—homely, stiff, ceremonious, noways beautiful. What a strange contrast they were! but I would rather have been without Flora than without my husband's kindest friend.

Mr. Osborne, who was also with us, gave his arm to Flora—like other people, he preferred the youthful beauty to the elderly goodness—Miss Saville came with Harry and me. As we went down the lane she talked to us of our duties; how we should educate our children; and of the system of religious instruction she should think it her duty to adopt with baby when she was old enough; while little Harry looked up with amazement from my side, and privately whispered to me to ask if Miss Saville was scolding papa or mamma. Harry did not comprehend how the infallible authorities of his little world should be lectured by anybody, and varied between amazement and indignation. We, for our own parts, took it with great good humor and respect, though, perhaps, it did not do us much good—for Miss Saville belonged to a bygone age, and to a class which greatly abounds in system—though I by no means despised her counsels and wisdom in training the little heir of Cottiswoode, who long ago had shown unmistakeable signs of possessing "a will of his own."

How beautiful the day was!—those glorious measureless depths of blue, yon floating snow-white islands—were they clouds or sunshine?—that curdled broken line, in its long oblique streaks, a vague beatitude of light and vapor, a real milky way. Then the green borders of the lane, with its tiny eyes of flowers looking through the matted herbage; the clear little rivulet of water singing through the meadow; the willows rustling their long branches as though vainly longing for the water, which these bristling boughs will never reach—I had the spring of returning strength, of added blessings—everything to be thankful for. I felt as if every step I took was somehow an expression of thankfulness. I was in no mood to listen to any discourse—my thoughts were all abroad upon the fresh air and sunshine, my heart was singing its own quiet song of jubilee and gratitude—I am afraid all the lectures in the world would have been lost on me.

And then we clustered round the humble font, in the homely little country church, many a kindly looker-on from the village following us softly, on tiptoe, to see the ceremony—that ordinance of all others most touching, most solemn, most simple, most like the first instinctive wish of nature. To claim by name and sign the protection of God for this little child, to lay down her helplessness, visibly in the sight of men, at the feet of the only strength that is Omnipotent, the only love that is Almighty; to say aloud before our neighbors, "She belongs to us only because she belongs to Thee—she shall be ours for ever, living or dying, because she and we are Thine." I leaned heavily upon my husband's arm, and looked up into his face. Harry's eyes were wet and glistening as mine were—we had not been together when our eldest born was dedicated thus, and it had been a hard, sad day to me—but the joy of this was almost more than I could bear.

When we left the church, it was not in the nature of mortal woman to help lingering to hear the plaudits which the admiring mothers of Cottisbourne bestowed upon my little Helen; some of them remembered my mother, and prophesied that this was to be "her very image;" others, loyal to the reigning monarchs, were divided as to whether she should be like her father or her mother; but there was no doubt about the principal fact, that such a beautiful baby never was seen. Little Harry by this time had deserted me for Amy, and the rest of the party had gone on before, so that I had only the Rector for my companion—the Rector, who, good man, had lingered with his natural ceremonious politeness, waiting for me. Mr. Saville was not great at conversation; and after we had exchanged a few remarks about the village and the parish, and the work which he was doing in both, I was much surprised when he, of his own accord, began another subject.

"We have heard from my brother in Australia to-day, Mrs. Southcote," he said; "Miss Saville is somewhat agitated—did you not observe it?"

"No, indeed," I said. "Is it painful news? oh, I hope not! or we only have been troubling her to-day."

"The trouble is an honor, madam," said my reverend companion, with one of his elaborate bows; "and the news is—not painful, certainly. My brother Richard, though unfortunate, was a man of mind—always a man of mind, Mrs. Southcote—and has, I am glad to say, recovered himself in his new sphere, as we are led to hope—he has, indeed," and here the Rector sighed a small sigh—"married since he went abroad—and with Mr. Southcote's liberal allowance I have no doubt he will do well."

And again the excellent Rector sighed. Why did the good man sigh? "You do not disapprove of his marriage, Mr. Saville?" said I, in my ignorance.

"Disapprove! no—far be it from me to disapprove of an honorable estate," said the Rector, looking wistfully up at the windows of the Rectory as we passed. "I have no doubt if Richard is mercifully supported in his changed ways he will be a happy man; but there are many men who never have it in their power to consult their own inclinations, Mrs. Southcote," he continued, with a sentimental air, shaking his head slightly, and looking after his sister, who was walking before us. I could not help blushing, though I was very much inclined to laugh, and I hurried on immediately to rejoin my husband, for I was afraid that the Rector was about to make a confidante of me.

The good man looked disappointed, but succumbed into his usual grim politeness, as I hastened on and took Harry's arm. My heart smote me when I saw his blank look, but I could not bear, knowing what a good man he was, to see him look ridiculous; and I am very much afraid that the Rector's love sorrows would have been little else to me.

Harry was in great glee and most exuberant spirits. "What do you think, Hester?" he cried, in a half whisper, when we were sufficiently far apart from our companions—"the Rector's going to be married—there's news for you—what do you think of it?"

"I am sure there is nothing at all laughable in it, Harry," said I, taking the opportunity, gladly, to resent my own strong inclination to laughter upon him.

Harry did not cease for my reproof, but his laugh was inward and subterraneous. "We must have the thing done in grand style," he said, "and astonish the bashful bridegroom by the reception we give him. Did they tell you the Ethiopian had changed his skin, Hester?—that Richard had 'settled?' I suppose I ought to be glad to believe it—but I have no faith in that fellow. And now what can we do for Martha,—my kindest friend?—not that I don't thank you, with all my heart, Hester, for what you have done already—she will never forget the honor you have given her to-day."

"I know exactly what we must do for her, Harry," said I.

"Do you?" he said, looking down upon me affectionately; "since when have you turned a good fairy, my rebellious wife?"

"Hush, Harry!" I said. "If I had not been your rebellious wife and very miserable once, I don't think I ever should have been good for anything; but I know quite well what we must do for Miss Saville to make her quite happy; you must see about building her a pretty, large, roomy cottage near Cottisbourne immediately, Harry."

"Must I?" said my obedient husband, "and pray, Mrs. Hester, if one might ask a reason—why?"

"Because it was her own project, her own desire—and it was in my black time," I said sadly. "I will tell you all about it after—but that is what you must do."

"When was your black time, Hester?" said Harry. "Was it when you and all the world were in mourning—when you found out that you had been deceived?"

"Don't, don't! I can't bear you to speak so," I cried. "It never was your fault,—never, Harry!—Why must I not speak?—what, you will not hear me? you are a tyrant, sir!"

"Very well," said Harry, laughing, "so be it—we will not quarrel over whose fault it was; but we know by whose blessing it is a white time now," he added more gravely, "and your orders shall be obeyed, though I will not call you a tyrant. I shall be glad to have Martha Saville still near us, and I think now it would be rather a heartbreak for her to part from these children and you."

He was quite right, though I wondered at it—Miss Saville had indeed grown fond of me. That she should love little Harry was nothing wonderful, but I was both proud and amazed at her affection for me.

We were to have a good many people with us that evening, and when Harry went up to the nursery with me to see the children, and how baby looked after her churchgoing, I started so much that I almost let my little Helen fall from my arms, when I drew off my glove—"My ring—my ring! what has become of it? I am sure I had it on my finger when I went out," I cried. "Alice, did you see it? I must have drawn it off with my glove."

Amy, Alice, the two Harries, great and little, were immediately searching for it in every corner; it was not to be found. "It is your father's ring, is it not, Hester?" said my husband; "you have dropped it in the church most likely. I shall walk down immediately, and see; don't be uneasy—it cannot be lost—any one who found it would know it for yours."

"Oh, Harry, stop! I am not uneasy," I cried eagerly; "wait a little, there is no hurry—pray don't go at all, then—I do not care—I shall be very glad if it is lost."

"What do you mean, Hester!" he cried in amazement.

I took him aside and whispered all the story into his ear; but Harry was sceptical, and laughed at my superstition. "Why, then, the ring is not yours, Hester," he said, laughing, "but your second son's—and you have no right to lose other people's property so coolly. Never fear, we will exorcise the demon—and, even on your own showing, it is better to look after it, that the mysterious powers who have it in charge may know you were unwilling to lose it. Now, let me go."

I was obliged to let him go, though very reluctantly—and, when he went away, Flora came running up stairs to condole with me. "Oh, Hester, have you lost your beautiful ring?" cried Flora; "and do you know Mr. Southcote is laughing about it, and says you do not want to find it again; tell me the story—do tell me the story, Hester! Mr. Osborne has gone with him, and the Rector and Miss Saville are in very earnest conversation, and I want my little goddaughter—oh, Hester, I do so wish you would give her to me!"

Yes, Flora was very envious; so we permitted her to hold the young lady in her arms, while Alice told her the story of Edgar the Scholar, and his revenge. Flora was very much awed by it, and full of eager interest now for the return of Harry: "She hoped—she did so hope, that he would never find that dreadful ring!—she should be quite frightened to look at it again!"

For my part, I was also a little anxious about it; but Harry's good example, and my own light heart, brought me out of the power of the supernatural. I knew already that love and peace reigned at Cottiswoode—that my own sins, my mother's wrongs, the lifelong sin and punishment of my father, had found a merciful conclusion in the happy family life which once more consecrated with daily thanksgiving the ancient family home. The constant feuds between the elder and the younger, had merged in the perfect union of the two branches of our house. God and Providence were with us, and we could afford to smile at Mystery and Fate.

But the ring was not to be found; though it was sought for in every direction, rewards offered, and every means tried—for Harry was obstinate in his endeavors to recover it—the ring of Edgar the Scholar never returned to Cottiswoode. I do not mean to confess that I am still superstitious about it—for, of course, such a jewel as that was no small prize, and some stranger might have picked it up upon the road, and I have no doubt, did—yet it was very strange, it must be admitted, that it should disappear so. We have not only a second son now, but a third, and a fourth! and Cottiswoode is almost overflowing, and our patrimonial acres will have enough to do to provide for all the children with whom God has blessed us. Sorrow has been in our house—sickness—once death,—but strife has never entered at the peaceful doors of Cottiswoode; and I should smile now, with the smile of perfect confidence and security, did any one whisper to me that discord could come between Harry and his brave brother Brian, our little knight-errant—our St. George—our eager champion of the distressed. The children are God's children—I do not tremble for them; and life comes to have a very different aspect, with all its unknown haps and chances, when one can say Providence, heartily, instead of Fate.

Margaret Oliphant – A Short Biography

Margaret Oliphant Wilson was born on April 4th, 1828 to Francis W. Wilson, a clerk, and Margaret Oliphant, at Wallyford, near Musselburgh, East Lothian.

She spent her childhood at Lasswade, near Dalkeith, Glasgow before moving to Liverpool.

Her youth was spent in establishing a writing style so much so that, in 1849, she had her first novel published: Passages in the Life of Mrs. Margaret Maitland based on the Scottish Free Church movement. It met with some success and was a good start to her career.

Two years later, in 1851, her third book Caleb Field was published. It was also now that she met the publisher William Blackwood in Edinburgh and was asked to contribute to his well-received Blackwood's Magazine. It was to be a lifelong endeavor. Over the course of the relationship she would have well over 100 articles published.

In May 1852, Margaret married her cousin, Frank Wilson Oliphant, at Birkenhead, and they settled at Harrington Square, Camden, London. He was an artist working primarily in stained glass. With the marriage she became Margaret Oliphant Wilson Oliphant.

Their marriage produced six children but three tragically died in infancy.

When her husband developed signs of the dreaded consumption (tuberculosis) they moved, on the advice of doctors, to warmer climes. In January 1859 it was to Florence, and then to Rome where, sadly, he died.

Margaret was naturally devastated but was also now left without support and only her income from her writing. She returned to England and took up the task of supporting her three remaining children by her literary activity.

By now she was being published both as an established novelist and regularly in Blackwood's Magazine, amongst several others. Her incredible and prolific work rate increased both her commercial reputation and the size of her reading audience.

Against this her domestic life continued to be tragic, full of sorrow and disappointment.

In January 1864 her only remaining daughter, Maggie, died and was buried in her father's grave in Rome. Her brother, who had emigrated to Canada, was shortly afterwards involved in financial ruin. Margaret generously offered a home to him and his children, adding another demand to her already heavy responsibilities.

In 1866 she settled at Windsor to be closer to her sons, who were being educated at near-by Eton School. That year, her second cousin, Annie Louisa Walker, came to live with her as a companion-housekeeper. Windsor was now to be her home for the rest of her life.

Her literary career for three decades was one of constant delivery and success. Whether she wrote historical works or across several genres in fiction: domestic realism, historical, romance or supernatural she was successful.

For more than thirty years she pursued a varied literary career but family life continued to bring problems.

The literary ambitions she wished for her sons were unfulfilled. Cyril Francis, the eldest, died in 1890, leaving a Life of Alfred de Musset, which was later incorporated in his mother's Foreign Classics for English Readers. The younger, Francis, who she nicknamed 'Cecco', collaborated with her in the Victorian Age of English Literature and won a position at the British Museum, but was rejected by Sir Andrew Clark, a famous physician. Cecco died in 1894.

With the last of her children now lost to her, she had but little further interest in life. Her health steadily and inexorably declined.

Margaret Oliphant Wilson Oliphant died at the age of 69 in Wimbledon on 20th June 1897. She is buried in Eton beside her sons.

At her death, Margaret was still working on Annals of a Publishing House, a record of Blackwood's Magazine with which she had enjoyed such a successful relationship.

Her Autobiography and Letters, which present a thoughtful picture of her domestic anxieties, was published in 1899. Only parts were written with a wider audience in mind: she had originally intended the Autobiography for her son, but he died before she could finish it.

Opinions on Oliphant's work are split, with some critics seeing her as a 'domestic novelist', while others recognize her work as influential and important to the Victorian literature canon. Critical reception from her contemporaries is also divided. John Skelton took the view that Oliphant wrote too much and too quickly. Writing a Blackwood's article called 'A Little Chat About Mrs. Oliphant', he asked, "Had Mrs. Oliphant concentrated her powers, what might she not have done? We might have had another Charlotte Brontë or another George Eliot." However not all of the contemporary reception was negative.

The esteemed M. R. James admired Oliphant's supernatural fiction, concluding that "the religious ghost story, as it may be called, was never done better than by Mrs. Oliphant in 'The Open Door' and 'A Beleaguered City'. Mary Butts lavished praise on Oliphant's ghost story 'The Library Window', describing it as "one masterpiece of sober loveliness".

More modern critics of Oliphant's work include Virginia Woolf, who asked in 'Three Guineas' whether Oliphant's autobiography does not lead the reader "to deplore the fact that Mrs. Oliphant sold her brain, her very admirable brain, prostituted her culture and enslaved her intellectual liberty in order that she might earn her living and educate her children."

Whatever the merits of their cases Margaret Oliphant has been shamefully neglected in modern years. She is now becoming more widely recognised as a leading writer of her day.

Margaret Oliphant – A Concise Bibliography

A canon of more than 120 works, including novels, travel books, histories, and volumes of literary criticism.

Novels
Margaret Maitland (1849)
Merkland (1850)
Caleb Field (1851)
John Drayton (1851)
Adam Graeme (1852)
The Melvilles (1852)
Katie Stewart (1852)
Harry Muir (1853)
Ailieford (1853)
The Quiet Heart (1854)
Magdalen Hepburn (1854)
Zaidee (1855)
Lilliesleaf (1855)
Christian Melville (1855)
The Athelings (1857)
The Days of My Life (1857)
Orphans (1858)
The Laird of Norlaw (1858)
Agnes Hopetoun's Schools and Holidays (1859)
Lucy Crofton (1860)
The House on the Moor (1861)
The Last of the Mortimers (1862)
Heart and Cross (1863)
Salem Chapel (1863)
The Rector (1863)
Doctor's Family (1863)
The Perpetual Curate (1864)

Miss Marjoribanks (1866)
Phoebe Junior (1876)
A Son of the Soil (1865)
Agnes (1866)
Madonna Mary (1867)
Brownlows (1868)
The Minister's Wife (1869)
The Three Brothers (1870)
John: A Love Story (1870)
Squire Arden (1871)
At his Gates (1872)
Ombra (1872
May (1873)
Innocent (1873)
The Story of Valentine and His Brother (1875)
A Rose in June (1874)
For Love and Life (1874)
Whiteladies (1875)
An Odd Couple (1875)
The Curate in Charge (1876)
Carità (1877)
Young Musgrave (1877)
Mrs. Arthur (1877)
The Primrose Path (1878)
Within the Precincts (1879)
The Fugitives (1879)
A Beleaguered City (1879)
The Greatest Heiress in England (1880)
He That Will Not When He May (1880)
In Trust (1881)
Harry Joscelyn (1881)
Lady Jane (1882)
A Little Pilgrim in the Unseen (1882)
The Lady Lindores (1883)
Sir Tom (1883)
Hester (1883)
It Was a Lover and his Lass (1883)
The Lady's Walk (1883)
The Wizard's Son (1884)
Madam (1884)
The Prodigals and Their Inheritance (1885)
Oliver's Bride (1885)
A Country Gentleman and His Family (1886)
A House Divided Against Itself (1886)
Effie Ogilvie (1886)
A Poor Gentleman (1886)
The Son of His Father (1886)
Joyce (1888)

Cousin Mary (1888)
The Land of Darkness (1888)
Lady Car (1889)
Kirsteen (1890)
The Mystery of Mrs. Biencarrow (1890)
Sons and Daughters (1890)
The Railway Man and His Children (1891)
The Heir Presumptive and the Heir Apparent (1891)
The Marriage of Elinor (1891)
Janet (1891)
The Cuckoo in the Nest (1892)
Diana Trelawny (1892)
The Sorceress (1893)
A House in Bloomsbury (1894)
Sir Robert's Fortune (1894)
Who Was Lost and is Found (1894)
Lady William (1894)
Two Strangers (1895)
Old Mr. Tredgold (1895)
The Unjust Steward (1896)
The Ways of Life (1897)

Short stories
Neighbours on the Green (1889)
A Widow's Tale and Other Stories (1898)
That Little Cutty (1898)
The Open Door (1918)

Selected Articles
Mary Russel Mitford (Blackwood's Magazine, Vol. 75, 1854)
Evelin and Pepys (Blackwood's Magazine, Vol. 76, 1854)
The Holy Land (Blackwood's Magazine, Vol. 76, 1854)
Mr. Thackeray and his Novels (Blackwood's Magazine, Vol. 77, 1855)
Bulwer (Blackwood's Magazine, Vol. 77, 1855)
Charles Dickens (Blackwood's Magazine, Vol. 77, 1855)
Modern Novelists—Great and Small (Blackwood's Magazine, Vol. 77, 1855)
Modern Light Literature: Poetry (Blackwood's Magazine, Vol. 79, 1856)
Religion in Common Life (Blackwood's Magazine, Vol. 79, 1856)
Sydney Smith (Blackwood's Magazine, Vol. 79, 1856)
The Laws Concerning Women (Blackwood's Magazine, Vol. 79, 1856)
The Art of Caviling (Blackwood's Magazine, Vol. 80, 1856)
Béranger (Blackwood's Magazine, Vol. 83, 1858)
The Condition of Women (Blackwood's Magazine, Vol. 83, 1858)
The Missionary Explorer (Blackwood's Magazine, Vol. 83, 1858)
Religious Memoirs (Blackwood's Magazine, Vol. 83, 1858)
Social Science (Blackwood's Magazine, Vol. 88, 1860)

Scotland and her Accusers (Blackwood's Magazine, Vol. 90, 1861)
The Chronicles of Carlingford (Blackwood's Magazine 1862–1865)
Girolamo Savonarola (Blackwood's Magazine, Vol. 93, 1863)
The Life of Jesus (Blackwood's Magazine, Vol. 96, 1864)
Giacomo Leopardi (Blackwood's Magazine, Vol. 98, 1865)
The Great Unrepresented (Blackwood's Magazine, Vol. 100, 1866)
Mill on the Subjection of Women (The Edinburgh Review, Vol. 130, 1869)
The Opium-Eater (Blackwood's Magazine, Vol. 122, 1877)
Russian and Nihilism in the Novels of I. Tourgeniéf (Blackwood's Magazine, Vol. 127, 1880)
School and College (Blackwood's Magazine, Vol. 128, 1880)
The Grievances of Women (Fraser's Magazine, New Series, Vol. 21, 1880)
Mrs. Carlyle (The Contemporary Review, Vol. 43, May 1883)
The Ethics of Biography (The Contemporary Review, July 1883)
Victor Hugo (The Contemporary Review, Vol. 48, July/December 1885)
A Venetian Dynasty (The Contemporary Review, Vol. 50, August 1886)
Laurence Oliphant (Blackwood's Magazine, Vol. 145, 1889)
Tennyson (Blackwood's Magazine, Vol. 152, 1892)
Addison, the Humorist (Century Magazine, Vol. 48, 1894)
The Anti-Marriage League (Blackwood's Magazine, Vol. 159, 1896)

Biographies
Edward Irving (1862)
Francis of Assisi (1871)
Count de Montalembert (1872)
Dante (1877)
Cervantes (1880)
Life of Sheridan in the English Men of Letters series (1883)
John Tulloch (1888)
Laurence Oliphant (1892)

Historical & Critical Works
Historical Sketches of the Reign of George II (1869)
The Makers of Florence (1876)
A Literary History of England from 1760 to 1825 (1882)
The Makers of Venice (1887)
Royal Edinburgh (1890)
Jerusalem (1891)
The Makers of Modern Rome (1895)
William Blackwood and his Sons (1897)
The Sisters Brontë. In: Women Novelists of Queen Victoria's Reign (1897)